In the near future, political and cultural divisions have pushed America to the brink of civil war over States' rights.

Daniel Ridley is a newly ordained missionary, raised in the heart of the separatist South and in ignorance of the broader world. He is sent to Boston as a missionary for the Christian Nationalist Evangelicals to preach the Word of God and to advocate for a government based on religious scripture. He's not sure why God chose to burden him with same-sex attraction, but he's confident his faith will give him the strength to resist that temptation. But he's not prepared for the hostility he faces up North, and his secret mission — to find an elusive killer and bring him to justice — only complicates his task.

Jaxtyn Keller is a young gay man and perpetual college student who leads a Buddhist worship group at his university in Boston. He believes everything in the universe is connected, and everything happens for a reason. Unlike most of the citizens in his terrorism-plagued city, he's convinced the only way to hold the country together is for both sides to truly see each other.

The two men meet by chance, and each sees in the other an opportunity to achieve his goal.

As the national crisis accelerates, however, Daniel's cherished beliefs collide with the harsh reality of separatist violence, and he is soon torn between duty to his church and his growing feelings for Jaxtyn. When their lives are threatened, the two men must find a way to overcome their differences and accept their love for each other, while they fight to both save themselves and prevent a civil war.

INTO THE
LION'S DEN

JOHN PATRICK

A NineStar Press Publication
www.ninestarpress.com

Into the Lion's Den

First Edition, October 2024

ISBN: 978-1-64890-809-5

Also available in eBook, ISBN: 978-1-64890-808-8

CONTENT WARNING:
This book contains sexual content, which may only be suitable for mature readers. Depictions of homophobia, religious shaming, domestic terrorism, mention of abortion, kidnapping, and Black erasure.

Prologue

"THIS IS NOT a test. Take cover immediately."

Daniel's cheek was squished against the bathtub wall. He breathed through his mouth while Jaxtyn — on top of him — frantically tugged at the blankets to cover their heads. Outside, sirens wailed, urging action. Through the closed bathroom door, Daniel could hear the announcements from the wall screen in Jaxtyn's bedroom.

"This is not a test. Take cover immediately." The warning repeated again and again, first in English, then Spanish, and then several more languages Daniel didn't recognize. Jaxtyn's foot slipped against the tub's wall, and his elbow dug into Daniel's ribs. "Sorry," he mumbled, his coffee-scented breath puffing against Daniel's face.

"This is not a test. Take cover immediately."

God was punishing Daniel. That much was certain. Not

even two months into his first mission, he'd failed to bring any of Boston's sinners to Jesus, and—worse, much worse—he'd violated God's sacred plan by succumbing to his own personal demons. Had it only been five minutes earlier that he'd condemned his soul to hell? Had he really almost *kissed* Jaxtyn?

Sure, it was a furtive, spontaneous thing, and in his panic, he'd pulled away before it truly began. But still. Did he really think he could flaunt God's will? Of course he couldn't. He'd failed. A spectacular, final descent into sin, and not five minutes later God announced his wrath through…whatever this was.

"This is not a test. Take cover immediately."

How had his life spiraled out of control so quickly? Only six months earlier, he was secure in his faith and his future, safe and cocooned in the loving community of his missionary college, confident and eager, ready to work God's will in the world. And now this.

"This is not—" The announcement cut off, immediately replaced by a series of shrill, sharp blasts. Outside, the sirens shut down, and an ear-splitting steady alarm took their place.

"Radiation detected! This is not a test. Take cover immediately."

Above him, Jaxtyn sucked in a breath and squeezed lower into the tub, pressing more tightly against Daniel.

Daniel closed his eyes and began to pray.

Chapter One

Six months earlier

DANIEL AND MARCUS sat on a bench enjoying hot apple cider and donuts as they waited to cast their ballots. Summer was lingering into November this year in South Carolina, and the students of Sangre de Cristo Missionary College formed a sea of white pants and red shirts as they spread out across the campus courtyard seeking spots in the sun, soaking up the last of the season's warmth. Surely it was another sign of God's favor to be blessed with such a day.

It was a festive atmosphere with the college choir singing hymns and the faculty manning the refreshment table. Victory was all but assured. This would be the year of the Christian Nationalist tidal wave. Everyone said so.

"I'm going to miss this place when we leave in the spring,"

Daniel said.

"Not me," replied Marcus. "I'm looking forward to getting out in the world."

It was the kind of thing Marcus would say — as if embarking on their sacred mission was like leaving for vacation. "Besides," Marcus continued. "We've been assigned to Boston! Aren't you excited?"

"Yes…" Daniel offered hesitantly. He touched the pistol in his shoulder harness for reassurance. "But it's a little scary. I mean, I know we've trained for this—"

"Yeah. Four long, suffocating years," Marcus interrupted.

Daniel rolled his eyes. "But Boston. That's going to be a tough nut to crack. They've told us from the beginning it's one of the most hostile cities we could be sent to."

"Sure it is," Marcus agreed. "But that means it has the most potential for success. Think of all the people there who haven't accepted Jesus into their hearts yet. Think of the political progress we can make if we can change even just a few minds."

The Galatian Hills mobile voting van arrived, rolling under the school's archway where a sign proclaimed, *Sangre de Cristo Missionary College, Bringing People to God and God to Government*. A soft smattering of applause rippled through the courtyard as it entered.

"And come on, Dan. If anyone can crack that nut, it's you. Top of the class four years in a row, not to mention your success with your community service assignments. Why, just the county jail alone—think of all the souls you've saved!"

Daniel wasn't so sure. The inmates had already been Christians before Daniel witnessed to them. In Boston, though, they'd been told they'd meet people who didn't even believe in God. Their missionary courses in bringing nonbelievers to Jesus seemed inadequate, too reliant on faith that God would work His will.

Listen to me! Too reliant on faith! It was absurd, and Daniel was ashamed for even having the thought. "Pray with me a moment?" he asked. Marcus took Daniel's hand without question, and both men bowed their heads. Silently, Daniel opened his heart to Jesus and offered himself as a vessel of God's will.

When he was finished, he released Marcus's hand. "Thank you," he said. "I'm glad they're sending us together." He and Marcus had been best friends since they were boys and had been roommates at Sangre de Cristo for the last four years. As trying as Marcus could be—always pushing the envelope, always questioning the wisdom of the church leaders—Daniel couldn't imagine going on his first mission without him.

"I think they're only sending me with you because I'm Black," he whispered. "I suspect they think it makes us look good to the outside world."

The settled peace that had come over Daniel while praying evaporated. "Marcus!" Daniel hissed, glancing around to be sure they hadn't been overheard. "You know that's ridiculous. Skin color might be important to the Northerners, but it means nothing here."

Marcus held up his hands. "Okay, Dan. I know. You're right."

Daniel relaxed, but not entirely. "We're Christian Nationalist Evangelicals. We're not White and Black; we're all one in God." He focused on the warm sun, the scent of cider in the air, and the taste of sugar on his tongue, and his unease disappeared. It was a good day and God's work was underway. He looked at the van with the town's slogan painted on the side: *Galatian Hills, God's Law Above All.*

Pastor Logan stepped into the courtyard, and a hush fell over the assembly. He also wore the missionary uniform, but his red shirt had silver crosses sewn into the tips of its collars, a mark of distinction and rank within the church. He was an older man with bushy eyebrows and obviously dyed black hair, a concession to vanity Daniel thought was inappropriate.

"Good morning, God's soldiers," he called out to the missionary students.

A robust "Good morning, Pastor Logan," echoed back to him.

"Today, we will bring our nation closer to God. His will shall be done. His justice served." Pastor Logan surveyed the rapt crowd and then held his hands to the sky. "Let us pray."

While Pastor Logan led them in prayer, Daniel's heart warmed. He thought of all the people in Boston who hadn't yet found faith in Jesus, who hadn't yet committed their lives to the service of God. He could do this. He could help those people find themselves and their purpose.

Yes. They were doing God's work for sure.

*

WHAT A DAY it had been! Daniel and Marcus stayed up late into the evening watching the Good News Network as the final votes were tallied. Pastor Logan had been right; the Christian Nationalist tidal wave had arrived.

And it all went so smoothly. Even in the Northern cities, there'd been no violence, no protests. The Good News Network was filled with images of cheering crowds waving the Christian Nationalist flag, long but orderly lines at voting stations, and entire families out celebrating the momentous day.

At the communal dinner that evening, Pastor Logan called it the start of a peaceful transfer of power, but Marcus frowned. Daniel nudged his foot under the table. It wouldn't do to have Pastor Logan notice Marcus's doubt.

Marcus knew things. Things he wasn't supposed to know. At least he claimed to. Daniel suspected Marcus was still in regular contact with his family, which was forbidden outside of one weekly letter. But unlike most of the other students, Daniel and Marcus had grown up in Galatian Hills, and Marcus snuck out occasionally, presumably to visit with them, although Daniel never asked.

He didn't *want* to know the things he wasn't supposed to know. He trusted Pastor Logan to tell him what was necessary. But Marcus had been gone that afternoon for two hours, and Daniel braced himself for some illicit revelation he'd need to pretend not to have heard.

Marcus had remained silent throughout the evening, although he seemed worried and uncertain. At 11:00 p.m., Daniel slipped under his covers and relaxed for the first time since Marcus had returned to their dorm room. He wouldn't have to acknowledge Marcus's unauthorized family visit after all. He wouldn't learn things he wasn't supposed to know.

Or so he thought.

"Don't you think it's weird, Dan?" Marcus asked from his

bed. He hadn't turned out the lamp on the table between them. "I mean, even the Good News Network has covered the recent protests and the marches on Washington and the…terrorism…"

Daniel lifted himself up on his elbows. "Stop it, Marcus. Stop right there. The terror attacks are only rumors." Marcus was about to respond, but Daniel cut him off. "And even if it's true, what do those people expect, living as they do in their godless cities with no moral grounding in Jesus. Of course it would be violent up there."

Marcus didn't respond.

"And the Good News Network is the *only* news. You've heard Pastor Logan. Everything else out there is lies and deception. It's why good Christians refuse to access the unfiltered internet. It's all just rumors meant to deceive us."

"Maybe," Marcus said. "But I heard a *rumor* today about Boston. That maybe there was more violence at the polling stations than we've been told. And since we'll be going there next year, I thought, well, what if Pastor Logan isn't telling us everything? What if he's keeping—"

"Marcus!" Daniel sat up and swung his legs over the side of the bed to face Marcus directly. "You have to stop. Do you think Pastor Logan would send you with me to Boston if he heard you talking like this? You need to trust in God, Marcus, which means trusting the church and that means trusting Pastor Logan." He waited a beat to see if Marcus would respond. He didn't. "We've *prayed* about this, Marcus. This is your greatest temptation to sin— questioning the wisdom of the church. Should we pray again now?"

Marcus sighed. "No, Dan. We're good." He reached over

and turned out the lamp, and Daniel slid back under his covers.

But a moment later, into the darkness of the room, Marcus asked, "But what about you, Dan? Do you think it will be more difficult for you up there? With your own temptation, I mean?"

Daniel was thankful for the darkness. *His own temptation.* Why God had chosen to burden him with same-sex attraction to men remained a mystery, but he knew God didn't give anyone a cross they couldn't bear, and he knew he'd continue to bear this one until God saw fit to remove the sinful urge.

"I'll be fine," Daniel whispered. "Jesus gives me strength."

Chapter Two

JAXTYN AND SYLVIE shuffled forward, elbow to elbow with hundreds of others, inching their way to the security tables in front of the polling station at Boston College High School. They'd been in the crowd for nearly an hour, and the low November sky threatened rain. Once inside the school, they'd have to wait even longer before they could cast their votes.

Protestors and advocacy groups lined the parking lot's perimeter. Jaxtyn was alarmed by how many Christian Nationalists there were. Banners proclaiming *God's Law Above All* and *Elect Christian Nationalists* appeared all around the edges of the massive crowd. He shuddered to think even here in Boston — the beating blue heart of the bluest state in the union — these radical fundamentalists were gaining traction.

Clouds of miniature camera drones swarmed overhead, attracted by the shouting and chanting. Banners with a white cross on a red background—the symbol of the Christian Nationalist Evangelical movement—hung from lampposts and traffic lights. Even as protestors tore them down, new ones replaced them, popping up like poisonous mushrooms after a rain. "Keep back!" the police shouted at the protestors, their voices amplified through their helmet microphones. But they were in full riot gear, and that only added to the sense of anxiety animating the crowd.

A plastic water bottle sailed through the air, and shrill whistles rang out from the parking lot.

Scientists say the entire universe is made of invisible particles of vibrating energy, and Jaxtyn believed it. He felt the power of those vibrations connecting him to everything else, and today that energy shimmered with foreboding. He moved closer to Sylvie so that their shoulders brushed together, and surprisingly, she seemed to welcome the contact. She must have a bad feeling about all this too.

Sylvie's choppy green hair and abundance of facial piercings mirrored her spiky personality. But Jaxtyn knew the image she projected was mostly a front to keep people at a distance until she felt safe around them. Jaxtyn's only nod to body ornamentation was a tattoo of a small, seated Buddha who smiled out to the world from Jaxtyn's neck, just above his collarbone. If people thought it was an odd tattoo for a tall, Nordic-looking blond, well, so be it. A little mystery was a good thing, and the guys Jaxtyn was attracted to seemed to think so too.

"Why is this taking so long?" Sylvie asked as they edged closer to the security tables.

Jaxtyn peered over the heads of the people in front of them to assess how much longer it might take. "Just a few more minutes," he said to Sylvie, whose view was limited to the shoulders of those around them. "It's the most important election in decades," he added. "Control of Congress hinges on today. This could be the end of the union as we know it and the establishment of religious governments in the separatist states. Everyone wants to vote."

"But two hours," Sylvie complained.

"I know," said Jaxtyn. He flinched when loud drumming began from somewhere behind the crowd. "At least we're only missing morning classes. Think about the people who work all day and need to do this in the evening. It'll be even more crowded then."

They shuffled forward again, and Jaxtyn felt a few drops of rain. "Look," he said, elbowing Sylvie and nodding off to the right at a group of Christian Nationalist Evangelical missionaries — or CeeNees as they were known from the acronym CNE. She craned her neck to see between the people beside her.

"Oh," she said when she spotted them. "CeeNees. They're fucking creepy," she whispered, as if even from a distance, and across the noisy crowd, they'd be able to hear her.

Jaxtyn had to agree. They *were* creepy, and in recent years they'd begun showing up everywhere. They wore white pants and red shirts, and anyone who'd ever been approached by one quickly learned to cross the street the next time. It was bad enough they wanted you to believe in their radical fundamentalist version of Christianity, but they *also* wanted the government to officially adopt their religion, to be able to force their Christian version of Sharia law on everyone.

They stood just outside the police buffer zone, praying,

handing out pamphlets, and trying to engage anyone they could pull into conversation.

"Fresh out of the factory," Sylvie said.

Jaxtyn stifled a laugh. Dozens of small missionary colleges had sprung up across the red states in the last decade. Their graduates fanned out across the blue state cities spreading the word of God and forcing political bullshit down the throats of anyone foolish enough to listen. Here in Boston, the colleges were referred to as missionary factories. And really, that's exactly what they were.

"We made it," Jaxtyn said as they approached the long table of poll workers. After their IDs were validated and their faces were scanned, they were directed toward the school. They passed through one of the new wide-arch style magnetometers and were nearing the main doors of the building when it happened.

pop, pop, pop, pop

The crowd screamed and surged forward, overwhelming the security tables. Jaxtyn grabbed Sylvie's arm as they prepared to sprint toward the safety of the building.

BOOM. A bright flash of light and a punch of air. Jaxtyn and Sylvie dropped to the ground.

A few more pops sounded, then silence, followed by pandemonium as cries for help rang out.

"You're okay?" Jaxtyn asked. His elbow hurt where he'd landed on the pavement. "We're okay, right?" He tilted his head toward Sylvie and noticed an abrasion on her cheek. She mouthed something, but he couldn't hear her through the ringing in his head.

Around them, people were beginning to stand. Other than

his elbow, he seemed fine, so he stood and dusted the dirt from his pants legs. Sylvie was beginning to rise, and he helped her up.

"I'm all right," Sylvie repeated, and Jaxtyn was relieved to be able to hear her. The sirens of emergency vehicles grew in the distance.

Guards rushed from the school, heading toward the security tables, and Jaxtyn turned to track their movements. The tables had been knocked into disarray by the surge of the crowd, and beyond them…no. Oh no.

Sylvie began to turn as well, but Jaxtyn blocked her. "No, Sylvie. Don't look."

*

"NINE DEAD AND dozens injured," Skylar said. "Fucking CeeNees."

Jaxtyn's tablet feed was displayed on the kitchen wall screen. All the news outlets were covering the Boston bombing while waiting for the election results to trickle in. "Are you sure you're both all right?"

Jaxtyn sat at the table nursing a beer, a cold pack wrapped in a bandage around his elbow. Sylvie was working on her third beer, and for once Jaxtyn didn't blame her. "Yeah, Sky, we're good." He glanced at Sylvie as she finished the bottle. "Just shaken up a bit; that's all."

The three of them shared an apartment less than a mile from the campus of UMass Boston, where they were each pushing the limits on how long they could justify staying in college. The apartment was a second-floor unit in a run-down triple-decker located in a part of Dorchester that had gentrified at the turn of the century and then fallen on hard times after the country began to tear itself apart. And even though the apartment was in a marginal neighborhood, they could only afford it because Skylar's parents paid most of the rent.

"But why would they do this?" Sylvie asked again. "Why us?"

It was a question Jaxtyn couldn't answer. It didn't make any sense, but the drone camera footage clearly showed two CeeNee missionaries making their way into the crowd from the rear as they pulled guns from beneath their red coats. They both wore suicide vests, but one of them hadn't gone off. And even though that attacker was quickly killed by security, the authorities were hoping the body would provide answers.

"Oh, come on," Skylar said. "All these recent terror attacks are purely political intimidation. It's no coincidence they're mostly targeting New England, New York, and California. They need us to give in."

"But it's not consistent," Jaxtyn said. "I mean, they're missionaries. They always seem so sincere. Sure, they're misguided and wrong, but they're not *killers*. Or at least they haven't been up until now. Why would missionaries kill innocent people?"

"Oh, sure," Sylvie scoffed. "So you know all about the CeeNees now, do you?"

"Have you ever even spoken to one?" Skylar asked.

"No," Jaxtyn admitted. But he saw with sudden clarity that's exactly what he should do. They *had* to find a way to connect with these people—otherwise, the entire country risked being torn apart. "But we *should* engage with them, don't you think? I mean, how are we going to find common ground and build bridges if—"

"Stop," Skylar said. "Don't you dare go all Buddhist-sacred-oneness-of-the-universe bullshit on us. Not tonight." Sylvie nodded her agreement, and Jaxtyn shut up. This wasn't the time for that argument, but still, the idea of an honest discussion with a CeeNee resonated. They *must* try to understand people who disagreed with them. He resolved to make the effort.

The election coverage was interrupted by an update on the polling station attack. The authorities had identified the man whose vest had failed to explode. He was a known member of a violent separatist group headquartered in South Carolina and was wanted for questioning in connection with the assassinations of several federal judges. The police now believed the two terrorists were only disguised as missionaries, but the motive for the attack remained unclear.

"See!" said Jaxtyn. "I knew something was off." But before anyone could respond, the news feeds on the wall switched again, this time to a map of the country with each state outlined in gray, red, or blue. Virginia flipped from gray to red, and Harrison — the Christian Nationalist from Florida — was declared the winner of the presidential race. "Oh, God," Sylvie groaned.

"Don't give up hope yet," Jaxtyn said. "It's Congress that's most important in this election. If they manage to peel off many blue state seats, it could mean the breakup of our country." But those numbers were looking grim too. The handful of remaining moderates in the red states had all been swept out of office.

As the night went on, it only got worse. Sylvie gasped when the results from New Hampshire came in. Jaxtyn shook his head. Even here in New England, the religious fundamentalists were gaining a solid foothold. Skylar's phone dinged, and he left the kitchen. A few minutes later he returned carrying a duffel bag.

"Guys, I'm going away for a few days."

"Why?" Sylvie asked. "Where?" She seemed bewildered, and Jaxtyn suspected the alcohol and the events of the day had pushed her to her limit. Skylar shrugged in response.

"Does this have to do with your new secretive friends?" Jaxtyn asked. Skylar shrugged again. "Promise us you won't do anything dangerous," Jaxtyn said.

Skylar nodded to the wall display. "A little too late to avoid danger, don't you think?" Then he picked up his bag and left the apartment.

Chapter Three

MARCUS WAS FIDGETING again, and nothing bothered Daniel more than when his roommate—*missionary companion* now, Daniel reminded himself—wouldn't be still. He was in the window seat, and his twitching leg bumped against Daniel's thigh in a staccato rhythm echoing Daniel's own rising sense of unease.

Marcus would push the tightly pleated curtain open as far as it would go, then remove his fingers and watch the fabric spring back an inch, again and again. They were stopped deep in a tunnel somewhere between Washington and Baltimore. The window was a black mirror.

"I wish we'd get moving," Marcus said. Daniel sighed. It was the third time he'd heard that during the last half hour. Marcus needed to learn patience. He made a mental note to pray with him about it soon.

"We're sitting ducks here," Marcus said. His face was turned to the dark window, his reflection a charcoal blur on the glass. Daniel didn't disagree with the sentiment. They were leaving the safety of their community and heading north where, ever since the election six months ago, acts of terror were increasingly common. There *could* be something wrong. There'd been no announcement explaining why they'd stopped.

Daniel pressed his knee against Marcus's. "Stop jerking around. People are going to think *you're* the terrorist."

Marcus stilled his leg and turned away from the dark window. "It's not funny, Dan. I wish I had my gun."

"Shh," Daniel whispered. They were on a Northern train, and it was packed with people. These folks didn't take kindly to talk of guns. But silently, Daniel agreed. He, too, felt the absence of the comforting weight of his holster. Marcus had chosen to retain his empty shoulder harness, but even that would have to be stowed in the secured luggage car before they entered New Jersey.

A horn blared and the tunnel was suddenly filled with light as an approaching train passed on the tracks beside them. A punch of air rocked the car, and anonymous faces flashed by in quick succession.

They look just like us.

"Oh, too bad," Daniel said. "It was just another train. Looks like you'll have to wait till Boston for a terror attack."

"Dick," Marcus said.

The door at the end of the coach opened, and the conductor stepped through.

These Northern lines still called themselves Amtrak, and the logo was blazoned across the woman's cap and shirt. "Tickets and

IDs," she called out.

Daniel grimaced when Marcus turned to him and said, "We had to show our documents twice already just to get on the train. How often are we going to have to do this?"

"Come on, Marcus, stop." Daniel let a little bit of his annoyance seep into his tone. Marcus was being overly dramatic, and that's the last thing they needed on this trip. "They went over all of this in our mission briefings. And we'll need to show our ID again when we change trains in Philadelphia, where you'll have to lose your holster—which you should have just checked into the secured container with your gun in the first place."

Marcus huffed. "Yeah, yeah, I know. And again in New York City, where we'll have to strip naked and get anal probed."

Daniel smiled. It wouldn't get quite *that* bad, but the rules did tighten the farther north one traveled. At least, that's what they'd been told. Neither of them had been north of Washington, DC, before.

The conductor made her way down the aisle, eyeing the two young men the entire time. Their red shirts and white trousers marked them as missionaries; Marcus's empty holster marked *him* as trouble. She reached them, and Daniel noticed many of the nearby passengers paying close attention.

She nodded at Marcus. "We don't want trouble."

They'd been told they'd hear that again and again.

"No, ma'am," Marcus replied. "You'll get no trouble from us."

"All right," she said and held out her hand. "Tickets and IDs."

She took the documents and ignored the silly name tags they

wore—Thomas and Paul. Daniel didn't blame her. They were a distracting affectation, and he wished the church didn't insist on them.

She studied the documents and then scanned them into her handheld. "All the way to Boston." It wasn't a question. "You know they don't want you there—" She read her screen. "—Daniel Ridley."

"Yes, ma'am," he replied. But it wasn't a matter of what the people in Boston thought they wanted. It was what God wanted that mattered.

"Fine. Into the lion's den with you." She handed back the documents. Did she know scripture or did she just happen to use the phrase?

"As for you, Mr. Johnson," she leaned in to address Marcus. "If you'd like to be a good neighbor and make people less nervous, I could check the shoulder holster for you right now."

"No thank you, ma'am," Marcus said. "I'll just keep my security blanket a little bit longer."

She shook her head and continued down the aisle. "Everything's fine," she said to anyone listening. "There'll be no trouble on my train."

*

THEIR MISSION TRIP had begun the day before with a traditional send-off service on the school's athletic field. The entire student body of Sangre de Cristo turned out to join them in prayer and to ask God for His blessing. The daffodils in the school gardens were just coming into bloom, and fog covered the river below the campus.

"Take these servants, oh Lord, as wholly Thine," Pastor Logan had prayed. "Use them today in Thy service. Abide in them and let all their work be wrought in Thee."

"Amen," a hundred voices responded.

A fox trotted across the edge of the field abutting the campus. Perhaps a mother with kits in her den, out searching for mice or voles. Surely, He had heard their prayer. Marcus and Daniel were leaving their warm, safe den too—heading into danger for the good of their greater Christian community.

Their first stop yesterday afternoon had been in Washington, DC, where they'd joined the vigil outside of Capitol Hill and spent the night with others from their church. The vigil had been in progress for a month, with tens of thousands of Christians praying on the Capitol grounds without pause, beseeching God to give Congress the strength to do the right thing.

A group of Catholics—temporary allies at best—had set up camp next to the Church's pavilion, and Daniel and Marcus had shared soup and bread with them and space under the propane heater, politely ignoring the Catholics' prayer beads and their Marian devotions.

But already, just one day into their mission, South Carolina felt like a world away. Dirty patches of snow clung to life in the deeply shaded corners of Pennsylvania's forests. They were told Boston would still feel like winter, likely colder than anything they'd experienced at Sangre de Cristo.

The train pulled into Philadelphia's Thirtieth Street Station and all passengers were required to disembark. Bags were inspected and tickets and IDs were validated. And even though he knew it would happen, Marcus complained when he was forced to surrender his empty shoulder harness. "But it's *empty*," he'd insisted to the station employee who was clearly just doing her job, had heard it all before, and didn't care. The harness went into their secured bin, which already held both their guns and Daniel's holster.

She checked their tickets again. "You're going to Boston?"

Marcus nodded. Daniel knew what she would say. "You know you'll need to store this bin at the station there, right? You won't be able to have them with you in the city?"

"It's a matter of principle," Daniel responded.

"All right"—she peered at his name tag and rolled her eyes—"Thomas." *How many Thomases had she seen come through here?* "It's a pretty expensive principle. You know they charge an arm and a leg to store firearms."

When neither man responded, she handed back their documents. "We don't want any trouble."

"No, ma'am. Neither do we."

The station itself was a magnificent structure, far grander than anything Daniel had ever seen. Windows rising four stories allowed thick bands of sunlight to spotlight the ancient wooden benches. The main hall had been divided into two sections, and the missionaries joined the other cleared passengers as they waited for their turn to reboard.

A statue stretched toward the high ceiling ahead of them—an angel with massive wings lifting the lifeless body of a young man—a fallen soldier, most likely—to heaven. Daniel blinked up at it, his eyes suddenly misty. There was a time when these people believed in angels and heaven, when God's grace had been real to them.

The passengers in the waiting area sat or stood patiently. Some stretched their legs, walking the length of the glass partition. Outside the enclosure, the people of Philadelphia rushed by. Few looked up at the angel.

A young woman their age approached. She had green, spiked hair and multiple facial piercings, both of which were unheard of at Sangre de Cristo. "Excuse me, gents," she said. "Do you know where I could find Jesus? I seem to have misplaced him."

They'd been told they'd get that a lot too.

"Sylvie," a tall, blond-haired guy called. "Stop. Leave them alone." He appeared to be roughly their age as well and was handsome in an athletic sort of way. *I can notice that; it doesn't mean anything.* The tattoo on his neck was mostly hidden by his jacket collar, and Daniel wished he could make out what it was.

"Is it true he's going to come again?" Sylvie asked, getting up too close. Daniel could smell her breath—gum and maybe alcohol. "I like a guy who can do that."

"Sylvie, come on. Stop." The young man started toward them. He wore a T-shirt showing an outline of the State of Texas getting kicked in the panhandle by a smiling cowboy boot. "Adios, Asshole," the shirt read. Perhaps he'd also been at the Capitol, protesting on the other side of the mall with his own people.

He reached them and smiled shyly. "Sorry," he mumbled before he guided Sylvie away by the elbow.

Daniel watched him walk away, thinking how little he knew of these Northerners. Marcus had ignored them both as missionaries were trained to do. Marcus was better than Daniel at not hearing minor slights and insults.

They reboarded the train, and several passengers smirked when they saw Marcus without his holster. The man who'd saved them from Sylvie was sitting a half dozen rows ahead. The fellow sitting next to him had to be gay. He had bright orange hair, wore makeup and a heavy, beaded necklace, and waved his hands about theatrically. Sylvie sat right behind them, and Daniel realized they must all be traveling together because she would occasionally lean forward and say something to the others.

The gay one let out an exaggerated shriek, and Daniel's face burned. Why did they have to behave that way? There were gays and lesbians in South Carolina, of course, even in the small town he grew up in, but they all acted normal. It wasn't illegal or anything, and they could even get married still—but there was talk of changing that soon. Homosexual acts were prohibited at school, of course, but even at Sangre de Cristo, there was a support group for students struggling with those feelings.

Daniel bowed his head in a brief prayer. *God loves us all. Jesus died for everyone, no matter the nature of their sins.*

Chapter Four

SYLVIE LEANED FORWARD in her seat and stuck her head between Jaxtyn and Skylar. She'd been drinking, and the tang of stale breath and gin hung between them. There was no way they would have let her bring alcohol onto the train in Philadelphia, so she must have been sneaking drinks from a hidden bottle during the trip up from Washington. "Did you see those freaks? They're sitting in the same car as us."

"They're not freaks, Sylvie," Jaxtyn said. "They're just..." He waved his hand, not sure how to finish.

"Why are you defending them, Jax?" Even closer now, Jaxtyn could detect the weed smell under the alcohol. "They're dangerous."

She's right about that.

Skylar craned his neck to peer down the aisle behind them. "I think they're kind of hot. I bet they have wild missionary sex each night in their hotel room."

"You think everyone is always having sex," Jaxtyn said. "And wild missionary sex is oxymoronic." Although Skylar was right about them being attractive. The one called Thomas was… not *hot*, exactly…but interesting in an intense way. "And don't stare," Jaxtyn added.

"You're wrong about the sex part," Skylar protested. "There's an entire porn channel about Mormon missionaries, and it gets pretty wild."

It had been a long three days, and Jaxtyn had had his fill of Sylvie and Skylar. A weekend road trip had pushed his tolerance of the pair to the breaking point. He rubbed his temples. "First of all, they're not Mormons; they're CeeNees—"

"Even worse," Sylvie interrupted.

She was right about that too. "And secondly, you do know porn isn't real, right? And there are better things to do with that VR set your parents bought you?" Once in a while, his annoyance at Skylar's wealth came through. Or, not his wealth particularly, but his wasting of it, his disregard for how lucky he was.

And the risks he took, as if money could protect him from everything.

"I can't think of one," Skylar responded. "And why are they called CeeNees, anyway?"

"Why did you even join us on this trip?" Sylvie asked. She liked to think of herself as a social justice warrior, but she was more of a social justice warrior groupie, traveling from protest to protest, taking on the cause du jour. She didn't wait for an answer before plopping back into her seat and slipping in her earbuds.

For a guy who spent so much time with his new group of

radical friends fighting against the breakup of the country, Skylar was remarkably uninformed about the details. "CeeNee stands for Christian Nationalist Evangelical, CNE. They love all the things your new friends hate. And you can tell these guys are CeeNee missionaries by their red shirts. The Mormons are all black and white."

"They look good in red," Skylar observed.

Hopeless. Jaxtyn followed Sylvie's lead and disappeared into his music.

*

IT SEEMED RIDICULOUS to have to disembark for yet another security scan less than two hours later at New York's Penn Station, but the New England States had their own set of rules and restrictions. In addition to restricting pepper spray, lighters, and matches, any passengers foolish enough to have brought tobacco products this far would need to surrender them unless they could produce a medical prescription.

Jaxtyn watched as the bin next to the security table filled with half-empty packets of cigarettes, the occasional cigar, and the rare tin of chewing tobacco. Unlike firearms and holsters, tobacco products would not be securely stowed away. They were to be destroyed, or, more likely, quietly distributed after hours by the guards working the desk.

"Tickets and IDs," the agent said to the two CeeNees in line in front of Jaxtyn.

"They're the same as they were when we got on the train in Charleston, and Washington, and Philadelphia," said the one whose nametag read Paul. But he handed them over anyway, and

Jaxtyn was glad the CeeNee was cooperating and wouldn't be delaying them by getting arrested.

The guard scanned the documents into his pad, then twisted it with his fingers so the screen faced the missionary. "Marcus Johnson," he said, "review this list of prohibited items and sign the attestation at the bottom."

So, not Paul. He wondered what Thomas's real name was.

"If you have any metal items on you, keys or such, you'll need to remove them and place them in the bin before you go through the scanner." Marcus swiped his finger across the screen. "Please wait over there until we announce boarding." The agent nodded to a small, enclosed area with a vending machine and only a few dozen seats already filled with passengers.

Marcus took his documents and moved away.

Now that Jaxtyn was right behind the other CeeNee, he realized he had a good four or five inches on the one whose name may or may not be Thomas. The overhead LEDs gave his hair a bright copper sheen. It looked like it would normally be combed into controlled waves. Or, more accurately, the CeeNee looked like the kind of guy who would normally make more of an effort. Right now, his hair was a mess, sticking out at odd angles, but he'd probably been traveling for some time and may even have spent the night at one of the DC rallies.

The CeeNee waited for the guard to look up and then handed over his documents without being asked. He must be the reasonable one of the pair. "Daniel Ridley. Read and sign, please." The guard spun the tablet around, and Daniel—a pleasant, old-fashioned name—swiped his finger, retrieved his documents, and went to join his companion.

I wonder if he's as tired of traveling with Marcus as I am of Sylvie and Skylar?

The crowded waiting area continued to fill with passengers. Marcus moved to the end of a line of people at the vending machine. Sylvie and Skylar were engrossed in Skylar's tablet, leaning in together, laughing.

Jaxtyn approached Daniel, and the CeeNee's glance darted across the room, looking for his missionary companion.

"Sorry about Sylvie back in Philadelphia," Jaxtyn said. "She's not usually like that." Jaxtyn wasn't sure why he was apologizing for Sylvie, or why he'd even approached Daniel in the first place. And he'd clearly made the man nervous by coming over to him while he was alone. "And I guess you're probably the ones who approach strangers, not the other way around."

He smiled to show Daniel it was intended as a friendly comment, that he knew they were missionaries and was still willing to talk to them. Daniel looked toward Marcus, who was inching his way forward in the vending machine line, then turned his attention back to Jaxtyn. His gaze was assessing, as if he had to think about how to respond. Jaxtyn thought it must be horrible to always expect a trap or hostility from people you didn't know.

"I'm Jaxtyn Keller." He held out his hand, and Daniel took it. "I live in Boston. Is that where you guys are headed?" He knew it was; he'd overheard the agent when he checked their documents, but he didn't want to seem like a stalker or anything.

"Daniel Ridley." He'd known that too.

"Boston then?" Jaxtyn prompted.

"Yes," replied Daniel.

Jaxtyn waited for more. *What kind of missionary can't make small talk*? But Daniel remained quiet, and Jaxtyn decided he needed to say something. It would be too awkward to just walk away now.

"Have you been to Boston before?"

"No."

More silence. It didn't seem hostile, or even unfriendly. Daniel simply appeared to be very nervous or deep in thought on some perplexing puzzle. Time for an open-ended question.

"It's a great city. What are you looking forward to most?"

Daniel's face relaxed. "Helping people find God's grace through faith in Jesus Christ," he replied.

Jaxtyn blinked. But before he could think of a possible response, Marcus returned, holding two bottles of water. He handed one to Daniel. "Everything all right?" he asked.

The presence of his missionary companion seemed to settle Daniel. "Sorry," he said. "It's been a long trip." He smiled at Jaxtyn. He had even, white teeth and a long, narrow nose. Jaxtyn's original opinion was confirmed. Not hot, exactly, but interesting in an intense way.

And clearly not the *"crooked teeth are the will of God"* kind of Christian.

"This is Jason," Daniel told Marcus.

Jaxtyn held out his hand. "Jaxtyn," he corrected.

"Good to meet you," Marcus said.

Jaxtyn felt the weight of Sylvie's rudeness hanging in the air. "Sorry about Sylvie, earlier."

"No worries," Marcus said. "We were told to expect that sort of thing."

"Well, you shouldn't have to tolerate disrespect." Jaxtyn felt embarrassed for his friends. Yes, the CeeNees were a threat to democracy, but it didn't solve anything to mock them and alienate them. If there was going to be some sort of country remaining after this was all over, they'd have to find a way to coexist.

"Were you at the rally?" he asked them.

"The prayer vigil, yes," Daniel replied.

"What do you think is going to happen?" Another good, open-ended question. Jaxtyn suspected they didn't share much in the way of political leanings, so he didn't want to assume they'd all like to see the same outcome.

"I think Congress will figure it out," Daniel replied. "We don't think it makes sense to dismantle the Union entirely; we just want the states to be in charge."

By *we*, Jaxtyn assumed he meant his church, or maybe the separatist states more generally. But they were all separatist states now, weren't they? No one wanted to see the current arrangement languishing on life support forever.

And besides, when you started drilling down into the details, the Union couldn't be broken up. Not in any practical way. Highways, military bases, currencies, and bond ratings—it couldn't be unwound without everything falling apart.

"But what about Texas?" he asked, holding apart the sides of his jacket to fully display his T-shirt.

Marcus laughed. "Nobody wants Texas to stick around."

It was true. That's why Jaxtyn had worn the T-shirt to the DC rally—it was a way of establishing common ground. Texas had jumped the gun last year and declared its independence unilaterally. The Supreme Court was taking its time deciding what to do about that.

Meanwhile, the other forty-nine states were all — for now — still committed to staying together in a new, much looser collaboration. But landing on the details of a new arrangement was proving to be elusive. Congress had been debating options for years, even before Texas pulled the trigger, with no apparent progress.

Jaxtyn noticed Daniel studying the tattoo on his neck, and he let his coat fall closed again. He wasn't embarrassed by it, and he'd happily have a discussion about religion and spirituality with anyone, but he wasn't sure what might trigger the CeeNees, and the whole point of coming over to Daniel was to apologize for Sylvie, not to start an argument.

At least, that was the whole point until he'd seen Daniel's smile. Now he was surprised to find himself wanting to linger, to see if he could get the young man to open up more. Maybe to smile at him again.

Sylvie and Skylar were looking at them. He knew how this would end. Skylar wouldn't be able to resist finding out what was going on, and soon they'd come over and Skylar would start embarrassing everyone talking about sex. Jaxtyn took out his phone and brought up the website of his sangha.

"The members of my…church," an entirely inaccurate word, but he didn't have much time, "enjoy talking with others about religion." He and Daniel both glanced nervously at Sylvie, who was headed toward them. "Respectfully, I mean. Can I send this to you? You'd be welcome to come."

He thought at first Daniel would say no. But Marcus nudged him, and Daniel took out his phone and accepted the contact information.

"What's going on, boys?" Skylar asked. He put his hand on

Jaxtyn's shoulder and gave the missionaries a conspicuous once-over. Daniel blushed. Marcus tensed and moved closer to Daniel in what Jaxtyn interpreted as a protective move. *Interesting.*

"Nothing," Jaxtyn said. "We're just getting ready to reboard. Come on." He gently turned Skylar toward the gate, where agents were scanning tickets, and passengers had already begun making their way down the steps to the platforms.

Sylvie winked at the missionaries before she turned and followed.

Chapter Five

WHEN THEY WERE boys, Daniel and Marcus would sometimes be invited on each other's family vacations. One summer, Daniel's family had taken Marcus along and gone on a driving vacation which included a visit to the Creation Museum in Kentucky. He remembered marveling at the dinosaur models in the full-scale replica of Noah's Ark. But even at age nine, he sensed something didn't quite make sense as he read the plaque describing how the flood had laid down the reptiles' fossils in rocks.

That night, Daniel and Marcus had stayed up late, shining their flashlights on the dinosaur models they'd gotten at the Creation Museum's gift shop. Marcus stomped his dinosaur across the bed toward Daniel's. "There's only room on this ark for one of us!" Marcus said as he lunged his tyrannosaurus forward. Daniel's brontosaurus didn't back down. "Actually, there's no room on the ark for either of us!"

The boys laughed, both because it was a funny idea — these enormous creatures squeezing onto an ark with all those other animals — but also because they were relieved. They both knew it was nonsense. They didn't have to pretend to believe it, not with each other. It was the start of a lifelong bond.

Once he was older, he began to use the idea of dinosaurs on the ark as a litmus test for people. It was truly a mark of someone beyond reason if they felt compelled to twist reality so violently to accommodate a literal reading of the Old Testament. It wasn't necessary, and it was counterproductive, making Christians look foolish. The whispered word "dinosaurs" became the secret code he and Marcus would use to call out anything absurd on its face, anything so filled with internal contradictions that it was embarrassing to watch people attempt to make it true.

Belief in the power of God's grace and salvation through His Son, Jesus Christ, was all that was necessary.

*

IT WAS EIGHTY degrees in their hotel room. A damp, moldy-smelling air blasted out of the wall unit, and no matter what they tried, they couldn't turn it off. The front desk manager said they'd send someone up, but that had been over an hour ago.

The King's Royal Court Hotel — "Five Star Luxury at a Budget Price!" — had proven to be a long subway ride from Boston's South Station. Many years ago, the room's cinderblock walls had been painted powder blue, as had the electrical conduits running along the baseboards and up the walls to the steel-gray outlet boxes. A small television had been bolted to the top of a massive chest of drawers, causing its laminated surface to warp and peel.

Marcus opened the bathroom door and stepped into the room. "The water is lukewarm at best," he complained, toweling at his hair. "I'd wait for a while to see if it heats up again." He was wearing a pair of white briefs, and he walked to the metal desk by the door and picked up the hotel's brochure with its absurd slogan on the cover.

"Dinosaurs," he said.

Daniel laughed. Dinosaurs, indeed. But Boston was an expensive city, and the church ran its missions on a shoestring.

Marcus bent over his bed and rummaged through his bag. He'd been a wrestler in high school and had a muscular, solid build. His white underwear stood out in stark relief against his black skin.

"You look like an Oreo cookie."

Marcus froze, just for a moment, then bent back to his task. "Ha," he said, and Daniel flushed in embarrassment. He shouldn't have commented on Marcus's appearance when he was only partially dressed. He wouldn't want Marcus to think he was looking at him like that, assessing him.

"I didn't mean…" Daniel began. "I wasn't looking there…at that."

"Chill, Dan," Marcus said. "It was a joke. I know you're not checking me out." He removed a clean pair of trousers from his duffel — white, of course; the uniform was required at all times — and slipped them on.

Did he rush to cover himself? Daniel wasn't sure.

Daniel's confession to Marcus of the sinful urges he was only beginning to understand himself was a new thing between them, and Daniel thought they were still trying to figure out if it changed anything. He hoped it didn't. Marcus claimed it didn't.

No one in the church kept secrets from one another. It was part of their covenant. No matter their struggles, temptations, or burdens, they were there for each other, praying together to ask Jesus to lead them back into God's grace. This was especially true for missionary companions.

They'd prayed together with their families as boys, and as teenagers they'd prayed together at school, but it was only since they'd become roommates at Sangre de Cristo that they'd begun praying together alone. In the evening in their dorm room, they would pray for Jesus to guide Marcus to accepting God's plan without question, to allow His will expression through Marcus, and for Marcus to resist the sin of prideful dominance and control. Sometimes, Marcus had confessed, he questioned God's wisdom — at least as far as His will was expressed through the church leaders.

But Marcus had the easy burden. It was a simple thing to pray for humility.

Daniel, on the other hand, was tempted by impure thoughts of men.

He remembered Marcus's involuntary flinch the first time they'd prayed together for Daniel. They were touching, clasping each other's hands, and kneeling face to face on the floor of their small room. He'd prayed that Jesus would give him the strength to ignore his impulses toward men, that He would provide a path for Daniel to have a loving relationship with a woman, to start a family as God surely intended for him.

Marcus's grip tightened as he puzzled through what Daniel was saying, and it was clear when the moment came and he'd figured it out. He hadn't disengaged, exactly, but his contributions of "Please, Jesus," and "Heal my friend Daniel, Jesus," had become more wooden, as if his mind had been pulled away from the prayer session—which it had, of course.

They hadn't spoken about it that night, but the next day, Marcus had asked the question Daniel knew he would. "You don't feel that way about me, do you, Dan?"

And the truthful answer, thank God, was no. "I don't really feel that way about anyone, Marcus. It's just a general thing I know God doesn't intend for me."

"I don't understand," he'd replied.

They were both sitting at the study table in their room, their essays and reflection journals pushed to the side. "Look, when you see a pretty girl, you can't help but notice her, right? And if it's the right place and time, maybe you even think about talking to her, asking her on a date."

Marcus nodded.

"Well, sometimes, I get that response with a guy." If he'd been very honest, he would have acknowledged it was more than just sometimes. "And I'm trying to...I don't know...*move it*, I guess...from guys to girls, as God intended."

"But you've never..." Marcus began. "I mean, you don't actually—"

"No! No, I'm going to get married and have a family someday. I mean, I notice pretty girls too." Maybe that was even true. He certainly was able to notice when a girl looked nice, with a new flattering haircut, for example, or a scarf that brought out the color in her eyes. "I just need Jesus to help me sometimes. To give me the strength to shift my gaze."

Marcus had accepted that, and their friendship had survived. There was no longer any awkwardness when they prayed together, and sometimes, when Marcus would notice Daniel's gaze on a fellow student, he'd touch Daniel's elbow, or ask a question about their studies as a distraction to help him.

But here in Boston, things felt unsettled again. The entire trip had been unnerving. He hadn't been prepared for the stares and for the hostility. But maybe he was imagining that?

"Did it happen again today with the tall blond boy?" Marcus sat on the side of his small twin bed, facing Daniel. His red shirt hung open in a concession to the heat.

"Jaxtyn," Daniel replied. "Maybe it did. I'm not sure."

"How can you not be sure?"

"We've been over this, Marcus." Daniel tried not to let his exasperation seep into his voice. "You could see he was attractive, right? Objectively?"

Marcus tilted his head. "Sure," he acknowledged. "Tall, blond, kind of athletic looking, I guess." He squinted, and then added, "White, if you like that sort of thing."

"Exactly," Daniel said. "And it doesn't make you gay that you can see the man is attractive."

"But I *don't* see him as attractive. That's the point, Dan. I'm not curious about how it would feel to touch him or kiss him. Just because I can see he'd make a good underwear model doesn't mean I'm tempted into sin by him."

The comment prompted Daniel to immediately conjure an image of Jaxtyn as an underwear model, and his face flamed.

"You're blushing."

"It's a hundred degrees in here," Daniel objected.

"Should we pray?"

They probably should, but Daniel was too confused to know what he needed—which was a sure sign he *should* be praying. But it was nearly time for their first check-in. And it hadn't been a big deal anyway. Jaxtyn was an attractive man, and Daniel had noticed. That was all there was to it.

"Not right now," he replied. "We need to get ready for our call with Pastor Logan."

*

THE WATER NEVER did get hot, and the pressure in the shower was disappointingly weak. The wall of the tub between the faucet and the drain was stained blue and green, and the tiny bar of soap they'd been given when they checked in had already been reduced to a sliver in Daniel's palm. He studiously avoided thinking about Jaxtyn as he tried, without success, to work the soap into a lather.

The water suddenly ran cold and then slowed to a trickle.

Five Star Luxury at a Budget Price! "Dinosaurs," he whispered to himself.

After toweling himself dry and slipping on his boxers, he entered the room to find Marcus busy at the small table, positioning his phone against the grungy coffee machine in preparation for their upcoming call.

"That should do it," he said as he studied the camera's field of view. There was only one chair in the room, but if one of them sat on the foot of the bed while the other took the chair, they'd both be visible on the screen.

Daniel finished dressing, combed his hair, and sat at the end of the bed. Marcus double-checked the phone's position, nodded, and moved the chair closer to the bed so he'd be sitting next to Daniel. "We've got five minutes," he said. "Can I tell you something serious, Dan?"

Marcus's eyes didn't meet his, and Daniel braced himself for more awkward questions about his reaction to Jaxtyn. "Sure," he said.

"You wouldn't have any reason to know this," Marcus said, "but the word 'Oreo' can be offensive when it's directed at a Black person."

That wasn't what Daniel had been expecting. "Oh." His mind raced to try to find what he might have missed, but he wasn't used to thinking about race that way—as a separate culture where words or phrases might cause offense unintentionally—other than the obvious slurs from the old days, of course. "Why?"

"Well," Marcus began, not meeting Daniel's eye. "It used to be something a Black person would be called if they acted White or thought of themselves that way. You know, Black on the outside, White on the inside."

How strange. The idea a color could act *like another color somehow.*

"Cripes, Marcus. I didn't offend *you*, did I? You know me better than that, don't you?"

"We're good, Dan. Don't worry. I just thought you should know how it could come across. To other people, I mean." He did look up then and met Daniel's eyes. "While we're up here."

He was still confused but appreciated his friend's efforts to help him out. "Okay, thanks. Is there anything else I should know?"

Marcus's eyes widened comically. "Hmm. Let's see… Is there anything arising out of five hundred years of subjugation and oppression you should *know*, so you don't accidentally embarrass yourself?"

And all right, put that way it was a foolish question. But he and Marcus never talked about these things. No one did.

The phone's alarm went off; it was time for the call.

"It's okay, Dan. I'll watch out for you." Marcus leaned forward and brought up the meeting screen. "Ready?" he asked.

*

OF COURSE, THEY had to wait three minutes before Pastor Logan joined the call. He made it a point, always, to be last to a meeting.

"Brother Thomas, Brother Paul."

"Good evening, Pastor Logan," the missionaries replied.

"I see you've made it to your destination. Did you have any difficulties on your journey?"

Daniel thought of the interminable train ride, the repeated validation of their IDs, the distrust and subtle hostility from fellow travelers, and the dismal hotel room. "No, sir."

"Good. I have news, but first, what is the Open Lotus?"

"What?" Marcus asked. He shot a blank look at Daniel, who began to answer, but Pastor Logan cut him off.

"It's the name of a new contact that appeared in Brother Thomas's phone this afternoon."

It was a startling reminder that their every move was supervised by the church. Daniel wondered if the subtle message was intentional — no matter how far they traveled, the church was with them, watching. "It's a church," Daniel said. "We met someone on the train who told us his congregation likes to meet with others and discuss religion. He seemed sincere."

He knew that wasn't quite right. The profile picture for the Open Lotus Jaxtyn had downloaded to his phone was an image of a seated Buddha with a multi-petalled white flower in his lap. He hadn't dared to click on the link; he wasn't sure his phone would allow him to access the site, and he didn't want to trigger any red flags.

"It doesn't sound like a church," Pastor Logan observed.

"It might not be Christian," Daniel admitted. He pictured the tattoo on Jaxtyn's neck—another seated Buddha. "Still, churches are good sources of converts for us. The congregants already have some sense of the importance of religion in their lives."

Pastor Logan closed his eyes. He did that when he was thinking, and it always made Daniel uncomfortable; he didn't know where to look. He resisted the urge to glance over at Marcus.

When he finally opened his eyes, Pastor Logan said, "Very well. But be careful with that one. Some churches are hostile to our message. It's best to focus your missionary outreach on the Catholics, or churches within immigrant communities." He paused, presumably leaving space for questions, then continued after a brief silence.

"Do not forget the youth centers either. Neglected young people are always eager to hear our message of salvation." Daniel and Marcus nodded. They already had the addresses of several social service organizations they'd begin visiting in the coming days.

"Good," Pastor Logan said again as if they'd all just reached some sort of agreement. "Now, I have an important update on your other mission."

Marcus leaned forward, and his leg started twitching. It wasn't in the camera's view, but Daniel reached over with his foot and lightly tapped Marcus's shoe to call attention to his fidgeting. Marcus resisted the idea of their other mission. In fact, they'd prayed on it together, asking Jesus's help to allow Marcus to accept the commands of his elders without question or objection.

Daniel wasn't convinced Marcus had found the humility to submit, and Pastor Logan had a sharp eye. He'd notice Marcus's discomfort if he wasn't careful.

"That's exciting news, sir," Daniel said, giving Marcus space to calm himself.

"Yes," Pastor Logan agreed. "We've uncovered surveillance footage of the suspect and Ruth together in North Carolina at a highway rest stop."

They'd been bound to come up with a video eventually. You can't travel by car from South Carolina to New York without your movements being captured. Daniel was surprised it had taken as long as it had. Beside him, Marcus remained motionless.

"It's only a five-second capture of the man from behind as he and Ruth get out of a car, and it's not very clear," Pastor Logan continued. "But there's one good thing. The young man evidently drove his own car. Can you imagine? God is surely leading us to him. His car has University of Massachusetts parking stickers on it for each of the last two years."

Daniel swallowed. *A student just like us.*

"It's a short subway ride for you. I won't send the pictures over the internet, but we're having them delivered to your hotel securely. You'll get them tomorrow."

"Jesus answered our prayers," Daniel managed.

"Yes," Pastor Logan agreed. "Now, let's pray together and thank Him for guiding us to our destination."

Chapter Six

SEVEN O'CLOCK IN the morning was far too early to be on campus. But the meditation group had been Jaxtyn's idea, and he owed it to the five brave souls who'd joined him to soldier on through the inconvenience.

He sat in a comfortable half lotus pose, and let his eyes rest on the slowly brightening blanket of clouds outside the window. Next to him, Sylvie knelt in a poorly executed Burmese pose, and Jaxtyn made a mental note to remind her to rest her weight between her feet, not on top of her heels.

He pushed the thought away. He should be emptying his mind, not cluttering it with notes.

He brought his attention back to the subtly shifting clouds. Behind them, far out across the ocean, the sun was beginning its westward arc across the sky. He straightened his back and pictured his spine being drawn up to meet the clouds, to meet the sun, his whole body opening to become one with the universe.

For the briefest of moments, he was there—that transcendent state all the mystics point to, where the sense of self dissolves and the limitless connections of life are revealed.

But only for a moment.

Once again, the CeeNees he'd met on the train that weekend intruded on his thoughts. There was something about them his mind kept picking at, kept coming back to, but he couldn't quite capture what it was. He decided to give up on his efforts to quiet his mind and, instead, opted to spend the last ten minutes of his meditation session letting his subconscious lead where it would.

The White CeeNee, Daniel—short and intense with nervous brown eyes—had seemed to hold so many contrasts. He'd been guarded and awkward, just the opposite of what Jaxtyn would have expected from a missionary. But it was the Black one, Marcus—muscled and watchful—whom his mind kept coming back to.

It was something in the way he'd rushed over when he saw Jaxtyn speaking with his missionary companion, something that felt out of context. At first, he'd thought perhaps Skylar's joke had had an element of truth to it. Perhaps the men had a relationship of sorts, and Marcus had intervened out of jealousy.

But the more he replayed the encounter in his mind, the more certain he was Marcus hadn't been motivated by anything like jealousy. Rather, it had seemed more…

Protective. That's what it was. Marcus had seen Jaxtyn as a threat to Daniel.

But why? He'd approached the man to apologize, after all, and he hadn't been threatening, or standing too close. They were missionaries; they'd have to be comfortable speaking with strangers. It wasn't just generalized nervousness. No. Marcus had specifically seen Jaxtyn as a threat, but not to himself — only to Daniel.

The timer on his phone chimed, and the meditators began coming out of their poses. "Ouch," Sylvie whispered.

"Namaste, everyone," Jaxtyn said, offering an easy smile around the circle. "That was a good session." There were murmurs of agreement and returned namastes. "I'll send a text reminder before the next meeting."

He stood and helped Sylvie up from her kneeling position. "Ouch. Jesus," she said, massaging her left knee. "How do you people do this?"

"Practice," Jaxtyn said, "But you really don't have to do it. There's a critical mass of people now, I think, to keep it going."

Sylvie linked her hands together and raised her arms above her head, stretching. "I know. But it's nice, peaceful even. I thought I'd be bored, but time changes somehow when I meditate." She tilted her head from side to side, and her spine made a popping sound. "It's just awfully early, Jax. Maybe you could reschedule for the afternoon?"

He didn't respond. They'd been over it before. Jaxtyn thought it was important to start the morning with meditation. It helped set the stage for mindful, attentive behavior the rest of the day.

"Come on, I'll walk you to the campus center and buy you a coffee," Jaxtyn offered.

"Throw in a muffin, and you've got a deal."

There was a steady, cold wind off the bay, so they hurried

across the campus, passing a handful of brave students out for a morning jog. Early-blooming snow crocuses shivered in a few protected garden beds.

They reached the campus center building, passed through the metal detectors, and hurried into the entry vestibule. "Still feels like winter out there," one of the guards at the table said as she scanned their IDs.

"And they say more snow is on the way this weekend," Jaxtyn replied.

"Yup," said the other guard. Jaxtyn thought he might be Jamaican. He wore a silver cross on a short pendant around his neck. "Who really knows what will happen?"

That was true about everything. The light above the inner door turned green, and Jaxtyn and Sylvie entered the main hall of the student center.

The guard's cross must have triggered the same thoughts in both of them. "I've been thinking about those CeeNees we met," Sylvie said. "I feel bad I mocked them. I mean, they're weird and their politics are shit, but I should have left them alone. I can't imagine what their lives must be like down there." She shivered in an exaggerated way, but Jaxtyn knew what she meant and thought she was sincere. "Do you think they live in one of those missionary factories?"

"Probably," Jaxtyn responded. "I mean, they were wearing the uniforms, so, yeah."

"I just can't imagine what their lives must be like," Sylvie said again. "It would be fascinating to talk to one."

"Well, you made a poor start at that," Jaxtyn said.

Sylvie sighed. "I know. I'm sorry. I was just so pumped from the rally. I couldn't help myself." They'd reached the café counter, and Jaxtyn ordered two coffees—one with cream and extra sugar for Sylvie—and a blueberry muffin. "I mean, we've got to watch out for our fellow citizens, you know? We can't let the CeeNees take over huge parts of the country and impose their religious beliefs on everyone, no matter how flexible we're trying to be."

Sylvie picked up their tray and took it to one of the round tables lining the wide, curving concourse of the campus center.

Two girls wearing hijabs passed by their table, and Jaxtyn noticed one frown when she took in Sylvie's green hair and facial piercings. Luckily, Sylvie was facing away from them. Already the peaceful ease from his meditation was fading, and he was in no mood for a confrontation.

"As your friend," he said, "I feel compelled to point out you weren't just pumped from the rally. You'd been drinking too."

Sylvie looked away. "I'd hoped you hadn't noticed."

Jaxtyn didn't say anything.

"I don't usually do that—drink during the day, I mean."

"You shouldn't do it all. You know how you get." Jaxtyn picked up his mug and took a sip. "And besides, you asked me to help you with—"

Sylvie put her hand over his on the table. "Stop. I know. You're right. I *am* doing better. Really. That was a slip." She pinched off a bite of her muffin. "And I appreciate your calling me out on it." She looked away as she popped the muffin into her mouth.

"I care about you, Sylvie."

She chewed and swallowed. "I know." She looked everywhere but at Jaxtyn. "And speaking of awkward, have you heard from Sky lately?"

"No. Not since he left on Monday." It was Jaxtyn's turn to look away.

"You know more than you're telling me," she said accusingly. "Does he talk to you about where he goes on these mysterious trips?" She broke off another piece of muffin and handed it to Jaxtyn.

"He doesn't. And I'm not sure I want to know. But I do worry about him, and he's never been gone for more than one night before. Wherever he is, I wish he'd reach out and let us know he's okay." Jaxtyn took the muffin and placed it on the napkin next to his coffee cup.

Sylvie glanced behind her, then lowered her voice. "You don't think he's gone into the Red, do you?" When Jaxtyn didn't respond, she continued. "I don't like those new people he's been hanging with. I'm afraid they might do something crazy."

That would be troubling. Skylar's heart was in the right place, and for someone so seemingly disconnected from the world around him he was always eager to help anyone out of a jam, but he'd recently fallen in with some dangerous people who did dangerous things, even if it was for the benefit of others.

But going into the Red would be a whole new level of risk. He took out his phone and scrolled through his contacts until he found Skylar. "*You good?*" he typed and sent it off.

"Maybe he's met a new guy," Sylvie suggested. "You know how he gets."

But they both knew that's not what had happened. He'd packed a duffel bag three days ago and told them not to worry. "Yeah, I hope so," Jaxtyn said, but he thought the universe was far more intertwined than they could see, and he didn't like the feeling he had of being pushed toward something dark.

Danger lay directly ahead; he could feel it in his bones.

Chapter Seven

DANIEL'S FIRST FEW days in Boston were difficult.

Everywhere he and Marcus went, people glanced nervously at their missionary uniforms. Community centers supposedly open to the public suddenly required permits for visitors. Pastors from churches proclaiming "All are welcomed" would chat with them outside their doors, then send them on their way. Police in patrol cars crawled along beside them as they walked down the street.

"We don't want any trouble," they heard again and again.

At some point during their first night, the heat in their hotel room had turned off entirely. The sudden silence had been a blessing, but they awoke hours later shivering in the cold. It seemed those were their only two choices—a blast furnace of eighty-degree air or nothing at all. They learned to attempt a balance by alternating the setting every few hours.

At least the photographs from Pastor Logan had arrived, although as he'd warned, the pictures didn't give them much to go on. Ruth was clear enough, but the camera had only captured the man who had taken her from behind. The good news was the University of Massachusetts parking stickers were for the campus in Boston—only a short subway ride from the hotel—and not one of the schools in other parts of the state. And there was a clear picture of the car too: an old green sedan with a hybrid gasoline engine.

Towards the end of their fruitless first week, they decided to visit the campus with the vague goal of wandering about the parking lot in hopes of spotting the car. It was a cold, windy morning with a thick cloud cover, and they'd blasted the heat in their room for half an hour to warm up before heading to the T, which is what people called the subway in Boston.

The King's Royal Court Hotel was a ten-block walk from the nearest Red Line station, and by the time they were halfway there, they could see people queued up ahead of them, stretching several blocks toward the station's security checkpoint. A cloud of miniature AI camera drones flew overhead, buzzing like mosquitoes.

"Is that a line for the subway?" Marcus asked.

"I hope not," Daniel replied. They made their way to the back of the line and asked the woman in front of them. She took in their white pants and red jackets, then looked away without answering. An older man standing in front of her turned and said, "Yes. The magnetometers are broken. They need to screen everyone by hand, not just the few normally selected at random."

"They'd have been selected anyway," the woman told him.

"Is there another station close by?" Marcus asked.

The woman rolled her eyes. "Do you think we'd be standing here in the cold if there was?"

People were already filling in the line behind them. A group of young men began to talk loudly about why the subway should charge CeeNees more to cover all the increased security costs. Marcus tensed. Even more than Daniel, he was particularly angered by people associating Christian Nationalist Evangelicals with violence. The violence—on both sides of the separatist debate—was perpetuated by secularists.

Daniel gripped his elbow to stop him from engaging.

"Get a load of that," one of the young men said. "They're sweet on each other." The others laughed. "Didn't think that was allowed where they come from."

"Hey, dude," another called, "do me a solid and have your friend Jesus speed things up here." More laughter, and the woman in front of them stepped out of the line and walked away. The camera drones zeroed in on the commotion. Marcus turned to say something to the men, but Daniel stopped him with a tug on his arm.

"Come on, Marcus. Let's go. We'll come back when the machine is fixed."

*

DANIEL STEERED THEM away from the subway and toward downtown Boston. The towers of the financial district rose in the distance. "The hotel brochure said it was less than five miles to the Back Bay."

"Dinosaurs," replied Marcus.

"Probably," agreed Daniel. But they continued walking, and as they did, the neighborhood around them began to change. There were fewer signs in English, and more people wore head coverings. The air smelled like the Punjabi Grill he'd eaten at once during a shopping trip with his mother to Charleston.

Everyone eyed them warily as they passed.

"It's these clothes, Dan. Do you think Pastor Logan would mind if we used some of our funds to buy street clothes?"

Daniel laughed, but then realized Marcus was serious. "You know he would. We're forbidden to hide who we are. It's like hiding the light of Christ." There were tables on the sidewalks in front of the stores, piled high with goods, and as if it was a sign, a merchant held out a pair of denim jeans.

"Better for you, yes?" the shopkeeper asked.

Marcus stopped. "Come on, Dan. I don't think Pastor Logan knew how it was up here, how much of a target we'd be."

Maybe. Marcus was right in a way. It didn't make their mission any easier to be confronted with hostility and fear at every turn. And their other mission—the secret one—might require them to operate a bit more discretely.

"We could ask him, I guess," Daniel said.

"Very good price on two," the merchant said, sensing an opening. "Safer for you."

"Better to ask forgiveness than permission," Marcus told him. And it was just the kind of thing he'd say too: going against the rules, thinking he knew better than the church elders. But just as Daniel was about to refuse, an emergency vehicle came up the street, squeezing its way through the traffic with lights flashing and sirens wailing.

In the distance, other sirens could be heard, and Daniel was reminded once again just how dangerous it could be up North. "I wish we had our guns," Marcus whispered. Thankfully, no one else had heard him. People were giving them dirty looks. Daniel reconsidered his resistance to buying something that would allow them to blend in with the people on the street.

"All right, but we can't spend much. We need to eat too."

They entered the small store, and within fifteen minutes, they'd acquired two pairs of jeans and two non-descript pullover sweaters. Daniel asked for a bag, but the merchant, who'd been checking his phone and looking increasingly worried, insisted they wear the new clothes.

"There is trouble today," he said. "You will be safer."

"We should listen to him, Dan. There are a lot of sirens out there."

There *were* a lot of sirens, a constant stream of them. So, they dressed in their new street clothes—the first time since the summer break Daniel had worn jeans—and headed back out into the city with their missionary uniforms in a bag.

The mood on the street had changed. Everyone was either talking on their phones or checking their screens as they hurried along. Merchants were beginning to close their shops, pulling down heavy metal covers over their storefronts. Marcus opened his phone and pulled up the Good News. "Nothing," he said after scrolling for a moment.

Daniel knew their access to the wider internet was blocked, but he'd never been so aware of it before or felt the restriction so acutely. "I guess if there was something we needed to know—" he began, but Marcus interrupted him.

"Oh, stop, Dan. Obviously, there's something we need to know. Look around."

Marcus backtracked to the shop they'd just left, Daniel trailing behind. Already the man was locking his front door, and he didn't open it when Marcus approached. "What's happening?" Marcus shouted through the glass.

"Go," the merchant shouted back, shooing them away with his hands.

"Please," Daniel said. "Our phones don't work here. Tell us what's wrong."

The man disappeared into his shop, and Daniel and Marcus looked at each other, unsure what to do next. Everyone who saw them glanced at them nervously, then looked away. No, Daniel thought, not nervously. Suspiciously.

He heard the key in the lock and the door opened only far enough for the shop owner to push two dark navy peacoats through it. "Here, take these. You won't be safe wearing the red jackets today. There's been a bombing downtown. Change now and go. I don't want you to be seen here." He locked the door and disappeared into the darkness of his shop.

"I don't like this, Dan," Marcus said as they shrugged off their jackets and put the peacoats on. "Why would he just give us these?"

"I don't know, but it was a Christian thing to do. When this is over, let's come back and talk to him about Jesus." In the distance, a thin tendril of gray smoke rose into the sky. A man who'd been standing in a doorway next to the shop stepped onto the sidewalk and approached them.

"You need phones," he said. It wasn't a question. He looked

young, maybe still in his teens, and he had a wide turban wrapped around his head and the beginnings of a wispy beard beneath his chin.

Daniel went to pull Marcus away, but Marcus said, "Yes."

"Here," the boy said, nodding toward the doorway and motioning with his arm.

"We're not going in there," Daniel insisted, gripping Marcus's arm.

"No, no. Here," the young man said again, and then Daniel saw the cardboard box hidden by the archway framing the door. It sat on a metal folding stand and the top of the box had been cut open to reveal boxes of phones.

"Burners. OpenSky system so you always have internet. Special deal on two."

"How much?" Marcus asked.

"Marcus, no!"

"Dan, we can't live here in ignorance. God helps those who help themselves."

It was a blasphemous thing to say. It wasn't their job to be partners with God; it was their job to submit to God's will. But Daniel remained silent while Marcus negotiated a price.

*

THE HOTEL ROOM had become uncomfortably cold by the time they returned, and Daniel turned on the heat even before removing his jacket. He took their missionary clothes out of the bag and neatly folded them, then tucked them into an empty bureau drawer. Marcus placed the two burner phones on the table.

Daniel stared at them, thinking of all the reasons they were prohibited. He knew the internet was filled with lies about the world, and with images and articles meant to obscure the truth and confuse the unwary, leading them away from God. Mostly, Pastor Logan had told them, it was a waste of time—a bottomless pit of distraction that either soothed and lulled or excited and enraged. Either way, the important work of doing God's will in the world was neglected.

The sirens of emergency vehicles continued to rise and fall in the distance. Daniel turned on his own phone and launched the Good News site, but there was still nothing being reported about what might be happening in Boston.

"Maybe we should try the television first," he said.

Marcus was already reading through the new phone's instructions. "Dan," he said. "Seriously? We have these now, and for all we know Pastor Logan booked us a room with no working television."

Daniel picked up the remote from the top of the bureau. "Still," he said, "the television seems more...excusable...for an emergency." He pressed the power button, but he could already tell from Marcus's expression he'd be using a phone anyway. The thrill of the forbidden was a powerful temptation for Marcus, and Daniel vowed to pray about it with him that evening.

The screen brightened. It had a ghostly purple glow around the edges and a faint image of a logo Daniel didn't recognize burned into the upper right corner. "Connect source," read the screen's message.

"Oh," said Marcus. "It's only a monitor." He turned to Daniel. "We'd need a phone to watch anything on it anyway."

Daniel tried to think of some reason to delay, to turn back

from this path of disobedience, but Marcus was already committed. "I'm doing it," he said as he pushed the phone's power button. "Hand me a piece of paper and a pen, will you? I want to write down what my number is."

There was a thin pad of paper in the top drawer of the bedside table, along with a tiny pencil, much like the kind one could find at a bowling alley or a miniature golf course. As he handed the items to Marcus, Daniel realized he'd been drawn into the crime and was now actively participating in it.

Marcus smiled. "I'll write down your number too," he said.

Daniel didn't say anything. There was no putting the apple back on the tree.

Marcus worked with the phones for a few minutes then handed one to Daniel. "Here you go, Dan. I've put my number into your contacts and yours into mine." Daniel picked up the phone and studied it. The lower half of the screen was a standard phone keyboard, the upper half an empty canvas, just waiting to tempt them away from the path of truth.

"The green circle is messages," Marcus said. Daniel's phone vibrated and binged as a message from Marcus arrived. *Hi*, it read. "Reply so we know both phones work."

Dinosaurs, Daniel typed, which startled a laugh out of Marcus when it arrived.

"There you go. You're getting into the swing of things now. The lightning bolt is the telephone, and the blue circle is the Open-Sky portal." He lowered his voice and whispered as if they were in an old horror movie. "That's where the uncensored internet is." This was just a daring adventure for him.

Daniel knew it was going to be difficult. "Marcus," he said, "promise me you understand this is only for emergencies, that we're only using it now to find out what's happening with the bomb."

"Dan, aren't you curious about the world?"

"Not in the way you mean, no."

"Fine," Marcus said. "You look then and find out what's going on. I'm going to hit the head." Marcus left the room and Daniel was left alone with his phone. He pressed the blue button and was immediately connected to OpenSky. He scrolled through the menus until he found News and had only touched the icon when his phone vibrated and chimed.

The screen changed to Incoming Call from Black Stud. He pressed Accept. "This isn't funny, Marcus."

"But there's no hot water." Marcus's tinny voice came from the phone's speaker. "That's an emergency, isn't it?" He was still speaking as he stepped through the door. "Sorry," he said. "Just testing the phone."

Daniel disconnected the call. "Black stud?" he asked.

"Sure," replied Marcus. "It's not like Pastor Logan is ever going to see it. And we're just throwing these away when we leave. You call me now."

Daniel did, and Marcus's phone chimed. He looked at the screen, hit Accept, and said, "Yep, it's working, White Worrier."

Daniel rolled his eyes. "This isn't a game, Marcus. We have important work to do. Now let's find out what's happening."

*

TWO HOURS LATER, the men were lying on their beds, slack-jawed as they surfed through the news on the internet. Marcus had linked his phone to the monitor while Daniel used his to independently verify some of what they were learning.

"How could we not have known all of this?" Marcus asked again.

"We don't know how much of it is true…" Daniel said again. But he was sounding increasingly uncertain as his own efforts at cross-referencing continued to validate the stories. "But the Boston polling station story must be true. Everyone but the Good News seems to have covered it." Daniel still couldn't make sense of what he was learning; it was overwhelming. "Why would they keep it all from us?"

"And why would someone do that? Kill all those people while they were standing in line to vote?" Daniel shook his head at what a horrible scene it must have been. The pictures from the news sites of the aftermath were bad enough. "And why would they have dressed like us? Why pretend to be missionaries when you're out to kill people?"

"Come on, Dan. They did it to make people afraid of us. And if the second one's suicide vest had gone off, they would have killed a lot more people and maybe nobody would have learned they were only posing as missionaries. And it worked, too, even though the truth eventually came out. You saw how people looked at us."

It was so unfair, that people up here could believe them capable of such things. They wanted to change Northerners' hearts and minds, not terrorize them into capitulating. "Do you think Pastor Logan knows?" Daniel asked.

"I don't see how he couldn't. But let's ask him."

"No," Daniel said. "We can't. Then he'd know *we* know, and

he'd know we used the internet."

"You're wrong, Dan. Think it through. There's no way someone wouldn't have told us about it up here. So, he's *expecting* us to learn about it. And in that case, we should ask him about it. Or, maybe he *doesn't* know, and then we should tell him."

Daniel gave that some thought, then said, "Right, I see what you're saying."

"Either way," Marcus said, "*not* asking him about it is what would make us look suspicious."

"How did you learn to think like this?" Daniel asked.

Marcus looked at him for several moments without speaking. Finally, he smiled — a wide, almost predatory smile, Daniel thought, that revealed his pink gums. "Stick with me, White Worrier. I've got your back."

Chapter Eight

JAXTYN FELT BAD for Professor Ringle.

He wasn't an *old* man—under seventy, most likely—but he had the wild look in his eyes all his generation got when they talked about how the country used to be. And he had the misfortune of teaching Constitutional Law to undergraduates, a field of study thrown into chaos when the Supreme Court overturned Marbury vs. Madison.

They weren't supposed to use their phones in class, but Jaxtyn held his under the desk and took a quick peek to see if Skylar had gotten back to him. He hadn't, and Jaxtyn was worried. He'd sent the text on Tuesday, and here it was—Friday already—with no word from Skylar all week.

"And so, it wasn't until 1947," Professor Ringle said, "in the Everson case, that the Supreme Court ruled the First Amendment's prohibition against establishing an official government religion applied to the states as well to the federal government." He pointed his stylus to the wallboard and pressed a button. The words "Doctrine of Incorporation" appeared on the wall.

Jaxtyn wrote the phrase in his notes. This was at the heart of why Congress couldn't reach a final solution. Many of the red states wanted to establish Christianity as their state religion. It's why so many CeeNee missionaries had fanned out across the country, trying to advocate for that position.

Most people in the blue states believed officially establishing a state religion was going too far, Jaxtyn included. It wouldn't be right to abandon so many of their fellow citizens, forcing them to live under whatever rules a religious government might impose.

"Of course, ever since the Supreme Court reversed Marbury vs Madison, and took itself out of the business of declaring whether or not state laws were constitutional—" and here, the wild look in his eyes intensified, as if he couldn't believe he was even talking about this "—legal scholars are split on whether the Doctrine of Incorporation still applies. *Are* states bound by the Bill of Rights?"

Jaxtyn's phone buzzed. He looked down, hoping it was Skylar finally responding, but even as he did so he noticed many students taking out their phones, and he heard the familiar tones of emergency alerts going off on phones throughout the classroom.

His screen lit up. There'd been a bombing in Boston.

"News?" asked the professor.

"Yes, professor. A bombing," replied a student from the front row.

A few more clicks on Professor Ringle's stylus and a local news feed was displayed on the wallboard. Live views from cameras in the area of the explosion showed broken glass and what appeared to be a collapsed brick wall, but no flames or widespread devastation. The plume of smoke rising into the sky was thin and light-colored. Unless it was a dirty bomb, it hadn't been a massive attack.

A campus lockdown was announced on the public address system, and everyone's phones went off again. A groan went up from the class; this was the second lockdown in the last month. People began texting, checking in with friends and family, advising about possible delays getting to jobs and other activities after class.

Jaxtyn's mind went to the CeeNees he'd met on the train last weekend, and he was immediately ashamed it did. There was no reason to suspect the missionaries had traveled to Boston to conduct a terror attack. But the spate of dirty bomb attacks in the last few years weighed heavily on people's minds, and the entire city was jittery.

Jaxtyn closed his eyes and took deep, cleansing breaths. When his mind settled, he visualized Daniel and Marcus and wished them well if they were still in the city.

*

BY SUNDAY, BOSTON was back to normal. No one had been killed in the explosion, but one of the women's health center's guards had been injured and was still in the hospital. The man who'd placed the bomb—left in a messenger's satchel draped over a bicycle's handlebars—had been found within hours and was in custody.

As Jaxtyn made his way across town on the subway, he

anticipated a difficult morning service ahead. The Sangha would be angry about the attack, and it would likely be challenging for most members to settle into relaxed mindfulness. He didn't envy Vishnu, whose job it was to moderate the sessions this month.

And he still hadn't heard from Skylar.

He tried to put it all out of his mind as he prepared for his meditation session. The Open Lotus Sangha met in the library where Jaxtyn worked part-time. He enjoyed the job, even though it was just reshelving books and helping people find what they were looking for. He would have liked to get more hours, but his availability was limited to evenings and weekends, and the library was already staffed during most of those hours. Still, it earned enough to help with rent and keep him in some spending money.

He arrived a half hour early, just as the library was opening at ten. He wanted to help Vishnu set up the space, and he also wanted a few minutes with Vishnu alone. The man was a good listener, and Jaxtyn hoped if he talked with him about his growing anxiety that something was *wrong*, that events were rushing forward somehow, leading toward disaster, maybe he'd be able to understand why he was feeling these things.

A small group had gathered by the doors waiting for the library to open—old people, mostly, but one teenage boy too. He had his back to Jaxtyn and his hands shoved tightly into his peacoat's pockets. He shifted from foot to foot and kept a noticeable distance from the others. He lifted a hand to tuck his hair behind an ear, and in the movement of his arm and shoulders, Jaxtyn realized it wasn't a boy, but a young man.

And there was something about the hair, a deep bronze

color and long enough to shift about in the stiff breeze.

Behind the library's large front window, a woman walked toward the front door, keys dangling from her hand. The young man's gaze shifted to follow her movement, and in profile Jaxtyn recognized him: Daniel, the CeeNee he met on the train.

He scanned the crowd for the other one, but Daniel was alone and not dressed in his missionary uniform, which was surprising, but also a relief. People were on edge following the bombing, and libraries had been targeted by terrorists recently, especially ones that had defiantly promoted the books banned by the Christian Nationalists.

Jaxtyn smiled as he approached Daniel. "You made it," he said and held out his hand.

Daniel looked startled and…something else. Disappointed, maybe? "Yes, hello." He reached out and grasped Jaxtyn's hand. He had a firmer grip than the tentative touch he'd offered at Penn Station in New York. "I *am* early, aren't I? I was hoping to scope things out before…"

Ah. So that was it. He hadn't finished the sentence, but Jaxtyn heard the implied *before I decided whether to stay.* And now he was trapped, or at least slipping away unnoticed had become impossible.

"Yes, we don't start until 10:30. Don't worry. I'm early too. I'm going to help Vishnu set things up. He's leading our sessions this month." He waved his arm toward the door. "Go on in. Explore the library. When you're ready, we'll be meeting in the Community Room. It's on the first floor in the back." There, that should put him at ease, and he could slip out if he wanted to, although Jaxtyn was surprised by how much he hoped the missionary would stay.

Daniel relaxed at the offer. "Thanks, I'll wander around. Sort of an odd place for a church."

"We're a small group, and I suppose I should warn you The Open Lotus is a Buddhist Sangha. We're very open-minded and curious about others, but we're not Christians." Jaxtyn waited to see if Daniel would object. "You'll be very welcome."

Daniel seemed to reach a decision. "Yes. I knew that. I looked you up on the internet before I came over, but I'm not sure what any of it means."

Jaxtyn wondered just how sheltered the CeeNee missionaries were. "No worries. Give me ten minutes to get organized then come find me if you want, and I'll walk you through what a service is like."

"Thanks, I will," Daniel said.

Jaxtyn turned and headed toward the community room, marveling at how much material there might be in the library the CeeNee missionary had never seen and had no access to at all. A thought occurred to him and he turned back to Daniel. "If you want to borrow anything, you can use my account."

*

"YOU'RE BRINGING A CeeNee here?" Vishnu asked. "Now? It's not the best week for that."

They'd finished arranging the chairs and mats in neat rows facing the front of the room where Vishnu had set up the small altar with its Buddha statue, bell, and battery-operated candles. "I know, but I met him on the train last weekend, before the latest bombing. And we *are* always talking about how we need to build bridges, find common ground."

"Common ground, yes," replied Vishnu. "But not with… with…" he waved his arm to finish his thought.

"They're not all terrorists, Vishnu. They didn't bomb the health clinic."

"But radicals aligned with them did. They all want the same thing: to impose some sort of religious government on half the country." Vishnu moved the meditation bell to the floor in front of his mat, and it released a muted, deep tone that floated in the room. Both men followed the sound as they'd trained themselves to do, until it melted into the ambient noises of the library around them.

Vishnu took a deep breath. "You're right, of course. He's welcome. But if you could ask him not to try to convert anyone until after the session, I'd appreciate it."

"Thank you, Vishnu. I think he's important, somehow."

Vishnu looked him in the eye. Jaxtyn's strange sixth sense about things had been a frequent topic of conversation between the two men. "Well, your intuition hasn't failed you yet. I hope he's important in a good way."

"I don't know yet," Jaxtyn replied. "I just feel he's connected to everything — somehow — to everything going on right now."

"We're all connected," Vishnu said. "That's what our spiritual practice shows. But it must mean something if you feel that way about him in particular." They both noticed Daniel hovering outside of the doorway, seemingly reluctant to interrupt. "That's him?"

Daniel had his heavy peacoat draped over his arm. He was wearing a tight, inexpensive-looking sweater and an old pair of jeans with a flair at the ankles in a style Jaxtyn hadn't seen in years. He looked like a refugee.

He also looked…good, Jaxtyn had to admit now. Attractive in a way that hadn't registered when Daniel had been in his missionary uniform.

Vishnu looked at the expression on Daniel's face. "This isn't just about you wanting to get laid, is it?"

Jaxtyn laughed and rolled his eyes. "Of course not."

Not just about that, anyway.

Chapter Nine

IT WAS THE periodicals section of the library that finally pushed Daniel past his limit.

There were the usual news magazines his church discouraged because of their secular biases, and a whole host of other publications Daniel had never heard of. He recognized *Christianity Today*, but what was it doing in the "lifestyle" section, right next to a magazine called *Queer Culture*?

His eye was drawn to a fitness magazine with two shirtless men on the cover, one on his back on a weight bench, the other standing behind him spotting. There was an eroticism to the photo that had to have been intentional. It was too much.

He turned his back to the racks of periodicals and made his way toward the front of the library. He'd slip out. He wasn't ready to be immersed in this world. He'd wait for Marcus to return from his visit to the AME church, and then they'd pray together on how to proceed.

As he walked to the front door, he glanced down the corridor toward the community room and saw Jaxtyn and another man moving stackable chairs into rows. Daniel paused, watching the men work. Jaxtyn had been nothing but welcoming and kind to him. He was letting his fears run away with him. He didn't need to understand Jaxtyn's world. All he needed to do was offer Jesus's light to the man and try to bring another soul to the grace of God.

Jaxtyn looked up and saw him. His face broke into a smile, and Daniel's pulse quickened. God had placed Jaxtyn before him for two reasons, Daniel suddenly realized. First, as an opportunity to present Jesus's good news to a person sincerely open to hearing it, and second as a temptation—a test—that he can accept the fact of his attraction to men without fear, that he can overcome it, put it aside, and redouble his efforts to spread the word of God.

Daniel returned Jaxtyn's smile, changed course, and headed into the room.

*

MEDITATION WAS *ALMOST* like praying, Daniel thought, only it was prayer without direction, with no listener, with no point. It was peaceful, though, and calming. He'd never tried to empty his mind before. It was strikingly difficult.

He sat on a thick cushion on the floor next to Jaxtyn. That had been a mistake—two mistakes, actually. He should have chosen the chair he'd been offered, but there were only two members of the meditation group in chairs, and they both appeared to be over seventy. He hadn't realized how uncomfortable it would be to sit cross-legged for a half hour, even with the pillow.

The second mistake was to sit so close to Jaxtyn. Their knees were mere inches apart, and Jaxtyn's upturned palms rested in his lap, distracting Daniel repeatedly as he tried to empty his mind and feel a connection to something larger — which was ridiculous, really. The connection these people were looking for was with God. And Daniel would share that truth with them if they'd listen, if they'd only open their eyes and see what was right in front of them.

Jaxtyn took a slow, deep breath, waited several heartbeats, then exhaled slowly. Daniel felt the air shift between them, and he took his own deep breath, trying to capture Jaxtyn's exhalation, to chase after those molecules and follow them into his own lungs.

Maybe sex is like this — sharing parts of yourself with someone else, becoming one.

Daniel blushed furiously. Meditation was messing with his head. Of course he and Jaxtyn were one. They were all one in God. It had nothing to do with sex, and it was dangerous, Daniel thought, to reach for spiritual experiences not anchored in Jesus. Surely this session must be nearly over.

As if reading his mind, Vishnu — the man leading the service — reached out and lifted a small metal bell, its chime resonating through the room. All around him, people shifted in their positions. Jaxtyn had told him the bell would mark the final five minutes of meditation, and that Vishnu would lead them through the last phase with a spoken meditation.

"Breathing in, my breath goes deep," Vishnu said in a slow, measured pace. Everyone took a deep breath. "Breathing out, my breath goes slow." A susurration of breath filled the room.

"Breathing in, I calm my body." A pause here, and Daniel felt it, something weighty leaching out of him. "Breathing out, I feel at ease." And he *was* at ease! It was almost as if his mind had left his body, as if his awareness was floating above the room, taking it all in, resting in something safe and all-encompassing.

He jerked, and his left elbow bumped into Jaxtyn's side. Had he fallen asleep?

Jaxtyn lifted his hand and gripped Daniel's arm to steady him. *Are you all right?* His look seemed to ask. Daniel nodded, transfixed by the sight of Jaxtyn's long, slender fingers grasping his forearm. He felt their heat on his skin through his sweater, and he felt the new ephemeral connection between them begin to slip away as he tried to see it clearly.

Vishnu repeated the breathing meditation three more times and then ended the session. "Namaste," he said to the room, pressing his palms together in front of his chest. "Namaste," responded the room as the people began stretching their arms or turning to greet each other. Jaxtyn smiled at him.

"I didn't fall asleep," Daniel told him. He heard how defensive he sounded and was about to clarify when Jaxtyn interrupted him.

"I know you didn't," he said. "You got in the zone. Not everyone does, you know, especially their first time. If you practiced more, your sense of balance would improve and keep you upright, allowing your mind to break free for longer periods." Jaxtyn raised himself from the floor in one smooth motion then reached his hand out to help Daniel. "You'll probably be stiff."

His knees complained as he came out of his sitting position, and Daniel was grateful for the help. Jaxtyn's hand was warm and larger than his own, enveloping his fully in a firm grasp. Once Daniel was standing, Jaxtyn said, "I'm glad you came," before releasing his grip.

"You may have noticed we have a visitor today," Vishnu said, and several faces turned to Daniel and smiled, most pressing their palms together before their chests and offering a slight bow. "This is Daniel Ridley. Jax met him on the train last week and invited him to join us today. Daniel is a Christian—" For a moment, Daniel panicked, fearing Vishnu would continue by describing him as a Christian Nationalist Evangelical or, worse yet, the acronym CeeNee, which was apparently synonymous with terrorist up here. Thankfully, he stopped at Christian. "And he'd be happy to speak with any of us during our social time about religion and spirituality."

That wasn't exactly what Daniel had said. He'd told Jaxtyn and Vishnu he'd welcome the opportunity to witness to people about Jesus's good news and the grace of God. But watching everyone's smiles turn to frowns, seeing their eyes shift away from him, Daniel was glad, in a pragmatic way, that Vishnu had chosen to be less explicit.

Daniel offered a wave, which drew more frowns, and he realized he would have been better off mimicking the pressed palms and head nod. "Hello everyone. Thank you for inviting me to your service." More frowning, and people began actively moving away from him, either shrugging on coats and heading to the door, or moving in small groups toward the coffee urn on the counter in the back of the community room.

"Come on," Jaxtyn said as he placed his hand on Daniel's elbow. "Let's get some coffee." He began steering Daniel toward a table containing mugs and napkins where several other members of the group had gathered. He was acutely aware of Jaxtyn's hand on his arm, and his focus on the touch clouded his thinking. His mind drew a blank as he approached the table and tried to think of how to begin.

An elderly woman turned to him, "Welcome to our Sangha, young man. I imagine that wasn't at all like what you're used to." Her smile was polite, but not warm. She didn't offer to shake hands. Daniel thought she was of the generation who knew how to maintain social niceties, even when they didn't want to.

"Yes, ma'am. Although it's closer to praying to Jesus than you might think."

"Is that so?" she responded in a tone making it clear a response would be both unnecessary and unwelcome. "How long have you been in Boston?"

"Just one week, ma'am."

Jaxtyn handed him a cup of coffee, and Daniel curled his fingers around it, absorbing its warmth. He was struck by how fundamentally unprepared he was to begin spreading God's word here in the North. All their training had failed to equip him with the tools necessary to respond to cool indifference.

"Well, I'm sure with that charming accent of yours, you'll soon have all of Boston's eligible young ladies hanging on your every word." Daniel wanted to object—it was Jesus's good news the people of Boston needed to hear, not his—but he knew a dismissal when he heard one and wasn't at all surprised when, after looking pointedly at Jaxtyn, she turned and began speaking with someone else.

Jaxtyn blushed, and Daniel wondered what subtext he'd

missed, and whether or not it had anything to do with the reference to young ladies.

They were alone now, effectively abandoned in the back of the room.

Jaxtyn took a sip of his coffee, then said, "Can I ask you something?" Daniel nodded, still replaying the exchange with the unnamed woman, wondering how he could have directed the conversation to where it needed to go.

"Why aren't you wearing your missionary uniform? Don't get me wrong; you're smart not to. I'm just surprised, that's all."

Daniel considered the question. He'd never needed to be concerned about how others perceived him. The uniform spoke for itself. He was God's messenger. But now, he wondered what people thought when they looked at him, what Jaxtyn thought. He knew his sweater was cheap, and his jeans outdated. He picked nervously at the sweater's cuff.

Jaxtyn waved his hands. "No, no. I mean, you look good without it." Then he groaned. "Sorry, that's not what I meant."

Daniel held up a hand to stop Jaxtyn from digging himself further into a hole. "We live very different lives than you do here," he said. "Marcus—my missionary companion—and I didn't realize what people thought about us. Until we got here, I mean. There are a lot of things we didn't know."

He paused to see if Jaxtyn would respond, but he didn't; he just sipped his coffee and waited patiently for Daniel to continue.

"Anyway, last week, when the bombing happened…" Daniel felt a flush of anger when Jaxtyn glanced about to ensure they were alone as if he was concerned others would think he'd brought a terrorist into their midst. "We learned we were attracting too much negative attention dressed as missionaries, but we don't have very much money, just enough to live on for a few months. So, we bought cheap jeans and a kind merchant gave us sweaters and coats."

"That was smart. The CeeNee uniform—" Jaxtyn stopped suddenly. "Uh, is that an offensive term?"

Daniel smiled. It was a simple question with a complicated answer. "I guess that depends on who's using it and what they mean by it."

Jaxtyn glanced around the room. Mostly everyone had left. Vishnu was inching his way closer along the table, loudly gathering cups into a plastic wash tub. "Well, what do *you* mean by it?" Jaxtyn asked. "What do you hope to achieve here?"

Daniel relaxed. That was easy. "I want to spread the good news of Jesus Christ." And yes, there was a political advocacy element to their work, but only because it was so important to create a country where Christian principles can be front and center in public affairs. And then there was his secret mission, but he wasn't going to tell Jaxtyn about that.

"Uh, okay," Jaxtyn said. "Go ahead. What is it?"

And once again, Daniel was at a loss. "You see, that's just it. I can talk about Jesus all day back home, but I realized this week I don't know how to *start* here. I wanted to talk to that woman, but—"

"Oh, don't worry about Margaret. She's a tough nut to crack. Tell us." Jaxtyn held out his arm in a silent plea toward Vishnu, urging him closer. "Think of it as practice." Vishnu looked as if being practiced on was the last thing he wanted to do, but he stepped closer.

"Daniel has good news," Jaxtyn told him.

"Oh yeah?" Vishnu asked suspiciously. "What's that?"

They both turned to Daniel expectantly. He could do this. It's what he'd been trained for. He took a deep breath. "You're mired in sin right now, but you can be saved from eternal damnation by the grace of God if you have faith in Jesus Christ."

"Oh," said Jaxtyn.

"Fuck this shit," mumbled Vishnu. He tossed the towel he'd been holding to Jaxtyn. "You clean up, and in case you didn't notice, everyone left early." Vishnu walked away, and Jaxtyn wrung the towel between his hands.

"Well," exclaimed Jaxtyn in a much brighter tone than the circumstances warranted. "That's the value of practicing then, isn't it? And good thing you didn't pull that on Margaret. Why don't you try again?"

Try again?

"But...but that's the good news. We're all sinners, and we can be forgiven because of Jesus's death and resurrection, and God's grace will cleanse our sins and bring us to Him." Daniel believed it to be fairly straightforward. And that was the point of mission work. Show people the truth, so they can be open to God working in them.

"Oh," Jaxtyn said again. "I see. Well, gosh, that *is* good news, isn't it? If that's, like, all part of your worldview, I guess. Especially the forgiving part — that was good." But Daniel thought he didn't look convinced. "Maybe you could start out differently though. Consider opening with the business about doing good works, being kind to strangers, that sort of stuff. That's all part of it, isn't it?"

"No."

"No?"

"No. It doesn't matter what you do. You can be saved only through the grace of God. You don't play a role in that."

"Oh." Jaxtyn turned to the table and began putting the remaining coffee mugs in the bin. "So, really, it's more just *news*, rather than good news."

Was he being teased? He straightened his back. "I'd say being saved from eternal damnation was pretty good news."

Jaxtyn put the last of the mugs in the bin and brought it to the small galley kitchen in the back of the community room, looking over his shoulder to make sure Daniel followed. "Okay," he said. "I think I get it. Death, resurrection, God's grace. Good news. Done." He put the tub in the sink and turned on the faucet, then squirted in some dish detergent. "So that's it? Now that I've heard the good news, I'm saved? That seems suspiciously easy."

As the tub filled with water, Daniel replayed their conversation to determine where he'd gone wrong.

Faith! He'd forgotten to stress the need for faith. What was wrong with him?

"Well, not exactly." He picked up a towel and prepared to dry the mugs after Jaxtyn washed them. "When I said it doesn't matter what you do, I meant that about things like giving to charity or feeding the homeless. There's nothing you can do to *earn* grace; it's only God's to give. But I should have pointed out God's forgiveness is available to you only through your faith in Jesus."

Jaxtyn was nodding. "Okaaaay." He began swishing the scrub brush inside the mugs and then rinsing them under the faucet. "So, it's free, but I have to sign up first? Create an account, download the app, that sort of thing?"

He held a clean mug out to Daniel, who took it and began drying. "That's an odd way of putting it, but basically, yes." He smiled when he thought about sharing this conversation with Marcus. "You need to have a relationship with Jesus. You need to truly believe, to feel Him in your heart. You need to turn your life over to Him."

They washed and dried in silence. Daniel had never considered how…daunting it might seem, the need to turn your life over to Jesus if you weren't already a believer.

"Um, how are you supposed to do that last part?" Jaxtyn handed the final rinsed mug to Daniel. "Hard to feel something in your heart if you don't believe it in your head first."

"But that's not true. You just need to pray, sincerely open yourself up to Jesus. It'll happen." Daniel hoped this wasn't misleading. It was what they'd been trained to say as missionaries. Sometimes, Daniel didn't always feel Jesus, but when that happened, he at least knew it was an aberration, and Jesus would return to him again. He worried, though, what would happen to someone new to prayer who, despite their sincere and earnest efforts, felt nothing.

Daniel finished drying the final mug and placed it neatly next to the others on the folded towel. He wanted to be able to offer Jaxtyn more, but there was nothing more. You either gave your life over to Jesus or you didn't.

He was surprised when Jaxtyn said, "Okay, I'm game. Show me how to do it."

"How to…how to pray?"

"Sure. We have the room for another twenty minutes."

Jaxtyn draped the hand towel on the hook attached to the wall cabinet's side and grinned. "I put myself in your hands."

Daniel's pulse quickened. This was it. He was poised to bring his first lost soul to Jesus. Heat crept up his neck as he thought about clasping hands with Jaxtyn in prayer.

None of that, Dan.

"Good," Daniel said as they headed back toward the chairs and cushions. "It would be best to kneel. Are you comfortable on your knees?"

An indecipherable look flashed across Jaxtyn's face.

"We could sit in the chairs if you prefer," Daniel offered. "The important thing is to be comfortable."

Jaxtyn raised his eyebrows. "As it happens, I'm able to spend quite a bit of time on my knees."

"Good," Daniel said again. He moved a few chairs out of the way and placed two cushions next to each other in the open space. "We'll face each other when we pray, but our eyes will be closed and we'll hold hands." He willed himself not to blush.

Don't fail this test, Dan.

"I'll do the praying out loud, but you can join in if you're moved to do so. Okay?"

"We're going to hold hands?"

"Yes. It's customary in my church, especially if it's only two people praying together. It reminds us we're all one in God, that we're all equal in His eyes. Does that... Will it make you uncomfortable? If it does, we can—"

"Oh, no." Jaxtyn interrupted. "By all means, let's hold hands."

Jaxtyn knelt on the cushion, and Daniel lowered himself to

his knees in front of him, then reached forward and took his hands. He was accustomed to Marcus's hands, small and thick and frequently damp. Jaxtyn's hands were big and warm. He was surprised when Jaxtyn entwined his long fingers through Daniel's. Normally, people simply clasped their hands together when they prayed, like a handshake.

This was more like what a boy and girl might do together on a date in the darkness of a movie theater. And he *had* told Jaxtyn they were going to hold hands, so it was an easy mistake. Daniel didn't want to break the flow just as they were starting, so he decided to leave things be.

Plus, it felt nice—intimate, but not in a threatening way.

Focus, Dan.

Daniel put all thoughts of Jaxtyn, the man, out of his mind and focused on Jaxtyn, the sinner. For he was as much a sinner as Daniel was; that was certain. Everyone was; original sin tainted all alike. Daniel watched as Jaxtyn closed his eyes; then he did the same.

"Jesus," he began, "please look upon these sinners. Fill their hearts with your love so they may be made ready to receive God's grace."

Chapter Ten

JAXTYN TEETERED BETWEEN amused and fascinated.

Daniel kept referring to him as a sinner—sometimes as a wretched sinner—while he carried on a one-way conversation with Jesus. That was the amusing part. The fascinating part was it was so *real* to Daniel. He truly believed he was talking to Jesus, and who knows, maybe he was, and maybe Jesus was talking back.

He snaked his fingers around Daniel's wrist to rest their tips on the pulse there. As he'd suspected, it was pounding. They'd been praying for ten minutes, and Jaxtyn had long ago opened his eyes to watch Daniel. Intense emotion played across his face. His neck had flushed a deep red, and his tightly closed eyes leaked moisture from the corners.

"Jesus, please!" he exclaimed and gripped Jaxtyn's hand even harder.

There was no denying it. Jaxtyn wanted to feel that pulse, see that flush, hear those pleas in entirely different circumstances. He wasn't sure how the CeeNee had moved so quickly from "not hot exactly, but interesting" to "I want this man," but he had.

The universe was a mysterious place, and Jaxtyn didn't believe in coincidences. Maybe Daniel's Jesus *had* brought them together.

The missionary had begun swaying in a side-to-side motion, his praying more intense, but quieter, almost incoherent at times he was speaking so quickly. Jaxtyn was reminded of Sufi dancers—dervishes, he thought they were called—swirling in hypnotic circles, or of the Jews at the Western Wall nodding in prayer.

It was fascinating, and a little bit scary, and strangely erotic.

He could have knelt there absorbed in Daniel's praying all day. But they only had the room for another five minutes. Already a few members of the ladies' mystery book club had gathered in the hallway. One was peering in curiously at the unusual sight.

"Daniel," he whispered, afraid of jolting the man out of his…what? Trance?

"Daniel." He tried again, untangling their fingers and pulling his hands away.

Daniel blinked and smiled—a wide, beaming grin that Jaxtyn would have normally associated with someone taking drugs. He was beautiful. "Jaxtyn, brother." He wiped the moisture from under his eyes with his fingers. "Did you feel him?"

He didn't want to lie, but… "Maybe?" He rose from the cushion. "I definitely felt something." And that was the truth. "We have to go. Our time's up for the room."

Daniel stood and seemed to come more fully back to himself.

He walked to the chair that held his coat. "Sure, of course." He was beginning to seem almost embarrassed, which Jaxtyn didn't understand. "Thank you for inviting me." He shrugged his arms into the heavy jacket. He paused as if he was unsure how to proceed. "But, Jaxtyn, seriously, did you feel him? Did Jesus come into your heart?"

Jaxtyn was putting the stacking chairs back where he'd found them. The mystery club ladies would arrange them in their own fashion. Already, one of the women had walked to the galley kitchen and had begun preparing the coffee. He took one last look around the room, then pulled on his jacket. "Maybe, Daniel. I don't know."

Inspiration struck. "Can we do it again? Maybe if you explained what to expect, or if we had a bit longer?" It felt manipulative. And it was. Jaxtyn had no real expectation of feeling Jesus in his heart or anywhere else, but Daniel had clearly had a transcendent experience of some kind, and Jaxtyn wanted to know more.

And he wanted to hold the other man's hands again.

But Daniel looked uncertain as they walked down the hallway toward the front entrance. "I don't know. I just thought you'd…that it would be easier, I guess."

Jaxtyn sensed him slipping away. "Hey, practice makes perfect. Give me your phone. I'll input my contact information, and you can let me know when you want to meet again."

Daniel pulled his phone out of his pocket, although he hadn't yet agreed to pray together again. It was odd, thought Jaxtyn. He didn't think Daniel wanted to give him his phone, but he held it out anyway as if he was unaccustomed to saying no to people.

It was a different phone than the one Jaxtyn had seen in New York, the one he put the Open Lotus contact information in. It was a bulky, cheap thing, without a folding screen and nearly the size of his hand. Oh. "You got a burner."

Daniel colored. "We needed to find out what was happening…after the bomb."

Jaxtyn absorbed that as he opened the contacts screen. If he understood Daniel correctly, the missionaries had no means of accessing the internet before they got burner phones. What kind of lives did these men live? The phone was unprotected with no face scan nor a thumbprint lock required to open it. He tried to school his expression when he saw the only other contact was Black Beauty. Marcus, surely. Could Skylar have been right about them after all?

He took out his own phone and scanned Daniel's number into it.

"Here you go," he said as he handed the phone back. "Hey, wait. I take it you got a burner so you could fly under the radar, away from the eyes of someone else?" Daniel didn't answer, but he didn't deny it. "The thing is, you could get a library card while we're here. As long as you have a temporary residence in Massachusetts, you can access the entire library, right from your phone."

He watched as Daniel thought through the ramifications.

"I mean, you could download anything, get access to information you might not otherwise have." He hoped he wasn't pushing too far, but he sensed these missionaries were more sheltered than even Sylvie suspected they were. Maybe worse than just sheltered, maybe imprisoned somehow — at least intellectually.

"Yes," Daniel said. "That makes sense."

"Come on, then. I'll take you over to the registration desk. You just tell them the name of your hotel, but they won't check." Daniel frowned. "Or," Jaxtyn rushed on, "we can just say you're a student and you live with us. Skylar and Sylvie and I share a little apartment just off campus."

"Campus?" Daniel asked.

"Yeah, we all go to UMass Boston."

"Did you say UMass Boston?"

Jaxtyn nodded, and Daniel looked like he'd just found a winning lottery ticket. The smile returned, and Jaxtyn didn't know what caused it, but he was glad to see it. "Jesus is here, Jaxtyn. You may not know it yet, but God is working through both of us. Let's get me signed up for a card. We will pray together again soon."

*

IT TOOK JAXTYN hours to get home, even though he was just going across the city. The subway didn't run as frequently on Sundays, and there was a security scare on a different line, which then caused a significant delay for his train, as the entire system was paused until they could sort everything out. At least they'd been brought to a stop aboveground, so Jaxtyn was able to gaze out the window as the light snow fell and melted away before whitening the landscape.

He thought about the water molecules in the snow, transforming themselves from solid to liquid, and how the water in his own body was connected to all the water in the universe. How many times had the atoms in his body switched places with the atoms in his surroundings?

Does it even make sense to think about my *body — on the atomic level?*

His mind drifted back to Daniel and what they'd shared while praying.

He'd never prayed before. It was *almost* like meditating, except focused on someone else, which only resulted in an increased sense of separation, rather than a sense of unity with the whole. He knew some meditators who focused on an image, even an image of a god — Krishna, perhaps, or Ram — but that was only to serve as a focal point preventing the monkey mind from leaping to other distractions. They never talked to the image, as if the god it represented was right there, listening to them.

Still, the similarities were intriguing. Jaxtyn didn't understand the neuroscience behind it all, but he thought Daniel's ecstatic glow after he'd finished praying was similar to what Jaxtyn himself felt after a successful meditation session when his mind freed itself from his body and he dissolved into a peaceful unity with the universe.

Jaxtyn's musings were interrupted by the hiss of releasing brakes, and the train started pulling forward. Daniel had said they'd pray together again soon. Jaxtyn smiled and closed his eyes, recalling the warmth of Daniel's hands in his.

*

HIS APARTMENT WAS a fifteen-minute walk from the JFK/UMass station on the Red Line. Greater Boston was more crowded than it had ever been, with so many people from the South flooding into the Northern cities at the same time economic refugees from around the world sought refuge in places that begrudgingly made space for them.

And even though the apartment was run-down and in a marginal neighborhood, they were still crammed into a two-bedroom unit. Jaxtyn and Skylar shared the larger, front room with its two windows overlooking the busy street while Sylvie had the smaller middle room with only one window facing a brick wall opposite the side alley.

A stinging sleet began falling as Jaxtyn hurried along the final block.

He was startled and relieved to see Skylar's old car parked illegally at the far corner, its hood sticking several feet beyond the painted line, nearly poking into the intersection. Then he was angry; Skylar hadn't called or responded to any of his texts. He resolved to find out what had happened before letting his anger settle deeper.

The lock on his building's front door was a cheap key-in-the-knob affair that wouldn't have deterred anyone intent on breaking in. Jaxtyn bounded up the steps to his own unit, unlocked the deadbolt, pushed open the door, and heard Skylar and Sylvie arguing in the kitchen at the end of the hallway.

"I hear Jax in the hallway," Sylvie said. "Maybe he can talk some sense into you."

Skylar was standing next to the table, holding a can of beer. He still had his coat on, and he'd shaved off all his orange-dyed hair since Jaxtyn had last seen him. The stubble on his scalp glistened with moisture. Sylvie sat in the room's only armchair—a concession to the fact the space served as the living room as well as the kitchen. She was scowling, her legs pulled up beside her and her arms crossed defensively.

"You're alive," Jaxtyn said as he shrugged out of his coat, flinging granules of sleet onto the fake wood floor, adding to the drops of water already accumulating beneath Skylar.

"Seem to be," Skylar responded. He took a swig from the can.

"Where were you, Sky?" Jaxtyn asked. He tried to remain calm, but the fact Skylar—who didn't drink often—had gone directly for a beer even before removing his coat was troubling.

"Oh, you know," Skylar remarked vaguely, waving his hand.

Sylvie stood. "No, Sky, he doesn't know. And neither do I. That's why we asked. Where the hell were you?"

"And why didn't you respond to any of my texts?" Jaxtyn asked.

"I was in jail, and they took my phone. They didn't give it back either." Skylar took another deep drink. "Hard to text when you don't have a phone."

No one said anything for a moment as the news sank in. "Jesus," Jaxtyn exclaimed, a strange echo from his prayer session with Daniel. He moved to the small refrigerator squeezed into the corner of the room and retrieved a beer. Sylvie collapsed back into her chair, and Jaxtyn sank into a chair at the table.

"Take your coat off and sit," he said, nodding to the chair across from him. "And start from the beginning."

*

AS SKYLAR TOLD his story, Jaxtyn became increasingly alarmed and concerned for his friend's safety.

"I can't believe they'd put you in jail for speeding," Jaxtyn said.

"That was just an excuse," Skylar responded. He took a final gulp of beer and placed the empty can on the table next to him. "They knew we were going to be trouble, so they decided to hold us for a while."

Sylvie stood when Skylar described the jailhouse and began pacing the small room. "Why did you go down there in the first place?" she asked. "Everyone knows to stay out of the Red. They hate us down there. And you're not exactly"—she waved her hand at him—"subtle."

Fair enough, Jaxtyn thought. But now that Skylar wasn't wearing makeup, and the orange hair was gone, he looked almost…inconspicuous. The rounded wooden beads draped around his neck could have been worn by guys anywhere, right? Well, maybe not in the Red. Jaxtyn didn't know.

"I don't like these new guys you've been hanging out with," Sylvie said. "They're getting you in trouble. Why did they want to go to Georgia anyway?"

Skylar took another beer from the fridge and then sat in the chair Sylvie had vacated.

"You have no idea what it's like down there," he responded.

"And you do?" Sylvie shot back. She leaned against the sink, arms crossed against her chest.

"I do now. Listen, I know you guys think I don't have an interest in what's happening in the world, and I don't keep up with what's going on, but the New Riders have opened my eyes. Now I—"

"New Riders?" Jaxtyn asked.

"Yes. That's what they call themselves. It's modeled after the Freedom Riders from the 1960s who helped desegregate the South. We drive into the Red with useful information for queer youth, things like—"

"We?" Sylvie asked.

Skylar took a drink. "Yes. We. I've joined their group."

Jaxtyn reached across the couch and placed a hand on Skylar's arm. "Sky, it's good you've taken an interest. We all need to do more to help our queer youth out. But there are plenty of things you can do right here without risking arrest."

Skylar tilted his head in acknowledgment but didn't offer his agreement.

"They didn't rough you up, did they?" Jaxtyn asked.

"Not me, no," Skylar responded, leaving open the possibility others in his group might have been.

"What is it you guys do down there?" Sylvie asked. She kept glancing toward the refrigerator, and Jaxtyn was proud of her for not grabbing a beer. He made a mental note to tell her so afterward.

"It's different each trip—"

"You've done this *before*?" Sylvie interrupted.

"Let him finish," Jaxtyn said.

"This time we were taking educational materials to Atlanta. Did you know there isn't even one healthcare facility left in the city serving the needs of trans youth? There's no place they can go to get information on hormone treatments, or surgery options, or even how to connect with their own community. No one is willing to talk to anyone under eighteen about gender identity, because it's illegal to encourage children to consider surgery or drug treatments of any sort without the written consent of their parents."

"I didn't realize it had gotten that bad," Sylvie said.

"Well, it has," Skylar responded. "And the few remaining queer community centers are constantly at risk of being shut down if they let teenagers into their space. And they're always being set up. Older-looking teens will be sent in by some church group to pick up a pamphlet or something, and then all of a sudden the police are there closing down the place, jailing the people working there."

"That's really grim," Jaxtyn said. He squeezed Skylar's arm.

"Yeah, it is. So, we brought loads of printed materials and hundreds of burner phones with prepopulated links to relevant websites. And also explicit instructions for how minors can move up here — what trains to take, how much they'll cost, how to dress and behave on the journey to avoid being stopped, where to find help and a place to stay once they reach New York or Boston."

Sylvie walked over and put her hand on Skylar's shoulder. "I get it, Sky. That's very brave, but I still think it's dangerous. I'm surprised they let you out of jail with all those materials."

"We were lucky. We got stopped in South Carolina on the way home after we'd gotten rid of everything."

Jaxtyn shivered, his premonition about things coming to a head resurfacing. South Carolina — where the CeeNees were from — so many interconnections. And what a close call. Sylvie was right. Skylar would still be in jail if they'd caught him with those materials.

"I don't know, Sky," Jaxtyn said. "Can you trust these New Rider guys? There's so much risk in what you're doing."

"They've put the rest of their lives on hold to help others. Of course I can trust them."

Sylvie and Jaxtyn exchanged a look.

"And what about you?" Sylvie asked. "Are you coming back to class? You've missed a whole week."

"Yeah. At least, I think so. Spending a few days in jail spooked everyone. We're trying to figure out how to do this without having to drive." He drank more of his beer. "And now I need to get a new phone. Anyway, I'm back now. What did I miss while I was gone?"

Sylvie filled him in on the bombing earlier in the week. Skylar had already heard a high-level account of the attack from a convenience store clerk in New Jersey, and he didn't appear interested in learning about what he'd missed in his classes. "How about you, Jax? Were you able to get more hours at the library yet?"

"No, not yet, but I do have other news," Jaxtyn said. "Remember those CeeNees we saw on the train last weekend?" Sylvie raised an eyebrow. "I held hands with the White one, Daniel, this morning as we prayed together."

Skylar dropped his can, and it rolled across the floor, beer sloshing out to mix with the puddles of melted sleet. Sylvie shook her head and stood. "I need to find new roommates." She grabbed a towel and handed it to Skylar, who bent and began sopping up the mess.

"I knew it!" he said. "So, they are gay, right?" He handed the now empty can to Jaxtyn as he continued to mop the spill.

"I don't know. Maybe." Jaxtyn put the can on the counter. "Daniel did ask me if I was comfortable on my knees."

His roommates gasped, and Jaxtyn laughed. "Relax. It's how they pray, evidently. But the Black one, Marcus, is in Daniel's phone contacts as Black Beauty. So, it's confusing." Jaxtyn handed Skylar a few paper towels and took the towel away to the sink. "The thing is, he was using a burner phone, and he was dressed in normal jeans and a sweater. He told me they bought them the day of the bombing."

"They're going rogue?" Sylvie asked.

"I don't think so," Jaxtyn replied. "I think they were just very uninformed about how they'd be received up here. I think a lot of important things are kept from them."

"We drove by one of those missionary factories last week," Skylar said. "They look all nice and countryside-ish, but I swear I got prison vibes just driving by."

"And you held hands?" Sylvie asked, bringing the conversation back to Jaxtyn's news.

Jaxtyn grinned. "It was nice," he said. "We knelt facing each other, and we held hands while he prayed."

Skylar threw the dirty paper towels into the trash bin under the sink. "What was that like?" he asked.

"Uh…weird," Jaxtyn replied. And suddenly, he was uncomfortable talking about it. It felt…private, something he'd shared on a personal level with Daniel.

"Did he pray out loud?" Skylar asked. "I saw that on the internet once, that they talk to Jesus like an imaginary friend who's right there in the room with them."

That was enough for Jaxtyn. "It wasn't like that," he said. Although, of course, it *had* been like that—probably even more dramatically than Skylar was imagining. But he didn't want to mock Daniel or cheapen what had happened between them in the library. He headed for the hallway. "I have to study. I'm glad you made it back safely, Sky."

Chapter Eleven

"HOW DID IT go at the church?" Daniel asked.

"Fine," replied Marcus. "It was smart for us to separate. I don't think they would have let me in if you'd been with me."

They were in their room at the King's Royal Court Hotel, shivering in heavy coats while they waited for the heat to come on. Daniel didn't know what to think about Marcus's comment. He knew the African Methodist Episcopal Church was mostly Black, but he wasn't accustomed to thinking his race would make anyone uncomfortable or make him unwelcome.

"Was it a successful visit? Did you pray with them?"

"I participated in their service, so we prayed, yes." Marcus's attention was as much on his phone as it was on Daniel.

"Pastor Logan was right to direct us toward churches where people already believe," Daniel said. "So, are they with us? Will they help persuade their government to support our cause in

Congress?"

Marcus turned his phone off. They were each sitting on the sides of their own beds, facing each other. Marcus flopped back and stared at the ceiling. "It's more complicated than that, Dan."

"Why?" It was worrisome Marcus was choosing not to look at him.

He sat up and cocked his head at Daniel. "Let's try this," he said. "Do you know how many Black people have moved here from South Carolina?"

Daniel shook his head. He'd noticed right away how many more Black people were around him than he'd ever seen in South Carolina, and he was pretty sure he'd heard more than one familiar accent from home. And it wasn't just the number of Black people, but all shades of brown, too, and so many foreigners. Or at least he assumed they were foreigners, given their head coverings and dress. He didn't know why Marcus had asked, but he knew enough to wait patiently while Marcus got to his point.

"I didn't either," Marcus said. "The answer is around fifty thousand."

"Wow. That's…a lot."

"Uh-huh. And that's just Boston. Nearly three-quarters of a million Black people have left South Carolina over the decade." Marcus stopped. He seemed to be studying Daniel, waiting for his reaction.

There was a loud *clang*, and hot air began blowing forcefully out of the wall unit. Daniel took his jacket off and draped it over the back of the room's chair, giving himself time to think. He knew he was missing something, and he didn't want to reveal his ignorance. But life back home was so much nicer than it was in this crowded, dangerous city. He truly couldn't understand why so many people would choose to live here instead.

Then he remembered the payment scheme that had been so controversial when it was introduced when he was a boy. It was one of the few childhood memories he had of his parents arguing about politics — or arguing about anything, for that matter. "It's *not* racist," his father had insisted, his voice raised in frustration. "Even if most of the people taking advantage of it are Black."

"Shh," his mother had responded, glancing toward Daniel. Then they'd moved the argument to their bedroom.

Marcus was waiting for him to say something. "Are these the ones who were paid to leave?" Daniel asked. He remembered learning in high school how successful the Pay-to-Go program had been — so successful, in fact, that shortly after South Carolina implemented it, half a dozen other states had followed suit.

It was a straightforward idea. The state would pay 10,000 dollars to any adult who agreed to leave, with 5,000 additional dollars for every minor they took with them. All that was required was for the person leaving to sign a legal contract promising not to return and forgoing any claims owed at that moment and in the future to any state funds.

Proponents had argued it would drain the state of the least desirable citizens — the ones who couldn't or wouldn't find meaningful employment, the ones who took more from state coffers than they contributed, the ones desperate enough to pick up stakes and move out of state for such a short-term gain.

And it had worked, too, at least financially.

But by the time it was obvious entire Black communities were disappearing and lawsuits were filed alleging discriminatory intent and disparate impact, the federal government had largely removed itself from the business of overseeing state laws, and the South Carolina Supreme Court gave the program its formal blessing.

A lot of White people had left too, after all.

Marcus nodded. "Many of the ones who moved here took advantage of the Pay-to-Go program, but not all of them." Daniel must have passed some sort of test because Marcus's expression relaxed. "I learned a lot today. They call it the Diaspora here." He took his jacket off and left it on his bed.

"Who does?" Daniel asked.

"The people from the AME church. The Diaspora. That's what they call the massive migration of Blacks from the South to the North in such a short period of time."

"Oh," said Daniel. He couldn't think of what else to say. It still didn't make sense so many would move *here*, but he sensed he'd gotten past a hurdle with Marcus and asking more questions might reintroduce an awkwardness he wanted to avoid. "I hadn't heard that before," he said.

"No," said Marcus, and he looked off to the side, not avoiding Daniel, exactly, but seemingly deep in thought. "Neither had I."

*

MARCUS WENT OUT and got lunch from a Pakistani vendor on the main shopping street a few blocks away and brought it back to their hotel where they planned to eat in their room while they strategized about their next steps. Daniel had told Marcus about meeting Jaxtyn at the library and explained their good fortune regarding their other mission—the secret one. They had a contact now at UMass Boston, and Daniel was certain Jaxtyn would give him a tour of the campus if he asked.

"Maybe we'll even get a better photo of the guy from Pastor Logan," Daniel said. "But even if we don't, we should at least be able to find his car if we spend enough time searching for it."

"I don't like it, Dan." Marcus tore off a chunk of his flatbread and scooped up a generous portion of…something…from one of the containers. Marcus had named each dish, but Daniel didn't know what any of it was. It tasted delicious, just spicier than he'd prefer, and he knew their room would stink for hours.

"Which part?" he asked.

"All of it," Marcus said. "I don't like the whole idea of the secret mission."

"Marcus." They'd been over it before, many times. They'd even prayed over it. Each time he was sure Marcus had recommitted to submitting to God's will in the matter—well, at least Pastor Logan's will, which they had to assume was the same thing—but then something would come up and Marcus would express uncertainty again.

But he'd never been this bold, out-and-out stating he didn't like the entire idea.

"It's just that it's so underhanded. Why can't we just let the authorities do their job?" Marcus asked, not for the first time.

"The authorities *will* do their job. We're just helping them by gathering some information that will be useful," Daniel replied, not for the first time.

Marcus sighed. "I know, I know. It just doesn't…feel right…"

"Marcus," Daniel put on his best Pastor Logan voice. "Ruth had her life ahead of her. Just because she wasn't going to be a missionary, and we hadn't kept in touch with her after her grandmother died—"

"It's not that," Marcus interrupted.

"You *saw* the guy with Ruth in the car."

"I *know*. I mean, I know he did it…" Marcus was winding down. He wouldn't defend what the guy had done; it was indefensible, and they both knew it. That's why it bothered Daniel so much that Marcus was so reluctant to get fully behind the mission.

Daniel played the ace card, which always ended the argument. "We're talking about murder."

"I *know*," Marcus said, in a tone indicating the discussion was over. Daniel waited for Marcus to add *You're right; I'm sorry*. But he didn't this time, and that worried Daniel more than anything.

*

RESIDUAL TENSION STILL hung in the air when they set the phone up and arranged the chair next to the bed in preparation for the call with Pastor Logan. They put their missionary uniforms back on and even remembered their name tags. Daniel shut off the heat and the room fell silent. It would gradually cool off until it became uncomfortable after an hour or so. Daniel hoped the call would be over by then.

"Were you touching each other when you prayed with him this morning?" Marcus asked as he checked the camera's screenshot. The question sounded casual, but Daniel heard the calculation in it.

He wasn't surprised Marcus had brought up Jaxtyn, but he wished he would have waited until after the call. "Of course. We clasped our hands together in prayer, just like you and I do."

"Was it…difficult? Did it trigger anything in you?"

Daniel sighed and looked out the window. It was getting dark, and the sleet had changed to rain. The streaks of water on the glass reflected a blurry, yellow light from a streetlamp below. Marcus's questions about Daniel's desires were getting harder to answer.

"Marcus, you'd be able to pray with a pretty girl, wouldn't you, even though all the while, you'd still know she was pretty, right?"

"So you think he's pretty? Or, handsome, I guess?"

"Yes, Marcus. Jaxtyn is a good-looking guy. You know that. You can see it too. It doesn't mean I can't help him find his way to God. It doesn't interfere with my mission." He thought of the pictures on the magazine covers at the library and how uncomfortable they made him. And he thought about the new library app on his phone and the entire world of danger awaiting him there — if he chose to explore it.

"Maybe," Marcus said, but he didn't sound convinced. "But if I notice how pretty a girl is when I'm praying with her, well, that's all part of God's plan for men and women. It's not sinful."

Not sinful like I am, you mean.

"I know, Marcus. I handled it. We're all tempted into sin, all the time. Jesus helps me stay strong."

Marcus nodded, satisfied. "Good, Dan. That's good. I'm here for you, brother."

*

PASTOR LOGAN WAS late, even later than last time. They were lucky, though, because five minutes after their call was supposed to start, Daniel's burner phone played a loud incoming-message tone. It was tucked out of sight under his jeans in the bureau drawer, but Pastor Logan would have heard the sound and surely would have asked about it.

They both got up to silence their phones.

"Was that him?" Marcus asked. Daniel was studying his phone's screen, trying not to smile. The profile read *Jax*, and had a picture of a seated Buddha next to the name, just like the one Jaxtyn had tattooed on his neck. He was consistently on-brand, that was for sure.

The message read: *Come to my meditation group Tuesday morning on campus? We can pray together again after.* This was followed by an emoji of praying hands and a smiley face. A smiley face? What did that mean?

Marcus had moved behind Daniel to peer over his shoulder. "What's with the smiley face?"

Daniel turned the phone off. "I don't know."

"Do you want to go?" Marcus asked.

"It would help with our other mission," Daniel responded without actually answering the question.

"We should both go," Marcus said.

Daniel pushed aside a brief flare of disappointment he wouldn't be alone with Jaxtyn. "Of course," he said. "We'll have better luck with two of us looking for the car. The sooner we find the guy, the sooner we'll be able to devote all our attention to the primary mission."

Marcus nodded, and a chime from the phone on the table announced the start of their meeting.

"Brother Paul. Brother Thomas."

"Good evening, Pastor Logan," they replied.

"How was your first full week in Boston?"

"Good," they replied simultaneously. "We're making slow progress," Marcus added.

Pastor Logan nodded. He was waiting for something.

"We weren't prepared for how hostile people would be," Daniel said. The silence stretched longer. "There was a bombing here last week. People thought maybe it was Christian Nationalist Evangelicals behind it." Pastor Logan still didn't say anything.

"You know," Marcus said, "because of the attacks on voters last year."

"Ah," said Pastor Logan. "We knew it had gotten difficult for our missionaries in New York. We didn't know what the public sentiment would be in Boston. That's unfortunate."

Marcus flinched. "What's unfortunate is we didn't know about the attacks before we came here," he said. Below the camera's view, Daniel kicked his shin. That was too far. Surely Marcus must know that.

A small smile appeared on Pastor Logan's face. Daniel's blood ran cold. "Are you *questioning* the Church, Brother Paul?"

Marcus looked down at his lap. "No, sir," he mumbled.

"Speak up!" commanded Pastor Logan.

"No, Pastor Logan. I am not questioning the church."

Some of the tension drained from Daniel's shoulders. "Had you heard about the bombing last week, Pastor Logan?" Daniel asked. "We pulled up the Good News Network right away but couldn't find any information about what was going on."

"Yes, Brother Thomas. I was aware of the situation." He let the silence drag on, and neither Marcus nor Daniel pushed further. "We have recently relaxed the dress code for missionaries in New York City. It seems we will need to do so in Boston as well if the people there are as hostile as you report. I'll deposit additional funds into your accounts to allow you to buy street clothes so that you don't attract unnecessary attention." He held up a hand. "Modest street clothes."

"Yes, Pastor Logan," they both said.

"As for what's going on in the world, pay it no heed. The news is simply a distraction, taking your attention away from doing God's work."

Daniel knew that and believed it to be true. He'd always gratefully accepted the limits on the outside world's intrusion into his life at Sangre de Cristo. It *did* allow him to focus all his attention on listening for Jesus's voice and filling his heart with God's grace. It's just that his…isolation…had never felt so immediately relevant before.

"And speaking of doing God's work," Pastor Logan said, "how did you make out with your church visit, Brother Paul?"

Marcus's foot was tapping wildly, and Daniel placed a calm, reassuring pressure against it with his own. He offered a quick prayer that Marcus wouldn't mention anything about a Diaspora—or anything at all about race—then chastised himself for treating the sacred act of prayer as if he was asking for a favor rather than giving himself up to God's will.

"I'm not sure," Marcus said honestly, which seemed to

please pastor Logan. "We talked a lot about Jesus — they were very receptive to that. But they seemed to think about their relationship with Him in a...I don't know...fatalistic kind of way, I guess. As if it was their job to just put their fate into His hands and accept whatever happens."

Daniel hadn't talked about this with Marcus yet, and he was curious about what Marcus meant.

"Go on," said Pastor Logan.

"Well, they seemed disinclined to think of themselves as tools God can wield to do his will. To them, being saved was all about what happens after death, not how they can be...useful...now in this life." Marcus nodded to himself as if he was confirming his own observation.

Pastor Logan nodded along with Marcus. "We've heard that before. Keep at them. The Black religious community is a strong voting block. We need them to advocate for religious freedom. Their state reps need to feel the pressure from all sides."

Pastor Logan shifted his gaze. "And you, Brother Thomas. How was your visit to the Open Lotus Church?"

"God works His will in mysterious ways, Pastor Logan. I met a young man there who attends UMass Boston. I'm confident we can manage an invitation from him to witness to students at the college." Daniel didn't dare look over at Marcus. This was a deceptively backward way of presenting what had transpired. "Getting onto the campus should hasten our success with our other mission."

"Excellent work," Pastor Logan offered. "Make that a priority. Let me know as soon as you've made progress. We need to identify that man." Marcus continued staring at his lap, and

Daniel knew what it was costing him not to speak up.

"I'll find a way for us to get there this week," Daniel said as if he hadn't already received Jaxtyn's invitation.

"Good. Anything else?"

They weren't going to pray together?

"No, Pastor Logan," they both responded, and then the call was disconnected.

Chapter Twelve

EVEN THOUGH THE bedroom Jaxtyn and Skylar shared was the larger of the two, it was still cramped with two full-size beds in it. Jaxtyn didn't have many things; he liked to be free of attachments. All the furniture and kitchen equipment in the apartment belonged to either Skylar or Sylvie. Other than a small Buddha statue that sat on a narrow shelf in the bathroom and the picture of a smiling, seated Buddha hanging on the wall over his bed, everything Jaxtyn owned fit into the three drawers of his bureau.

Skylar was pretending to be asleep. Jaxtyn knew he was pretending because he was perfectly still and silent. Skylar tossed and turned and made all manner of grunting and snorting sounds when he was sleeping.

"Sky, are you awake?" Jaxtyn whispered.

He waited a few moments, and just when he was sure Skylar was going to blow him off, he heard, "Yeah."

"Are you telling the truth that they didn't hurt you? In jail, I mean." He hoped it didn't come across as purely being concerned about sexual abuse, but he did worry about that. Skylar wasn't exactly subtle about his sexuality. But he worried about all the other forms of abuse too. Did they hit him or threaten him? Spit in his food? Play loud music at night?

"No," Skylar said. "It was a neat and clean county lockup. We each had our own little room—I wouldn't even call it a cell—with a sink and a toilet behind a half wall. We weren't even technically arrested. At least that's what they said. I think if we had been arrested and charged with a crime, we might have gone somewhere worse." Skylar rolled onto his side to face Jaxtyn. "They did make me eat grits in the morning."

"I can't believe they could just keep you locked up without charging you." But Jaxtyn knew they could. It was one of the things Professor Ringle kept going on about—how each state had different ideas now about what due process rights had to be afforded to citizens, and since the Supreme Court no longer viewed itself as having authority to set a national standard, some states proved to be more zealous in their detention policies than others.

"And Mark—the guy who drove us down in his van—found a tracking device under his hood. Thank God he knew to look for one. He threw it into the cab of an eighteen-wheeler at a rest stop."

"I'm glad you weren't driving. You wouldn't have driven your own car down there, would you?"

"My car's too small to fit us all for such a long drive." That wasn't an answer, and Jaxtyn wondered if Skylar *had* driven down on one of his trips. He didn't want to push for an answer.

"What's it like down there?" Jaxtyn asked.

Skylar sat up and then swung his legs over the side of the bed. Across the small room, Jaxtyn did the same. "It's weird, Jax. At first, nothing seems different, except for all the guns—everyone there carries a gun. And at first, they're all super friendly, even people like the clerks at the convenience stores, asking about your day and stuff, like they know you or something."

Skylar shook his head. "But they're not friendly. Not really. Once they heard our accents, they closed up tight."

Like we do with them, Jaxtyn thought, recalling his sangha's response to Daniel's presence at meditation.

"But then you start noticing all the other differences," Skylar continued. "Like how conservatively everyone is dressed, and how the young people don't dye their hair, or get tattooed, or wear piercings." Skylar leaned forward.

"And then you're, like, 'Hey, everybody's White.' And then you start noticing the Christian cross. It's everywhere! On advertisements of all kinds and billboards and store windows. And then, the first time you see a cross on the side of a police car, you realize you've traveled to somewhere different."

Jaxtyn tried to imagine it—the world Daniel lived in.

"But, Sky, what more do they *want*? Why all this fighting?" It was the question everyone kept asking. Why wouldn't these states just accept the religious freedoms they had already? Why couldn't they all just move on?

"That's what we asked the folks at the Queer Community Center in Atlanta. Those people are scared, Jax. They were so grateful for our help but wouldn't even let us bring the pamphlets or the burner phones inside their building. Instead, they told us where to drop them so young people were likely to find them.

They're under constant surveillance, and even though they aren't doing anything illegal, the police are getting more and more bold about harassing them."

Jaxtyn shook his head, trying to reconcile this picture of an overbearing police force with Daniel, who seemed so kind and sincere. "But why?" he asked again.

"Well, here's how they explained to me," Skylar said. "Every time the state or local government does something to promote Christianity, the ACLU sues, claiming it's against the constitution. The constitution still exists after all, even if it is just the state courts enforcing it, and even down South, there might be a line deemed by the courts to be too far, although nothing they've done so far has come close to it.

"And last year, when Georgia mandated grade schools teach children homosexuality is a sin and that sexual relationships need to be limited to a married man and woman, well the Atlanta Queer Community Center joined the ACLU's lawsuit, saying the new state law harms queer youth. Which it does, of course."

Jaxtyn stood and crossed the short distance between them, sat next to Skylar, and put his arm across his shoulders. "That's awful."

"Right," Skylar continued. "So, the Unified Christian States — that's what they call themselves down there — want any new federal arrangement to explicitly permit states to establish a state religion. To make it official the state can enforce Christian values and teachings and make all these lawsuits and challenges go away once and for all."

"But what about all the people who aren't Christians?" Jaxtyn asked. "It would be like living under Sharia law or something."

"Come on, Jax. Why do you think they pay people to leave?"

Jaxtyn blew out a breath. "Jesus," he said.

"Exactly," agreed Skylar.

*

THE FOLLOWING MORNING, Jaxtyn was making coffee, and Sylvie was hurrying about the apartment collecting what she'd need for the day and stuffing the items into her carryall. She looked like she hadn't slept, and she'd only bothered with her eyebrow and nose piercings.

"Tough night?"

She squinted her eyes at Jaxtyn as if she suspected a trap, then shook her head. "No." She rolled her shoulders and then looked at him more openly. "Yes, actually, and thanks for asking. To be honest, I could have used a drink…or something…last night, after everything Skylar told us. But I've been taking your advice to heart. Stone sober for a week now." She offered a weak smile.

"Good for you, Sylvie." Jaxtyn poured a cup of coffee, added lots of sugar and cream, and handed it to Sylvie. "If there's anything I can do to help, or if you need to talk…" He poured his own cup.

"I know. You're a good friend, Jax." She took a sip, and it seemed to brighten her mood. "Listen though," she whispered as she glanced down the hallway. "I don't think Skylar is telling us everything. I think he's doing more than just bringing educational pamphlets and burner phones down there."

Jaxtyn had suspected there might be more, too, but he couldn't point to anything specific and hadn't wanted to say anything. He was glad Sylvie shared his hunch. Unless it was more than just a hunch for her.

"Why do you think that?" he asked cautiously.

Sylvie cocked her head. "You think so, too, don't you? Your Spidey sense is tingling, isn't it?"

Spidey sense. That's what people who knew him well called his uncanny ability to sense the patterns unfolding in the world around them. Jaxtyn didn't see it as anything special; he just felt the interconnectedness of the universe very deeply, and if something was off somewhere, his subconscious mind couldn't help but connect the dots, and anticipate how things might play out. His meditation practice deepened those associations.

"I do think so, yes," Jaxtyn admitted.

"You don't think this new gang of his has gotten him involved in anything illegal, do you?"

It was a good question. "The New Riders? To be honest, I don't know what's considered illegal down there. I mean, if they're providing minors with information on how to run away from home and where to find support in Boston or New York, then…maybe? That might be considered a crime."

Sylvie took a deep drink of coffee, and even though there was already plenty of cream in it, she poured in more. "I *hate* this!" she said. "Why does everything have to be so complicated? Why can't people just let others be?"

"I suspect that's what they say about us. They just want to practice their faith, why can't we let them?" Jaxtyn held up a hand when he saw Sylvie was about to tear into him. "It was rhetorical. I know the answer. Not everyone down there wants to live under these church's religious laws, and we need to look out for them, especially the ones who might have a harder time looking out for themselves."

Sylvie seemed to deflate. "Exactly. I just wish there was more we could do without putting ourselves at risk."

"Well, there's not," said Skylar, coming out of the hallway. "But I appreciate your concern for me."

"Oh, Sky," Sylvie sighed. "You know we support the objectives; it's just that antagonizing people isn't going to help, and it might even set us back. I mean, the terror attacks haven't exactly been helping their cause, have they?"

Jaxtyn nodded his agreement with Sylvie's point and poured Skylar a cup of coffee.

"But they *have* been working," Skylar insisted. "You hear the way everyone talks on campus. They're willing to give the Christian states anything they want at this point. People just want to end all the drama and get back to something closer to normal — whatever that's going to end up being."

"Just don't do anything that's going to get you into real trouble, Sky," Sylvie said. "We don't want to see you get hurt."

"She's right," Jaxtyn agreed. "Bad enough you had to spend so much time in jail. And Congress is working on it, and the courts too. We should just let them do their jobs."

Skylar accepted his mug from Jaxtyn and lifted it in a salute. "Not all wars can be fought in court."

Jaxtyn was about to respond, but Sylvie cut in. "All right, we've all made our points. Sky, it looks like you're coming back to class this week?" Jaxtyn heard the hopeful note in her voice, a silent plea that this week, at least, would be a normal one, and that Skylar's attention would be focused on school and not whatever his new group of friends might be plotting next.

"Yes," he replied. "We've all decided to lay low for a while. The tracking device in Mark's van had him spooked."

"Good," said Sylvie. "A nice, quiet week then."

Jaxtyn picked up his own mug. "Uh, guys, just so you know… I invited the missionaries to my meditation group tomorrow morning. I think they're curious about the campus. And, well, I think Daniel wants to pray with me again."

Skylar laughed. "Oh, I can just see it! The two of you in a corner of the student center, holding hands and praying to Jesus."

"Right," Jaxtyn said. "So, that's the problem. I was thinking for the praying part we might come back here?"

Sylvie shook her head. "That's just weird, Jax. I think you're becoming obsessed with these guys."

"One of them, anyway." Skylar smirked.

Sylvie finished her coffee and placed the empty cup in the sink. "Well, if you're bringing CeeNees here, I'll be sure to be somewhere else."

"Not me," said Skylar. "I want to check out Daniel more closely, now that I know you have a hand-holding type of relationship."

"Sky, don't be obnoxious," Jaxtyn pleaded. "Please?"

"Don't worry. I won't cramp your style. I'll just say hello, and then I'll get out of your hair."

Chapter Thirteen

THE BOSTON PUBLIC Library was an ornate, imposing structure anchoring an urban square with a beautiful nineteenth-century church opposite. The symbolism wasn't lost on Daniel. Public education and faith in God were two of the foundations upon which this nation was built. His eyes swept up the church's columns to take in the stained-glass windows.

Why had these people moved away from God?

"Come on," said Marcus, placing his hand on Daniel's elbow and nudging him toward the library. They got in the line of people waiting their turn to pass through security. When they reached the front, an elderly Black man with short gray hair asked for Marcus's ID.

"Long way from home, son," he remarked in a familiar Lowcountry accent as he scanned the document into his computer.

"Yes, sir," Marcus replied.

The guard handed Marcus's ID back to him. "Glad you made it safe. If you need any help settling in, come see me. There are lots of us who can help you out."

Daniel was right behind Marcus in line and overheard the exchange. *It's the clothes. We don't look like missionaries, and the guard assumed…what? That Marcus had moved here?* He handed over his own ID, and the guard scanned it, then looked back and forth between them.

"Travelling together then?" he asked. Marcus nodded, and a look of comprehension dawned on the guard's face. "You're not... Are you fellas…?"

"We're missionaries," said Daniel. Marcus remained silent.

"We don't want any trouble," the guard said.

"No, sir," Marcus replied.

They passed through the metal detectors — one of the newer wide arches using radar and artificial intelligence to scan crowds — and made their way into the library. "I'm still not sure we should be doing this," Daniel said. "Pastor Logan would have a fit."

"Well, he's not here. Plus, you have a library app, so I don't see any reason why I shouldn't too."

Daniel saw lots of reasons. He didn't think Marcus would be self-disciplined enough to avoid following rabbit holes into forbidden territories. He also didn't think Marcus would be as cautious as he should be in making sure he doesn't say something to Pastor Logan revealing he knows things he shouldn't.

"Besides," Marcus said. "Pastor Logan knew we'd learned about the bombing last week, and about last year's terror attack on voters. He *knows* we're figuring things out on our own. I think it's expected of us." They walked toward the information desk so Marcus could set up his own account.

"Look at all this," Marcus said as they passed row after row of periodicals. "I could spend days in here."

"And meanwhile, sinners out in the real world would be going without the benefit of knowing Jesus for your neglect."

Marcus grinned. "Well, Pastor Logan says you need to know the people you're trying to save, right? I'm just trying to follow his guidance."

"Dinosaurs," muttered Daniel.

*

THEY SET MARCUS up with his own library account, spent some time looking through the forbidden magazines—both of them uncomfortably ignoring the two smiling men on the cover of *Queer* magazine—and then began making their way to the exit. It was a springlike day and sunny, and they wanted to take advantage of the weather and see if they could begin making headway on their primary mission.

As they prepared to leave the building, Daniel's attention was drawn to a large bulletin board near the coat racks by the door. *Help Southern Refugees* read one flyer tacked high up in the corner. *Do you have a room? A pull-out sofa? A job to be filled? Citizens escaping religious tyranny need your help!* It was a single sheet of paper with a dozen or so precut strips along the bottom printed with a phone number. Most of them had been removed.

Daniel brought Marcus to a stop in front of it. "Seriously?" he asked. "Refugees? Religious tyranny?" He looked for a response from Marcus, but his missionary companion was simply staring at the notice, then he reached forward and tore off one of the strips.

"What are you doing?" asked Daniel.

"Maybe we can talk to them…find out what they think is going on."

Maybe, thought Daniel. But whoever answered that number was unlikely to be a candidate for inviting Jesus into their heart.

Marcus must have read the doubt on his face. "Don't forget about Saul on the road to Damascus."

Daniel grinned, as he always did when Marcus surprised him with a particularly on-point Bible reference. "All right then, Brother Paul. Let's get out there and save some souls."

It was approaching noon when they stepped into the square across the street from the library. "Do you think we could get into that church?" Daniel asked, indicating the ornately columned brick building across the plaza. "It must be magnificent inside." Daniel scanned the front of the building for a security line but couldn't see one.

An enormous banner was strung across the width of the building just above its tall entryway. *We Stand with Freedom. We Stand with Love. Keep Church and State Separate.*

"I don't know," Marcus replied. "Looks like it might be closed. But let's walk over and see if there's any information about visiting."

A signboard by the entryway announced the church was temporarily closed to visitors until after the "current situation is resolved." It looked like it had been there for a while. Daniel frowned at the sign, uncertain of its meaning. He was about to ask Marcus for his thoughts when a voice from behind them called out, "You won't find your answers in there, gentlemen."

Two young men approached them—missionaries, judging by their white pants and red shirts and jackets. The lone white star sewn onto their coats' lapels identified them as Texans. "Can we share our good news with you?"

Daniel smiled. "No, we're actually—"

Marcus put a hand on his arm. "Sure," he said. "We can use some good news. What is it?"

Daniel recognized the gleam in their eyes as they finally found someone willing to hear them out. He wondered how long they'd been in Boston and whether or not they'd met with any success. He didn't imagine the Texans would be any more welcome here than he and Marcus were—less so, probably, given the chaos caused by Texas's self-proclaimed independence.

The shorter of the two came forward. He was a Latino, and his name tag read "Brother Emanuel." Daniel thought it was lucky for them they didn't have to take on the names of apostles.

"There is a path for you away from sin. You can be reconciled with God," said Emanuel. The other missionary, Brother Jeremy, smiled and nodded his agreement.

"Oh, that's all right," Marcus replied. "We're good. Thanks anyway."

The four men stood looking at each other, and Daniel realized what Marcus was doing. He was testing these missionaries, mirroring the kind of refusal they'd been getting themselves since they arrived. Perhaps he was even searching for a breakthrough—some way to get around the roadblocks they faced over and over.

But the two Texans seemed just as stymied by a polite refusal as Daniel had been at Jaxtyn's sangha.

"But you're not," said Jeremy. "Not good, I mean. You're mired in sin. You need to have faith in Jesus to receive God's grace." Emanuel smiled and nodded.

"*I* don't think I'm mired in sin," Marcus said. "Are *you* mired in sin, Dan?" Daniel shook his head. He knew in his heart he was mired in sin, and it felt like a betrayal to deny it, but he saw what Marcus was attempting and decided maybe they could all learn something if he played along. "Why do you guys think that?" Marcus asked them.

The Texans looked at each other. "It's the natural state of humanity," Emanuel said. "We're all born that way, as sinners, estranged from God. We need to reconcile with God to receive his grace."

"How do you know that?" Marcus asked reasonably.

"The Bible tells us that—" began Jeremy, but Marcus cut him off.

"Okay, stop," he said, holding up a hand. "You've totally lost them right there."

The Texans blinked at him, and Marcus held out his hand. "I'm Marcus. This is my missionary companion, Daniel." Comprehension slowly dawned on their faces as they shook hands. An older couple crossing through the plaza looked at them suspiciously.

"You're missionaries?" asked Jeremy.

"Why aren't you in uniform?" Emanuel asked.

"You must have just arrived in Boston," Marcus observed.

"Yes, this morning," Jeremy said. "The people don't seem very friendly."

This startled a laugh from Daniel. "You haven't seen anything yet. We got the okay from our mission director to wear street clothes so we don't attract so much hostility." The Texans looked at each other nervously.

The older couple passed by. "Don't talk to them," the man said. "You'll just encourage them." The woman hooked her arm through her husband's, and they continued on their way.

Marcus nodded toward them. "You'll have to get used to that. We've spent a week getting nowhere with people here. But I think I learned something just now." Daniel was curious about what that might be. The conversation they'd just had with the Texans was one they'd been having over and over again recently. "We need to start with these people right where they are."

That was a core tenet of their training. Meet people where they are. Had they been failing to do that? A breeze gusted into the plaza, and the windows of a tall, glass-clad tower next to them shimmered like water on the surface of a pond.

Daniel saw it then. "Most of these people don't believe in the Bible, or if they say they do, they don't really mean it. We need to show them why their lives need to change, not just tell them they're mired in sin." It was obvious now that he thought about it. They shouldn't use the language of the church; they should use the secular language of these people's lives.

"Right," said Marcus. "We need to start by getting them to acknowledge they're stuck somehow, unhappy or unsatisfied, feeling something missing in their lives."

There was so much potential in this idea. "Yes!" agreed Daniel. "We just can't tell them what's missing. We can't start with Jesus. We need to lead there."

The Texans didn't look convinced; in fact, they looked

overwhelmed.

A vibration in Daniel's pocket was accompanied by an insistent buzzing noise. At first, he thought it might be a message from Jaxtyn, but then he noticed Marcus reaching his hand into his pocket and pulling out his phone. The Texans looked perplexed as all around the square people simultaneously paused to check their phones.

Daniel read the alert on his burner phone's screen. There'd been a bombing in New York City at a women's health clinic. The extent of casualties was unknown. Everyone in the vicinity glanced over at the missionaries, then shifted their gazes away.

"What's going on?" Emanuel asked. He pulled out his own phone and looked at the blank screen.

"There's been a bombing," Marcus said. "New York this time."

"This time?" asked Jeremy. He turned to his missionary companion. "Are you seeing anything?"

"No," Emanuel said. "I don't understand."

Marcus handed his phone over so they could see the story. "You'll need to get burner phones. The Good News Network doesn't cover the attacks."

"And street clothes," Daniel added. "Everyone up here assumes we're responsible when these things happen."

"What? How often—"

But they were interrupted by a shout from across the street, opposite the library. "Fuck you, CeeNees!" It came from a group of young men standing by the sign marking what used to be the finish line for the Boston Marathon. Daniel and Marcus had walked past it on their way to the library. "We look forward to welcoming the runners back once things return to normal," the sign read. It had been bolted into the brick façade of a building, and the screws holding its plexiglass cover in place were rusted. "Stop the fascists now!" had been scratched into its surface.

The young men who'd cursed them began making their way toward them.

"You guys should go back to your hotel," Marcus told the Texans. They were smart enough to see the truth in that, at least, and they hurried away.

"Scared 'em off, did ya?" one of the young men asked as they approached. "Good."

It was dizzying how quickly things had changed. It didn't even occur to Daniel to try to bring these men to Jesus until after they walked by.

"God help us," he said to Marcus. "We've gone native."

*

"HOW ABOUT HER?" Daniel asked, pointing to a woman shrouded in multiple jackets, despite the early spring sun. She stood by a bus stop, resting one hand on a shopping cart filled with plastic bags. Daniel didn't think she was waiting for a bus.

"I don't know," Marcus replied. "We're supposed to avoid people who might react violently or who might be unpredictable because of drugs or alcohol." They slowed as they approached the woman. She spotted them, eyed them suspiciously, and pulled her frayed wool hat down low over her ears.

"She's homeless," Daniel said. That much had become obvious as they got closer. They could smell her unwashed body, see the smudges of dirt on her knuckles and chin. "But she doesn't look dangerous. This is our chance to try it out." Since their encounter with the Texans, they'd been talking about a new way to approach people—connecting with them on a human level before attempting to bring them to Jesus.

"Let me go first," Marcus said. "She's Black. She might feel threatened by you."

Daniel pushed down a surge of resentment. It was a ridiculous idea. He wasn't the least bit threatening, especially now, when he wasn't cloaked in the raiment of a man doing God's work. And Marcus's increasing focus on race was a cause for concern. "Jesus doesn't see your color." Wasn't that a message they'd heard all their lives? Daniel made a mental note to talk to Marcus about it later.

"Good morning, ma'am," Marcus called out in a soft voice when they were still a good distance away. She leaned protectively over her cart, then glanced around to see who else was nearby. "Nice afternoon, isn't it?" Marcus continued.

"I got nothing worth stealing," she said. "I don't want no trouble."

It wasn't an anti-missionary statement; she couldn't know what they were. She was simply afraid, and Daniel wondered again at how these blue states can go on and on about compassion and human rights, and yet still allow so many of their citizens to live in fear on the fringes of society. "No, ma'am," Marcus said. "You'll get no trouble from us."

She didn't relax.

Marcus slowly pulled his wallet from his pocket and removed a five-dollar bill. It was a gold-backed New Dollar—not one of the increasingly worthless old dollars that were still widely used. She looked at the money and squinted. "We found this right on the sidewalk, just around the corner," he said. It was a lie, and Daniel was uncomfortable with that. "We thought it might rightly have been meant for you to find, not us." He held it out to her, allowing plenty of space between them. She could reach forward and take it or not.

It was a lot of money for them. They didn't have much, and everything was more expensive in Boston than they'd anticipated.

She took the bill, studied it for a moment as if she were expecting a trap, then nodded and stuffed the money into a pocket deep in one of her jackets. "Well, God bless you, boys." But she was still wary, and she turned back to her cart.

"Yes!" Daniel exclaimed. "God will bless each of us if we let Jesus into our hearts." Her eyes widened, and Marcus grimaced. "Would you like to pray with us now?" Daniel reached his hands toward her.

"Help!" she yelled. "Help!" She pushed against her cart, groaning with the effort to get it moving.

"Come on, Dan," Marcus said as he tugged Daniel's arm, pulling him away. "We're going," he called over Daniel's head. "Sorry to have bothered you." She stopped calling for help, but others on the street were casting wary glances their way.

They turned the corner, and Marcus kept a hurried pace until they'd put two blocks between them and the homeless woman. "I can't believe you gave her five NDs," Daniel complained. They'd slowed but were both breathing hard, more from the adrenaline than the workout. "We need to eat, too, you know."

"Well, I can't believe you tried to get her to pray with us when we clearly hadn't gained her trust yet," Marcus replied. He sounded angry at Daniel, and that was entirely unfair.

"Opening their hearts to God is what we're here for, isn't it?" Daniel heard the frustration in his own voice. Their lack of progress, the hostility of everyone around them, the run-down hotel—it was all getting to him. Something needed to give.

"Is it?" Marcus asked.

"Of course!" Daniel said. Why would Marcus even ask such a thing? "We're Christian missionaries. Spreading the good news of Jesus is the only reason we're here. We're bringing people to God..." Daniel slowed and let out a sigh. "And we're failing."

They'd paused under a shop awning, getting out of the way of the people rushing by. *Everyone was always in a hurry here.* Daniel longed for a lazy summer afternoon, sipping a sweet tea in the shade of one of the campus's live oaks.

"Dinosaurs," Marcus mumbled.

"*What?*"

"I said dinosaurs. We're Christian *Nationalist* Evangelicals, Daniel. And from everything Pastor Logan stresses, I'd say the nationalist part of our mission is far more important than the Christian part."

Daniel wanted to close his ears. This was unthinkable. Nothing—*nothing*—was more important than believing in Jesus and, through Him, receiving God's grace. How had Marcus fallen so far from the path? How had Daniel not seen it earlier?

"What has gotten into you?" Daniel demanded. "It's that Black church, isn't it? You've been acting funny ever since you visited there."

Marcus leaned back as if he'd been punched, and Daniel began to suspect he'd overstepped—somehow—as he watched the emotions play across his friend's face. *Anger? Fear? Embarrassment?* Finally, Marcus's features settled into a closed, guarded look.

He nodded. "Yeah, Dan. That's right. It's always the Blacks, isn't it?"

What was that *supposed to mean?*

And then it hit him. Despite all his training, despite the unceasing message he'd grown up with—that color doesn't matter, that it's not even a thing people notice anymore—he subconsciously leaped to blaming the Black church for Marcus's confusion. "I'm sorry, Marcus. I shouldn't have said that. I shouldn't even have *thought* it. Color doesn't matter. We should pray—"

Marcus turned away. "No, Dan. You're wrong. Color *does* matter. My being Black is a part of me, just like your being…being…"

Daniel waved his hands. "No, stop!" He shot a panicked look at the people flowing past them on the sidewalk. "We need to go back to the hotel. We need to pray. Something's off with us. I think it's this city. It seeps under our skin like a poison."

Marcus let out the breath he'd been holding. "Sure, Dan. It's okay. Let's go back and pray." *Why did he sound so defeated?* "We'll tackle saving souls again tomorrow, and you can visit the campus to get to work on the secret mission."

Daniel wanted to ask then, to make sure Marcus intended to come with him to the campus, so they could both search for the guy seen with Ruth in the photos. Pastor Logan had said it was their highest priority. But even as he had that thought, he realized it confirmed Marcus's accusations—that Pastor Logan valued finding the killer over the work of saving souls.

He didn't want to have that argument again with Marcus—not while they were so unsteady with each other. He wasn't sure he'd be able to keep steering Marcus back to their obligations, back to their submission to God's will. He'd talk to him about the campus trip later after they'd prayed together.

*

THAT AFTERNOON, AS they knelt together in prayer, Daniel found himself comparing Marcus and Jaxtyn: How Jaxtyn had warm, enveloping hands and was eager to twine his fingers through Daniel's, while Marcus's sweaty palms were often cold, and his fingers lay loosely against the back of Daniel's hand. How if he opened his eyes while praying with Marcus, the two men would be face-to-face, and Marcus's eyes would be scrunched tightly closed. With Jaxtyn, if Daniel opened his eyes, he'd be staring at Jaxtyn's elegant, slender neck, his Adam's apple rising and falling hypnotically, and Jaxtyn would be staring back at him with a quizzical look, as if asking an unspoken question.

These were entirely inappropriate thoughts at any time, but especially so while praying—which might explain why Jesus was forsaking him, refusing to fill his heart with His presence. "Jesus, please blind us with your glory," Daniel pleaded. "Please fill my brother Marcus with the wisdom to understand your will."

Marcus squeezed his hand and whispered, "He's not Santa, Dan."

This was their way of calling one another out while they were praying if one of them started *asking* Jesus for things, which was both selfish and hubristic, as if Jesus was there to work miracles for them personally.

Daniel returned Marcus's squeeze. "Thank you," he whispered. He was really off his game, and he redoubled his efforts to put all thoughts of Jaxtyn out of his mind and to turn his attention to opening himself to God. Marcus had returned to mumbling his prayer. He seldom prayed out loud, and Daniel was often curious about what Marcus was actually saying as his heart swelled with Christ's presence.

They'd turned the heat on in their room when they got in, then turned it off again right before they settled into prayer. It was quieter that way, but it allowed the sounds of the city to filter into the room. Sirens, some near and some far, were a continual background distraction, as were the brakes of the buses and the horns of private automobiles.

Daniel pictured the green car from the photographs. He hoped they'd spot it on campus; it would be easy then to set up an arrangement where one of them would always be stationed nearby until the owner appeared. Thoughts of campus nudged his mind to Jaxtyn and to the meditation session he'd be attending the following morning.

He wondered if he'd have a similar experience as the first time, recognizing the essential aspect of meditation as closely aligned to prayer, but without the focal point of Jesus. Of course, that made the entire exercise pointless—like a man stumbling toward a desert mirage. No matter how eloquently Jaxtyn went on about the interconnectedness of all things, or becoming one with the universe, he was missing the fundamental value of a transcendent experience—which was to connect with God.

And here in the King's Royal Court Hotel, kneeling on the none-too-clean carpet, clasping Marcus's damp hands, he finally began to feel Jesus entering him, filling his mind and heart with divine light. *I submit to your will, Jesus.* An all-encompassing warmth and light shone upon and through everything in the room, everything in the entire city, in the world.

It was as if Jesus had taken them into Himself, and they'd taken Jesus into themselves, everything melding together, becoming one.

He *was* Jesus and Jesus was —

Wait. What? I'm not Jesus! That was blasphemy. He took a deep breath to try to calm himself. It was all Jaxtyn's fault, filling his mind with talk of universal connections. It was a bracing slap in the face to be pulled out of his prayers with such thoughts.

"Jesus!" Daniel exclaimed.

Marcus raised an eyebrow. "Was that *Jesus,* as in *please fill my heart with your love, Lord,* or was that *Jesus!* as in taking the Lord's name in vain?"

Daniel reddened. Such an outburst was entirely unlike him. "I…I was…praying," he offered, but he knew it sounded weak and defensive. Marcus smiled and closed his eyes, then he took up his mumbled praying again. *Dinosaurs,* Daniel imagined him saying.

Chapter Fourteen

IT WAS THE first truly mild day of spring. A soft breeze carried the briny smell of low tide to Jaxtyn as he waited for Daniel at the JFK/UMass Red Line station. He'd been told it never used to be this warm in Boston in March, but no one talked about the changing climate anymore. The perils of global warming didn't seem as pressing when the country was tearing itself apart.

A train pulled into the station, and soon hundreds of commuters poured out of the exit. At this hour of the morning, everyone was in a hurry. Even the line at the coffee kiosk moved quickly, and soon the crowd cleared—on their way to classrooms, offices, or perhaps home after a long night shift.

Jaxtyn liked to pay attention to the voices in crowds. As he waited for Daniel, he counted nine distinct languages, most of which he could easily identify. He still struggled to differentiate Vietnamese from Thai, at least when he only caught fragments of conversation in a thick crowd. But there were new members of the Open Lotus Sangha who were Thai—refugees fleeing the chaos caused by rising sea levels, like so many of the thousands of other Southeast Asians arriving in Boston—and he was getting better at picking up on the nuances of the language.

If Daniel wasn't on the next train, Jaxtyn would have to leave him and Marcus to their own devices and hope they managed to find the athletic center, and his mediation group, in time for the session. Students were still allowed to invite visitors onto the campus, but they had to be preregistered with security. Daniel had almost balked last night when Jaxtyn called him for the information, but after a quick consultation with Marcus, which Jaxtyn heard only half of, he relented and provided the minimum details necessary to allow security to conduct background checks on the missionaries.

It felt a bit intrusive—underhanded, even—but with that information Jaxtyn had done his own digging, and discovered Daniel was, as Sylvie had predicted, enrolled at one of those missionary factories in South Carolina. But other than its Christian Nationalist objectives, little information was available online about Sangre de Cristo. Daniel and his family were also conspicuously absent from all the common social media sites. He wondered if that was normal for people down there.

There was slightly more information available about Marcus Johnson. He'd been a successful wrestler in high school, and the photos Jaxtyn managed to find showed Marcus to be the only Black guy on the team. His father was a doctor and the family seemed to be well off, which explained his presence at the private all-boys high school. He was also enrolled at Sangre de Cristo, and

Jaxtyn wondered if he and Daniel were roommates, or if Skylar might be right, and they were more than that.

He recalled Marcus's contact information on Daniel's phone—*Black Beauty*—and felt a stab of jealousy. He pushed the thought aside and closed his eyes. He wished for nothing but peace and kindness for the two men, and he directed those positive thoughts into the universe.

He opened his eyes, and there they were, two stragglers exiting the station and looking around in confusion even as Jaxtyn heard the next train pulling in. They'd managed to find clothing that didn't look quite so much like charitable hand-me-downs, and Marcus wore a shirt with a subtle tribal pattern Jaxtyn associated with Nigerians.

Jaxtyn pushed himself off the wall he'd been leaning against and waved to attract Daniel's attention. Daniel shielded his eyes from the sun and then offered a quick wave in acknowledgment. He looked around as if the action had embarrassed him. Marcus kept shifting his gaze between his phone and his surroundings as if he were checking their location on a map.

When they reached him, Marcus held out his hand. "Hi, Jaxtyn. I'm Marcus. We met already in New York. Sorry we took so long. We hung back to let everyone who knew what they were doing pass us on the way out."

"Yes, I remember you. And no worries. We have time to make it across campus for the session." People from the last train were already beginning to stream through the station exit. "This way," he said, indicating the flashing pedestrian crossing sign. The first wave of commuters caught up with them and everyone hurried through the intersection before the light turned.

They'd made it across the wide intersection and Jaxtyn slowed his pace when he saw Daniel and Marcus were lagging. "Why does everyone move so fast here?" Daniel asked. "I can barely keep up."

"Sorry. I have longer legs than you guys," Jaxtyn said. "How have you been making out this week? I bet you miss South Carolina." He figured he could ask without seeming like a stalker, now that they'd given him the information necessary for the background checks.

Marcus shrugged, and Daniel said, "A little."

"Do you have families back home? Do you miss them?" And, okay, he was digging and he already knew from his research they both had families, but he was curious about these men, and what their lives must be like.

"Yes, we have families," Daniel said. "But even when we were at school, we were only permitted to write and receive letters once a week, and now that we're on our missions, we're not allowed phone calls with them at all. So, we're used to not being in regular contact." The crowd they'd crossed with surged around them, then dwindled. Jaxtyn stopped and put a hand on Daniel's elbow.

"You can't contact your *family*?"

Daniel turned to face him and took a couple of deep breaths, seemingly grateful for the pause. "We can, but just once a week, and only by letter."

Jaxtyn didn't want to betray his shock. Daniel didn't seem to think it was so unusual, and Marcus stared at Jaxtyn with a quizzical look, perhaps wondering why he was asking personal questions.

"Oh, that must be difficult," Jaxtyn said.

"No, not really," Daniel said. So, they were back to that again—short, impersonal responses. But Daniel didn't seem as nervous as he had when they'd first met in New York. Instead, he appeared distracted, and both he and Marcus were looking around as if they were tourists, which, Jaxtyn figured, they were in a way.

As they got closer to the campus Daniel's agitation seemed to increase. Both of the missionaries kept looking behind them and off to the sides as if they were trying to memorize the neighborhood's layout. "Where do people park?" Daniel asked.

That was a strange question. Jaxtyn pointed to an open-air lot on their left as they walked down Mount Vernon Street. "That's the Bayside lot. It's got the most spaces but it's several blocks to the campus. There are other lots across campus too. There's a big garage, but it's expensive, and the faculty who can afford the monthly fee like to park there. Most of the students don't drive. Some students live in the dorms, but most live off campus in small apartments like we do."

"I see you need a sticker to park in the lot," Daniel said. Again, it was an odd observation, and Jaxtyn worried he was missing something. And how had Daniel even noticed such a thing? It's not like they'd walked through the lot. He could see hundreds of cars parked at Bayside across the street, but Daniel would have had to pay close attention—and from a distance—to notice the stickers.

"Uh, yes. Space is at a premium here. Most of the students live close enough that they don't need to pay for a campus parking sticker. Well, Skylar has one, but his parents are richer than

God." Immediately after making the comment, Jaxtyn realized it was probably an offensive thing to say to a Christian missionary. "Sorry."

Marcus laughed. "How rich is God, anyway?" he asked.

"Marcus," Daniel cautioned in a disapproving way.

"Oh, come on, Dan. Lighten up. It was just a joke."

Dan. Jaxtyn weighed the nickname in his mind and concluded he preferred Daniel. It suited the man's serious nature. He was surprised by the note of tension between the missionaries. Daniel didn't respond to Marcus. Instead, he peered intently at an old Catholic church as they walked by it. "Did we know about this one?" he asked Marcus.

"I don't know. I'd have to check our list."

Do they have a list of every church in Boston?

"There could be students who go there," Daniel told Marcus. "They always make good candidates."

Jaxtyn knew they were talking about converting people to their idea of God, and also, maybe—because they were CeeNees—convincing them of their politics, but he was still struck by how calculated and clinical they sounded. It was as if they were recruiting soldiers or spies.

"I think it's just a handful of old people who still go there," Jaxtyn said.

They continued toward the campus in silence, which Jaxtyn found increasingly uncomfortable. "Thanks for coming this morning," he said. "Have you ever meditated before, Marcus?"

"No."

"But we are going to pray afterward, right?" asked Daniel once it was clear Marcus wasn't going to offer any more information.

"Yes. We'll go over to my apartment. Sylvie won't be there, but Skylar will." Marcus and Daniel exchanged a look. "I don't think he'll want to pray though."

"He's the one with the orange hair, right?" Marcus asked.

Jaxtyn grinned. "Not anymore. His hair was orange when you saw him on the train. He's shaved it since then."

"He's gay, right?" asked Marcus.

"*Marcus*," Daniel hissed.

"What? There's nothing wrong with that, is there?" Marcus looked to Jaxtyn. "Up here, I mean. It's treated as normal, isn't it?"

There was a subtext here Jaxtyn was missing, and Daniel was clearly angered by Marcus's question. Or, perhaps not the question itself, but by the fact Marcus had raised the topic at all. Daniel's face blazed with embarrassment, and the color clashed with his coppery red hair. Jaxtyn liked it. A lot. But there were hidden land mines here; he was sure of it.

"Yes, Skylar's gay." No harm in acknowledging that. Skylar would be the first one to proclaim it from the rooftops. "And you're right. There's no stigma associated with being gay here." Jaxtyn decided to risk stepping on a mine. "Are you gay?" He left the *you* vague. He could have been asking Marcus, or he could have been asking both of them.

"Me?" asked Marcus with what Jaxtyn thought was feigned disinterest, as if they were talking about the weather. "No. Not at all."

"Stop it, Marcus," Daniel snapped. "It's not something to be talked about." He turned to Jaxtyn. "He's just baiting you. He knows there's a difference between unnatural desire and the sin of acting on it. Everyone has his own cross to bear; it's how we respond to our sinful natures that's important. We need to let Jesus bring us into God's grace."

They covered the remaining few blocks in silence, Jaxtyn wondering about what Daniel *didn't* say and about why Marcus hadn't asked Jaxtyn if *he* was gay.

"Well," Jaxtyn said as they crossed the final street and entered the campus. "Welcome to UMass Boston." They passed through several not particularly attractive public spaces, and then finally reached the athletic center, a new building, generic and low to the ground. They entered the short queue at the security line.

"It's early still," said Jaxtyn, "so the line will move fast. Have your IDs ready."

They entered the security vestibule, and the guards confirmed that the missionaries' information had been entered into the system. Photos were taken, the printer whirred, and two temporary plastic ID badges were produced for Daniel and Marcus. The green light came on over the doorway into the facility and the men went through.

Jaxtyn checked his phone. They didn't have much time. "We're just down this hallway," he said.

Marcus stopped. "Actually, I'm suddenly not feeling that well. I think I'll just go for a short walk instead."

"Oh, um…" Jaxtyn didn't think it was a good idea to leave him wandering around the campus on his own. What if he tried to convert someone, or got lost, or got in trouble somehow? But he didn't have time to think of what to say, and Daniel didn't seem concerned.

"Okay," Daniel said before Jaxtyn could come up with a reason to object. "Text me if you need me. But be back here in forty-five minutes so we can head over to Jaxtyn's together."

*

THEY SETTLED INTO practice and the room fell silent. Jaxtyn was pleased to see the number of meditators was growing. There were at least a dozen students, and a few faculty members had shown up also. Daniel had wisely chosen a chair this time rather than a floor cushion. Several others were seated in chairs as well, and the circle filled the perimeter of the space. If more people came next time, Jaxtyn would have to arrange the room in rows.

It was impossible for him to calm his mind. He sat on a floor mat next to Daniel, and he was acutely conscious of the man's knee just inches from his face. He was worried about Marcus wandering the campus on his own, and he was still distracted by the talk of being gay on their walk from the train. At least Marcus's comments had made it clear he and Daniel weren't a couple, but was it possible Daniel *was* gay after all? Jaxtyn *thought* there might be reciprocal interest, but maybe he was just projecting his own desires.

He tried again to clear his head, but the stillness wouldn't come. Marcus had denied he was gay. Why hadn't Daniel? And what had he meant by everyone having a "cross to bear?"

Jaxtyn hated when he could see the pieces of a puzzle but couldn't fit them together. Why the interest in where people parked? Why had Marcus gone for a walk? He knew it was all connected, but he couldn't see how.

He risked a glance up at Daniel's face. His eyes were tightly closed, and Jaxtyn knew he must be praying to Jesus. What would that be like, he wondered, carrying on a conversation with someone who wasn't there? Or maybe Jesus *was* there, for Daniel at least, in some meaningful way Jaxtyn couldn't understand. He closed his own eyes and conjured an image of Jesus, hoping to catch a glimpse of what Daniel might be experiencing.

But it was the ridiculous Hollywood version of Jesus that came to mind, with his coarse woven robe and flowing brown hair, and those absurd blue eyes smiling out of a serene, wise face. Jaxtyn muffled a laugh. But the image of Jesus didn't falter. Instead, it approached him, reached out, and embraced him.

He didn't know what was happening, but he let the vision unfold, intently trying to be welcoming and open to a new experience. The embrace was warm and tight. Jaxtyn swore he could feel the muscles in Jesus's back, but somewhere along the way, he realized, Jesus had become Daniel, and he gripped the back of Daniel's head, breathing in the scent of his hair.

The figure pushed away from him, and it was Jesus again, with Daniel standing behind him and off to the side, both men smiling. Then it was Daniel who came forward and ran his fingers along Jaxtyn's cheek. Then Jesus again, then Daniel, and then he couldn't tell the difference between the two. He was overwhelmed by a sense of peace and belonging, a comforting embrace, both physical and not physical, and he so wanted to sink deeply into it, to disappear into—

He felt a nudge against his head—Daniel's knee, tapping him. He had the puzzling sense Daniel had been trying to get his attention for some time. His phone was vibrating in his pocket. Had he set the alarm incorrectly, for four minutes rather than forty?

He opened his eyes and saw the entire circle looking at him, some smiling, some with looks of concern. "Jaxtyn," Daniel whispered. He looked up at the missionary, who was beaming down at him, tears in his eyes. "You saw him." Daniel was still whispering. "I know you did. He came to you."

Jaxtyn slowly realized nearly an hour had passed. He pulled his phone out of his pocket and deactivated the vibrating alert.

What the hell just happened?

"Namaste," he tried to say, but his throat felt constricted, and he had to swallow thickly before trying again. "Namaste," he said, more clearly. He folded his hands in front of his chest and bowed to the circle. "Well, that was something."

"Namaste," the circle replied, all smiles now, with knowing looks of satisfaction and wonder that Jaxtyn had lost himself in the universal connectedness of all things, and for so long. Jaxtyn could only recall reaching that state a handful of times, and then for only a few minutes before it slipped away.

People were rising from cushions and greeting each other. Daniel stood from his chair and reached out a hand to help Jaxtyn up. He took it, gripping it tightly as he stood. His mind was still reeling from the clarity of his…vision? Mystical experience? He could still feel the ghostly presence of Daniel's hair between his fingers.

"He filled your heart as he did mine," Daniel said.

That earned a strange look from the woman next to Daniel, and Jaxtyn said, "Shh. Not here," as the slowly returning rational part of his brain insisted, hesitant to assess a new and profound experience until he had a chance to fully consider it.

"You can't shut him out now," Daniel said. It wasn't a plea so much as it was an assertion. And that was the thing about radicals of all stripes—political or religious—they were so sure of themselves. Jaxtyn found that unsettling. What gave Daniel the right to claim he understood what had just happened when Jaxtyn himself hadn't even begun to process the experience?

"Yeah, well, I make my own decisions," Jaxtyn said. Daniel looked hurt by the comment, and Jaxtyn mentally kicked himself. He didn't need to be rude. It was brave what Daniel was doing, coming to a hostile city, trying to spread what he saw as the truth—even if it was misguided. And dangerous. But he wasn't going to fake an apology for his statement. "Come on, let's go find Marcus."

Chapter Fifteen

THEY EXITED THE athletic center, and Daniel raised a hand to shield his eyes against the low March sun. Marcus was waiting for them, and he responded to Daniel's questioning gaze by shaking his head; he hadn't found the car. It was obvious Jaxtyn had noticed the exchange because he frowned but said nothing.

"How did the meditation go?" Marcus asked.

"Good," replied Daniel. He wanted to say more, to say he was certain Jesus had filled Jaxtyn's heart. But he knew he'd already pushed too far when he'd told Jaxtyn he couldn't turn away from Jesus now, and he didn't want to compound the error. Marcus had been right; Daniel needed to learn restraint and to commit to meeting people where they were, spiritually. He had to stop pushing people beyond their limits. Jesus will come to people when they're ready to receive Him.

But Jesus *had* come to Jaxtyn. Daniel knew it. He'd just have to be careful how he talked about it until Jaxtyn was ready to acknowledge the truth.

"It's going to be warm today," Jaxtyn said as he shrugged off his winter jacket. He wore a loose-knit blue sweater over a white T-shirt, and Daniel admired the movement of the man's shoulders as he pulled his arms through his coat's sleeves. When he reluctantly shifted his gaze, he saw Marcus giving him a direct look, not challenging exactly, but knowing. "Are you guys ready? It's about a fifteen-minute walk to my place."

"Lead the way," Marcus said.

Daniel was uncomfortably aware of how much he wanted to see where Jaxtyn lived. *How* Jaxtyn lived—what his kitchen looked like, what kind of art was on the walls, what books were on the shelves. What his bedroom looked like.

He sighed. God wouldn't give him a heavier cross than he could bear. He knew that. He fell in behind Marcus who was at Jaxtyn's side saying something Daniel couldn't hear. They passed through the campus and had only gone a few blocks when their phones chimed—all their phones, including the official Sangre de Cristo ones.

Daniel pulled his church phone out of his pocket and noticed that Marcus chose to check his burner phone instead. They read the news alert, and Jaxtyn said, "Oh, this is bad."

"It doesn't seem *that* bad," Daniel said after he'd read the message on his church phone. "I mean, I can see how some people may not like that it happened…" Marcus cocked his head at Daniel, and Jaxtyn seemed surprised by Daniel's statement.

"Oh," Marcus said. "I think I get it. What does yours say, Dan?"

He scrolled to the top of the alert and began reading. "A number of unjustly accused patriots were released from detention overnight after a daring rescue by a group of Christian freedom fighters. The patriots, all from Tennessee, had been taken into custody after they'd protested the Federal government's unlawful efforts to force citizens to support social policies in clear violation of their sincerely held religious beliefs. The brave men and women who came to their rescue included—"

"Enough," said Marcus, holding up a hand. Jaxtyn's eyes had widened in an expression of disbelief as Daniel was reading. "Jaxtyn, would you read what's on your phone please?"

Jaxtyn looked at his screen and began reading. "A coordinated terrorist attack last night on three federal facilities in Tennessee resulted in the deaths of at least seven guards and the release of nearly 3,000 convicted felons. The facilities were low-security prisons, dozens of which have been built over the last decade to house nonviolent prisoners convicted of tax evasion. The prisons are part of a national effort to stem the rapidly rising tide of businesses and individuals who refuse to pay federal taxes until the government guarantees what the separatists call full religious freedom for the states. Currently, there are over 70,000 prisoners incarcerated in—"

"That's enough," said Marcus.

Jaxtyn looked up from his phone, a bewildered look on his face. "Jesus," he said. "Oh, sorry."

Daniel shook his head in disbelief and looked back at his phone. "But how? I mean, how is it possible the same event can be seen so differently?" He remembered thinking how similar praying was to Jaxtyn's meditation, except for the fundamental flaw that meditation denied the experience of God in the process. An idea began to form at the edges of his mind, but he lost the thread when Marcus spoke.

"Why did you say this was particularly bad, Jaxtyn?"

Jaxtyn slipped his phone back into his pocket. "Federal agents targeted for assassination? I don't think that has happened before. It escalates things."

Marcus pulled out his other phone and began comparing the two stories side-by-side. "Jesus," he said.

"Marcus!"

"Oh, right, sorry." But Marcus grinned, not seeming sorry at all.

"Come on," said Jaxtyn. "We should get going. I'm glad you guys aren't wearing your CeeNee uniforms."

Daniel noted the grim looks of the people around them, tucking their phones away and hurrying about their business. He knew it wasn't rational, but he sensed calamity approaching, much like the unknown beast slouching toward Bethlehem. There was nothing to be done about it. He put his faith in God and offered a brief prayer for the safety of the Texan missionaries.

*

JAXTYN SET A quick pace through the streets of Dorchester, expertly weaving his way through the morning crowds. The men didn't speak much, each lost in his own thoughts. Daniel was trying to understand the source of his increasing sense of foreboding and was startled out of his inner reflections when he heard Jaxtyn say, "Just one more block."

And suddenly, there it was. The green sedan parked at the

end of the street, the one they'd been looking for, the one the killer had used to carry Ruth away. Its front end poked into the intersection, and its windshield was tagged with multiple parking fine notices. Marcus must have seen it, too, because both he and Daniel came to an abrupt stop, staring at the car. Jaxtyn stopped and turned to the missionaries. "Everything all right? My apartment is just around the corner."

Daniel tried not to betray his surprise. The secondary mission was a secret after all, and he feared Jaxtyn would think less of him if he knew his mission to Boston had been…what exactly? Diluted? Compromised?…by an objective not related to bringing people to God. With a blinding flash of recognition, Daniel understood that was his own projection. *He* was the one who was beginning to question the wisdom of putting so much importance on the secondary mission over their primary objective.

Maybe Marcus had been right all along.

But whatever he felt inside, Marcus had always been faster on his feet than Daniel. "You know, Dan," he said, "we promised to take pictures during our mission, and we haven't been doing a very good job of that."

Jaxtyn looked skeptical. "Here?" he asked. It was a narrow street, deep in shade, lined with tired-looking triple-deckers on both sides and crowded along its length with older cars. "It's not a very nice view."

"No," Daniel said, pulling his official church phone from his pocket. "Marcus is right. This gives you a good sense of the neighborhood." He aligned his phone's camera to capture Marcus in the foreground, and the green sedan behind him. He made sure to include the license plate and the UMass parking sticker as well as the street sign at the intersection. He was certain it was the car in the videos but knew Pastor Logan would want to have proof.

"Good. Thanks," he said to Marcus after he took the shot. He looked around for a vantage point he could come back to, somewhere he could spend time without arousing suspicion so he could be there when the driver returned, but there was nothing—no café or coffee shop, no charging station or market stand.

"You know," Jaxtyn said after they were ready to move on, "I can't quite figure you guys out."

No. Of course you can't.

*

ONCE HE WAS inside Jaxtyn's apartment and had walked along the narrow hallway leading to a kitchen at the far end, Daniel decided he was disappointed. It was dark and smelled faintly of foreign cooking, although that was probably seeping in from one of the other units. On the way down the hallway, they passed two closed doors—"Bedrooms," Jaxtyn told them—and a small bathroom.

"It looked like it would be bigger from the outside," observed Marcus.

"They used to be," Jaxtyn said. "Originally, each unit occupied an entire floor. They're mostly all divided up now like this." In the kitchen, the guy from the train, the one who'd had wild orange hair, was leaning against the sink and eating from a takeout container. His head had been shaved since Daniel had seen him, and he wasn't wearing makeup as he'd been then. Daniel thought he might have seen him again someplace but couldn't think where.

"Hey, Skylar," said Jaxtyn. "You remember Daniel and Marcus, don't you?"

The man removed a pair of chopsticks from the white box and waved to them. "Sure I do. The hot CeeNees."

Daniel felt himself blush, and Marcus jutted out his chin, ready for an altercation.

"Sky, you said you wouldn't cause trouble," pleaded Jaxtyn. "They're my guests."

Skylar waved the chopsticks again, then scooped up some noodles. "Chill, Jax. I'm just saying the boys look good. No harm in that, is there, gents?" This last he directed at Marcus, who simply squinted at Skylar like he was trying to figure him out.

"There *could* be harm in that," Marcus said.

Skylar lifted his eyes from the box and smiled. "Oh. Nice. Is that a threat?" He turned to Jaxtyn. "I like this one; he's got balls." Daniel wanted to melt into the floor, and Marcus was about to respond when Jaxtyn interrupted him.

"Listen, Sky, I'm serious. We're here so I can learn more about their religion, maybe find some common ground with people I don't think we always need to be at odds with." Daniel was slightly disappointed to learn Jaxtyn had his own agenda, that he wasn't just open to receiving Jesus into his heart. Still, it was interesting what he had said — about finding common ground — and it echoed something that had been circling in Daniel's thoughts since the meditation session.

"We're going into the bedroom, and they're going to show me how they pray." Again, Daniel would have preferred hearing Jaxtyn say, "…and we're going to pray together," but it was a start. "You can join us if you promise to be respectful and serious;

otherwise I don't want to hear a sound from you out here, understood?"

Skylar stared at Jaxtyn, and a whole world of communication passed between the two men Daniel couldn't read. He dreaded the idea of Skylar joining them in prayer. It was bad enough he had to fight against his physical attraction to Jaxtyn and the sinful longings that attraction prompted. But he wasn't sure he could settle into communion with Jesus if a hostile party was in the prayer group, mocking him. He glanced at Marcus, but his missionary companion was poker-faced, and still staring quizzically at Skylar.

Did Marcus think he recognized Skylar too?

"We're good," Skylar said, standing up and breaking the impasse. He took the box to the sink and began rinsing it. "I'm going out. We don't have any beer, so I'm going on a packie run to Quincy to stock up. Want me to get you anything?"

"No," Jaxtyn replied. "And it's good you're heading out. You need to move your car. It's too close to the corner and covered in parking fine tags."

Daniel froze as time crawled to a stop. He saw Marcus's eyes widen. Could *Skylar* be the man they were searching for? Yes, of course! They'd only seen him from behind in the video, and he'd shaved off the wild orange hair he'd had on the train. That's why Skylar looked familiar. Surely, God had led them here.

Skylar groaned. "My folks don't like to see lots of debits on that account. I'll put it in the campus garage after I unload the beer." He put the empty takeout container in a trash bin next to the sink and lifted his jacket from the back of a chair.

Once again, Marcus recovered first. "Is a packie run going

to a liquor store? I've never been to one. Mind if I come with you?"

Both Jaxtyn and Skylar seemed surprised by the request, as well they would be. But Daniel thought it was a clever ploy and was the best way to establish Skylar really was the owner of the car in question, the man seen in the video with Ruth. But Daniel didn't like the idea of leaving Marcus alone with him, or of Marcus going into a liquor store for that matter. Marcus was questioning too many things lately to be trusted with those types of temptations.

"Are you guys even allowed to drink?" Skylar asked.

"No," replied Marcus. "But, when in Rome…you know?"

"He's kidding," Daniel said. At least he hoped it was only a joke. Still, the prospect of praying alone with Jaxtyn was appealing, and he didn't try hard to stop his missionary companion or warn him against getting into trouble.

"Suit yourself," Skylar said. "I'd never want it said I shied away from the challenge of corrupting an innocent."

Chapter Sixteen

JAXTYN WAS SURPRISED when Marcus asked to go with Skylar. Those two were like oil and water, and he hoped they'd be able to avoid an all-out fight. Skylar was becoming more radicalized against the separatists every day, and Marcus...well, Marcus was a CeeNee, with all that implied.

The intense young man standing next to him in the kitchen was a CeeNee too. Jaxtyn had to keep reminding himself of that — not just that he was a Christian, but that he proudly let his Christian faith determine his politics and was set on wreaking havoc, in Jaxtyn's opinion, on the entire country in the name of his God.

Daniel's gaze darted across the small space, never landing anywhere for long, and never meeting Jaxtyn's eyes. He had a pronounced Adam's apple, and Jaxtyn followed its rapid rise and fall. Daniel was nervous, and Jaxtyn didn't know why.

"I hope they don't kill each other," Jaxtyn joked. It was

intended to lighten the mood.

"Marcus can take care of himself," Daniel responded, as if he took Jaxtyn's statement literally. "I'm sure he wishes he had his gun though."

Jaxtyn blanched. He was uncomfortable around guns, even talk of guns. And Marcus was a missionary. What use would he have for a weapon? "He brought his gun with him?"

"Of course. We both did." Daniel patted his hip, indicating where he normally carried his pistol. "We can't carry them here though. They're in a secured storage container at South Station. It's weird to be without them." He looked out the window, but South Station wasn't visible from here if that's what he was looking for.

"You…carry your guns a lot?" As alarming as the reality of the guns was, Jaxtyn was embarrassed to realize a small part of him thought the idea of Daniel with a gun was sort of hot.

Daniel turned back to Jaxtyn. "Yes. All the time," he said. "It's normal back home. It's why crime is so low." Jaxtyn had a moment of mental dizziness as he tried to make sense of the statement. "If law-abiding citizens here carried guns, you'd be much safer."

Jaxtyn wasn't in the mood for a debate. He wanted to get to the praying part of the morning—well, the handholding part, if he was honest with himself—as soon as possible. Two men holding hands, kneeling on a wobbly mattress—the upside potential was limitless. And he couldn't help but hope Daniel's nervousness might include an element of sexual tension. Surely, he felt this attraction too.

"Shall we go into my bedroom?" He phrased the question in

a suggestive way, and he let some of that tone come forward in his voice. Daniel simply nodded, his Adam's apple rising and falling.

Jaxtyn considered taking Daniel by the hand and leading him down the hallway but rejected the idea as being too forward. He didn't want to scare the man off, and he reminded himself even a chaste prayer session would be a win, as he was sincerely interested in Daniel and wanted to learn more about him. He motioned to the hallway. "After you," he said. "It's at the end of the hall on the left."

They entered the bedroom, and Jaxtyn flipped the light switch by the door. He watched Daniel for any reaction to Skylar's Mapplethorpe posters, but other than a startled raising of his eyebrows, he chose to ignore them. Skylar's bed was a rumpled mess, his VR set tossed onto the pillow. There was one chair in the room, and a small desk, but both were piled with Skylar's clothes. It had been neater when he'd left for campus in the morning, and he was angry at Skylar for intentionally trying to undermine him.

"Sorry about the mess," he said, waving toward Skylar's bed and the covered furniture. "I could clear off the chair if you want to sit, or we could kneel like last time either on the floor by the bed or on top of it."

Daniel took in the room, and Jaxtyn waited for his judgment. The only contribution Jaxtyn had made to the room's decor was a small framed picture of the Buddha seated in a lotus pose. It hung on the wall above his pillow. Daniel eyed both beds, and then the door, and Jaxtyn was afraid he was going to suggest going back into the kitchen or skipping the prayer session altogether.

"Come on," he said, preempting any move by Daniel. "We'll

get on the bed, and you can face me and the Buddha, so you don't have to see…all the other stuff." He scrambled onto his bed and into an awkward kneeling position, then offered a hand to Daniel to help him climb into place. It took some doing and wobbling—Daniel even let out a soft laugh at one point, which Jaxtyn took as a very good sign—but finally, they were in place.

"Okay," Jaxtyn said. "Let's do this."

He reached forward and clasped tightly onto Daniel's hands, as much to keep him in place as to prepare for Daniel's prayer instructions. They were close—very close. If they leaned toward each other, their foreheads would touch. Daniel's eyes gleamed like polished wood in the low light, but Jaxtyn saw worry in them.

"They'll be fine," Jaxtyn said, assuming Daniel shared his own concerns about how Skylar and Marcus might be getting on. Daniel offered a weak smile in response, then closed his eyes, seeming to direct his attention inward. "Should I close my eyes too?" Jaxtyn asked.

"Yes, if it will help you open your heart and become receptive to Jesus."

"Okay." Jaxtyn spoke softly. He already felt as if they were entering a sacred space. The outside noises faded, and his mind began to reach for that transcendent state he sought when he meditated. But he kept his eyes open so he could look at the man in front of him, to study him. A lock of Daniel's hair slipped out of place and came to rest over one eye. Jaxtyn let his long fingers slide across the backs of Daniel's hands, almost a caress if one was inclined to see it that way. Daniel stiffened, and both men wobbled slightly on the mattress.

Enough of that. Pay attention and give him the benefit of the doubt.

After a moment, Daniel started speaking. His eyes were tightly closed and his hands trembled, ever so slightly, in Jaxtyn's grasp. "Jesus, please come to this sinner. Fill my heart with your love. Give me the strength to push out the demons plaguing me. Make me worthy of God's grace."

Demons? Daniel continued in that vein until a tear slid from the corner of his eye. His prayers faded into mumbling—incoherent, but intense. "No," he said at one point, shaking his head for emphasis. His hands clenched into fists beneath Jaxtyn's. "Please." It was a desperate plea. "Give me your strength, Jesus." He appeared to be in pain as he fought off whatever these demons were.

Jaxtyn hated seeing Daniel tormented like that, and he reminded himself that offering compassion was always the right thing to do. He took a deep breath, pushed aside his concerns about looking silly, or feeling foolish, and joined Daniel in prayer. "Jesus, if you're there, please ease Daniel's suffering. I...I don't like seeing him so upset." He squeezed Daniel's hands and risked sliding his fingers up Daniel's arm to his elbow. A show of concern, of support, nothing more.

Daniel shuddered and made a choking sound that could have been a suppressed sob. Tears were flowing freely down his cheeks, and he began trembling in earnest. "Please," he begged. "*Please.*"

Jaxtyn had had enough. He leaned forward and pulled Daniel to his chest. "Daniel, what's wrong? What demons?" He held Daniel's head against his shoulder, felt the sobs shaking the man's body. "Shh," he whispered. "It's all right. There are no demons here."

Daniel lifted his head from Jaxtyn's chest. His eyes were swollen, and his face was wet. But in his vulnerability, in his naked exposure and pain, Jaxtyn thought he was beautiful.

"You are so, so wrong," Daniel said. "*You* are the demon."

And then, to Jaxtyn's utter surprise, he moved his lips to Jaxtyn's and kissed him.

*

THE KISS HAPPENED so quickly; Jaxtyn could almost convince himself he'd imagined it. Immediately after their lips met, Daniel threw himself backward onto the bed in frustration and rolled onto his side to face the wall. "I've failed," he whispered to the wall. He sounded defeated and surprised at the same time as if he wasn't used to failing or having to admit it.

Jaxtyn still knelt on the bed, one hand touching the wall for balance as the mattress slowly stopped undulating. More than anything, he wanted to lie down next to Daniel, envelop him in a comforting hug, tell him everything would be all right — explore the kiss that he might have imagined. But he knew that would be a mistake.

Things were beginning to make sense. *He* was Daniel's demon.

He'd been right that there was a strong mutual attraction between them. He just hadn't realized how important it would be to Daniel to deny that attraction, to pretend it was nothing more than a distraction. He slid off the bed in an awkward shuffle, avoiding touching Daniel, avoiding brushing the hair away from his damp face, or kissing his temple, or resting a hand on his bony hip, anticipating the electricity that would shoot between them. "I'm going to make you a cup of tea. And then, once you're back to yourself, you and I are going to talk." He paused in the doorway. "Milk and sugar?"

"Yes, please," Daniel mumbled to the wall. His sobs had turned to sniffles, and his breathing was returning to normal. Jaxtyn smiled and headed into the hallway.

*

IN THE KITCHEN, Jaxtyn filled a mug with water and popped it in the microwave for two minutes. He removed a teabag from the box in the cabinet and pulled a carton of milk from the fridge. He gave it a sniff and decided it would do.

As he waited for the microwave timer, he thought about what to do with Daniel.

It was too late for the prayer session. His main concern now was making sure Daniel would be all right. He couldn't imagine the pain of feeling tormented by your very nature.

The timer dinged and Jaxtyn smiled again. Daniel had kissed him, or at least he'd attempted it. It was awkward and over nearly before it began, but it was heartfelt, even if it had nearly killed Daniel to do it. Once he'd had his tea and calmed down, they would talk about what it had all meant to Daniel. Jaxtyn promised himself not to push, not to use labels, and to avoid politics and social conventions. He wanted to get Daniel to admit his desires, maybe come to see it's not as bad as he feared, or he'd been taught.

He finished preparing the tea, and carried it down the hallway, offering a silent prayer to Jesus, or the Buddha, or the unifying power of the universe, or anyone or anything that might be listening that Daniel would kiss him again, for real this time, before Skylar and Marcus got back.

Daniel had gotten off the bed, removed Skylar's clothes from the chair, and taken a seat. It was a mild disappointment, but under the circumstances a perfectly understandable retreat. Plus, it allowed Jaxtyn to push a pile of Skylar's socks out of the way and place the tea on the desk in front of Daniel.

"Here you are," Jaxtyn said. Daniel nodded his thanks but didn't look at him. "Take your time. Have some tea. Everything's fine. You'll see."

Across the city, a cacophony of sirens started blaring.

Chapter Seventeen

DEAFENING AT FIRST—it became a continuous wailing that seemed to go on forever, only to wind down before taking up again. Daniel was reminded of the air raids in the old war movies he used to watch with his parents on Sunday afternoons. In the lull between the sirens' peaks, horns and other alarms could be heard in the distance as emergency vehicles began racing through the city streets.

"Bathroom," Jaxtyn said as he hurried about the bedroom, pulling the blanket off first his bed and then from Skylar's too. "Get to the bathroom, Daniel."

Daniel rose from the chair. "What's going on?" He had to raise his voice to be heard over the sirens, the confusion and shame from the kiss temporarily pushed aside.

Jaxtyn thrust the blankets into his hands. "Take these. Go to the bathroom. I'm grabbing Sylvie's. I'll be right there."

Daniel pushed awkwardly through the doorway with his load of blankets and made his way to the bathroom. Behind him, Jaxtyn moved into Sylvie's room. He must have activated the wall screen there, with the volume cranked high, because even as he entered the bathroom, Daniel could hear an announcer's voice repeating "Take cover immediately. This is not a test." The same message repeated, over and over, first in English, then Spanish, then two more languages he didn't recognize.

Daniel could hear a soft thumping from the apartment above them, then an object being dragged across the floor. The foreign cooking smell was gone; he'd either gotten used to it or it had dissipated.

Jaxtyn began to squeeze into the room behind him, his arms filled with Sylvie's blankets and a thick, flower-patterned comforter. There was barely enough space for the two men to stand. It was a windowless room, and a small shower/tub combination filled one side. The remaining space was occupied by a tiny pedestal sink and a toilet. A square mirrored cabinet hung on the wall above the sink, its glass was smeared with fingerprints along the edge where the door hinged open. A precarious wicker stand forced into the corner held soap and shampoo, two rolls of toilet paper, a box of tissues, and, on the top shelf, a tiny Buddha statue. The bathroom door pressed against the stand as Jaxtyn maneuvered his bundle into the room.

"Sorry," he said, as he bumped into Daniel when he turned to shut the door behind them. "Drop yours on the floor. Let me get the comforter down first." Daniel searched for a spot on the floor to put the blankets, but he and Jaxtyn already filled the space, so he simply dropped them at his feet. Jaxtyn placed the comforter in the tub and began spreading it out.

The television's announcement, still audible through the closed door, cycled back to English. "Take cover immediately. This is not a test."

"I'll get in first," Jaxtyn said. "I'm bigger than you and don't want to crush you." Jaxtyn stepped over the low tub wall and began contorting himself to fit.

Daniel's brain caught up to what he was seeing. He balked. "I'm not getting in there with you. You can barely fit yourself."

"Dammit, Daniel. You have to. If there's going to be a blast, we'll need to protect ourselves from debris. There's no window here, so that's good. Just get in and pull the other blankets on top of us."

Left on his own, Daniel would have stood there, considering his options, scrolling through his phone for news or advice. But he was good at following direct orders, doing what he was told without question, so he began to climb into the tub, assessing where he might be able to settle that wouldn't be *entirely* on top of Jaxtyn.

"Hurry!" Jaxtyn said, reaching up a hand and pulling Daniel down. "Tug the other blankets over us."

He still wasn't sure what was happening, but the wailing siren urged action, and it was easier to do what Jaxtyn told him rather than ask questions. He settled on his side — partly on top of Jaxtyn, partly squished against the side of the tub — then blindly flailed one hand above him, searching for the edge of a blanket he could pull it into place. The tub wasn't long enough for either man to stretch flat, and when Jaxtyn kicked up with a foot to try to catch the end of a blanket and nudge it into place, his knee jabbed into Daniel's stomach.

"Oof."

"Sorry." Jaxtyn finally got a grip on the blankets and began carefully shifting them until he was satisfied. "There," he said as the blankets settled over them. Daniel's cheek rested on Jaxtyn's shoulder, which was far too intimate, so with great effort, Daniel managed to wriggle around half a turn. His nose then pushed against the vinyl wall of the tub, but that was better than feeling the rise and fall of Jaxtyn's chest.

The bathroom light filtered weakly through the covers, but Daniel could only see the tub wall. It was warm in the tight space, and a faint smell of soap—botanical, but not flowery—competed with Jaxtyn's own smell, the coffee he had that morning, the incense he must burn in his room. Daniel took a deep breath. He was concerned about what his own breath smelled like. He felt dampness under his arms and tried to remember if he'd put on deodorant that morning.

"Take cover immediately. This is not a test."

"What's happening?" Daniel asked. He tried to reach his hand toward his pocket to retrieve one of his phones, but he wasn't able to do that without sliding the back of his hand tightly along the length of Jaxtyn's torso, so he gave up on the idea.

"You won't be able to use your phone. They block the signals at times like this, you know, so the terrorists can't communicate with each other if there's a group of them."

This has happened before?

Jaxtyn shifted slightly, and the men settled into a spooning position. It was more comfortable, but also more awkward with their bodies forced so tightly against each other. Daniel's butt pressed solidly into Jaxtyn's lap, but each time he tried to create even a little space between them, he ended up merely grinding into Jaxtyn, which wasn't his intention at all.

"How long are we going to be here?" Daniel asked.

"Well, it depends on what's going on. We should know soon if—"

He was interrupted by a change in the siren's cadence—five short, quick blasts, followed by more wailing, then the blasts again. The cycle repeated itself.

"Depends on what?" Daniel asked.

"Shh." Jaxtyn squeezed Daniel's elbow to keep him still.

When had Jaxtyn managed to put his arm across me?

The television repeated its message in several languages, then, "Radiation Detected. Take cover immediately. This is not a test."

Radiation!

"Oh," said Jaxtyn. He took a deep breath, pressing Daniel tighter against the tub's wall.

"What…what?" Daniel struggled to rise and lost his grip on the wall. Jaxtyn pulled him in even tighter.

"Daniel, it's all right. It was a dirty bomb. It's happened before. If it was a full-on atom bomb, we would have heard the blast. Hell, we'd probably be lying under rubble right now."

"But…radiation. Are we going to get sick? Are we going to die?"

Jaxtyn rubbed his hand along Daniel's arm where they pressed together. "No, you're not going to die. They've always just been minor blasts, something like a pipe bomb, but they're packed with radioactive materials stolen from medical facilities or research labs, that sort of thing. Now we just have to wait to see where it happened. Then they'll know when it's safe to move around."

Daniel's calf tightened in a cramp, and he jerked about trying to straighten his leg, but all he managed to achieve was a sharply banged knee.

"Oh, that was nice," said Jaxtyn. "Do that again."

"Stop. It was a cramp. You're not funny." Daniel tried to hold himself as still as possible and willed his leg to return to normal.

"Sorry. I make jokes when I'm nervous."

Daniel didn't respond. Instead, he tried to calm his mind by focusing on his body. The cramped muscle had eased, but twinges in his lower calf threatened its return. His heartbeat seemed normal—all things considered—and his breathing was shallow but steady. He maneuvered a quarter twist, so he faced up rather than having his nose pressed against the tub's wall. Jaxtyn still gripped him in a semi-embrace.

He took several deep breaths, acutely aware of Jaxtyn's forearm rising and falling along with his stomach. The blanket inches above his face puffed out with each exhalation. Now that he'd turned his head, he could feel Jaxtyn's warm breath against his ear.

"Um, if it's radiation, do we need these blankets?"

"No," Jaxtyn responded, but he made no move to push them aside. Daniel waited for him to do something. He was the one who'd been through this before, after all. "But it's nice, isn't it?"

"No," Daniel replied. With some difficulty, he extricated his arm that had been trapped against Jaxtyn, very intentionally not focusing on all the various parts of the man's body he felt as he did so. He pushed aside the blankets and cool air pooled into the tub. "And we don't need to stay in here, do we?"

Jaxtyn sighed, and his coffee-scented breath caressed Daniel's face. "No," he said with an air of resignation, almost as if he'd been caught out at something. He pressed an arm against the side of the tub behind him, and as he did so, he pressed even more tightly into Daniel. But the contact was fleeting, and with a grunt, Jaxtyn managed to stand. With one hand pressed against the wall, He stepped over Daniel and out of the tub, then offered a hand to help Daniel to his feet. It was a relief to move his limbs again, and Daniel shook his arms once he was standing on the floor, He stood on his toes to stretch his calf muscles.

"We should stay in here until we know the explosion wasn't close by. The solid walls are better protection than glass." Jaxtyn ran some water in the sink and splashed his face. Then he combed his wet fingers through his hair, forcing it into some kind of order. Daniel glanced into the mirror over Jaxtyn's shoulder and winced at his unruly reflection. His hair was sticking out at an odd angle and his cheek was bright red where it had been pressed against the vinyl. "Don't worry. You look good disheveled," Jaxtyn said as he met Daniel's eyes in the mirror.

A wave of emotions crashed through Daniel—embarrassment about the earlier kiss, confusion about how to respond to Jaxtyn's newly emboldened comments about their mutual attraction. He couldn't just ignore the innuendos anymore, but he didn't want to encourage them, did he?

But most of all he was disappointed in himself. He'd failed to honor God's will, failed to overcome something so simple as an inappropriate sexual attraction, failed to bring Jaxtyn to Jesus. He pulled out one of his phones and confirmed Jaxtyn's prediction he wouldn't have service.

"Do you think Marcus and Skylar are all right?" he asked. That was safe ground at least and allowed him to stop focusing on his own shortcomings.

"Yes. Sky will know what to do." Jaxtyn had turned and was resting his butt against the rim of the sink, his arms crossed in front of his chest. Daniel stood awkwardly in front of the toilet, trying to maintain a distance from Jaxtyn without looking like he was desperately shrinking away.

Jaxtyn rolled his eyes and seemed to be about to say something when the recording on the television abruptly switched to a live broadcast.

"This is the Massachusetts Emergency Management Agency. A shelter-in-place order remains in effect for the City of Boston. Radiation detectors at the Federal Court House, Rowes Wharf, and South Station have all registered heightened levels of radioactivity. Those facilities and surrounding buildings are being evacuated. There are no immediate reports of deaths or injuries, and structural damage to the affected locations appears to be minor. Phone service will be restored when authorities conclude there is no longer an imminent risk of attack. The shelter-in-place order will be lifted once all civilians are evacuated from the affected areas, and the extent of the radiation contamination is determined."

The announcement continued with evacuation instructions for people in the immediate area. "Okay," Jaxtyn said. "We can leave the bathroom." He opened the door and then disappeared into the hallway. Fresher air spilled into the room, and Daniel tried to get his thoughts together. They were okay. Marcus was okay. Sure, he'd made a horrible mistake by trying to kiss Jaxtyn, but nothing was stopping him from redoubling his efforts to resist temptation. He was God's servant, and he was determined to act like one.

He knew Jaxtyn was in Sylvie's room because the wall screen's volume was lowered. But he turned right in the hallway, heading toward the kitchen. He didn't want to be alone with Jaxtyn in his bedroom, and they obviously weren't going to try praying again. As soon as Marcus returned, they'd leave. Assuming they were right—that God had led them here because Skylar was, in fact, the killer—then the secondary mission was accomplished, and they could put all this behind them and get to the serious business of saving souls.

He sat in a kitchen chair and hoped Jaxtyn would offer to make him another cup of tea, or even bring him the cold one from the bedroom. Minutes passed as he listened to the instructions given to the people evacuating, on how much iodine they should take, and where to go for decontamination. He didn't envy the people on the upper floors of the Federal Reserve building; they would need to stay in place until it was deemed safe for them to pass through the lobby.

They stockpile iodine here. Just for this type of event.

He thought about his gun and how it wouldn't have helped him at all. He checked one phone and then the other, but there was still no service. Jaxtyn hadn't returned to the kitchen. He stared out the window, wondering if there was invisible radiation in the air, as the announcer read out the names of the detection stations reporting normal levels—Chinatown, Beacon Hill, the warehouse district, the North End, and Back Bay. The last was where the library was, he remembered.

He assumed these were all the closest stations to the affected areas, but he didn't know how close they were to the campus or if it was safe now for them to go outside. He left the kitchen in search of Jaxtyn, and found him back in his bedroom, sitting on Skylar's bed fiddling with his roommate's VR helmet.

"You can heat your tea in the microwave if you want." Jaxtyn didn't look up. "You don't need to sit in here with me."

Daniel stood in the doorway, confused by the change in Jaxtyn. "What's wrong?" he asked. "I mean, you know, beyond…all this." He waved his arm to take in the apartment and the city beyond.

"What's wrong? Seriously?" Jaxtyn put the VR set down and looked up. "I don't get you, Daniel. I mean, I get that you're uncomfortable around me, but it's rude to treat me like I'm repulsive. The whole time we were in the bathroom, I could feel you flinching each time we touched, how desperately you didn't want to be in physical contact with me. Hell, when we got out of the tub, I thought you were going to crawl into the toilet to get farther away from me."

He put the headset down and curled his hands into fists, pressing them into Skylar's mattress on either side of him.

"And okay, I was maybe a little forward in hinting at how attractive I found you, but you could have just said you weren't interested, and I would have let it drop. It's done that way up here, you know. No harm no foul."

Daniel tried to make sense of what he was hearing. Of

course, he was attracted to Jaxtyn; that's what kept getting him in trouble. He replayed what had happened between them, and realized his efforts to create distance, to avoid triggering the attraction, were misinterpreted as the exact opposite of how he felt. And now he'd have to admit his feelings because he couldn't be so cruel as to allow Jaxtyn to think he found him repulsive.

"The thing is," Jaxtyn continued, "I'm confused about the kiss. You did kiss me, right? I didn't imagine that?" Daniel took a step into the room. "Why did you do that? Was it just some sort of twitch? Was it a test?" Jaxtyn swallowed. "Pity?"

Daniel couldn't stand the look of confusion and rejection he saw in Jaxtyn's eyes.

"Because it was a pretty mean thing to do, actually," Jaxtyn continued. "I thought…well, I thought maybe you liked me too. Maybe, even though we live in such different worlds, you might have been interested in getting to know me. So, yeah, that was pretty harsh."

The siren's wailing stopped and was followed by three short blasts.

"That's the all clear. You can wait outside for Marcus if you want. Or you're welcome to stay in here. I promise not to bother you."

Daniel entered the room and sat next to Jaxtyn. Skylar's bed was a mess, and Daniel avoided looking too closely at the state of the sheets.

"No, you have it wrong," Daniel said. "It would be easier to let you believe that, but it wouldn't be right." He thought about how to tell Jaxtyn the truth, then laughed out loud. Telling the truth was always easy and straightforward. It was lying about things—trying to make them something they weren't—that was difficult.

Maybe he could bear this cross after all.

"I *am* attracted to you," Daniel said. The mattress shifted as Jaxtyn sucked in a breath.

"But—" Jaxtyn began.

"No. Wait." Daniel held up a hand. "I don't *want* to be attracted to you. That's the truth. I don't know why God saw fit to plague me with same-sex attraction. But it's no different than the burdens others have, not really. We're all tested in our own ways."

Three more short siren blasts outside, then the sounds of traffic returning to normal, Boston going about its business.

"So, I'm…I'm a burden for you?" Jaxtyn asked with a frown.

"No. You're my own personal demon. Tormenting me, or more accurately, enticing me into thoughts of doing sinful things."

That seemed to please Jaxtyn. "I *entice* you?" He grinned and risked moving his hand to Daniel's knee.

Daniel swatted it away. "Stop. See? You do that, and you grin, and your eyes get all sparkly and I end up wanting to kiss you. Which is what I did—or almost did, anyway—but I shouldn't have. It was weak of me to give in. I betrayed my commitment to God."

"Huh," said Jaxtyn, who had removed his hand but scooted closer to Daniel on the bed. "But how do you *know* God doesn't want you to kiss me?"

"Oh no, I'm not getting into that with you. It's my church's teaching, and it's based on the Bible, and I believe it. I'm not debating it with you." Daniel *thought* he'd communicated his position appropriately, and it felt good to open up about his temptations — there was nothing wrong with feeling a same-sex attraction, after all, it was only acting on it that became problematic, that deviated from God's plan for men and women. And he'd certainly cheered up Jaxtyn, who had a certain glow about him now he hadn't when Daniel had come into the room.

That thought brought him back to the morning's meditation session. "Jesus *did* come to you this morning, didn't he?" He turned to face Jaxtyn, simultaneously inching a bit farther away, "I mean, you seemed to lose all track of time, and the look on your face…"

Jaxtyn thought for a moment before answering. "Honestly? I don't know."

Daniel was disappointed in the answer. He suspected Jaxtyn was trying to disavow a legitimate visitation by Jesus. "What *did* you see?" he prompted.

"Well, Jesus, yes, but—"

"I knew it!" interrupted Daniel.

"*But,*" continued Jaxtyn. "I think I…conjured him, or something. I mean, it was the Hollywood version of Jesus. That can't be right, can it?"

"Of course it can! Jesus can come to you in any way that works. The important thing is that you let Him into your heart. It's through Him that God fills us with His grace."

Daniel had snatched victory from the jaws of defeat. He was going to be the vehicle through which Jaxtyn came to know God. And if he hadn't succumbed to his own weaknesses, if he hadn't had to confess the nature of his sins, he wouldn't have been having this heartfelt conversation with Jaxtyn. The Lord truly does work in mysterious ways.

"It wasn't just Jesus, though, in my…vision, or whatever it was."

"That's fine," Daniel said. "It's all good. God's presence can be felt in many ways. Some find peace and tranquility in reading scripture or singing songs of praise. What did you see?"

"Well, I saw you. Jesus brought you to me." He squeezed Daniel's fingers, and it was only then that Daniel realized Jaxtyn had reached over and taken his hand.

"I…me?" He swallowed and didn't pull his hand out of Jaxtyn's grip.

"Yes," Jaxtyn said, his head suddenly much closer to Daniel's. "It was confusing at first because the images of you and Jesus kept shifting back and forth. And Jesus was embracing me and then it was you who was embracing me, and then time just sort of stopped and I floated in this beautiful state. Then you tapped me on the head with your knee."

Daniel didn't know what to say. It was all so…complicated.

"It was almost like Jesus brought you to me," Jaxtyn concluded.

And isn't that exactly what Daniel had been thinking? Hadn't he just convinced himself that God had led him to Jaxtyn? Not just to find the killer, but also to save Jaxtyn's soul? But had Jesus been leading Jaxtyn to Daniel too? That's too extraordinary to be a coincidence.

He couldn't tell Jaxtyn about the secret mission, and he'd assumed finding the killer and leading Jaxtyn into God's grace was the reason he'd been led here. But what if there was something else? What if Jesus was leading Jaxtyn here for his own reasons?

"But why?" He'd been lost in his own thoughts and hadn't meant to ask the question out loud.

"I don't know," Jaxtyn answered. "Maybe Jesus wanted us to meet, maybe he wants us to like each other. Maybe he thinks we have something we can teach each other."

Could that be it? Had Daniel been so preoccupied with his own work he failed to see the Lord acting in others? Was he so self-important to think Jaxtyn had nothing he could teach him? Certainly, that was wrong, especially if Jesus was working His will through Jaxtyn.

"Isn't it possible," Jaxtyn continued, putting his arm across Daniel's shoulders, "that maybe Jesus wants you to be a little more humble, less certain you know His will in all things?"

And wasn't that also *exactly* what Daniel had been thinking? He would need to talk to Marcus about all this. Maybe he should learn to listen more and be less sure about everything.

"Maybe Jesus wants you to keep an open mind, to test what you think you know." Jaxtyn's breath was a soft caress along Daniel's cheek. "Maybe he wants you to confront your demons, not run from them."

His demons? But that would be Jaxtyn, and, oh…

Jaxtyn leaned in and kissed him. Everything ran together in a confused muddle, but before he could think it through, before he could take the time to make *sense* of things, he found himself deepening the kiss. His first kiss! And it was everything he'd feared it would be. He clutched the back of Jaxtyn's head, pulling him even closer, letting his demon in.

A throat-clearing noise interrupted them. "Look, I'm not

judging," Skylar said from the doorway. Marcus stood behind him, his eyes wider than Daniel had ever seen them. "But if you're going to go all the way, could you do it on your own bed?"

Chapter Eighteen

IT WAS NEARLY midnight by the time Sylvie got home.

"Sorry," she said as she came into the kitchen. Jaxtyn could smell the alcohol as soon as she entered, and he exchanged a look with Skylar. The day had been very difficult for everyone in Boston, but still, Sylvie had a hard time stopping drinking once she'd started. Jaxtyn didn't like to see her backsliding this way. He didn't feel he had a right to lecture her, though, as he and Skylar had already gone through one six-pack of beer and started in on a second.

She moved to the kitchen table with extraordinary care — the kind of precise, cautious movements the inebriated use when pretending not to be drunk. Even so, she missed her first grab at the back of the chair.

"Good thing you don't drive," Skylar said.

"That's very funny," Sylvie said as she reached for a beer.

Jaxtyn cringed but held his tongue. "I'm glad you're all right. Did you have to work this evening?" Sylvie had a part-time job at a small tattoo and piercing shop, but Jaxtyn was pretty sure she only had afternoon hours right now.

"I worked earlier today, and then a bunch of us went out to decompress after everything that happened." She certainly looked decompressed.

"We were beginning to worry you got caught up in one of the decontamination sites," Jaxtyn said.

Sylvie shuddered. "Thank God, no. What's the latest? How serious was it this time?"

"Not very," said Skyler. "It turned out to be pretty low-grade stuff. No one was seriously injured, and only a small section of the federal courthouse is going to have to be sealed off." He took a swig of his beer.

"No one has been seriously injured *yet*," Jaxtyn chimed in. "We don't know if there will be any long-term exposure effects." Sylvie hadn't opened her beer. Either she'd forgotten about it, or she was rethinking her decision.

Skylar grinned. "Ask Jaxtyn what his big news is."

"I don't have big news, Sky." But he couldn't hide his own grin even as he offered the complaint. "If you hadn't come in when you did, I might have had news."

Sylvie looked between the two men. "Okay," she asked Jaxtyn. "What's your not-big news."

Skylar was nearly bouncing with excitement. "Jax had sex with the CeeNee!"

Sylvie popped the tab on her can of beer. "Jesus Christ."

"Almost!" Skylar agreed. "Nearest thing Jax will ever come

to it anyway."

"Stop," Jaxtyn said. "I did *not* have sex with the Cee…Daniel."

"Only because I stopped you." Skylar turned to Sylvie. "You should have seen it! The CeeNee was practically humping Jax's leg, and he had his tongue so far down his throat—"

"Enough," Jaxtyn said. He pushed his chair back and stood. "It was nothing like that. It was sweet and innocent."

"Uh-huh," Skylar said. He turned to Sylvie. "It was like in the Mormon porn, only better, because it was real, and on my own bed too."

"I've heard enough," Sylvie slurred. She picked up her beer. "I'm going to bed."

"Your comforter might be a little damp," Jaxtyn told her.

"Oh, gross!" she said.

"No!" Jaxtyn replied. "From the tub. We used it to shelter in place."

She just looked at the two men and shook her head, which seemed to make her a little dizzy because she steadied herself with a hand against the kitchen doorframe. Jaxtyn vowed to talk to her in the morning, support her if she wanted to get back on the wagon. He had an early class, and she would surely sleep in, but maybe in the afternoon.

"I worry about her," Jaxtyn told Skylar after she left.

"I know, but she's a grown woman," Skylar said.

"Doesn't mean we shouldn't look out for one another." Jaxtyn took his unfinished beer to the sink and dumped it. What would have happened if Skylar and Marcus hadn't returned when they did? Marcus's shock was almost comical, but Daniel's panic at being discovered was a gut punch. He hated to think he was responsible for causing that kind of pain.

"I was a manipulative dick," he told Skylar. "I wouldn't be surprised if Daniel never wants to see me again."

"Oh, come on, Jax, don't be so hard on yourself." Skylar took another swig from his can. "From where I was standing, it didn't exactly look forced."

"No, it wasn't." Jaxtyn smiled at the memory of Daniel's eagerness, of his guard slipping away completely. "But I might have misled him some. I told him I had a vision of Jesus."

"But you *did*, didn't you? Isn't that what you said happened during your meditation?"

Jaxtyn ran his hands through his hair. "No. I *envisioned* Jesus, intentionally, just to see what praying might be like for Daniel. That's different from some sort of mystical vision. Those just… come upon me."

"Seems like splitting hairs to me. Besides, you had one of your mystical experiences too, didn't you? Isn't that what you're always aiming for, some transcendent feeling of oneness with the universe?" Skylar used air quotes to indicate his disdain for the entire idea.

"Well…yes…"

"Jax, don't look a gift horse in the mouth. You had a vision of Jesus, or you pictured him in your mind or whatever, then you tripped into one of your headspace things where you become one with everything, then Jesus pimped Daniel to you — which is awesome, by the way — and then Daniel was all, like, 'Bring it on; fill me with your spirit, dude.' Really, it's a win-win." Skylar took a final swallow of his beer.

"How is it," Jaxtyn asked, "that you can make a sacred mystical experience sound like a cheap hookup?"

"Talent," Skylar replied.

Jaxtyn shook his head, then walked to the refrigerator to root around for something to snack on. He found some leftover noodles in a bowl, grabbed a fork, and started eating.

"Besides," Skylar said, "I know it's all good because Marcus told me Daniel was attracted to you."

The noodles Jaxtyn had been carefully twining around his fork slipped to the floor in a wet *plop*. "What! When did he tell you that? Why didn't you tell *me* that?"

"Chill. I'm telling you now. And we had a lot of time to spend huddled in the refrigerated storage room of the package store." Skylar grabbed a paper towel from the roll on the counter and began scooping up the fallen noodles.

"You told me you talked about politics," Jaxtyn said.

"We did. He had a lot of questions about us. Northerners, I mean. He's pretty smart actually, for a CeeNee." He finished cleaning the mess on the floor and tossed the towel into the garbage bin. "And then we got onto the gay stuff."

Jaxtyn squinted suspiciously. "How did you get onto the 'gay stuff'?"

"Well, I may have asked, at one point, if it was going to be the last day of his life, wouldn't he maybe want to experiment a little? I might even have placed my hand on his knee, you know, to emphasize the seriousness of the situation." Skylar batted his eyes.

"I'm surprised you're not bloodied." He made a show of studying Skylar's face for wounds. "And you told me you wouldn't cause trouble."

"No worries, Jax. Marcus is pretty cool. He laughed and said he'd need to be *certain* it was his final minutes, but that he'd keep an open mind."

Keep an open mind. Isn't that what Jaxtyn had told Daniel Jesus wanted from him—to keep an open mind?

"But then he started asking me lots of questions about being gay," Skylar continued, "like the kind you get from young people just realizing who they are. How did I know? When did I know? Was it difficult for me? That sort of thing. But I knew he wasn't asking for himself, so I figured he was asking for Daniel."

Jaxtyn nodded. That made sense—it explained the dynamic he'd noticed between the two missionaries from the very beginning. Marcus was protecting Daniel.

"So," Jaxtyn asked, "Marcus knows about Daniel? Well, he does now of course." Jaxtyn blushed at the memory of Marcus seeing them kissing. "But he knew even before?"

"Yes, but it's different for them down there. He tried to explain it to me. It seems there's a huge difference between having—excuse me, 'suffering from'—same-sex attraction and acting on it. Like, you know, sucking face with another guy. He says it's not a sin to be tormented by 'those demons,' just a sin to give in to them."

He grabbed another beer and sat back down at the table. "Weird shit, huh?"

Jaxtyn cringed, recalling the pain in Daniel's voice when he spoke about the demons dragging him down. "Daniel called me his demon." Could he truly be the source of so much of Daniel's anguish?

"Oh. It's cute you have pet names for each other already. Do you call him your angel?"

Chapter Nineteen

DANIEL AND MARCUS prayed together that night, silently, urgently. Both men were desperate to recapture some of the normalcy their lives had held before they arrived in Boston. They agreed not to speak of the events of the day prior to praying. There was just too much—the terror attack, the horror of sheltering in place, fearing for their lives, the confirmation Skylar was, indeed, the killer, and, of course, Daniel's shame. It was too much to unpack piecemeal.

They needed Jesus's centering presence to help them make sense of it all.

After nearly an hour, Marcus let his grip on Daniel's hands fall. "I can't," he said. "It's too much. I can't settle my mind enough to open my heart to Jesus."

"I know, me too." Daniel leaned back in the chair. Marcus was sitting on the edge of the bed, and Daniel had dragged the chair across the room to face him. They were scheduled for a call with Pastor Logan in less than an hour. "What are we going to do?" Daniel asked.

Marcus picked up his phone—the burner phone—and began thumbing across the screen. "Well," he said, "I think we shouldn't lie to Pastor Logan." Daniel nodded eagerly in agreement. "So, I guess that means," Marcus continued, looking up from the phone, "we tell him part of the truth, but not all of the truth."

Daniel swallowed. What part of which truth? He knew he'd sinned, but he was finding it increasingly difficult to distinguish between the sin of action and the non-sinful state of unnatural desire. "I'm not sure I know what the truth is anymore."

Marcus stared at him for a moment. "Do you feel like you can continue your mission, Dan?"

Daniel shrugged his shoulders. "See? I'm so confused, I don't even know what that question means. Are you asking if the shock of the terror attack was too much for me? Or if I'm too afraid to stay here after what happened—after learning how vulnerable we all are? Or are you asking if my descent into the depths of sinful behavior rendered me too impure to witness to anyone?"

Marcus flinched. "Um, that last one, I think?" Then he grinned. "But the way you put it makes it sound pretty ridiculous, doesn't it?"

"I don't know, Marcus. I'm confused about everything." He stood, walked to the heating unit, and flipped the power switch. He was anticipating the clunking, grinding sound of the heat coming on, but there was only silence. "Do you think they fixed it?"

Marcus grinned again. "More likely they disabled it entirely to try to get us to leave. Even though we don't wear the uniform, they know who we are."

Daniel felt the metal grill of the wall unit and confirmed Marcus's fears. "It's not working at all." He turned to face Marcus, who'd gone back to studying his phone. "So, what are we going to tell Pastor Logan?"

"I guess that depends on you, Dan. Did your…episode…today, with Jaxtyn, teach you anything? About yourself, I mean. Anything you need to tell Pastor Logan?"

Daniel shook his head. "No. I don't think I'm any different than I was yesterday. I mean, we both know this is my struggle. I'd just never…given in to it before. I have to be stronger."

"But do you *feel* different, Dan? Do you feel changed?"

Marcus sounded almost like they were discussing something acceptable, not a shameful surrender to sinful urges. "No." But that was a lie. He *did* feel different. He felt like something had opened inside of him, a floodgate that had been holding back a deluge. But he had no way of explaining that to Marcus. He couldn't even explain it to himself. "There's no need to tell Pastor Logan about it. It was a mistake. It won't happen again."

Marcus looked as if he might challenge him, but instead, he turned his attention back to his phone, then said, as if he were changing the subject, "Skylar said he'd always known he was like that. Gay, I mean. They don't separate the wanting to do it from the actual doing of it up here, the way we do. To them, it's just who you are, an identity." He paused but didn't raise his eyes to meet Daniel's. He was leaving space for Daniel to respond, but Daniel didn't know how he could. "It's an interesting idea, isn't it? A different way of looking at it."

"That seems like an odd thing for you and Skylar to have talked about."

"Well, we spent a lot of time together in the refrigerator. Better than a bathtub, I guess."

Daniel shuddered as he remembered his time in the tub with Jaxtyn. He was embarrassed by his response to what he saw now as attraction and desire, and how he'd hurt Jaxtyn by making him think he was repulsive somehow. He hated lying to Marcus too. The kiss had changed everything. An electric current had run through him, and it had yet to shut off. He'd been transformed… but into what?

"Anyway," Marcus continued, "Skylar was pretty convincing. I just wanted to put it out there — that maybe there's more to the same-sex attraction thing than it just being a sin."

Daniel was grateful for the sentiment. At least Marcus didn't think his slip made him a monster, or unredeemable. No matter how mired in sin we become, Jesus will come to us. Marcus saw that.

"But I don't actually want to *see* it again, you know? So, if you're going to pursue anything along those lines, just do it privately, okay?"

"I'm *not* going to pursue anything! It was wrong, a mistake, a sin. I'm going to ask Jesus for His forgiveness, and we're not telling Pastor Logan anything. It doesn't need to be raised with him." Daniel tried to put a note of finality in his voice. "And I don't think you should be listening to a killer when it comes to understanding moral behavior."

"Maybe," Marcus allowed. "But I kind of liked him. I mean,

once you get beyond the intentional rudeness, he seems like an okay guy. I learned a lot about how people up here see us. There's a lot we're not told, you know. And he's very loyal to his friends. He's looking out for Jaxtyn. I think that's why he told me so much about being gay. He knew Jaxtyn liked you, and I think he was worried you might end up hurting him, if you were…into him, and acted on it."

"Well, I'm not. Or at least I'm not going to live that way." Daniel sat down on his bed. "I wish we weren't talking with Pastor Logan now. He's going to know something's off with me."

"Just chalk it up to the terror attack. And I won't tell him about what happened with you and Jaxtyn. We'll pray together about that when we're calmer."

"Thanks, Marcus. You're a good friend. Plus, once he learns we positively identified the killer, he'll be so pleased, he'll forget about anything else."

Marcus put down his phone and stood. "You know, maybe we don't have to tell him about Skylar either. I mean, he did seem like a decent guy. Maybe he's *not* the killer."

Daniel couldn't believe what he was hearing. They'd finally wrapped up their secondary mission, the one Marcus had been lukewarm on all along, and now they had the chance to put it behind them. Why was Marcus balking? "What are you talking about? We'll tell him what we learned, he'll share it with the authorities here, and Skylar will face justice. Even if he's not the actual killer, he played a crucial role. He's the one who took Ruth. We have proof now."

"I know," Marcus said. He walked to the window and looked out into the gloomy night. "But *we* could go to the authorities, couldn't we? We could go to the local police right now, tell them what we know and show them the videos of Skylar and Ruth. Why would Pastor Logan want to handle it all from back home? The crime wasn't even committed there."

"The *murder*, Marcus. We're talking about a murder."

"I *know*, Dan. But they should handle it here. It's where Skylar lives."

Daniel just looked at him, trying to figure out what he was missing. "What's happening here, Marcus?"

Marcus let out a breath. "All right. You were upfront with me about Jaxtyn, so I should be upfront with you. I don't trust him, Dan. I don't trust Pastor Logan when he says he's going to take the information to the authorities. I don't think we should tell him about Skylar."

A silence fell over the room. This was bad. It was Marcus's biggest weakness—his mistrust of God's will, especially as expressed through the authority of the church. Before they'd come to Boston, he'd always managed to limit himself to expressing doubt, and he and Daniel had always been able to pray together for Jesus's guidance. And then Marcus always came around, came back into alignment with his religious community. But this was different. He was being defiant, not just doubtful.

And on the same day Daniel had sunk so deeply into his own sin. This city was destroying them. But as forgiving and accepting as Marcus had been about Jaxtyn, Daniel couldn't betray the church. He would pray with Marcus over his failings, but he wouldn't turn his back on his obligations. "I'm telling him, Marcus. I have to." Then a horrible thought occurred to Daniel. "If that means you have to tell him about Jaxtyn, then so be it."

Marcus looked like he'd been slapped. "I'm sorry you think I'd blackmail you, Dan. I wouldn't." He gathered his things from the table and stuffed them in his jacket pocket. "I'm going out."

"But the call…" Daniel said.

"Tell him I'm out saving souls." And with that, Marcus was gone.

*

"BROTHER THOMAS." PASTOR Logan acknowledged him with a nod. "Where is Brother Paul."

"He's sick, sir. He needed to go to a clinic." A lie. Daniel felt miserable. He'd never lied to Pastor Logan, and he was still embarrassed by the accusation he'd made against Marcus, that he thought Marcus would threaten him like that by disclosing Daniel's kiss with Jaxtyn in order to blackmail him into not sharing what they'd learned about Skylar. Where had that come from? He knew Marcus better than that.

It was the kiss. It's screwing with my head. And it was more than a kiss, wasn't it? It was a revelation.

"Nothing too serious, I hope? He wasn't harmed in the incident up there today, was he?"

The incident.

"No, sir. The terror attack was frightening though. We had to shelter in place for a long time."

Pastor Logan raised his eyebrows at Daniel's phrasing but didn't follow up. "All in service to the Lord, Brother Thomas." He closed his eyes and pressed his fingers together. Daniel waited. Finally, Pastor Logan looked into the camera. "If only these Northern people would wake up and recognize the folly of defying God, they could be spared these incidents." He narrowed his eyes at Daniel. "You must convince them of that, Brother Thomas."

Daniel didn't know how he could do that, and he didn't like the implication he could speak to the people here about what type of punishment God chooses to bring to sinners. It was time to change the subject.

"We found him, sir. The killer, I mean."

Pastor Logan's eyes blazed. "Where is he? What can you tell me?"

"We were right. He's a student at UMass Boston. I have a picture of his car parked at the address where he lives."

"You found out where he lives!" Daniel had never seen Pastor Logan this enthusiastic about anything, which seemed wrong somehow. But he had no time to follow the thought. "Are you sure you identified his apartment? Does he live alone or with others?"

"Yes, he lives there with two other students—"

"What's the address?" Pastor Logan had pulled a pad of paper in front of him and had begun taking notes.

Daniel's unease intensified. "Marcus and I thought we could go directly to the police here and let them know about the video with Ruth."

"*Marcus*?" Pastor Logan sneered.

"I'm sorry. I meant Brother Paul. It's been a long day, and—"

Pastor Logan leaned into the camera. He was so close Daniel could see the drops of sweat that had suddenly appeared on his forehead. "Listen to me, Brother Thomas. Don't fuck this up."

The blood drained from Daniel's face, and the room closed

in around him. It was so out of character. He'd never even heard Pastor Logan use the word damn before.

"God is counting on you. *I* am counting on you." He leaned back away from the camera.

And at that moment, Pastor Logan seemed more threatening than God.

"Now, I need the address, and a description of the entrance." Daniel stumbled his way through providing the information. He couldn't remember the address, but he forwarded the photo of Skylar's car to Pastor Logan, his fingers fumbling across the keypad as he sought out the contact information. Pastor Logan studied the photo on his screen. "Good. The killer—do you know his name?"

"I…no." More lies, a day spent damning his soul to hell. But Marcus's voice echoed in his mind. *I don't trust him, Dan*, and Daniel was surprised to find he was beginning to share the sentiment.

"This was good work," Pastor Logan said. "Learn as much as you can about the killer, see if you can get his name and find out anything else you can about the apartment. And then you're done. Don't tell *anyone* about any of this."

Pastor Logan stared into the camera. *Don't fuck this up* hung in the air between them. "Anything else?" he demanded.

So, they weren't going to pray or discuss saving souls here in Boston.

"No, sir. I'll tell Brother Paul you wish him a speedy recovery."

Pastor Logan cut the connection.

*

IT WAS HOURS before Marcus returned. Daniel had considered texting him several times—had even gone so far as to type out a "Just let me know you're okay"—before reconsidering and deleting it. Marcus needed time alone with his thoughts, and it wasn't Daniel's job to mother him. Besides, Daniel had had a chance to think about how he'd treated his missionary companion and knew he owed Marcus an apology.

The room had grown continually colder, and when Marcus finally came through the door, he shook his head in disgust. He banged his fist against the wall unit, but they both knew it was only to vent frustration and not a serious effort to produce heat. "You know, if there really is a hell," said Marcus, as if questioning the existence of a central aspect of the church's doctrine was perfectly acceptable, "this is what it must be like."

Daniel had put his own jacket on hours ago, and he shoved his hands deep into the pockets. "I thought hell was supposed to be hot. You know, all fire and brimstone?"

"No, Dan. Hell is Boston. Cold as fuck. And lonely." He didn't look at Daniel.

So, it was a day for destroying boundaries—behavior, language, trust. Daniel hoped he could repair at least one of them.

"I'm sorry, Marcus. I was an ass to imply I didn't trust you. I'm just so confused, and I haven't had a chance to figure out what all the new stuff in my head means. So, I lied to you."

Marcus looked at him then. "I know you lied, Dan. I was just hoping you'd tell me the truth before I had to drag it out of you." He gave the wall unit one more half-hearted slap, then came and sat on the edge of his bed. "It's Jaxtyn, right? That changed things for you, didn't it?"

Daniel sat next to him. "Yes. I see now more clearly who I am. But I can't live the way they do up here. I don't know what the answer is, or whether or not I'll be able to fight off sin for the rest of my life, but I do know I can't see Jaxtyn anymore — not until I figure out what's happening to me and how to control myself."

"You can't just walk away after what you two did this afternoon. That wouldn't be fair to him. I think you should at least explain yourself. He deserves that."

He was right, and Daniel was embarrassed he'd even considered just walking away without an explanation. He'd hurt Jaxtyn enough. "You're right, Marcus. Pastor Logan wants more information on the apartment where Skylar lives anyway. I'll go there tomorrow, take a few more pictures from the outside, and then explain to Jaxtyn why I can't see him anymore." Marcus tensed next to him, and Daniel turned to face him directly. "I lied to Pastor Logan; I told him we didn't know Skylar's name. You're right about that, too, I think. Something's wrong there. He was too interested in where Skylar lived."

"Why take any more pictures at all then?"

"Well, it was a direct command. I can't pretend we don't know where the apartment is now. I'll just take a few not-very-good shots of the front of the building, talk to Jaxtyn, and be done with it."

Marcus flopped backward onto the mattress. "You're funny," he said, looking up at the peeling paint on the ceiling. "Talk to Jaxtyn and be done with it."

"What?" Daniel asked impatiently.

Marcus only smiled. "Nothing. We'll see how that goes."

Daniel stood and then moved to his bed. "Where did you go

tonight?" He tried to keep his voice neutral, but he feared it still sounded accusatory. "You were gone a long time."

"I was at Pastor Ashton's house." Marcus sat up and looked to Daniel for a reaction.

Pastor Ashton, the head of the AME church where Marcus had been spending so much of his time, and where he discouraged Daniel from joining him because a White missionary might make people uncomfortable. "Oh?" Daniel tried to keep his growing sense of unease at bay. "You went to his house? Have you…have you been having success with him? Converting him to our faith and way of thinking?" But even as he asked the question, Daniel suspected he wouldn't like the answer.

"No… not exactly." Marcus shot him a smile, an awkward, forced thing that pleaded silently with Daniel not to judge. "More like maybe he's been having success with me."

Daniel's stomach sank to the floor. "Oh, Marcus…"

"Look, Dan. We're both learning a lot here, right? I mean, there are lots of ways to see things, different ways to spread the Word of Jesus." Daniel wanted to interrupt, but Marcus rushed on. "It's not like he's trying to discourage me from my mission — not the primary one, anyway." Daniel didn't say anything. He didn't know where to start. "And we have…deep discussions about politics. I'm learning a lot."

A weighted silence descended between the men. Marcus was clearly waiting for…what? Daniel's condemnation? His rejection?

"And this is why you're suddenly okay with my same-sex attraction? You hope it takes the heat off of you for falling away from God completely?" It wasn't a fair thing to say; Daniel knew that, and before Marcus could close up, he lifted his hand and apologized. "No. Wait. I'm sorry. That was an awful thing to say. I know you didn't mention anything about falling away from God. But…but the *church*, Marcus. It's our whole lives."

"Pastor Ashton is part of a church," Marcus countered.

As if there could be more than one true church, as if lots of pastors could offer competing versions of God. Daniel's head was spinning. "And he's teaching me things about my people I never knew. Things they don't teach us where we come from."

"Your…your *people*?" Daniel was honestly perplexed. Did he mean Christians? What could he possibly not know already?

"*Black* people, Dan."

So, they were back to that. "Marcus, I know people up here think about skin color differently than we do, but, come on, it's not like…like…"

"It is, though, Dan. There's an entire history — an entire culture — we've been taught not to see. Pastor Ashton has opened my eyes. We pray together all the time. Jesus comes to him too."

Daniel was relieved to know Marcus's relationship with Pastor Ashton was centered around Jesus, but he had no idea what to do with all the other things Marcus was telling him. "Marcus, listen. I need time to think about this. I appreciate your instincts were right about Pastor Logan, and I want to trust you know what you're doing here, too, but it's all too much for me. At least today it is. Let's talk more about everything tomorrow. We'll pray about it then, too, all right?"

"That's good, Dan. I like that you're keeping an open mind." He stood and walked to the temperature controls. He turned it on and then off. Nothing happened. "We've got to find a new place to stay."

Daniel couldn't argue with that. "Thanks for being such a good friend, Marcus."

"You got it, brother. We're going to be fine. Everything will be all right."

*

THE NEXT MORNING, as Daniel angled his church phone for one more picture of the front of Jaxtyn and Skylar's apartment, he found himself even more conflicted about what Pastor Logan had asked of him. No, not just conflicted—he was suspicious. The more he let Marcus's fears about Pastor Logan sit in his heart, the more certain he became that Marcus was right. Pastor Logan was up to something.

He waited until a bus came by to take his shot. The vehicle blocked the building number affixed to the wall by one of the front doors. Two women, one quite elderly, came out of the door which must lead to a unit on the first floor, and Daniel took a picture of them too. He began to formulate a story for Pastor Logan, explaining how he saw the unnamed murderer enter the building with two other people who looked to be about his age, and that was why he assumed he lived with other students.

He would acknowledge he could be wrong of course. In fact, the murderer might have only been visiting friends, which would explain both his car parked on the street and his presence at the triple-decker. Pastor Logan might not even recognize what all the parking fine tags were or understand what they implied about how long Skylar's car had been parked at that corner.

Once he was satisfied he'd gotten enough unhelpful photos

and had adequately fleshed out his story for Pastor Logan, Daniel realized he hadn't planned at all for the more important task he had ahead of him—explaining to Jaxtyn why he couldn't see him again. He hadn't even thought to send Jaxtyn a text asking if they could meet. It was midmorning; he was probably at class. They all were, most likely.

He considered sending a text right then, but decided "Hi, I'm outside your apartment taking pictures" was just too creepy. And what if one of them *was* home, and had been watching him standing there for so long? Enough. Daniel put his trust in God, marched across the street, climbed the rickety steps, and rang the doorbell to Jaxtyn's unit.

He didn't hear anything from inside but concluded he wouldn't necessarily. The bell would ring somewhere on the second floor, after all, possibly even in the kitchen at the far end of the hallway. He waited and then pressed the button again.

On the street, someone got out of a car and slammed its door. Daniel jumped and reached instinctively for his gun. He felt suddenly very alone and wished Marcus was with him. Sirens rose and fell in the distance—the ubiquitous background music to the City of Boston.

He wanted to go home.

He was deciding whether he should try the bell once more when the door pulled open.

"Oh, fuck me." It was Sylvie, the girl with the green hair and all the facial piercings. Only this morning, her nose, lips, eyebrows, and even her ears were devoid of ornamentation. Her eyes were puffy and red-rimmed, and her hair was a sticky mess.

"Good morning," Daniel responded. *Was she ill?* He tried not to stare at the gaping holes of her elongated earlobes

"He's not here," she said. She began to close the door.

"Wait!" Daniel put his foot in the doorway, a questionable technique they'd been taught at Sangre de Cristo, but one that came in handy now. "I just want…I want…"

Sylvie stared pointedly at his foot, then cocked her head. "What?"

He smelled the alcohol then and noticed the dampness on her cheeks. Sylvie was in pain.

"I need to leave a message for Jaxtyn."

She stared at him for a moment, then glanced up the stairs. "And what, you don't have a phone?"

"No, I do. It's just…not a good message for a text. I want to leave him a note."

She sighed and Daniel didn't pull back from her alcohol-scented breath. "Fine." She held out her hand. "Give it to me. I'll make sure he gets it."

"I haven't written it yet." Daniel waited to see if she'd crush his foot. When she didn't, he said, "Please. Just a piece of paper and a pen, and I'll be gone in ten minutes."

"I need a drink." She turned and began climbing the stairs, leaving the door open behind her. Daniel followed. "You're going to fuck him over, aren't you?" She was unsteady on the steps and didn't turn to face him. She paused near the top before putting her hand on the railing and continuing to hold it until she reached the landing. "And not in a good way."

She'd left the apartment door open, and she shuffled down the hallway toward the kitchen without pausing. Daniel avoided looking into Jaxtyn's bedroom as he followed the cloud of alcohol-infused breath and sweat. She began rummaging through a drawer and pulled out a notepad and pen. She put both on the kitchen table next to an open bottle of vodka.

The notepaper had a border of unicorns and rainbows. "Uh…do you want a drink?" she lifted the vodka and tilted it toward him. There were no glasses on the table or the counters.

"No, thank you."

She looked at the bottle and sighed, then she put it on the counter by the sink. She even held it over the sink first, as if she was contemplating dumping the vodka down the drain before deciding she wasn't ready for that. She turned then and faced him. "Are you even gay, or do you just like messing with people's heads?"

Daniel hadn't reached for the pen yet. His instincts had been screaming at him to pay attention, to be on guard. He considered her question. Could he simply say no? Not after yesterday's kiss. But he wasn't gay, not in the way Sylvie meant, not in a way that implied a lifestyle. But he also couldn't begin to explain how his same-sex attraction was nothing more than a temptation to sin, a test of his faith in Jesus's strength and his belief in the grace of God. That was too nuanced for this moment.

And Sylvie was drunk. Alcohol was her demon, obviously, and she seemed to be having just as much success fighting hers as Daniel had fighting his. They were alike that way at least, as were all God's children.

"Yes. I'm gay." He was surprised to hear himself say it. It was the first time he'd clearly articulated the thought, let alone spoken the words out loud.

Sylvie blinked; she was surprised too. "Oh," she said.

And then…something happened.

He was infused with warmth, and Jesus filled his heart so suddenly and powerfully he shook, as if a jolt of electricity had run through his body. The room brightened with the blazing light of God, which was surely pouring out of Daniel, because Sylvie must have seen it too, her eyes widening when he rose from the chair and approached her. She stood exposed before him—a sinner just like Daniel, in pain and distress, estranged from God, cut off from the truth.

"Sylvie," he said, his voice choked with emotion. "You're in pain. I see that. I *feel* that." He wanted to reach for her, but he didn't. Even through his tear-blurred eyes, he saw she was leery. "I'm in pain too," he continued. "We all are. But you don't need to be. You don't need to be anyone other than who you are. You can put aside your burdens. Just lay your fears down and allow yourself to be loved for who you are."

She swallowed, then let out a soft gasp.

"Sylvie, I *love* you." Jesus loves you, he almost said, but at the last moment, he heard Marcus's voice reminding him to meet people where they were, to be present with them from the very start of their journey to Christ, even if that journey started with stepping away from a bottle. She looked confused, and her hands shook silently at her sides.

"Sylvie, let me acknowledge your pain, let me sit with it. No judgment, no lectures. Just let me offer you the little strength I have, so you can learn to love yourself again. Do you want that? Do you want to feel loved?"

"Yes." It was a barely discernable whisper. Daniel wasn't even sure she knew she had spoken.

God's grace flowed through Daniel. A river. A flood. "Sylvie, can you feel it? The small flame in your heart? Love waiting to blossom?"

"Yes." This time more certain, she seemed surprised, and she let out a soft sob.

Daniel reached out his hands, and she leaned forward and clasped them. They would pray, but Sylvie didn't need to know that's what they were doing. "Feel the flame's warmth. Let it grow. Know you are loved. You are perfect just as you are."

Another sob, this one accompanied by a puff of vodka. Daniel pressed forward. *Jesus,* he prayed silently, *fill this sinner with your love. Open her spirit to receive God's grace. She's ready, Lord. She's waiting for you.*

"Do you feel the love, Sylvie?"

"Yes." She leaned into him then, and he pulled her into a tight embrace.

"That's Jesus. He loves you. He died for you. You don't need to understand that or even believe it—not right now. Just know his love is holding you up. He'll always hold you up, Sylvie, forever." He ran his palm across the top of her head, and she began sobbing in earnest. Her whole body shook against him.

"You feel him," Daniel whispered into her ear. "He'll never leave you now."

She could only nod her assent, and Daniel took the full weight of her into his arms. *Thank you, Jesus. Thank you for leading me here to this godforsaken city and to this sinner. Thank you for filling her heart with your love.*

Thank you for allowing me to serve your will.

Chapter Twenty

"WHAT THE *FUCK*, Sylvie?" Jaxtyn read the short note Daniel had left for him again. "He was here, and you didn't text me? And he left *this*?" He shook the note for emphasis.

Sylvie sat at the kitchen table. Fragrant steam wafted from the cup of tea in front of her. "I told you, Jax. I didn't see the note until this afternoon." She wrapped her hands around the mug. "He must have written it when I was sleeping."

"And you left him here *alone*?" Jaxtyn demanded. He read the brief note again.

> *Jaxtyn, Thank you for helping me to understand myself.*
> *I'm sorry, but I can't see you again. Don't shut Jesus out*
> *of your heart. Yours in Christ, Daniel.*

He dropped the note in front of Sylvie. "Tell us again exactly what he said."

Skylar, who'd been resting his butt against the sink, watching the back and forth between his roommates, stepped forward. "Jax, I think you're missing the most important part where Sylvie claims to be a Christian now."

Sylvie shook her head. "I didn't say that."

"No?" Skylar persisted. "You said the CeeNee showed you Jesus."

"Not...exactly." Sylvie looked more thoughtful than offended. "He talked to me about love, and how...profound love can be, how healing it is." She sipped her tea. "And then he spoke about Jesus as a physical presence, and...I know this sounds weird...but it was like I could feel him, deep inside of me, a peaceful, loving presence."

"See," said Skylar. "I would have sworn *Jax* would have been the first one to feel the CeeNee deep inside of him."

"Not the CeeNee, Skylar," Sylvie said. "Jesus."

"Jesus," Jaxtyn repeated, in an entirely different tone than Sylvie had used. "Can we get back to what he said? Why won't he see me again?"

"I don't know, Jax. He showed up in the middle of the morning looking for you. When he learned you weren't here, he said he wanted a notepad so he could leave a message for you. Then, you know...the whole Jesus thing happened." She waved her hands to encompass the events of the day—her "conversion," as Skylar mockingly put it. "Then, I remember he helped me dump the vodka down the drain—"

"Not the chocolate-flavored vodka—?" Skylar interrupted.

"Sky! Let her finish."

"And then the next thing I knew, I woke up in bed. It was

midafternoon, Daniel was gone, and the note for you was on the table."

"I hope he didn't steal anything," Skylar said.

"You should have texted me as soon as he got here," Jaxtyn said.

"Jesus," Sylvie exclaimed, clearly frustrated with the onslaught of advice and questions. "All I know is he was here for me when I needed someone."

"Wait," Skylar said. "Which 'he' are you talking about? The CeeNee or his imaginary friend?"

Sylvie stood. "Make fun all you want. It was a very real experience for me. I *felt* it. I think there's something to the Jesus stuff." She picked up her tea and began walking toward the door.

"Oh, come on, Syl," Jaxtyn called to her. "You had a transcendent experience. Just like we have during meditation. You don't need to make anything supernatural out of it."

She turned in the doorway. "No, Jax. You're wrong. This wasn't some temporary glimpse of something bigger than us, some 'cosmic interconnection.'" She made air quotes with her fingers when she said cosmic interconnection, and Jaxtyn was hurt she intentionally made the phrase sound ridiculous. Sylvie noticed his discomfort. "Sorry. What I mean is when that happens during meditation it makes me feel so small, like I might just disappear into some vast, incomprehensible…nothingness. This was different. It was *personal*—feeling a power greater than myself, that somehow still connected with me as a human being needing love and support."

Sylvie looked between the men. Jaxtyn thought she was hoping for validation, some confirmation they understood what she was saying, but he could only shake his head. Skylar walked to the refrigerator and opened the door. Then he turned to Sylvie. "You dumped the beer too, didn't you?"

*

"HE SAID HE won't see me again," Jaxtyn told Vishnu. "He's ignoring all my texts."

Sunday's meditation session at the Open Lotus Sangha had not gone well. The dirty bomb attack had everyone on edge, and there was a palpable sense something had to give. Things couldn't keep going this way indefinitely. "Let's just give them whatever the hell they want and be done with it," one of the meditators had blurted out, only five minutes into the session. No one seemed surprised by the interruption.

"No," insisted someone else. "That's just giving in to the terrorists. It's what they want."

"So let them win. Who cares anymore? I want my life back."

"What about all the people down there who don't want to live under a Christian dictatorship? Don't we have an obligation to them?"

"We'll help them move here—"

"Let's take the war to them—"

"Let's join Canada—"

And so the meditation session deteriorated into a maelstrom of anger and conflicting opinions. Vishnu hadn't even tried to keep things on track. Afterward, he and Jaxtyn met privately in one of the library's study rooms, where they were able to focus on the immediate, tangible problem of Jaxtyn's rejection by Daniel.

"I mean, the kiss was amazing," Jaxtyn repeated. "Why

would he just decide to ghost me?"

"Well," Vishnu replied carefully, "you did say he called you a demon."

"Not *a* demon, *his* demon. It was possessive, almost romantic."

Vishnu shrugged. "Uh-huh." He took a deep breath. "Look, Jaxtyn. I appreciate your keeping an open mind and all, and I'm not saying there's anything wrong, exactly, with dating a CeeNee, but—"

"His name's Daniel."

"Daniel then. But my point is maybe this isn't the best time for you two. Maybe he understands that. Things are too tense—"

"But, Vishnu, aren't you the one who's always saying we all need to figure out a way to live together? That we need to get along somehow?"

Vishnu threw his hands up in exasperation. "And how's that working out for us?" he shook his head. "Maybe they're right. Maybe we're all better off if we go our separate ways."

Jaxtyn had no response to that, and both men sat quietly for a few moments.

"But I really like him, Vishnu. I've said it before; he's important somehow. I can't just let him fade away."

Vishnu sighed. "Fine. It makes no sense to me. I think you're letting yourself get carried away by an infatuation. But I'll always support you. You know that."

Jaxtyn let out a breath he'd been holding. "Thank you, Vishnu. So, what should I do? How do I get him to talk to me again?"

To kiss me again.

Vishnu pushed his chair back and stood. "To start, you're going to need to bone up on the boy." He smiled. "No pun intended."

Jaxtyn stood also. "How do you mean?"

"Let's head upstairs to the religion section of the library and find out what makes him tick."

Chapter Twenty-One

"IT WAS A miracle, Pastor Logan. Jesus turned me into a vessel for his will. I brought that woman to God." Daniel knew he sounded boastful, and he could almost feel Marcus rolling his eyes next to him. He'd had to…manage the truth, just a bit, for Pastor Logan. They'd already decided not to reveal they'd been inside Skylar's apartment, so he and Marcus agreed to relocate the episode with Sylvie to the student center on campus.

It was frightening how the lying got easier the more he did it.

"Yes, so you said, Brother Thomas. That's certainly good news." There was a brief stuttering noise as the cell signal faded then reconnected. "Now, have you learned anything more about the killer?" Marcus tapped his foot against Daniel's. *See?* He was saying. *The guy's obsessed.*

"No, Pastor Logan."

That was followed by silence. Was he waiting for an apology? A promise to try harder? He'd saved Sylvie's soul! Why weren't they talking about that?

"Very well," Pastor Logan said. "We've identified him through the car registration and the university's records. His name is Skylar Martin. He's twenty-one years old. He lives in one of the units on the second floor of the building you identified. Get back to the campus. Ask around and see if you can find anyone who knows him. Meet him if you can. See what you can learn."

"Yes, sir. We will," Marcus replied. He tapped Daniel's foot again. "I'm very proud of Brother Thomas for having brought a sinner to God. I'm encouraged we can make progress here."

"Yes, yes. Of course. Let me know when you learn more about Skylar Martin." He signed off.

Marcus exhaled. "Jesus," he exclaimed.

"Marcus," Daniel cautioned.

"Yeah, yeah, I know. But come on, Dan, that was nuts."

Daniel agreed. It was as if Pastor Logan had completely abandoned their purpose of doing God's work. "Well, I am proud of you, Dan. I didn't just say that to needle Logan. That was good work you did with Sylvie. And…well, it's too bad about what happened…with Jaxtyn, I mean."

It had been several days, and already there were a half dozen text messages from Jaxtyn on his phone. He'd obviously read Daniel's note but wasn't willing to accept the fact Daniel wasn't willing to meet with him again. His last message ended with: *And what did you do to Sylvie?* It was a teasing piece of bait dangled in front of him—an invitation to engage. Daniel wasn't biting.

"I just wonder," Marcus began, "If maybe you weren't a

little premature with—"

"Marcus, no. Stop. We've been over it. I can't see him again. God put him in my path to teach me a lesson about humility. I've learned the lesson. It's over."

"Okay, okay," Marcus sighed. "Hey, it's early still. Do you want to go out?"

"Out?"

Marcus punched Daniel's shoulder. "Yeah, Dan. Out. Like, outside. We've been here for weeks, and we've never even eaten at a restaurant. Let's go into the North End and splurge on an Italian meal."

"We're not tourists, Marcus." Daniel stood and walked to the window. "We're here to save souls. And now that the secondary mission is behind us—"

"Is it? Are we just going to ignore Logan's demand we find out more about Skylar?"

"Yes. Or, we can just tell him we tried, but no one on campus seemed to know who he was." But that would mean lying. Again. Still, something was off about the entire secondary mission, and Marcus was right—they needed to be cautious with Pastor Logan now. "I mean, I guess we could try, just ask one or two people. Then it wouldn't be a lie."

Marcus nodded. "Sure, Dan. Whatever you need to do to feel good about it. Personally, I'm learning I don't mind lying to Logan."

Daniel frowned. "Look, I know a lot of things are changing, but—"

He was interrupted by a knock on the door.

"Expecting anyone?" he asked Marcus.

"No. Maybe they've come to fix the heat." Marcus went to the door and peered through the peephole. "Oh." He shot Daniel a guilty look and opened the door.

Jaxtyn stood in the doorway. A canvas bag was slung over his shoulder, clearly weighted down with its contents. His hair was disheveled, and his cheeks glowed from exertion. "I can't believe this building doesn't have an elevator," he said, bracing a hand against the doorjamb while he caught his breath.

"It does," replied Marcus. "It just doesn't always work."

Jaxtyn shook his head and ran his tongue across his lower lip. Daniel remembered the taste of those lips, and his face heated. "Can I come in?"

"Um, actually—" Daniel began before Marcus interrupted him.

"Don't be such a dick, Dan." He pulled the door fully open. "Come on in."

Jaxtyn stepped through and dropped his heavy bag on the floor. He eyed the small room. "Uh, nice place you have here. Cozy."

"Dinosaurs," Marcus said.

"Huh?"

"Never mind him," Daniel said. "You can't stay. We were just heading out to dinner."

Marcus rolled his eyes. "No, we weren't. We're not *tourists*, Dan."

"I just have a few questions," Jaxtyn said as he bent into the bag at his feet and began pulling out books. Was that the Bible? "I've been doing a lot of reading—you know, so I can understand you better, and your religion. Building bridges and all that." He held up a book. Yes, it was the Bible. And it had sticky notes throughout its pages. "It should only take a minute."

*

THREE HOURS LATER, Daniel's head was spinning. Marcus had excused himself to go rinse the remains of the biryani takeaway container in the bathroom sink. He'd been in there a long time, and Daniel suspected he was just trying to avoid the conversation. He'd never been a fan of Bible studies.

"But it still doesn't make *sense*," Jaxtyn said again. "If it represents the infallible word of God, how can parts of it be wrong?"

Marcus shook his head as reentered the room. "Guys," he began. "Please. You've been over this—"

"It's not *wrong*, Jaxtyn," Daniel insisted. "It's just two different perspectives of the same event."

"But you can't have different perspectives of the facts," Jaxtyn insisted. "Either the stone was already rolled away from the tomb when the women got there or it wasn't. Either an angel appeared in the tomb or it didn't. Either guards were present or they weren't."

They'd pulled the little table near the bed so Jaxtyn could sit in the room's one chair with his books and notes spread out on the tabletop while Daniel sat on the bed's edge, elbows propped on the table opposite Jaxtyn. "I think it's not as simple as that," Daniel said. "You may be taking things out of context."

"Oh, come on, Daniel. It's the most important part of the story, right? The resurrection? You'd think the Bible would only have one version of that."

Daniel simply shook his head. He knew there were accounts

in the Bible, especially in the Old Testament, that at first glance seemed to conflict with each other. But he also knew the church had answers to all them, and he didn't burden himself with trying to make sense of the arguments—they could be pretty arcane. And the important thing was the message of the Bible—not how all its pieces fit together.

Marcus, on the other hand, was always interested in anything that seemed to challenge the church's authority. "Let me see," he said. He sat next to Daniel on the bed, squeezing against him to get a better view of the books on the table.

Jaxtyn turned his notepad in so Marcus could see it and tapped his pencil on a sentence he'd underlined. "Look, it says two women went to visit the tomb, and there was an earthquake and an angel appeared and rolled back the stone and then sat on top of it." He turned to Daniel. "Which one was this again?"

Daniel sighed. "The gospel of Matthew," he answered reluctantly.

"Right," Jaxtyn continued. "And the angel told the women Jesus was gone—"

"Risen," interrupted Daniel. "He didn't just disappear."

"Okay," Jaxtyn said. "But then the women hurry off to tell people. They didn't even look inside the tomb, even though they just watched an angel open it up by rolling away the stone!" He looked between the two missionaries for a reaction.

Marcus leaned forward. "Well, that *is* interesting," he said.

Jaxtyn nodded and turned a page in his notebook. "But then over here, the Bible says three women went to the tomb, and the stone was already gone, and some guy was already inside, but it wasn't Jesus. And he told them Jesus was…what was the word again, Daniel?"

"Risen."

"Right," Jaxtyn continued. "But then this guy tells the women to go tell others, but they don't! They just leave and they don't tell anyone, because they're too afraid. Which one was this again, Daniel?"

Another sigh. "The gospel of Mark."

Marcus reached across the table and slid the Bible to him. He opened the book, found the passage he wanted, and read for a moment. "Huh," he said at last. "I thought I remembered something about men in shining garments."

"There is!" Jaxtyn exclaimed. "That's in yet another version. It's in…" He began flipping through the notebook, "It's in—"

"Luke," interrupted Daniel, pushing himself off the bed. "It's in the gospel of Luke. And enough already. This is ridiculous. It doesn't change anything. The important part is that Jesus suffered and died for our sins, was resurrected, and belief in Him is the only true path for receiving God's grace."

Jaxtyn leaned back from the table. "Okay," he said, correctly reading the finality in Daniel's voice. "I just think it's odd, that's all. I mean, only one of these versions can be true, so these others are wrong, and this is the most important part of the whole story, so why not just stick to one version—even if they couldn't be sure which one was true?"

Daniel had walked to the window. "I don't know, Jaxtyn," he said to his own reflection in the glass. Then he turned. "The Gospels were written nearly two thousand years ago. We can't hold these men to modern standards of accuracy." Marcus simply shrugged. This kind of thing didn't bother him, but he had a more pragmatic view of authority.

Jaxtyn tilted his head. He didn't seem convinced. "So, when it says in Leviticus a man should not lie with a man the way he does with a woman, that's maybe not fully accurate either?"

Marcus groaned. "No, please. Not Leviticus." He stood from the bed. "Does anyone else want me to run out and get some dessert?"

Jaxtyn ignored him and leaned over his bag on the floor, rummaging about in it before withdrawing two more books. "And this one," he said, holding up a small textbook titled *The Epistles of Paul*. "I mean, seriously, why on earth were they arguing about whether the first Christians needed to be circumcised?"

Marcus smiled. "Dan isn't circumcised," he added helpfully.

"*Marcus!*"

"Uh…" Jaxtyn said.

"They weren't arguing about it," Daniel said. "Paul traveled throughout the Mediterranean founding new Christian communities among the pagans. These epistles are letters he wrote afterward helping them stay on track and clearing up confusion for the first Christian communities."

"Confusion about circumcision?" Jaxtyn asked. Clearly, he thought that was as odd as it sounded.

"Not just that. Most of the confusion was around whether or not new Christians had to become Jews first and obey all the Old Testament laws, like dietary restrictions and keeping the Sabbath and, yes, circumcision."

"And do they?" Jaxtyn asked. "Need to follow the old laws?"

"No," Daniel replied. "Those laws were a covenant between

God and the Jewish people. Jesus's death and resurrection ful-filled that covenant, and the old laws don't apply anymore."

Jaxtyn slowly nodded his head. "That's convenient. And men not having sex with men—was that part of the old law too?"

Daniel sighed. "Well, yes. But—"

"Well, case closed, then!" Jaxtyn exclaimed. "So, what's the problem?"

"You know," Marcus interrupted them. "When Skylar and I were stuck in the refrigerator, he told me Jaxtyn was studying to become a lawyer. I get that now."

This was getting out of control. Daniel tried to regroup. "There are other reasons why God's design for love and procrea-tion is—"

"Wait." Jaxtyn held up a hand. "Paul was going around in-troducing people to Jesus? Telling them about how to get God's grace and stuff?"

Daniel sensed a trap. "Yes," he replied cautiously.

"That's what you guys are doing, too, right?"

Marcus nodded.

"But these people—they kept getting off track, and Paul had to keep circling back, correcting them, right?"

Where was he going with this?

"Well, that's what you need to do with Sylvie. And with me too. She keeps getting confused and isn't sure how she should pray. And you need to keep teaching me too; I didn't completely get it the first couple of times."

Daniel barely managed to suppress his grin at the obvious ploy. *He's refusing to accept the fact I don't want to keep seeing him. But, well, maybe I've changed my mind?*

Marcus laughed. He saw it too. "Clever," he said.

Jaxtyn struggled to maintain a straight face. "No, I'm serious. We need you to send us epistles. Show us how to do this. And since you're right here in Boston, you don't even have to write anything down. You can just come visit us." He left a brief space for an objection, but Daniel remained silent. "Wonderful! Does Friday afternoon work?"

Chapter Twenty-Two

"OH, FOR CHRISSAKE, Sylvie, give it a rest." Skylar slammed the refrigerator door shut and took a deep drink from a carton of orange juice.

"That better be the one with your name on it," Sylvie said. She was sitting at the kitchen table playing Jesus videos on her tablet. That's what Skylar called them, always sounding disgusted with the entire situation.

Jaxtyn was simply glad she wasn't drinking. He'd just removed the coffee pot from the machine, and he surreptitiously eyed Skylar as he carried it to the table. The orange juice carton had masking tape on it reading *Jax*, but he wisely remained silent about that. He poured Sylvie more coffee and watched silently as she dumped spoonfuls of sugar into the mug.

One vice at a time.

The Jesus videos were more in the nature of testimonials—

people telling their stories about how a relationship with Jesus helped them kick their addictions. On the screen, an older, balding man described how Jesus's love had allowed him to love himself, and to develop enough self-confidence to quit gambling.

"What the hell does self-confidence have to do with gambling?" Skylar asked. Sylvie ignored him, but Skylar seemed determined to get a rise out of her this morning. "You know, you don't need the CeeNee's imaginary friend to help you get your life in order."

"Maybe Jesus could help you with your porn addiction, Sky," Sylvie shot back.

"Yeah? Maybe he has a stash of demon porn he'd be willing to share?" Skylar put the juice carton down on the counter and picked up a mug. He held it to Jaxtyn. "Although I guess demon porn is your specialty now, isn't it?"

Jaxtyn filled the mug and then replaced the carafe in the machine. "Not yet, but I think I'm making progress." He sat across from Sylvie. "He's coming over on Friday afternoon, by the way."

Sylvie looked up. "Good. I need to talk to him. It's already starting to feel like maybe it was a dream—the experience I had when we prayed together."

"Maybe it was," Skylar said. "Or a delusion or something. Is he bringing the one with the muscles again? I liked him. I wouldn't mind spending more time locked in a refrigerator with him."

"I don't think Marcus is coming, no." Jaxtyn exchanged a glance with Sylvie. "And I think it would be best if you weren't here either."

Skylar was already heading out of the kitchen with his coffee. "No worries, kids. I have a super-secret meeting with my cool friends on Friday night, so you'll have to handle Bible camp by yourselves."

"He's such an asshole," Sylvie said after Skylar had left the room.

"I know. He is sometimes. I worry about him though. I was wondering how long it would be before he and his new friends got up to something again."

Sylvie shut her tablet. "Do you think they'll be going back down there?"

He would have liked to say no, but he couldn't. The New Riders may have gotten spooked by their detainment last time, but Jaxtyn suspected they'd be back at it. He didn't fault them—they were helping queer youth, after all, kids at real risk of harm—but he did worry. He wished everything was different.

"Why is everything so fucked up?" he asked.

"I don't know, Jax. But speaking of fucked up, the lady downstairs told me three more of the security cameras in our neighborhood were vandalized last night. Why would people do that?"

A sense of foreboding washed over Jaxtyn. "Could be just kids?" But he didn't think so.

"I don't know," Sylvie said. "It's a lot of work to take out so many cameras, and all within just a few days. If there was something valuable around here—like a jewelry store or something, I'd be worried someone was planning something."

"It's probably nothing," Jaxtyn said, despite all his instincts screaming otherwise. "But we should be careful."

*

AFTER CLASSES ON Friday morning, Jaxtyn arrived home to find Sylvie cleaning the kitchen. She'd brought the desk chair from Jaxtyn's bedroom and pulled the table out a few feet from the wall, so all three of them would be able to sit around it. A potted plant with a balloon reading "Happy Birthday" sat on the counter.

Sylvie rubbed at a spot on the sink's faucet. A bit over the top just for Daniel, but Jaxtyn wasn't going to criticize. "Whose birthday is it?" he asked. He was usually pretty good about remembering such things and was certain both Skylar's and Sylvie's were late in the autumn.

Sylvie twisted the sponge under the water. "Someone thinks it's Skylar's. This was waiting on our steps inside the front door." She nodded to the plant. It was a sad-looking thing, scrawny and without flowers, in a cheap plastic pot. It didn't look like it came from a florist. "The woman downstairs said a man knocked on her door this morning asking where Skylar lived. She said he left them on our steps. There's no note."

That was odd, and the sense of unease that had been clawing at Jaxtyn all week ratcheted up a notch.

"I figure it was probably some guy Skylar laid who didn't get the memo that he only does one-night stands," Sylvie said.

"Why the birthday greetings, I wonder?" Jaxtyn asked.

Sylvie shrugged. "Beats me. Maybe he lied to the guy to throw him off. Or maybe he couldn't find a balloon that said, 'Thanks for the Blowjob.'"

Jaxtyn snorted. "Well, we'll have to wait till tomorrow to find out. He told me he'll be on the Cape tonight with his new friends. One of them has a house there. Or his parents do, I guess."

"Plotting," Sylvie said. "It's dangerous."

"I won't argue with you." He looked around the kitchen. "Looks nice in here."

"Thanks," she said. "We'll have to meet here. Praying in your bedroom would be too weird after what happened with you guys last time. And I don't want us all in my room."

Last time. There certainly wouldn't be a repeat of that this afternoon, not with the three of us here. But that was all right. Jaxtyn was just glad he'd gotten Daniel to agree to come over. He felt a twinge of guilt over the circumstances. He didn't want to mislead Daniel, but the more he thought about it, the more convinced he became Jesus was simply a manifestation of the need for spiritual connection and grounding—a familiar model, and a very personal one, that people could use to explain the experience of universal connection.

Sylvie had more or less admitted as much when she described her experience of Jesus as being more powerful than meditating because it was focused on another being, someone who would love her and forgive her despite all her faults. It was the opposite of the transcendent experience of melting into the oneness of the universe Jaxtyn aimed for when he meditated.

He'd never realized before how that might frighten some people—make them feel too insignificant. Of course, Jesus or some god or goddess or whatever was better if you were concerned about such things. Sylvie wanted a higher power to *care* about her. It wasn't healthy, but if it was a first step on the road to sobriety, Jaxtyn was happy for her.

Still, if he was going to have any kind of a relationship with Daniel—and he did want that, as hopeless as it might seem—he would have to try to convince him there was more than one way of understanding spirituality.

As if on cue, a knock on the door announced Daniel's arrival.

*

DANIEL LOOKED GOOD—smiling and confident, a man on a mission, so to speak. He wore new well-fitting trousers and a tight, button-down shirt in a moss green color that highlighted his dark copper hair, which was beginning to grow long, winging out over his ears and falling across his forehead. It was a good look for him. Jaxtyn reminded himself this wasn't a date, but he wondered if Daniel hadn't put a little extra effort into his appearance.

He was becoming accustomed to how the whole praying-to-Jesus thing went. Occasionally, Daniel would pause to explain something to Sylvie before returning to beseeching Jesus to fill their hearts. Jaxtyn didn't interrupt, but ever since he'd been reading up on Christianity and the Bible, questions kept arising he'd love to ask—respectfully, of course—about the nature of Jesus, both physically and spiritually. How did Daniel think it *worked*, mechanically, for Jesus to fill his heart? What did that *mean*?

But for Sylvie's sake, he decided to remain silent and go with the flow.

And she did seem to be getting something out of it. She smiled and nodded, and honestly seemed to mean it when she told Daniel that yes, she *could* feel Jesus in her heart. Yes, she *could* feel his love and forgiveness. Jaxtyn was amused by his brief stab of jealousy when Daniel and Sylvie clasped their hands together.

He shook his head and tried to bring his attention back to what Daniel was saying, to the words he used in prayer. But it was no use. He only wanted to run his fingers through the man's hair, to taste those lips again.

Sylvie and Daniel were both glowing when the prayer session finally came to an end. It was early evening, and Sylvie had clearly regained the sense of peace and inner strength her first exposure to Jesus had brought to her. Jaxtyn thought Daniel would be exhausted, but he looked energized, ready to take on anything. Maybe even his demons. Jaxtyn had a few ideas about that.

"Thank you," Sylvie said. "That was beautiful." She stood and walked to the sink, leaving the two men alone at the table.

Daniel looked at Jaxtyn and raised a questioning eyebrow. Jaxtyn read his silent questions as: *Did Jesus come to you again? Does it make more sense to you now? Do you see how important it is for Sylvie?* Jaxtyn wanted Daniel to mean: *Can we go into your room and make out?*

"Tea?" Sylvie asked.

"No," replied Jaxtyn. "We're going out to dinner."

"Oh," Sylvie replied. "Great. Where should we go?"

"No," Jaxtyn said. "I'm taking *Daniel* out to dinner." He looked across the table and raised his own eyebrow. *You know you want to. We don't have to call it a date, but we both know it is. Don't you dare say no.*

Daniel colored, and some of the confidence slipped from his face, but he nodded his assent.

"Oh," Sylvie said again, this time with a knowing smile. "In that case, have fun you two."

*

"I SHOULD HAVE asked if you like pizza," Jaxtyn said as they slid into opposite sides of the red vinyl booth. The waitress left a pile of menus on the table—specials, wine list, cocktails, microbrews—and left with a smile aimed at Jaxtyn and a promise to be back in a minute.

"Who doesn't like pizza?" Daniel picked up the food menu. A frown appeared as he scanned the menu.

"It's my treat," Jaxtyn said. "I invited you."

"No. Don't be ridiculous. I can't let you pay for me. That would seem like...like..."

"Uh-huh," Jaxtyn grinned. "And that would be bad because..."

Before Daniel could respond, the server returned. She stood very close to Jaxtyn. She was likely a couple of years on either side of thirty, with heavily applied makeup. "And what are you two handsome boys having to drink this evening?"

"Two of the local microbrews please," Jaxtyn said.

"Sure, I'll need to scan your IDs." She placed her device on the table and swiped her finger across the screen while she waited for them to hand her their IDs.

"Just water for me, thanks," Daniel said.

"Sure thing," she said. "But I'll still need your ID if there's any alcohol at the table."

Jaxtyn handed her his card, and she passed it over the screen which beeped and turned green. He supposed he should have asked first if ordering beer was okay with Daniel. He suspected he didn't drink, but he didn't think it would be horrible if he let his hair down a little, maybe just had a taste? But now as he watched Daniel nervously hand over his ID, he regretted his decision.

The machine turned red, and the waitress looked at the card. "Oh, South Carolina. We can't take these. Do you have your federal ID?"

"What's wrong with this one?" Jaxtyn asked. He took it from her before she could hand it back to Daniel. He scanned it quickly, in part because he was curious to learn how old Daniel was. It was a bad photo, but wasn't that true of all IDs? A quick look at his birthdate revealed he was twenty — old enough to drink in Massachusetts. After the Supreme Court ruled the Minimum Drinking Age Act was unconstitutional, most states reverted back to eighteen to increase tax revenue.

"My federal ID is in the hotel safe."

The waitress frowned. "I'm sorry." She seemed honestly sympathetic. "I'm glad you made it out of there, but we can't accept IDs that don't have a date of birth."

Jaxtyn turned his attention back to Daniel's ID. Wasn't that his birthdate right there, next to the expiration date? He looked more closely. *Date of Life*, it read. That was an odd way of putting it. Daniel reached across the table and retrieved his ID from Jaxtyn's fingers.

"We'll both just have water," Jaxtyn told her.

She placed her hand on Jaxtyn's shoulder and gave it a squeeze. She leaned in and whispered, "If you went to the bar and ordered a beer, I won't notice if you bring it back to the table."

"Thanks," Jaxtyn replied. "But that's okay. I didn't know about the South Carolina IDs. My boyfriend is new here. We're still figuring things out."

Daniel kicked him under the table.

"Oh," she said as she took a step back. Her face transformed and then relaxed. "Got it. Well, good for you, then. Now I'm doubly glad you got out of there," she told Daniel. "Back with the water in a flash, and an order of fries on the house." She winked and headed off.

"Why did you *do* that?" Daniel moaned. He flushed a deep red, and Jaxtyn decided he'd never tire of seeing it. "I'm not your—" He lowered his voice to a whisper. "—boyfriend."

"A guy can dream, can't he?" Jaxtyn reached forward and motioned for Daniel to hand him the ID again. "Besides, I wanted to let her know she doesn't have to keep flirting with me. This will be easier for her, and she'll still get a nice tip." He looked at the ID again. "So, what's with this? Is 'date of life' what I think it is?"

"Probably." Daniel sounded defensive. It wasn't an attitude Jaxtyn had seen from him before. "We don't believe in waiting until you're nine months old before you start calculating your age. I mean, you exist from day one. That defines how old you are—not some random event almost a year into your life."

Jaxtyn schooled his expression. "Well, being born isn't exactly *random*…"

"No," Daniel acknowledged. "I shouldn't have put it that way. But it also doesn't mark the start of your life. The day before you're born, you're alive and kicking. Ask any woman who's given birth, and she'll tell you the truth of that. It's not like you just spring into existence for the first time at the moment of birth. In fact, you're pretty much the same the day before you're born as you are the day after. God breathed life into you the moment you were conceived. So, it only makes sense to start counting your age from that moment."

Daniel gripped the paper-wrapped bundle of silverware beside his menus. It was obvious he was expecting pushback. Jaxtyn needed time to think about what he was hearing. His immediate instinct was to reject it out of hand. Fetuses in the womb weren't at all the same as newborn babies, even if it is only one moment in time separating the two.

But Daniel seemed sincere, and Jaxtyn didn't want to offend him. Not if he didn't have to. And, so far, other than his insistence on a complicated relationship between Jesus and God's grace and being saved by faith, Daniel hadn't come across as *irrational*, exactly, just…zealous. He was on a mission, after all.

"I… I don't know what to think about that yet."

Daniel's grip on the silverware loosened, and he ran his fingers lightly over the bundle as if to smooth it out, making sure everything was in its place. "Okay. Fair enough. I know that's not how you think about things up here. But it's important to us."

Jaxtyn breathed a sigh of relief. Daniel didn't expect agreement, which was a relief, because Jaxtyn didn't agree. But as long as neither wanted to fight about it, it looked like they'd be able to sit comfortably with the difference between them, at least for now. "Is it hard for you?" Jaxtyn asked. "Always having to be prepared for a fight? To have people reject what you share with them?"

Daniel studied his hands and then looked up. "Thank you for asking that. Yes, sometimes it's…difficult. But we're trained to deal with it." He paused and opened his menu, flipping its pages without really looking. He closed the menu. "It's just…I don't like being on guard all the time, you know? I mean, the whole point of the Christian community is that we're one with God, united by Jesus's love. It's hard to hold yourself at a distance from everyone.

It's hard to be afraid all the time."

Jaxtyn reached across and touched Daniel's elbow. He wanted to hold his hand but knew that would only scare him off. "You don't need to keep a distance from me."

Daniel nodded and then turned back to the menu. "Pizza?"

"Yes. Anchovies?"

"Ew, no. Mushrooms?"

"Gross. No."

"Pineapple?"

"Absolutely not."

They both studied the menu. "Pepperoni?" they asked simultaneously.

Jaxtyn grinned. "See? There's always common ground."

The conversation flowed freely after that, and Jaxtyn could almost convince himself it *was* a first date. He learned about Daniel's childhood and the storybook setting he thought only existed in old movies. A loving mother and father, actively involved in their only child's education. A small but tidy house in a suburban neighborhood. They even had a dog. In his imagination, Jaxtyn filled in the picture with a picket fence and gingerbread trim on a wide front porch.

He told Daniel about his own childhood, as different from Daniel's as could be. His mother was Swedish, and she was in the United States on a student visa when she became pregnant and decided to stay. She was a wild, free-spited woman who would have been called a hippie decades ago. If she ever knew who Jaxtyn's father was, she didn't share that information. They roamed from spot to spot when he was a boy, and as a teen, he gradually learned to live more and more independently. Although they exchanged messages occasionally, he didn't know where she was living at that moment.

Daniel seemed appalled, so Jaxtyn changed the subject.

He asked about Marcus's use of the word "dinosaurs," and Daniel told him the story of his visit to the arc, how the exhibit tried to explain the fossils were laid down by the flood, and how he and Marcus used "dinosaurs" as code for calling bullshit on someone when they said something clearly not true—when they were trying too hard to convince someone else, or perhaps even themselves, of something they wanted to believe but couldn't.

"Dinosaurs," Jaxtyn said, grinning. "I like it."

Daniel hinted that his hometown was a religious community of sorts, built around the central presence and power of their church. But they were careful not to get too far into controversy—nothing about federalism or states' rights or government-sponsored religion. Certainly nothing about race, gender identity, or sexual orientation. Although they'd have to talk about all that eventually, wouldn't they, if anything were to become of…this.

And Jaxtyn was surprised to realize he already thought of them that way—as if they were at the start of a possible relationship. It was a crazy idea, though, wasn't it?

As they were finishing the pizza, the conversation had turned more personal. Jaxtyn told Daniel about his part-time job at the library where the Open Lotus met. It wasn't much money he explained, but Skylar covered most of their rent, or, well, his parents did. And State schools were free in Massachusetts—at least until you turned twenty-six. So you could attend part-time for up to eight years before you had to earn a degree.

"Which is good for me, because prelaw is hard work,"

Jaxtyn said.

They both laughed when Jaxtyn described Sylvie's job at the body ink and piercing studio and they both rolled their eyes at Skylar's ability to coast along on his parent's dime. "Are either of them dating anyone?" Daniel asked. It was an interesting question, and Jaxtyn suspected Daniel didn't care what the answer was—he just wanted to broach the topic of dating. Jaxtyn smiled.

"No. Sylvie's always so busy, and Sky only does one-night stands—so far anyway. I suppose he'll settle down someday."

"Have you been friends with Skylar for a long time?" There was something to the question Jaxtyn couldn't put his finger on. The answer was important to Daniel, but why?

"Not really. Only for the last few years, since we've been roommates." He watched Daniel for a reaction and then got distracted when he licked a drop of pepperoni grease from his thumb. He remembered their kiss and wondered if he'd get to experience that again. He hoped so.

What had they been talking about? Skylar. Jaxtyn thought of all the recent drama with Skylar and his detention by the police in the very kind of place Daniel came from. "Sky can get himself into trouble sometimes."

"Yeah, he seems the type."

"How about you?" Jaxtyn asked with what he hoped was at least a passable degree of casualness. "Are you seeing anyone…back home, I mean?"

Daniel looked at his plate and the last of the pizza there, only a sliver of crust remaining. "No. I…tried once. In high school. It didn't go well."

Of course it didn't, Jaxtyn thought. "Look, I know you don't date guys as that's not done in your world. But I also know you find guys—well, me at least—attractive. Right?"

Daniel blushed but nodded his agreement.

"Well, do you like girls that way too? I mean, is that a possibility for you?"

Daniel picked at his napkin. "I can't imagine not having children someday."

"That's not an answer." Jaxtyn waited to see if Daniel would respond, but he didn't. "I'm sorry if that's too personal. I'm not trying to make you uncomfortable. I'm just trying to figure out where I stand, you know? In my role as your demon, I mean." He smiled to show he was trying to keep things light.

"Demons are to be cast out," Daniel said. But he smiled when he said it, and Jaxtyn decided he wouldn't push it.

He nudged the empty pizza platter a few inches. "Should we order another?" Jaxtyn asked.

Daniel's phone—the burner, not the official one—sat next to his plate, and he checked the time. "Probably not. I should get back." He didn't seem certain. No, Jaxtyn thought, he was definitely leaving an opening.

"But it's early. Let's at least go for ice cream first."

Daniel was quick to agree, and Jaxtyn signaled the server for their check. She brought it and scanned Jaxtyn's phone for the payment. "Can't I at least pay half?"

"No. Like I said, my treat. You can pay next time." He didn't leave room for Daniel to object to the assumption of a next time before rising from the table. There was an ice cream shop just three blocks away in the direction of his apartment. They set off down the street, and Jaxtyn began formulating a plan where he would have to buy ice cream for Sylvie and bring it back to her, so they'd need to go back to the apartment together before Daniel headed to the subway.

The streetlamps, which had come on while they ate, cast pools of light onto the sidewalks. It was a chilly evening, and the bustle of pedestrians and lines of slow-moving cars generated the buzz Jaxtyn loved about this city. "Do you like it here?" he asked Daniel. In the distance, the sounds of sirens ebbed and flowed.

"No. Not at all." That was awfully abrupt, but Jaxtyn was beginning to expect direct and unvarnished honesty from Daniel.

"Why not?" Jaxtyn touched Daniel's elbow to indicate a need to turn right at the corner.

"It's dirty and loud and far too crowded. And there's always violence." As if to prove his point, a police car weaved through the traffic next to them, its siren blaring. "I'm constantly reaching for my gun. I can't believe people here feel safer without the ability to defend themselves."

"I've never seen an actual gun." He couldn't imagine what it would be like to live in a place where everyone was armed.

"And the poverty," Daniel continued. "A lot of people here are truly destitute. And people are rude and in a hurry all the time. It's like there are thousands of strangers all crammed together but without any real community." He stopped and looked at Jaxtyn to see if he'd gone too far with his criticism. "I guess I just mean I don't feel like I belong. How do you know who you can trust?"

They were approaching the ice cream shop, and Jaxtyn slowed his pace. "Well, Boston's a big city. The way you described your hometown it sounded very small, and your missionary fac—

school is probably pretty close-knit too. But I bet the bigger cities…" He paused to try to come up with any big cities in South Carolina, "Charleston, for instance, would feel busy and crowded too."

"But it doesn't. I've been there. People are friendly."

To you maybe. Jaxtyn recalled Skylar telling them how everyone closed up as soon they realized he and his friends weren't like them. And besides, didn't most of those states pay people to leave if they didn't fit in?

"We're here," he said. He pulled open the door and motioned to Daniel to go first. It was a small space, with an enormous blackboard filling the back wall behind the freezer cases. Three employees were busy taking orders and scooping cones. Customers queued behind a rope barrier as they studied the many flavors handwritten across the board.

"Even this place is crowded," Daniel said. "And it's barely spring."

"We're big on ice cream in Boston year-round. Look at all those options. What strikes your fancy?"

They read through the list, and Daniel had just asked, "What do you suppose 'bear tracks' is?" when the power went out. The room quickly filled with the glow of phone screens, and a moment later the emergency light by the back exit blinked on. "No news yet," someone murmured as he studied his phone.

"Sorry, folks," a woman behind the counter called out. "We need to keep the cases closed, try to keep the inventory." A groan went up from the crowd. "Hopefully it'll just be a moment or two and we can start scooping again." But the multiple sirens picking up outside cast doubt on that, and someone who stepped out came back in with news the outage stretched as far up the street as he could see.

After a few minutes, people began to leave, then everyone else followed when word came of a fire several blocks away. On the sidewalk, people peered at the flickering orange glow in the sky and sniffed at the faint trace of smoke in the air. "How do I get to the subway from here?" Daniel asked.

"Well, the nearest redline station is less than a mile away,' Jaxtyn replied. "But we should make sure it's open before you head off." Phones began buzzing all around them, and Jaxtyn checked his. "Oh, a transformer station exploded. Big outage throughout South Boston and Dorchester." The flickering light made the darkness seem sinister, and the mood of the crowd on the street shifted from inconvenienced to alarmed.

"A transfer explosion?" Daniel asked. "Do you think it was…"

"What?" Jaxtyn asked. "Do I think it was religious terrorists intent on imposing their laws on everyone else and trying to scare us into letting them have their way?"

Daniel recoiled from the outburst. "We don't do those sorts of things," Daniel insisted. "We're not like that."

"Dinosaurs, Daniel," Jaxtyn said. "You may not have come here to blow up transformer stations, but you do have a political agenda, and it does involve imposing your will on the rest of the country. And the terrorists are associated with your tribe. They're acting on your behalf."

Daniel was silent, and the two men stood on the sidewalk as the sky flickered above them. Jaxtyn regretted snapping at Daniel. He didn't believe Daniel was at all involved with the terrorist side of the separatist religious movement. But Jaxtyn was angry. Not just angry about the explosion, but angry at how accustomed he'd become to having his life disrupted that way.

And he was angry at himself for having become attached to someone so blind to the realities of his world.

"I should go," Daniel said.

It would be easier, surely, for Jaxtyn to let him walk away. He was an adult; he'd manage to find his way back to his hotel, then eventually back home to South Carolina, where everything was safe because of all the guns, and people were kind and God ruled the land. He shook his head. He couldn't send him into this chaos.

"No. I'm sorry I lashed out at you—none of this is your fault." Although, in a way, it was. The people down there had to open their eyes and take some responsibility for the actions of their radicals. "Come back to the apartment. We'll get in touch with Marcus, see if things are okay there. Then we'll check the status of the red line."

Daniel looked down the street, seemingly assessing his chances of making it to the subway. The traffic lights over the corner intersection were dark, and the cars and buses had come to a standstill.

Jaxtyn groaned and took hold of Daniel's elbow. "That's not even the right direction. Come on." They turned and began moving through the dark city, the headlamps of idling vehicles the only illumination.

*

"THEY SAY IT could be days before it's repaired," Sylvie told them when they came into the apartment. "They still don't know the cause." She looked at Daniel, and then quickly turned away. The harsh white light of a battery-powered lantern threw their faces into stark relief.

"I'm going to call Marcus," Daniel said. He stepped out of the kitchen into the dark hallway to place the call, but he was clearly uncomfortable going into either bedroom or the bathroom for privacy, so they were able to hear his end of the conversation while he paced the length of the hallway.

"Okay," Daniel said in the hallway. "Right. Is the hotel telling you when it will be back on?" There was quiet as Daniel walked up and down the hallway. "Well, what about the subway? Any word on that?"

Jaxtyn stepped into the hallway. "Is the hotel out too?" he asked Daniel, even as Daniel listened to Marcus's response.

"Yes," he mouthed.

"Let me talk to him." Jaxtyn held his hand out for the phone. Daniel passed it to him without question, and Jaxtyn was amazed once again how ready Daniel was to do whatever was asked of him. It must be the missionary training, he thought. But it would be better for Daniel to be a bit more assertive in his own self-interest. Maybe they could work on that. And there he was, right back to thinking of the two of them as having some sort of future together.

"Marcus? It's Jaxtyn. Everything all right there?"

Jaxtyn nodded as he listened to Marcus, and Daniel stood awkwardly in the dark hallway, looking unsure if he should rejoin Sylvie in the kitchen or insist on having his phone back.

"Yeah, we're good. Thank you for lending us Daniel today. We had an instructive afternoon." He waited, and then laughed at something Marcus said. Daniel reached for the phone, but Jaxtyn turned aside. "Listen, it's not safe for him to make his way back in the dark, so he's going to spend the night here." Daniel waved frantically for the phone. "Uh-huh. Right. You too. Message us if you need anything." He disconnected the call.

"What!" Daniel looked at the closed phone Jaxtyn handed back to him. "You can't… Why would you…?"

Jaxtyn grinned. "Oh, come on, there's really no other option. And besides, Skylar isn't here tonight. I'll sleep in his bed, and you can have mine. I just washed my sheets." They went back into the kitchen. "Daniel's staying tonight," he told Sylvie. She raised an eyebrow but didn't comment. "You can keep the lantern. I have my meditation candles."

"Romantic," she said.

Jaxtyn was sure Daniel must have been blushing behind him. He went to the refrigerator and opened the door — there wasn't much in it. He grabbed two waters. "Your yogurt will go bad," he told Sylvie. "You should probably eat it now."

"Thanks, Dad," Sylvie said. "See you guys in the morning." She waved them off down the hallway.

Chapter Twenty-Three

THE BLUE GLOW of Jaxtyn's phone illuminated the hallway as they made their way toward the bedroom.

Daniel's head spun with questions and self-recriminations. Why had he given his phone to Jaxtyn without question? Why had he let Jaxtyn tell Marcus he wouldn't be coming home? Why had he agreed to come back here after the power outage instead of making his way to the hotel? He was an adult—he could have figured it out.

Maybe. But this city was so…off-putting.

They stepped into the bedroom. The lights from the street traffic cast slow-moving blocks of white across the walls. Jaxtyn went to his dresser and pulled two candles from a drawer. "I use these for meditating sometimes," he said as he lit them and placed them on the table between the two beds.

Daniel eyed Skylar's bed. That was where they'd kissed.

And everything was leading back to that, wasn't it? Of course it was.

And let's be honest, I want it to.

He shouldn't. He knew that. He wished he *didn't*. But he and Jaxtyn were already not looking at each other, not doing anything to put a question mark on the unspoken inevitability of what was to follow.

Jaxtyn sat on the edge of his bed, even though he'd already said he'd sleep in Skylar's, and patted the mattress beside him. "Sit," he said. And of course, Daniel did.

Even though he was expecting it, Daniel was surprised when Jaxtyn leaned in and kissed him. His hand rested against Daniel's shoulder, and he kept a steady pressure there, not allowing either of them to lean in and close the gap or to deepen the kiss. After a moment he carefully pushed away from Daniel. "There," he said. "I *had* to do that. *We* had to do that—to get it out of the way."

Daniel licked his lips. Jaxtyn tasted of pizza, and he surprised Daniel once again by saying, "We need to talk about a few things." The flickering candlelight made the little Buddha tattoo on his neck shimmer. Daniel nodded.

"First," Jaxtyn said. "I like kissing you and you like kissing me. I know your church says that's wrong, and I know it bothers you to go against your church's teachings. Can you help me understand why it's considered to be wrong?"

Daniel took a deep breath. All the missionaries had been instructed on this in a generic sort of way. He could cite all the Old Testament sources condemning sexual immorality, and he could talk at length about the beauty of God's plan for men and women.

But his instructors had never considered how to respond when one of their own willingly and enthusiastically engaged in such behaviors himself.

And Jaxtyn was smart. He'd already gotten Daniel to acknowledge much of the Old Testament's restrictions didn't apply to Christians because Jesus's sacrifice on the cross fulfilled the original covenants God made with Abraham and then Moses. So he couldn't just spout some archaic law found in Leviticus and be done with it. But beyond that, Daniel himself had been struggling with this very question and not coming up with any compelling answers.

Even Marcus had seemed, lately, to be willing to reconsider their assumptions.

So, the truth then: "No, I can't help you understand why it's wrong," Daniel answered. "I *believe* it to be wrong. We're taught that very firmly, and up until now I've had no reason to question it." Jaxtyn was about to say something, but Daniel held up a hand to stop him. "But…I do realize I may not have all the answers, and it's unfair to judge others or even myself, I suppose, if I can't point to a strong justification for doing so."

Jaxtyn nodded. "I'm glad to hear you say that. I've done research, you know, on Christianity." Daniel grimaced, remembering all the books and notes Jaxtyn had brought to their hotel room earlier. "And I'm pretty confident that as far as anyone can tell, Jesus never mentioned anything about homosexuality."

Daniel couldn't resist rising to that bait. "Well, of course, he didn't. There would be no need for it. Everyone understood it was immoral. There's no record of him talking about human sacrifice, either, but that doesn't mean he approved of it."

"Well," Jaxtyn said, "actually, given how everything turned out—"

"All right," Daniel interrupted. "Bad example. But you know what I mean."

"I do, yes," Jaxtyn agreed. "But doesn't that show all these ideas about sexual behavior might be a little more…flexible than your church chooses to see it? I mean, morality has changed a lot in the last two thousand years. I'm sure your church would agree slavery, which was a widespread practice at the time, is appropriately considered immoral today. Same with the abuse of children and women."

Daniel had to agree, at least with the sentiment. He'd had the same thoughts himself.

"And societies grow and mature," Jaxtyn continued. "And as they do, their understanding of right and wrong deepens too."

Daniel shook his head. "Still," he said. "Scholars and theologians have studied this for centuries. The church's teachings aren't just based on whimsy. Greater minds than mine have come to the conclusions the church bases their teachings on."

"Oh, listen to you! You're going to leave all the heavy thinking to others now, are you? You can't abrogate your responsibility to think for yourself, Daniel. That only leads to fanaticism—and dirty bombs going off in Boston."

Jaxtyn was right. They'd reached what felt like a stalemate. But at least it was one based on honesty and a willingness to listen to each other and learn. That was progress.

"We're not all like that, you know. I mean, about the terror attacks." But despite his insistence, Daniel's time in Boston had convinced him his church *was* complicit somehow—in a loose way, perhaps—in the violence being wrought on Northern cities. You can't stir up radical extremists and then wash your hands of responsibility for the havoc they wreak.

"I do know that," said Jaxtyn. "But average people in the red states need to know what's being done up here in their name. You can't all keep your heads buried in the sand."

Daniel knew that was true. He'd had no idea what life was like up here until his mission. And the possibility the leaders of his church who he knew and trusted could be involved somehow in the violence that had been going on...well, that was unconscionable. Maybe Jaxtyn and Marcus were right about how Daniel needed to change. Maybe he did need to start questioning what he was told to believe, what he was told to do.

"And besides," Jaxtyn said, "Would I be so desperate about wanting to kiss you and stuff—" Daniel's mind latched onto "and stuff" and wondered what it could mean. "—if I thought you were a terrorist."

"What sort of stuff?" Daniel asked.

Jaxtyn smiled, and in the candlelight, his blue eyes glittered like ice.

"Well, as your demon, I feel a certain sense of obligation to—"

But Daniel cut him off and pulled him in for a kiss.

Maybe he'd regret it. Maybe after he and Jaxtyn did...whatever it was they were about to do, he would come to realize it was wrong and against God's will, and he'd see with clarity why he needed to deny himself this. But maybe not. And right then, he couldn't understand why God would want him to hold back, why he should deny himself this pleasure.

He combed his hand through Jaxtyn's hair, eliciting a soft groan of approval.

"Are you sure?" Jaxtyn whispered.

"No," Daniel replied. "But I have to find out for myself, don't I?"

"Anytime you want to stop—"

"Shut up, demon. Stop talking and start kissing."

Jaxtyn did.

*

AFTERWARD, DANIEL KEPT searching for some revelation proving what they'd done was wrong—overwhelming guilt, perhaps, or embarrassment, or even simple regret. But it hadn't felt wrong at all. In fact, resting in Jaxtyn's arms, feeling his chest rise and fall against Daniel's back, seemed like the most natural thing in the world. A moment very possibly *designed* by God—surely not one he would prohibit.

Jaxtyn twined his fingers through Daniel's hair. "That was beautiful," he said. Daniel watched the headlights from an automobile sweep across the walls. Traffic had cleared, and most of the time the room was in total darkness, the candles having spluttered out during the last few hours. "Tell me what you're thinking," Jaxtyn whispered. There was a note of fear in it.

"It *was* beautiful,' Daniel said. "I keep waiting for something else, some condemnation maybe."

Jaxtyn's breath brushed Daniel's cheek when he laughed. "What? Like, lightning coming through the ceiling or something?"

Daniel arched his back and pressed more tightly against

Jaxtyn, an echo of their time in the bathtub. "No. I don't think God would do that, even if this was wrong. I guess…maybe I'm expecting an *internal* condemnation, some self-criticism about weakness, and giving in to sin. But…"

He trailed off as Jaxtyn's arm closed around him and his hand came to rest low on Daniel's belly. "But…?" Jaxtyn asked.

"But I feel…validated. And angry." Daniel surprised himself with the truth of that. "I don't think there *is* anything wrong with me." He was surprised by that too. "I don't think what we did was wrong."

Jaxtyn moved forward and kissed the top of Daniel's head. "I should get a damp cloth and clean us up," he said. But he made no move to push himself away from Daniel.

"No," Daniel said. "Not yet. This is perfect. Let's just rest a while."

They fell asleep that way — warm and safe and vulnerable.

*

BANG.

Daniel startled awake when Sylvie yelled, unintelligible and abruptly cut off.

Jaxtyn pushed himself up behind Daniel and was throwing off the blanket just as the bedroom door crashed open and three men burst in, one with a flashlight and two with guns drawn. The bright beam danced across the room, taking in Skylar's empty bed before coming to rest on Daniel and Jaxtyn. "For fuck's sake," the one with the flashlight said. "Sodomites. Figures."

Daniel recognized the accent from home. Jaxtyn swung his legs over the edge of the bed, and Daniel reached out a hand to restrain him.

One of the men pointed his gun at Jaxtyn. "Don't move." Jaxtyn froze in place.

"Which one of you is Skylar Martin?"

Oh, no. God, please no. What have I done?

Jaxtyn shivered behind him. He'd told Daniel he'd never even seen a gun. "He's…" Jaxtyn began. But he was having a hard time forming words. "He's not—"

"I am," Daniel interrupted. "I'm Skylar Martin."

"Get up!" The gun swiveled to Daniel. "And for God's sake, put some clothes on." Daniel moved from the bed. The flashlight shifted to illuminate the pile of clothes Daniel and Jaxtyn had hastily discarded earlier, and one of the intruders hissed his disgust at the intermingled clothing. "Beasts," he spat.

Daniel found his underwear and pulled it on, then did the same with his jeans.

"Hurry!"

Shirt, then socks, and then he was trying to pull on his shoes while standing in the dark when Jaxtyn said, "I'm Skylar Martin."

The flashlight's beam bounced to Jaxtyn, and Daniel hoped it was the glare of the light making him look so pale "What the hell are you two playing at?"

"We don't have time for this," the one holding the gun trained on Daniel said. "She'll come to in a few minutes, and she'll call the police. Take them both. Come on. Get dressed," he commanded Jaxtyn.

Jaxtyn stood unsteadily from the bed and began searching for his own clothes. "Is Sylvie hurt?" he asked.

"Never mind her," said the man aiming a gun at him. "She's

out right now, but she'll come to in a few minutes. If either of you don't do exactly as we say, we're coming back and putting a bullet in her head."

Daniel stood quietly, careful not to make any sudden movements while Jaxtyn finished dressing.

"We're going to leave here and get into a van out front. One word from either of you and the girl gets shot. Understood?"

Jaxtyn and Daniel nodded.

"Phones," he demanded, holding out his hand. They pulled them from their pockets and turned them over. "All right then, sinners. Let's go meet your judgment day."

Chapter Twenty-Four

ONCE THEY CLIMBED into the back of the van, gags were stuffed in their mouths, and tape was wrapped around their heads to hold the gags in place. Their hands were tied in front of them and knotted at the wrist. Jaxtyn listened for the sounds of gunfire but heard nothing. He tried to convince himself that meant Sylvie was okay.

They were alone in the windowless back cargo area. A ceiling dome light cast a dim yellow glow across the interior. Blankets had been piled on the floor, and Jaxtyn didn't know how to feel about that. If the plan was to kill them, why provide blankets? On the other hand, what did those blankets mean about how long they'd be in there?

Their abductors clearly weren't experts, and Jaxtyn figured out right away that with his fingers free — even severely restricted in range and flexibility due to his bound wrists, he could still work at Daniel's ties. It took half an hour, hampered as they were by the continual jostling of the moving vehicle, but once Daniel could use his hands, they made short work of freeing each other.

Jaxtyn assumed they were still in the city, as their progress seemed slow and they kept jolting to a stop. Of course, the power outage would slow them down, and Jaxtyn had a sudden shocked realization the outage had probably been orchestrated by their kidnappers, along with the dismantling of the security cameras and…something about Skylar's odd birthday flowers tickled at his mind, but he quickly lost the idea. Their abductors had been planning this for days. But why?

He crawled to the back doors and tested them, finding them locked. He moved back to Daniel and grabbed a blanket. "I'm sorry," he said, "but I really need to take a piss." He took the blanket to a far corner, knelt with his back to Daniel, and directed his stream into the pile. At least the urine wouldn't run across the van's floor.

When he was finished, Daniel did the same, and then they came back to the wall separating the cargo area from the front passenger compartment and sat with their backs against it. Jaxtyn could hear voices on the other side, and even though they seemed to be arguing, Jaxtyn couldn't make out their words.

"You okay?" Jaxtyn asked.

"Yeah." Daniel rubbed his wrists where the rope had been tied. "You?"

"Yeah."

"I tried the door but it's locked." He was stating the obvious, but Jaxtyn was having a hard time thinking about what was happening to them—organizing it in some way that made sense. "I thought maybe we could make a run for it when the van stops, but it doesn't look that way."

"Do you think Sylvie is okay?" Daniel asked.

"Yes." he tried for a level of confidence he didn't feel. "They said she'd only be out for a while. They probably drugged her. I didn't hear any shots, did you?" Jaxtyn thought Daniel shook his head, though it was difficult to see him in the dim light. "Besides," Jaxtyn continued. "They were looking for Skylar, weren't they? Not Sylvie? What could they have wanted with him?"

Daniel was shaking silently, and Jaxtyn was concerned he was going into shock. "Hey," he said, putting his hand against Daniel's cheek, which is when he realized he was crying. Of course, that didn't mean he *wasn't* going into shock. "Hey, talk to me, Daniel," he whispered.

"It's all my fault," Daniel said.

He pulled Daniel into his side. "No. No, of course, it isn't." He spoke right into Daniel's ear. The road noise was picking up from outside as the van's speed increased, but they couldn't risk being heard and having the kidnappers realize they'd gotten their gags out.

But then he remembered the details of what happened right before they'd been shuffled out of his bedroom, and a cold dread blossomed deep in his stomach. "Why did you tell them you were Skylar?"

Daniel sucked in a shaky breath. "Why did *you* tell them you were Skylar?" He leaned away from Jaxtyn. "If you had just kept quiet, everything would be fine."

"Fine? You'd be in this van with a gag in your mouth and your hands tied! What's fine about that?"

Daniel's crying had subsided into sniffing and soft hiccups. "At least you'd be safe, and I'd be going home."

The dread deepened, a coil of anxiety tightening inside him. "Home? Daniel, what's going on? Who are these men?"

"I'm sorry, Jaxtyn. This *is* my fault." Jaxtyn's vision had adjusted to the dim interior. The ride smoothed out as they began speeding along a highway, and Jaxtyn leaned forward to study Daniel's face.

He wanted to deny that assertion again, to reassure Daniel but found he couldn't. "Why is this your fault?"

"I…directed them here. I gave them the address…told them it was where Skylar lived." Daniel thumped his head against the wall behind him. It was intentional…as if he wanted to hurt himself.

"Shh," Jaxtyn cautioned. He wavered between concern they'd be heard and fear that if he gave himself the space to understand what Daniel had just said, his world would change irrevocably. He didn't want that. But Daniel's words kept repeating in his head, over and over. "But…why?" he managed to ask.

Daniel spoke as if he was in a trance. He *was* in shock, Jaxtyn thought, maybe he was confused about all this. "It was our secret mission. To find Skylar and bring him to justice." Jaxtyn shook his head. This made no sense.

"You…what, tracked us?" Jaxtyn couldn't believe he was even asking the question—after everything he and Daniel had shared.

"No. Jesus surely led me to you. You don't believe that though, so I suppose you would say it was fate, or the universe acting according to some plan." Daniel shook his head at the absurdity of the idea. But wasn't it exactly what Jaxtyn had thought? That they'd been led to each other for a reason?

"And now I'm being punished," Daniel continued. "For believing I knew better than God and for thinking I could willfully sin without consequence, without accountability." He laughed then, right there, hostage in the back of a van going who-knows-where. Jaxtyn was sure he was in shock. But…it was true what he was saying, wasn't it?

"Why Skylar?" It was the only thing he could think to ask. He put aside — for now — all his questions about Daniel's belief in sin and punishment.

"I didn't know it was Skylar in the beginning. I only knew we were looking for a murderer. We had some photos, and we knew he lived in Boston."

The van swerved into a curve and Jaxtyn leaned into Daniel, then pushed away. "That can't be. You've got it wrong. Skylar's a lot of things, but he's not a killer."

"But he is," Daniel insisted. "He took Ruth from a park and drove her north." The road hissed underneath them. Rain began to drum on the roof. "Did you know?" Daniel asked. "Did he tell you he traveled to South Carolina? That he was breaking the law? That he was dishonoring God's will?" He sounded disgusted, and Jaxtyn raced to keep up. "We have pictures of the two of them in his car. Did you know what he was *doing*? Didn't it bother you?"

Daniel was getting angry. Jaxtyn's head spun. Yes, he knew Skylar went South. But it was to help queer youth in desperate circumstances. And sure, down there what Skylar and his friends did probably *was* against the law, but he wasn't a killer.

"I don't think Skylar would kill anyone, Daniel." Had it

really only been hours ago they'd been in bed together, discovering each other?

Daniel shook his head. "No? Well, perhaps he wasn't the actual killer, but he was an accessory, which is the same thing. He drove her there." Daniel clenched his fists. "And now Leah is dead, and her killers need to be brought to justice." Daniel closed his eyes, and part of Jaxtyn was trying to make sense of what he was saying while another part of him was trying to remember how to treat a person going into shock.

Keep him awake. Keep him talking.

"But then," Daniel mumbled. "Everything went wrong. We were just supposed to hand him over to the police, and Marcus said…he said…"

Keep him awake. "What Daniel? What did Marcus say?"

"That Logan couldn't be trusted."

"Who's Logan? No wait, who's Leah? I thought you said someone killed Ruth?"

"Leah was Ruth's unborn baby. She was only three months old." And then Daniel did shut down. He may have even fallen asleep, and Jaxtyn—finally comprehending the full reality of what he was hearing—sank into a pit of grief and despair.

*

AT SOME POINT, Jaxtyn must have slept, too, because he was jolted awake when the van pulled onto a rough surface and came to a stop. Daniel was propped into the corner, staring at him. Jaxtyn was glad he hadn't slipped into a coma—or whatever happens to people in shock—but he felt like he was looking back at a stranger.

He hadn't had time to process anything he'd learned.

An abortion? All this over an abortion?

The doors of the cab opened, and footsteps came around to the back.

"Quick, hide your wallet," Jaxtyn said. "They don't know who we are yet." He reached into his pocket and slid his underneath the blankets behind him. Daniel leaned to the side and did the same. One of the back doors banged open, and Jaxtyn was momentarily blinded by sunlight. When he could see, he was staring at a gun pointed at him by a masked man.

"Told you they'd get the ropes off," the one with the gun said to the other who was also masked and was busy opening the second door. "Pissed themselves too. Get their wallets and IDs." The second man climbed into the van while the first kept his gun trained on Jaxtyn.

"They're still on the dresser in the bedroom," Jaxtyn said.

"Search them," the one with the gun said.

The other one patted them down. "Nothing," he reported. Then he shrugged. "We'll figure it out one way or another." He threw a bag into the van. "Water and food," he said. Behind him, Jaxtyn could see a thick forest. There was no traffic noise. "We were going to offer you a chance to piss in the woods, but too late for that, I guess. Either of you need to crap?"

They both shook their heads. "Where are you taking us?" Jaxtyn asked. The one without the gun laughed. "You'll find out." He lifted his phone and took photos of Jaxtyn and Daniel, and then turned to the other. "Should I tie them back up?"

The man with the gun cocked his head. "You guys know to keep quiet? Any trouble and we're heading back to Boston to kill the girl."

"We're good," Jaxtyn said. "Thanks for the water." He'd read once you were supposed to befriend a kidnapper — humanize the relationship. The man laughed again and closed the doors. The lock slid into place with a scrape of metal on metal.

*

ONCE AGAIN, THEY were speeding down the highway. There was less traffic here, Jaxtyn surmised, and they kept a steady pace.

"Do you know where they're taking us?"

Daniel didn't answer at first. He was flat on his back with his head resting on a rolled blanket, but he wasn't sleeping. He looked more alert, more present, which Jaxtyn thought was a positive sign. But he also appeared disconnected somehow, like he was simply waiting for his fate to reveal itself.

Jaxtyn was sitting cross-legged in the corner. He had tried to meditate for all of about two minutes before giving up on the idea. "Are you just going to ignore me now?"

Daniel sighed. "I suspect they're taking us to Pastor Logan."

That didn't clarify anything for Jaxtyn, but he sensed he wasn't going to get too much information out of Daniel, and he needed to understand why they'd been kidnapped before he pressed Daniel on the specifics of who these people were. "We're talking about an abortion, right? You're telling me Skylar helped bring a woman to a state where she could legally have an abortion?" It made sense, he could see Skylar and his new friends doing that.

Daniel tilted his head to look at Jaxtyn. "That's what you call it." He turned his head back to stare at the roof of the van. "But it's murder, plain and simple."

Fanatic fundamentalists were kidnapping him. It was hard for Jaxtyn to wrap his head around. And he knew not to argue with people who put faith above reason, but he'd hoped he could find common ground with Daniel. What a fool he was. Still, he couldn't help himself. "Oh, come on, Daniel, do you seriously believe aborting a three-month-old fetus is equivalent to murdering a person?"

Daniel tilted his head toward Jaxtyn again. "Do you really want to get into this right now?"

No. No, he didn't. But he was angry, and he felt betrayed. "You have something else in mind? Maybe we could pray together, and we could hope Jesus comes into our hearts and shows us how threatening to kill Sylvie is part of God's plan. Or how kidnapping us under gunpoint leads to God's grace?"

He was glad to see Daniel wince as that hit home.

"Or, no, wait. I know. Maybe we could have sex again? You remember that, right? You enjoyed it, as I recall."

Daniel groaned as if he'd been hit. "I'm sorry I hurt you, Jaxtyn. I didn't intend for that to happen. But you don't need to punish me. God will take of that." He closed his eyes, signaling he'd had his say and was finished.

Jaxtyn wasn't finished. "What *did* you intend?" When Daniel didn't respond, Jaxtyn pushed on. "I mean, after you handed Skylar over to your Gestapo religious police. What did you think would happen next?"

Daniel rolled onto an elbow and pushed himself up. It was difficult to maneuver in the confines of the jostling van, but eventually, he managed to sit upright. "We just wanted to see Skylar brought to justice. Pastor Logan told us they wouldn't do anything about it in Boston, but I thought if we brought all the evidence to the police—Ruth's testimony, the pictures of him with Ruth, the pictures of his car—that they'd do *something*, arrest him at least. Maybe send him to South Carolina to face charges."

Jaxtyn recalled the photos Marcus and Daniel took of Skylar's car parked on the corner.

He shook his head. "You thought the Boston police would arrest Skylar for helping a woman get to a place where she could exercise her fundamental right to health care?"

A fire lit in Daniel's eyes. "Why do you people always say that? There is no fundamental right to kill another person."

"Another per—" Jaxtyn broke off and took a deep breath. It would do no good to antagonize Daniel now. But what a warped view of the world! He recalled Daniel's assertion when they were eating pizza that a baby is no different right before birth than right after, and he'd used that as evidence an unborn baby was a person just as much as a baby newly delivered.

And that perspective made a certain *emotional* sense, Jaxtyn supposed, but it didn't change the fact that—no matter how developed—a fetus that has never taken a breath and was entirely dependent on an umbilical cord for its survival could hardly be thought of as equivalent to a fully developed person. Besides, it wasn't about an unborn baby just before birth. Ruth had only been three months pregnant.

"Look," Jaxtyn said. "You wouldn't call an unfertilized egg still in a woman's ovary a person, would you?"

"No, of course not," Daniel replied warily.

"And what about the sperm cells? They're not people, are

they? You don't have the sticky remains of thousands of dead people drying on your belly right now, do you?"

Daniel frowned at the reminder of what they'd done the night before. "Of course not. But don't make light of that. I knew I was committing a sin, and I'll take responsibility for it before God. But it's not something to joke about."

Jaxtyn had hoped the physical reminder of last night's intimacy would at least give Daniel pause, arrest the relentless push of dogma. But no, just the opposite. "Sorry. But tell me, when *does* your church say it becomes a person? As soon as a sperm cell makes its way in and the single egg cell splits into two cells? Are those two cells a person?"

"Yes," Daniel said. "Exactly then, when God breathes life into the unborn person."

It was absurd. Jaxtyn's head raced with a thousand reasons why a divided cell wasn't a person. The fertilized egg wasn't even in the uterus yet! But it wouldn't matter. He saw that now. Daniel believed those were actual people making their way down a woman's fallopian tube. It wasn't an argument about science. It was something else.

"I guess we just disagree then," Jaxtyn said.

"I guess so," Daniel agreed.

After that, there didn't seem to be any way to continue a conversation. It was as if the question of abortion, and who is a person and who is not, had become an insurmountable wall between them rendering all other dialogue impossible.

"I wish they hadn't taken our phones," Jaxtyn said, as much to himself as to Daniel. Daniel looked at him and seemed to be about to say something. "I need to warn Skylar," Jaxtyn continued, and Daniel looked away.

Jaxtyn lay down flat and tried to sleep.

*

PERHAPS THE SHOCK of events had simply overwhelmed him and his body had shut down, but when he woke next, it was to the sound of crunching gravel as the van came to another stop. When the back doors opened, the masked gunmen said, "Break time. Get out. Stretch your legs." Both Jaxtyn and Daniel began to struggle to their feet. "One at a time," the man pointing a gun at Jaxtyn said. "Skylar first."

Jaxtyn and Daniel looked at each other.

"Told you that wouldn't work," the other one said.

"Doesn't matter," the first one said. "We're almost there, and we should hear back on the photos soon anyway." Daniel swallowed audibly, and for the first time, Jaxtyn realized how much trouble Daniel might be in when the mysterious Pastor Logan learned how he'd been found in bed with Jaxtyn.

"You first." The gun wavered to indicate Jaxtyn. "And don't even think about running. We're deep in the woods, and there's nowhere to go. Plus, we'll put a bullet in your boyfriend if you try anything."

"They won't though," Daniel said to Jaxtyn as he clambered unsteadily out the back doors. "They'll want to make an example out of Skylar, and they can't do that if they shoot me and dump my body."

Both gunmen did a double take when they heard Daniel's accent. "What the hell is a local boy doing up in Boston?"

Jaxtyn climbed out of the van and the other man tied a thick rope around his ankles. "Pretty obvious what the sodomite was doing up in Boston," he said. "Couldn't get away with that down here." Then he nodded at Jaxtyn. "Go ahead. Hobble around the parking area. Relieve yourself if you need to. I won't be more than four feet away with a gun trained on you the whole time."

Jaxtyn followed orders and took three loops around the small clearing. They were right, there was nowhere to run through the dense forest. He took a piss against a massive pine tree. When he finished, the gunman said, "Okay, back in the van."

Next, it was Daniel's turn, and Jaxtyn watched as he was escorted outside. "I didn't know sex between consenting adults was illegal down here," he said to the man guarding him. He shouldn't have; it wasn't at all helpful to bait your kidnappers into an argument. But the gunman only laughed.

"I didn't say it was illegal, son. I said you wouldn't get away with it." He turned his head and spit, and Jaxtyn was glad it hadn't been aimed at him. "And besides, sodomy has always been illegal under God's law." There was nothing to say to that. And to think these people wanted to establish a state religion.

After a few minutes, Daniel came back, the doors were locked, and they resumed their journey.

It was getting hot in the van. Surely, they must be nearing their destination. Jaxtyn kept mulling over Daniel's understanding of the personhood of the fetus. Sometimes it almost made sense. Sure, a fetus one hour before birth is pretty similar to that same baby an hour later, other than the fact that once it's born it's an independent, breathing entity, no longer submerged in fluid and reliant on an umbilical cord for…well, for everything. But still. It was even more absurd to think of that fertilized single cell nine months earlier as a person.

You had to draw the line somewhere.

But where? And how?

He was missing something. Forgetting something he already knew, but what? A sudden image of Sylvie, shaking her head in disappointment brought clarity. Ruth, of course.

"Was Ruth kidnapped?"

Daniel grimaced. A sore spot then. "No," he admitted.

"So, she didn't want to have a baby then? She went to all the effort to find someone who could help her seek appropriate medical care — took all that risk — and that means nothing to you? You think your opinion is more important than hers?"

"It's not my opinion. It's God's will."

"Uh-huh. And you know this because…?"

Daniel just shook his head.

Jaxtyn sighed. "Well, I think you shouldn't be so cocksure about what God intends. Maybe he didn't mind our having sex last night and maybe he didn't mind Ruth making her own decisions about her future. Maybe you should be a little more humble."

They turned away from each other.

A half hour later, Jaxtyn heard shouting from the cab. He couldn't make out the words, but someone was angry. The van slowed then turned sharply onto what must have been a dirt road, based on the bumps, then crunched to a stop.

"They heard back on the photos," Daniel whispered. He was scared, and despite everything, Jaxtyn felt a surge of protectiveness. He shifted closer to Daniel.

The back doors banged open. Both kidnappers held guns,

and they looked like they wanted to use them. "Un-fucking-believable! Neither of you is Skylar!" There was nothing to say to that, and Jaxtyn and Daniel remained silent. "And you were a missionary!" A gun shook in Daniel's direction. Jaxtyn didn't miss the past tense. "You fucked up big time."

Daniel nodded.

The kidnappers just stood there for a few moments pointing their guns. "Come on," one of them finally said. "There's nothing to get out of them. We're only an hour out, then they won't be our problem anymore." The other grunted his agreement, but he still looked like he wanted to shoot someone. They slammed the doors shut, returned to the cab, and took the van back on the road.

One more hour. "What's going to happen to us?" Jaxtyn asked. He wished he sounded less frightened.

"I think they'll just let you go," Daniel said. "They kept their masks on the entire time. I don't think they would have done that if they just planned on killing you."

It hadn't even occurred to Jaxtyn anyone would kill him until Daniel mentioned the possibility. He swallowed thickly. "What's going to happen to you?"

"Oh, I sealed my fate last night." He offered Jaxtyn a weak smile signaling…what? He didn't blame Jaxtyn? He enjoyed it but regretted it? Life is so unfair? All the above probably. "I'm going to burn in hell for all eternity. I don't care what happens between now and then."

That seemed pretty final.

Jaxtyn closed his eyes and tried to settle his mind. He wouldn't be able to meditate, of course, but he could try to prepare himself for whatever lay ahead. But whenever he came close to calming his thoughts, they insisted on returning to Daniel, and his fatalistic belief he was doomed for eternity.

He was surprised to find he cared as much as he did. He should feel angry and betrayed. And he did feel both of those things, but what he and Daniel had experienced last night was real, and Jaxtyn was convinced it could have developed into a profoundly beautiful new reality for Daniel if it had only had a chance to grow and mature.

But no longer. If only Daniel wasn't so certain about his fate. He seemed to be certain about everything — the good and the bad. *Oh, wait.*

"Hey," he said. Daniel sniffed wetly. He'd been crying. "I'm no expert," Jaxtyn continued, "but isn't the point of your religion that you can be forgiven, that there's always hope?"

Daniel took in a deep, shaky breath. "But I knew what I was doing last night. I *knew* it was a sin. But I wanted to do it, so I did it anyway." He looked to Jaxtyn and then lowered his eyes. "And I liked it." He whispered this last, deep confession.

Jaxtyn's heart warmed. "Daniel. I can't believe I'm going to say this, but talk to your Jesus about it. Don't give up believing in the power of God's grace. Maybe what's important is that you're *trying* to do what's right, trying to figure out what the answers are. Maybe Ruth was trying to do that too."

Daniel didn't say anything, He remained very still.

"Your church can't answer those questions for you, Daniel. You have to search your own heart to find the truth. Let Jesus help you. Don't block him out of your heart now."

The van turned and continued more slowly for a while. Based on the occasional short stops and increased outside noise,

Jaxtyn concluded they must be traveling through a town. They pulled to the side of the road and stopped.

"We're here," Daniel said. He reached under the blanket behind him. "Don't forget your wallet. And, here, take this. They didn't think to look for two phones." He slid the burner across the floor to Jaxtyn.

The doors opened. The masks were still on, but the guns were gone. "You're free to go," one said.

Jaxtyn suspected a trap, but he stood and held his hand to Daniel to help him up. Daniel smiled but remained sitting. "*I'm not free to go*," he said.

"Got it in one, darlin'." The man smirked.

Jaxtyn looked between the doors and Daniel. "I'll stay with you."

"Get out of my van," one of the men said. "We're not going to kill the little cocksucker, but we sure can rough him up if you give us trouble."

Daniel nodded, and Jaxtyn shuffled to the open doors and then jumped down.

"Go in God's grace, Jaxtyn," Daniel called to him. "And thank you."

*

AS SOON AS he hit the ground, one of the men shoved him hard, and he fell. The back doors slammed shut, and Jaxtyn heard the men scramble into the cab and speed off. He hadn't had time to catch the license plate number and hadn't thought to do it when he'd been out of the van earlier. He stood and dusted the gravel off his legs. His scraped elbow spotted blood.

He turned and took in his surroundings—a small rural town, clean and tidy with widely spaced buildings. The road he was on seemed to be a two or three-block stretch comprising the town's main street. A car passed by slowly, and the passenger—a woman with a colorful scarf tied around her hair—peered curiously at him. Half a block away, a work crew of three men cleaned a storm drain. They each wore a shoulder harness with a pistol strapped into it, and if they'd noticed him being tossed from a van that sped away, they gave no sign of it.

He was standing in front of a church. Its tall metal steeple rose high above the rooflines of the town's other buildings and was topped by an enormous cross. There was a flagpole in front of the building, which Jaxtyn thought was odd for a church, and it became odder still when he noted the order of the three flags flying from the pole. The United States flag was on the bottom, immediately below what he recognized as South Carolina's state flag, with its palmetto tree, crescent moon, and white cross. At the top of the pole was the CeeNee flag—a blood-red field with a centered white cross.

A uniformed police officer stepped out of the… No, not a church. "Galation Hills Police" the sign above the door read. This was Daniel's hometown.

"You look lost, son," the officer said, almost as if he'd been expecting him.

"I need to report a kidnapping."

"Uh-huh," the officer said, nodding. He seemed to have been expecting that too. "Who'd you kidnap?" He chuckled at his own joke.

"No! I was kidnapped." Jaxtyn said frantically. He pointed

in the direction the van had sped off. "You can still catch them. They can't be more than a mile away."

"Uh-huh," he said again, then he nodded to a young woman who'd just turned a corner and was approaching the front of the police station. She had a large mixed-breed dog on a leash, and the dog began pulling frantically when it saw the officer. "Lori," he said. "Roscoe!" He patted his chest, and the dog stood up, pawing at the officer's belly. Jaxtyn was afraid the dog would set off the gun somehow. The man reached into a vest pocket and pulled out a dog biscuit. "Here you go, boy." The dog nearly took his hand off, grabbing at the treat.

"Roscoe, down," the woman corrected and pulled the dog away. "Thanks, Chief. Tell Moira I said hello." She didn't look at Jaxtyn, didn't even acknowledge him standing there, frantically motioning down the street.

"Your dad doing better?" he asked.

She'd already continued on her way, but she turned and smiled. "Yes, thanks. I'll tell him you asked."

"Sir, *please*," Jaxtyn pleaded. "There's another kidnapping victim still in the van. They couldn't have gotten far. If you could just—"

The officer—the police chief, he supposed—finished buttoning the flap on his dog treat pocket. "Now just hold on a minute, son. We don't go sending police cars chasing off after alleged kidnappers just on the say-so of someone not from around here."

"*Alleged*? But I—"

The chief held up his hand. "Come on in. We'll fill out a report and see where we go from there." He turned and proceeded up the stairs, leaving Jaxtyn no choice but to follow. A sculpture of the Ten Commandments — taller even than Jaxtyn — dominated the reception area. A desk with a monitor, unoccupied for the moment, filled one side of the space, and a half dozen chairs and small tables occupied the other. A hallway led into the interior, and a cross hung on the wall above the doorway.

Chief Stiles — according to his name tag — led Jaxtyn down the hallway and into a spacious office. He sat behind the desk, indicated Jaxtyn should take the seat in front, and then turned his attention to his monitor. Another cross hung on the wall behind him, and a Bible held pride of place on the top shelf of a small bookcase, next to a framed picture of his family — the chief, an attractive middle-aged woman with long hair, and two teenage boys, all grouped together on the open deck of a boat, a lake spreading out behind them.

Jaxtyn was briefly distracted by the idea a policeman could feel comfortable displaying pictures of his family in public.

"So, a kidnapping?" Chief Stiles began typing on his keyboard.

"Yes, from my apartment in Boston. They broke in the night before last and took me and…my friend. They were armed!"

The officer tilted his head. "Of course they were." He typed something else and then looked up. "Boston? You've come a long way."

As if he was on vacation or something. Jaxtyn looked through the large glass window into an open area of the station but didn't see anyone else.

"ID?" the chief asked, reaching out his hand.

Jaxtyn retrieved his wallet and pulled out his identification card. "I managed to hide this from the kidnappers. There were three of them," he added, willing the officer to work faster.

Chief Stiles took the ID and scanned it. "Clever of you to hide it." He read the screen. "Jaxtyn Keller. No arrest warrants." Did he sound disappointed?

This was getting weird. No, it had been weird from the moment he got out of the van.

"Please—" Jaxtyn began again. But he was interrupted when the chief called out, "Woodrow." A uniformed officer entered.

"Yes, chief?" she said. She was Black with closely cropped hair. A gold cross hung from a chain around her neck, and a gun nestled in the holster at her hip.

Stiles handed Jaxtyn's ID back to him but picked up the wallet and held it to Woodrow. "Dust this for prints. We have ourselves a kidnapping." And this time Jaxtyn heard the mocking tone. They didn't believe him, or they didn't care.

"No," he said, reaching for his wallet. "They didn't touch it; I hid it under a pile of blankets."

"Uh-huh," the chief replied. "Like I said, clever boy." Woodrow disappeared with his wallet. "Now, can you describe these men?"

"No. There were three of them. They wore masks all the time."

"Uh-huh. Anything unusual about any of them? Could you recognize their voices, maybe?"

"No. They all sounded the same."

The chief stopped typing and smiled. "We do down here, don't we?"

"No...no, that's not what I meant." Jaxtyn leaned forward. "It's just that everything was so chaotic, and—"

Stiles waived away the objection. "Now you say you had a friend with you?"

"Yes, it was the middle of the night. They broke into my bedroom and—"

"Oh, your *bedroom*." Stiles drew out the word meaningfully. "So, a female friend, was it?" He cocked an eyebrow at Jaxtyn.

"No," Jaxtyn said carefully, trying to get control of the situation. "The other victim is a male. He—"

"Uh-huh. Same bed though, wasn't it?"

What was going on here? Sweat began dripping down Jaxtyn's sides.

"Please. He's still in the van. His name is Daniel—"

"Ridley," Chief Stiles interrupted. "A promising young missionary, last I heard. Such a shame. They shouldn't send those kids up there. Nothing good ever comes of it."

He knew! Jaxtyn's heart raced. "I…I want to talk to a lawyer."

"Sure, son. Of course, you can do that. Probably should, in fact." He stopped typing and turned from his monitor to Jaxtyn. "Do you have one in mind?"

Did I? No, he'd never had occasion to hire a lawyer, and besides, his phone with all his contact information had been taken. Daniel's burner wasn't going to help him, and there was no way he was going to let these police know he had it anyway. Weren't they supposed to assign a lawyer if you needed one?

"A…a court-appointed lawyer?" But even as he asked, he knew it was useless.

Chief Stiles laughed. "A court-appointed lawyer? Oh, that's funny. You're not in Kansas anymore, son." Still chuckling, he turned back to his monitor and swiped his finger across the screen. Then he pushed a tablet across the desk toward Jaxtyn. "Anyway, you're not under arrest. Just sign your statement here describing the alleged crime and you're free to go."

Jaxtyn read the statement. It was brief and to the point—not *wrong*, exactly, just very mundane, as if describing a minor auto accident. He pressed his thumb to the print reader and slid the tablet across the desk. "I'll need my wallet back."

Stiles leaned back in his chair and rubbed the back of his neck. "Well, wish I could help you there, son. But you just signed a criminal complaint. That wallet is evidence of a potential crime. We'll need to hold onto it until the investigation is complete."

Jaxtyn's face heated and his nervousness transformed into anger about how he was being railroaded. "So, what the fuck am I supposed to do now?"

"Language, son, language," Stiles cautioned. "You don't *want* to be arrested, do you?" He stared hard at Jaxtyn, and Jaxtyn suspected he really could be arrested for cursing at this man. He took several deep breaths.

The chief nodded. "Better. Now, I suggest you make your way home. We'll be in touch after the investigation is complete."

"I don't have any money," Jaxtyn said, although this man already knew that. "My payment card is in my wallet, and my phone was taken by the kidnappers."

"Well now, that's a conundrum, isn't it?" He rubbed at the back of his neck again, playing at thinking through a tricky problem. "Funny, isn't it? How you start making bad decisions in life, and they just keep piling up, one after the other, until…well, until you're screwed." Jaxtyn didn't reply. He knew there was more to come. "Woodrow," Stiles called again.

She came back into the office immediately. She'd obviously been waiting for the call. "Here you go, Chief." She handed him an envelope.

Stiles opened the envelope and spread out a number of bills. Jaxtyn eyed them wearily; they weren't new dollars and they weren't old dollars. Instead, they were red and white with a cross prominently displayed on each. "These are good throughout the Christian States—better than the useless federal paper you have in your wallet. This is enough to get you on a bus down to Charleston. The bus station is two blocks up."

"And once I'm in Charleston…?"

Stiles spread his hands. "Up to you. I'm sure you could find a few odd jobs to earn money for a trip back North. There are several charities there that will put you up and feed you in the meantime. Maybe you'll even learn a little something about our Good Lord and how you failed Him."

Jaxtyn didn't want to ask, but he couldn't help himself. "What's going to happen to Daniel?"

Stiles's face hardened as did his tone. "Go," he commanded and pointed to the door. Jaxtyn rose and stepped to the door.

"Son," Stiles called. Jaxtyn had opened the door but turned to face the man. "You've got some piece of filth on your neck.' He motioned with his hand to the side of his neck to indicate where the problem was. Jaxtyn raised his hand to brush whatever it was off—something from the floor of the van?—when he realized what Stiles was referring to. His Buddha tattoo.

Jaxtyn dropped his hand, stepped through the door, and out into the bright sunlight, Chief Stiles's cackling laugh fading into the background.

The street workers had moved on, but traffic had picked up. Everyone stared at him as he passed by. He headed toward the bus station, but he had no intention of going to Charleston. Once he was a couple blocks away from the station, he pulled out Daniel's burner phone. He'd never memorized Skylar or Sylvie's contact information; there'd never been a need.

He opened the phone and touched the contacts button. There were only two. One was his own, with a picture of the seated Buddha. He touched the other and called Black Beauty.

Chapter Twenty-Five

PASTOR LOGAN'S BUSHY gray eyebrows sliced angrily down toward the bridge of his nose. His flushed face became more and more red as it rose to meet his artificially blackened hair. The entire appearance was clownlike, and Daniel wondered how he'd ever respected this man. Feared? Yes, Daniel still feared him.

"You fucked up!" It wasn't the first time he'd said it, and each time he'd pound his fist against the desk, and more and more spittle would fly from his lips. "You are an *abomination*, Ridley."

It wasn't the first time he'd said that either.

Ridley. Not Brother Thomas, not even Daniel. Ridley. Ridley the fuckup. Ridley the sodomite.

Somewhere outside the office, Daniel's parents were waiting. He hoped they were across the campus, safely out of earshot. He looked at Pastor Logan, waiting for his next outburst, waiting to learn his fate, and for a brief moment he was tempted to say,

"Let's pray to Jesus and ask him to fill our hearts with love and lead us to God's grace."

It would be worth saying if Pastor Logan suffered an apoplexy. He stifled a giggle. His world had come apart, and he was losing it.

"Do you find something *funny*?" Logan demanded.

"No, sir." There was no sense antagonizing the man. He knew he'd be expelled from Sangre de Cristo. After all, he'd been sent on his mission, and he'd…failed. But every time he thought about Sylvie and her seemingly sincere interest in Jesus, he thought perhaps it hadn't been a total failure. But then he'd think about Jaxtyn.

Daniel knew now he was gay. It was difficult to even think it, to divert from the word *sodomite* before it crept into his thoughts. Even still, even with his new self-awareness, he also knew he'd made behavioral choices that were against God's will, or at least he thought they were. Or used to think they were. Maybe they weren't? Maybe Jaxtyn was right, and Daniel needed to be a little more humble about all his certainties. But there was so much to think about. He needed time. Which brought him back to his parents.

He didn't know what Pastor Logan planned on telling them. Or, more importantly, *not* telling them. He wasn't ready for a discussion about his sexuality. What would they think of him? Would they ever forgive him? Was there anything *to* forgive?

As if echoing his own thoughts, Pastor Logan said, "Your parents would be *devastated* to learn what you did."

Would be, not *will be*. That was…interesting.

Pastor Logan waited. He seethed with anger, but Daniel

sensed he was waiting for something, something from Daniel. "Say something," Logan demanded.

"How can we be so sure?" Daniel asked. "I mean, of things that aren't in the Bible? Like, how do we know certain forms of love are against His will?"

Pastor Logan simply shook his head. It seemed as if all the negative energy had poured out of him, leaving him spent and exhausted. "So, we can add blasphemy to your list of sins. You'll burn in hell, you know, Ridley, and I, for one, won't shed a tear over it."

And wasn't that exactly what he'd told Jaxtyn? But it was Jaxtyn—Jaxtyn!—who had to remind him that Jesus's love was always available, that salvation was always possible. "But how do we *know*," Daniel pleaded again, not sure any longer who he was asking, or even what he was asking.

"Enough!" snapped Pastor Logan. He steeled his fingers under his chin and closed his eyes.

What was he waiting for? Why didn't he just end it all now? "Into the lion's den with you," the Amtrack conductor had said when he'd started his journey. If only she'd known.

"Your parents would be so ashamed."

There it was again, as if maybe they didn't *need* to be ashamed. *He was…what…threatening me? But why? He held all the cards. He could do what he wanted.* But Logan got tired of playing with him and cut to the chase. "My men made a mistake."

Yeah, kidnapping seems like a pretty big mistake.

"They were supposed to drop him in the woods so Stiles could find him and bring him in for questioning—keep him locked up for a few days, put the fear of God into him."

Daniel felt shame again for what he'd brought onto Jaxtyn, and disgust for how Logan had planned all this. He wasn't even surprised to learn his hometown police were in on it.

"Instead," Logan continued, "they took him to Stiles directly and even gave the chief a heads-up he was coming. And Stiles didn't even detain him. He took his wallet and let him go." Logan shook his head in disgust. "I'm surrounded by fuckups. And now your sodomite friend—"

"Jaxtyn Keller," Daniel interrupted. He wasn't going to let Logan strip Jaxtyn of his dignity.

Logan narrowed his eyes but continued. "Now he knows the police were in on it."

And suddenly, it began to make sense why Logan could use Daniel's cooperation.

"'Course, there's nothing he could do about it. It would be his word against the police. A Northern troublemaker down here claiming he was kidnapped. Crazy." He eyed Daniel carefully.

I could corroborate Jaxtyn's statement. And then Logan would be exposed for what he was—a vigilante bent on pursuing his own justice outside of the law.

"I see," said Daniel because he finally did.

Logan nodded. "So, here's what happened. You *were* kidnapped, but it was by Northern terrorists out to blame Christian Nationalist Evangelicals for all the problems they have up there. Brother Paul managed to get a message to us, and the Church rescued you and brought you home. Your sodomite friend wasn't with you, and you have no idea what he's talking about."

Logan waited.

Fuck you, CeeNees. Daniel still heard the young men's taunts from outside the Boston library. He couldn't find his voice.

"Your parents will be told the good story, not the shameful one. Of course, you'll need to lie low for a while. We'll say you're recovering from the ordeal. I expect you to decide to remove yourself from our community entirely and take this indelible stain of sin with you."

What had Jaxtyn told him? *Don't give up believing in the power of God.*

"Do we have an understanding?" Logan asked.

"Oh, yes. I understand you completely now."

Chapter Twenty-Six

AFTER USING DANIEL'S burner phone to talk to Marcus, Jaxtyn followed his instructions and soon found himself standing on the porch of a carefully restored Victorian home two blocks off Main Street. It looked like a museum replica, and he was almost afraid to press the ornate brass bell built into the wooden doorframe.

He didn't need to. The door opened and a man with Marcus's eyes and smile waved him in. "You must be Jaxtyn," he said. "I'm Walt, Marcus's father."

"It's nice to meet you," Jaxtyn replied. "Thank you for doing this."

"Well, I don't know what *this* is yet, but Marcus filled us in on what happened to you and Dan, and we're happy to help."

"I'm worried about Daniel. They dumped me at the police station…" He remembered all the crosses on the walls, the cars, the uniforms. It was hard for him to think of that place as anything other than a church. Maybe that was the point. "But they kept him in the van and sped off. The police wouldn't go after them." He wasn't sure if it was safe to mention the police knew about the kidnapping, that there was a conspiracy of some sort going on.

He truly was a stranger in a strange land.

"They're probably bringing him back to Sangre de Cristo. We'll make some calls and see what we can learn."

"Thank you. Those men were so angry. They thought—"

"Wait," Walt said. "Come into the living room. Cassy is making tea." He led the way into a large corner room that, despite the heavy wood trim throughout, was bright and cheerful. There were plenty of plants in decorative pots placed next to comforta-ble-looking overstuffed furniture. Gauzy curtains draped all the way to the floor alongside tall windows. "Cassy," Walt called. "Jaxtyn is here."

A woman who looked less like Marcus entered from a door-way on the far side of the room. She was tall—taller than Jaxtyn—and had a willowy frame and nearly black eyes. A girl of about ten followed behind her, looking like she hadn't yet settled on which parent she would ultimately take after.

"Cassy, Ella, this is Marcus's friend Jaxtyn." He rose and shook their hands. Ella was shy about the introduction and took a step back. "Ella, Jaxtyn will be staying with us tonight." He ex-changed a glance with his wife. She put a hand on her daughter's shoulder. "Bring in the plate of cookies, sweetheart, and offer one to our guest, then the adults are going to talk privately for a while, okay?"

After the cookies and tea were served, Ella left the room, and

Walt said, "So, Jaxtyn, Marcus has filled us in on the basics—as best he knows it, anyway—but why don't you tell us what happened?"

He began telling the story and found himself constantly tripping over what he could share and what he couldn't. How would they feel about Skylar's role in Ruth's abortion? Or about the fact their son sheltered in place with him at a liquor store?

When he got to the part about the kidnapping, he froze. These people deserved the truth, but they knew Daniel, and it wasn't his place to tell them Daniel was gay. Or that he had been gay, anyway, for one night at least, before having that closet door slammed shut in his face again.

"It was the middle of the night. We were in…we were asleep. And they barged into my room…I mean, the apartment we all shared, and—"

"Jaxtyn," Cassy interrupted him by reaching forward and putting a hand on his knee. "You don't need to worry about us. Not everyone down here is a bigot. Marcus told us Daniel seemed to be… How did he put it, Walt?"

"Discovering himself."

Elizbeth smiled. "That's it. And that he had you to thank for that."

Daniel blushed at the memory of their night together, and how thoroughly committed Daniel seemed to have been to the act of discovering himself. And despite everything that had happened, he hoped there might be opportunities to continue those discoveries.

"Truth is," said Walt, "we'd often wondered about Dan—always so quiet and thoughtful. Like, even as a boy, he knew he was guarding a secret, even if it was a secret he wasn't sure of himself. And the boys were so close growing up, sometimes we worried Marcus might—"

"Not *worried*, dear," interrupted Cassy, flicking her eyes to Jaxtyn. "Wondered, that's all."

Walt harrumphed. "Well, you may have *wondered*. I worried." He turned to Jaxtyn. "I support you one hundred percent, son, and I'm glad Marcus does, too, but that would have been a hard life for a boy growing up down here." He lowered his voice and looked around, and it would have been a comical "the walls have ears" moment, but Jaxtyn was beginning to suspect that was dangerously close to the truth in Galatian Hills. "We even considered moving, if Marcus turned out to be like that, going up North."

Cassy shook her head at the memory. "We felt so enlightened, preferring to move away from everything we knew rather than deciding to send our child to a conversion camp. That's generally what happens here." She sighed. "We should have moved anyway, but we didn't know how bad it was going to get, and the missionary schools were still new, and then Dan and Marcus decided they wanted to go to Sangre de Cristo together. And who wouldn't be proud of a child who wants to commit his life to witnessing for Christ?"

Just about every parent he knew in Boston, Jaxtyn thought. But maybe that's all part of the problem.

"Anyway, that was when Pastor Logan started putting his fingers in everything around here—town hall, the police, the schools." He searched the room again, looking for those ears. He didn't seem to be aware he was doing it.

"And we worried about Ella," Cassy added. "The idea of moving her into such a…secular…"

"She means 'violent,'" Walt said.

Cassy scoffed. "No. Well, a little." She offered Jaxtyn an apologetic look. "It's just, there *does* seem to be a lot of danger up there, and—"

Their phones went off with alerts as if summoned by the very idea of Northern violence. Walt checked his first. "Oh no, there's been a bombing."

The familiar shudder of fear ran through Jaxtyn, and even before knowing the details he was conducting a mental inventory of where each of his friends was. *I shouldn't be used to this.*

"It was a church," Walt said.

Elizabeth swiped at her phone, and the wall screen lit up. "Six confirmed dead," read the headline scrolling on the bottom of the feed, followed by, "Authorities in Atlanta—"

"Atlanta?" everyone said at the same time. Terrorist violence hadn't come to civilians in the South before. *Please, please, please don't let Skylar and new his friends be involved.*

But no, it wasn't secular terrorists from the North—if they even existed—it was Christian Nationalists targeting one of those new liberal Christian unification churches. They'd been established in recent years to counter the violent, separationist language coming out of the mainstream CeeNee churches.

Cassy stood. "I'm going to make sure Ella hasn't seen this before we have a chance to explain it to her."

When she was gone, Walt said, "This can't go on."

"No," Jaxtyn agreed. Although he couldn't see a way forward. But he kept thinking there was something about him and

Daniel that held a clue, a piece to the puzzle. "I hope Daniel's okay."

*

LATER THAT AFTERNOON, they finalized arrangements to get Jaxtyn home on the train, but there were no tickets available for the next day, so he had to book for the day after. "It's no problem at all," Cassy had insisted. "We're happy to have you." But she'd been rattled by the news out of Atlanta, and even though she and Walt were privileged, proud members of the new South, they were still Black, and a firebombing of a church must have resonated in a painful way.

"Come on," Walt said. "You can help me with the grilling." It was a gas grill and easy enough to get going. Walt brought out a platter piled high with steaks. Jaxtyn tried to pretend he'd seen a grill before, or that much meat all at once. It was like something out of a storybook, and he wondered if this was what Daniel's life was like too. Walt went back into the house and reappeared with a metal bucket filled with cans of beer.

Jaxtyn thought a cold beer or two would be just the thing after his ordeal. "Cassy only approves of drinking when we have other men visiting. I'm taking advantage of this situation, so we'll have to hit these hard." He smiled and handed Jaxtyn a can of beer. Then he froze. "Please tell me you drink."

Jaxtyn popped the tab. Tiny shavings of ice melted on his palm. "I don't think I've ever wanted a beer more than I do right now."

"Good man," said Walt. He opened his own can and appeared to drink nearly half of it in one long swallow. "So how do think my son is getting along up there? Whenever we talk to him, he sounds fine, but…I worry."

"To be honest, I haven't spent that much time with him. When the dirty bomb went off, he was out with Skylar, and when Daniel and I were arguing about the Bible, Marcus pretty much avoided us and hid out in the bathroom."

"That sounds like Marcus," Walt said. "He was never one for lengthy debates. He's told us about that AME Church and its pastor. It's a Black church, mostly, right?"

Jaxtyn wasn't sure. He didn't know anything about what churches Marcus visited. But he had a vague sense there was something called the AME Church and that its congregants were mostly Black. "I think so. I'm sorry, Walt, but I don't know too much about what Marcus has been doing. Daniel and I didn't talk about that."

Walt finished his beer, and Jaxtyn took another sip of his. "I don't think he wants to come home," Walt said. It was a whispered confession, and he didn't make eye contact when he said it, as if it was something he was ashamed of. "I mean, I can see how a young man might find a…looser…environment appealing. But, what kind of life would it be? All that violence and anti-Christian sentiment." He cast a glance at Jaxtyn's tattoo. "I don't mean you, of course."

"Well, to be fair," Jaxtyn said, "the violence isn't something we do to ourselves." Walt winced. "And we're not all against Christians. Well, Skylar is, but even he liked Marcus. I think Marcus fits there, and if, as you say, he's found a church…?"

Walt cracked another beer, and they talked about inconsequential things for a while. Jaxtyn was on his second beer, and

Walt was on his fourth, when Cassy came through the door from the kitchen. "I just talked to Dan's mother." She made a sour face.

Walt leaned in close to Jaxtyn and made a face. "We don't like her," he whispered. The alcohol had loosened him up. Cassy heard her husband's comment. "We adore Dan," she said. "But his parents are too sanctimonious, even for here."

He'd always assumed society would be monolithic in small Christian towns, where everyone shared the same values and belief systems. But no. Evidently, even in places like Galatian Hills — the heart of Christian Nationalism — people naturally formed their own tribes.

"Is he all right?" Jaxtyn asked.

"Yes, he's home. They know he'd been kidnapped, but I think they got a different version of that story than the one you and Marcus shared with us."

Jaxtyn exhaled as relief coursed through his body. Daniel was safe.

"Can I see him before I go back to Boston? We didn't get a chance in the van to, you know, say goodbye."

Marcus's parents looked at each other. "Probably not, Jaxtyn," Cassy said. "His parents are very strict. Even if they didn't know you were…" She waved her hand about.

"Gay," Jaxtyn supplied.

"Right." She took a deep breath. "Gay. Well, they wouldn't want you in their home. Don't take it personally —"

"It *is*, personal, Cass," her husband interrupted.

"Yes, you're right. You see, Jaxtyn, they view the outside world as a threat to their identity and lifestyle. They would never associate with anyone other than Evangelical Christian

Nationalists. And they certainly wouldn't invite you into their home."

Jaxtyn was developing a better idea of why it was hard for Daniel to be open about his sexuality. If only they'd had more time together, Jaxtyn was sure he could have helped Daniel ease into the new awareness of himself. Instead, they'd been kidnapped and threatened, and now Daniel was back with his unsupportive family.

"Could I at least call him?"

"No," Cassy shook her head. "He doesn't have a phone. His mother said they agreed with Pastor Logan that Daniel should, and I quote, 'withdraw from the world for a while until he recovers from the ordeal.'"

I bet that's what Logan thinks. Withdraw from the world and the ability to share the truth of what had happened.

"I have his burner phone. It's how I got in touch with Marcus."

"Dan's parents would be furious if they'd known he had one," Walt said. "We asked Marcus to get one so we could stay in touch, even though the mission rules prohibit that."

It was good to know some families—even down here—had enough perspective to look out for each other, even if it was against the church's strict rules. Maybe especially if it was against the rules. So much about Daniel and Marcus and their behavior toward each other made more sense now.

"Marcus seemed like he had a good head on his shoulders."

Walt smiled. "We like to think we raised him right."

Dinner was a revelation. Jaxtyn never knew families could be like that, cooking and eating together, spending an hour just talking about whatever was on their minds. Ella proved to be a delight, asking Jaxtyn an endless series of questions about what life was like in Boston. He tried to answer as honestly as possible, always being respectful of her parent's religious sensibilities, without trying to hide how much more culturally diverse Boston was, and how much more interesting, in Jaxtyn's opinion, that made living there.

As he finished the best steak he'd ever had and slowly sipped his third beer, Jaxtyn acknowledged why some people would want to stay here. The peace, the certainty, the *security*. But was it real? Or was it so artificially propped up by rigid expectations of conformity that it was ultimately an illusion? As he mulled all this over, a light buzz and exhaustion catching up to him, he was struck by an idea—a plan that just might work.

Late that evening, alone in the guest room, he pulled out Daniel's phone and texted Marcus.

Chapter Twenty-Seven

DANIEL'S PARENTS KNEW there was more to the story than Logan had told them, but they didn't press for details. It was a pattern of willful ignorance they'd deployed his entire life, although he was only just learning to see it. "But you *were* kidnapped?" they'd asked. "Yes," he'd replied, and he was grateful not to have to lie. "Did they hurt you?"

They destroyed everything I believed in. They ruined what might have been something special with another man. They shook my faith, leaving me uncertain and confused. "No," he'd said.

By his second day at home, Daniel was ready to scream. He had no phone, he wasn't allowed to leave the house, and he was beside himself with worry over Jaxtyn's fate. In Logan's story, Jaxtyn had been erased. "Who?" his mother had asked when Daniel had mentioned his name, momentarily forgetting he'd been rescued, not kidnapped, and that he'd been driven back to Galatian

Hills alone by heroes of the church. Something had to give.

"I feel like a prisoner," he'd said at breakfast that morning, before his father left for work, before his mother set about doing whatever it was she did to fill her days. "Nonsense," snapped his father. "You should be grateful for God's protection." He finished his orange juice, and then reached his hands across the kitchen's small round table. "Let's pray to Jesus and thank Him for His protection and for leading us to God's grace."

The Ridley family clasped hands and prayed. Except Daniel couldn't. Jesus had abandoned him, or he'd abandoned Jesus. He wondered if there was a difference, and that kind of ridiculous speculation made him think of Jaxtyn, and his stomach twisted. He closed his eyes and tried more earnestly to bring Jesus into his heart—but received only silence.

"Amen," his father said. He nodded, confident in the belief Jesus had, indeed, come to all the Ridleys and that their eternal life in heaven was secured.

Since the day Logan had tossed him out of Sangre de Cristo, Daniel hadn't spoken to anyone outside of his home. His parents deferred calls until another time and turned away the handful of visitors who came by. He wanted to talk to Jaxtyn or to Marcus, but without a phone, he had no way of reaching them. He did ask his parents to talk to the Johnsons and confirm Marcus was all right. They did and told Daniel the Johnsons had already heard about the kidnapping from Marcus.

His head spun in an attempt to separate truth from fiction. How did Marcus know about the kidnapping? And did he know about the real one or the fake one? He gave up trying to figure it out. It wasn't his intention to keep everything secret for long anyway.

His mother began clearing the breakfast dishes, and his father slipped on his overcoat and picked up his car keys. Daniel braced himself for another day filled with isolation and fruitless attempts at prayer. His father had just reached the front door when his parents' phones alerted, and Daniel had a moment to wonder if his burner phone would have alerted, too, or if this was something more local. The news the day before of the church fire-bombing in Atlanta had set his mother off. "But what do they expect?" she'd asked. "With their heresies about personal freedoms and universal salvation. And they call themselves Christians."

She activated the wall screens, and their lives changed in an instant.

*

FOUR HOURS LATER the news continued to pour in, the announcers shaken by what they were describing. The images were harrowing: thick black smoke billowing out of the United States Capitol building, several dead bodies in the middle of the Mall. A group of heavily armed rioters—Christian Nationalists, Daniel was ashamed to see—had built a barrier at the top of the Supreme Court steps and seemed to be indiscriminately firing their guns into the air.

Was it the start of a civil war, or just rioters releasing their rage against an impotent government and its lack of progress? Pastor Logan sent out a message activating the Galatian Hills militia—as if swarms of liberal atheists might descend on the town intent on wreaking havoc. For a moment, Daniel saw the events unfolding through Jaxtyn's eyes. Why would the pastor of the local church be able to activate a militia? Why wouldn't that be the responsibility of the police?

It wasn't just Christian Nationalists rioting in the capitol. Daniel saw masked groups of heavily armed anarchists and hundreds, maybe thousands, of ordinary-looking young people. Well, not ordinary-looking for Galatian Hills, but ordinary-looking for what he'd come to expect in Boston—a wildly diverse group, some with tattoos and piercings, others in head scarves, hijabs, and even bicycle helmets. They all carried signs insisting, in one way or another, on reclaiming their futures.

For two days it appeared the end of the country had finally arrived. Air travel was grounded, all trains were stopped, and the interstate highways were shut down. The president declared martial law. Roadblocks popped up everywhere across the country, and grocery stores were quickly emptied.

But on the third day, it ended almost as suddenly as it began. Dozens had died in the riots, but just when it seemed the country would tip over into the abyss, the nation took a deep breath and paused.

But what did it all mean? He couldn't stop thinking about Jaxtyn and Marcus, and even Skylar and Sylvie. Had Jaxtyn made it home? What was it like up in Boston? There'd been no news coverage locally about conditions in the Northern cities. He even worried about those poor Texan missionaries, so far from home.

He needed to get out of the house.

On the fourth day, the local emergency was declared to be over, his father went back to work, and Chief Stiles urged the citizens of Galatian Hills to go about their business as normal. His mother told him she was going grocery shopping and reiterated he wasn't to leave the house.

"Yes, ma'am," he replied.

As soon as she left, he went into the garage and pumped air into the tires of his bicycle.

Twenty minutes later, he was standing on the porch of an old Victorian-style home—not like one of the grand ones he'd seen in Boston, but a modest farmhouse showing its age and its lack of upkeep. He hadn't been there for years, although he'd visited a few times when he was a boy.

The door was opened by a thin, White woman—strikingly white as if she hadn't seen the sun in ages. And strikingly thin, also—too thin.

"Dan?" she said. "I heard you were back."

Of course she'd heard; Galatian Hills was that kind of town. Even with all the recent chaos, rumors spread quickly.

He nodded. "Mrs. Deveraux." She hadn't moved aside, and he peered over her shoulder into the gloom. The curtains were pulled closed. And even standing on the threshold he smelled the dust and closeness of the air inside.

"It's not a good time," she said.

"No," he agreed. "It hasn't been for a while."

"You should go." She sounded embarrassed, or maybe apologetic.

"Please, ma'am, I just want—"

"No, Dan. She's—"

"Mama!" A young woman interrupted them as she came down the stairs. "For goodness' sake. It's not like we get visitors every day." She came forward and stood next to her mother, squeezing her aside.

"Dan," she said.

"Ruth," he responded.

"I'm going out on the porch," Ruth said.

"It's not a good idea, honey."

"Oh, stop. He's not here to harass me or lecture me." She looked Daniel in the eye. "Are you?"

"No. I just want to talk."

She stepped onto the porch and there was an awkward moment when neither Daniel nor Ruth knew how to greet each other. They settled on an unsatisfying handshake.

"I'll be right inside by the door," Mrs. Deveraux said, but she looked directly at Daniel, so he said, "Yes, ma'am."

The summer chairs hadn't been set out yet, so they leaned against the wooden railing. "I'd offer iced tea," Ruth said, "but it's just overwhelming for her." She tucked her hair behind an ear and peered sideways at Daniel. "Having company, I mean. Well, everything, really."

They stood quietly side by side. Daniel realized he hadn't prepared well for this meeting.

"So, um, how are you, Ruth?" He knew it was lame, but he didn't know how to ask his real questions. *Are you the same? Do you regret it? Does God love you?*

She huffed out a laugh and held her left leg out. She lifted the hem of her pants and moved her foot in a short circular motion, displaying her ankle monitoring bracelet. "Oh, you know, same old, same old."

Daniel grimaced, and they fell back into silence. "When's the trial?"

She sighed. "Don't know yet. But there's no point to it, is

there? Still, they'll have one, just for form's sake. My lawyer said they'll want to wait until…" She paused. Daniel could tell she was about to say Skylar's name but knew she shouldn't. How much did other people know, anyway? Even Daniel and Marcus hadn't known his name when they started their secret mission.

"Until the guy who took me is captured. The lawyer thinks I might get a good plea deal if I cooperate by testifying against him." She looked at Daniel, waiting for a response. He could tell it was a test of some sort. Daniel was certain everyone had been telling her Skylar was the criminal, not her. That he'd been leading her astray and taking her from the stabilizing influence of her family and church.

But Daniel had learned a few things since he'd escaped that influence himself.

"Funny, isn't it?" he said. "They'd treat you like a bystander, like you had no agency in this at all. Even though you were doing exactly what you wanted to do." He said it without judgment, and he was surprised to realize he didn't feel any judgment. It was the simple truth, after all.

He'd passed the test. "Thank you," she said. "No one else sees that." They were silent together for a while, listening to wrens claiming their territories in the nearby bushes. "Your mission changed you."

"I met him up there," he said. She froze. "Skylar," he added. "Would you think it's funny he and Marcus ended up sheltering in place together in a liquor store when a dirty bomb went off in Boston?"

She smiled. "Nothing's really funny anymore. But that comes close." She glanced meaningfully at the security system beside the front door, drawing Daniel's attention to the fact her mother would be listening to them, then led him farther down the porch. The curtain in the front window moved and then went still. She lowered her voice. "How is he? Did you…bring him back?"

"No," Daniel said, matching Ruth's quiet whisper. "Logan's goons thought they were kidnapping him, but they ended up with me and…someone else instead."

She smiled. "Logan's goons! You *have* changed, Dan."

"More than you know." He bit his lip. This was so hard. "I wish you didn't have that bracelet. There's something I want to talk to you about, but I'd rather walk when I do."

She took his hand. "I can go throughout our yard. Let's head to the back garden." They started down the steps, and the door opened.

"Ruth!"

She didn't turn around but acknowledged the call by raising her hand. "I can walk in the yard, Mother. Relax." They continued around the side of the house.

Daniel figured it was now or never. He wasn't particularly close to Ruth. They'd played together as kids and might have even shared a dance at a school social. But she, too, had changed, and they shared something now — a secret knowledge about a world they'd been shielded from.

"I met someone in Boston. Someone who…opened my eyes to things."

She squeezed his hand. "Is this a romantic someone?"

Even though he wasn't looking at her he felt himself blush. He nodded and hoped she saw it.

She must have because she said, "Good. I'm glad that

happened for you." She looked off to the side. "It should happen to everyone at least once."

"Did it for you?" he asked. He'd always assumed her pregnancy was something done *to* her. And even if it wasn't exactly against her will, then at least it was probably something unintentional, an accident. "Was it like that?"

"No." She shook her head. "If I'd been in love, I may have kept it."

It. The word made Daniel uncomfortable. They reached a shade garden with tall flowering bushes, providing some privacy from the house. There was a stream in the woods beyond, and they could hear its spring rush over the pebbles lining the bed. They sat on a bench in the shade.

"I've always been a bit of a rebel, Dan. No one could talk any sense into me. You know what they called me when I was younger?" Daniel shook his head. "Boy crazy." Nearer the house, a black cat strolled across the yard, hunting. "And I was! Still am, I guess. I *like* sex—" She paused and looked at Daniel. "I hope I haven't shocked you?"

She had, but he denied it. "No. I...I think I might like sex too."

"Well, that's a surprise! You never seemed the least bit interested. All the girls gossiped about you. They said you were the godliest of all the boys, but secretly they all had crushes on you and just hoped they'd be the one to stir your heart. Why, sometimes I even wondered if...oh."

He watched her face as the pieces of a mysterious puzzle fell into place. "Yeah," he said. "Oh."

"A boy?"

He nodded. "Skylar's roommate, if you can believe that."

She took his hand again. "The Lord works in mysterious ways."

The back door opened. "Come closer to the house, Ruth."

"She thinks we're having sex," Ruth whispered. "She's worried she'll have to go through all this again. As if this could ever happen twice."

Daniel stood and helped Ruth up. "Come on. Let's walk where she can see us."

It was only April, but the day was heating rapidly, and the grass in the yard was too long. An electric lawnmower sat by the shed, its cord trailing toward an untended flower bed. A bicycle was propped against a shed, and a hand pump sat next to it. "I can't even just go out for a bike ride anymore." She shook her head. "I miss that."

They continued along a well-worn path through the lawn. "My dad disappeared," she said. "He couldn't take it anymore."

Daniel hadn't known that, but why would he have? No one ever talked about the family, just the crime.

"I don't blame him. But I do wonder where he went. Like, did he get out entirely?"

Did she mean from the South? From the church? Or from this narrowly defined life they were all trapped in?

"If I didn't have this shackle, I'd get out too. Have you told anyone else?"

It took Daniel a moment to remember what they'd been talking about, and he laughed when he did. He'd just told someone he was gay, and he'd nearly forgotten. "Just a girl I was trying to save. I think I might have brought her to Jesus. She was the only one up there I made any progress with at all." That is, if he didn't count Jaxtyn. And how could he count Jaxtyn at his point? "Other than that, no. You're the only person I know, and who knows me, that I've said it out loud to. I've only just told myself."

"Well, I'm happy for you, Dan." They turned a corner of the house, and inside, her mother moved into the dining room, tracking them. "Is this boy a Christian?"

"No. At first, I thought maybe I could bring him to Jesus, but now I'm not sure I can, or even if I want to."

"Don't say that, Dan. These things take time. We all need Christ in our lives." She looked to the house as a window curtain settled back into place. "Especially now."

Did she mean now that the country was falling apart or now that her life had fallen apart? Maybe both. Or maybe neither. Maybe nothing ever really falls apart; maybe instead, everything just keeps changing into something else. He thought about Jaxtyn explaining impermanence.

"He has a tattoo on his neck of the Buddha."

She smiled. "Oh, Dan. Maybe *you're* the wild one. I'm glad you came. I don't get any visitors."

They were making their way back toward the front of the house. "Can I ask you something, Ruth? Something personal."

"Not if it's about who the father was. I'm tired of people asking that. It's nobody's business."

It hadn't occurred to Daniel to ask. "No, Ruth. The baby was yours. That's all that matters."

"That's right," she said, nodding. He'd passed another test. "Go ahead, ask."

Daniel stopped walking. "Do you think it was a person?"

Ruth cocked her head. "What an odd thing to ask, Dan. Of course it was a person! What, did you think I was going to have a puppy or something?"

"No. I mean, like, a real person, a full person, like you or me?"

Ruth started walking again, slower this time. "Well, not just the same as us, no. How could it be? I mean, it didn't have the right to vote or carry a gun."

Daniel smiled at the thought of how appalled Jaxtyn would be by the image of a gun-toting fetus. "No, I just mean…I don't know. Do you think God breathes a soul into everyone at the moment of conception?"

"Oh, Daniel. Souls, really?" She took his hand again as they passed a small brush pile. "Honestly, I have no idea. I don't think we're meant to know such things. Do you remember my grandma?"

He was surprised by the abrupt transition. He hadn't thought about her for years. She'd been the talk of the town when she first started wandering off on her own in the middle of the night, confused about who she was. The family had begun locking the doors, something no one did in Galatian Hills, and that was when all the kids stopped going over to Ruth's house to play.

It went on for years. Boys used to bike by and slowly circle the block, hoping to hear the moaning coming from inside. Even after she finally died, the rumors kept up that the house was haunted.

"I can't imagine how hard that must have been for your family," he said.

"It was such a relief when she died," Ruth said. "If God

breathed a soul into her when she was conceived, I have no idea why he waited so long to suck it back out."

He didn't know how to respond to that, and they continued their walk in silence until they reached the front of the house again, where they stopped. "Look, Dan. Millions of people die every day, and millions more are born. I don't know if God gets involved in each birth and death, but I do know we have some impact on how others live, or don't. We send people off to war to die all the time. They might try to kill Skylar, or even me, for what I did. We let entire countries full of desperate people die slow deaths because we think we can't solve their problems, or we just don't care. How many grandmothers in how many homes have been given an overdose of sleeping pills?"

Daniel swallowed. How was it Ruth had come to know such suffering?

"The thing is, Dan, people are going to live and die, and we're all going to be involved one way or another in those outcomes. Sometimes we help people, sometimes we hurt people. Sometimes we let people die, sometimes just through ignoring or neglecting them, sometimes more directly. We all make choices, Dan. All the time. I'm going to help Skylar if I can. I'm not going to testify against him. He did a good thing. He helped me when I needed him. It was my choice to make, and I made it. Do you understand what I'm saying?"

Maybe. He *felt* what she was saying. He pulled her into a hug, and after her initial surprise, she relaxed and hugged him back. "I can see what you're thinking, Dan. You want to *know*, for sure, what's right and wrong. You want it to be black-and-white. Am I a good person for wanting to help Skylar or a bad person for killing my unborn baby? You want to be able to judge me."

Up until that very moment, it was exactly what Daniel had wanted. But when she showed him the truth, that need evaporated. He couldn't judge her any more than she could judge him.

"I'm not going to judge you, Ruth," he whispered. "I...I don't think anyone can judge us but ourselves." God could, maybe. He didn't know anymore.

"That's good," she whispered back. "Because I won't be judged by you, or anyone else. I'll make the decisions in my life as best as I see fit. I'll let God judge me in the end."

But when he stopped to think about it, Daniel imagined God was going to be pretty busy—there was a lot of judging to be done. How would Ruth fare, compared to Logan, with his kidnappings, vigilante justice, and, yes, most likely terror bombings and maybe even murders? Daniel's money was on Ruth.

And what about me? Would God see my hubris and find me lacking? What about the night I spent with another man? What if that became something more—something beautiful and transforming?

"Don't give up believing in the power of grace," Jaxtyn had said.

His vision blurred with unshed tears as he looked at Ruth. "You've thought about this a lot," he said.

"Yes. I've had to."

Chapter Twenty-Eight

THE JOHNSONS LIKED to clasp hands when they prayed, and they prayed a lot during the days of the riot, and they always invited Jaxtyn to join them. He hadn't been able to take the train home. Once martial law was declared, the only way to travel between South Carolina and Massachusetts was by private car, and from what he could learn on the internet, that was an unpredictable, arduous process, what with the interstates being closed and private roadblocks appearing at random locations along the state highways.

But it would have to be done for his plan to work.

Marcus had been against it in the beginning, but as they talked it through, and the riots worsened, he came around. Sylvie had been fully supportive, and even Skylar, who wouldn't be able to participate, thought it was a good idea. Finally, on the third day after the riots had started and things had begun to settle down,

Marcus informed Jaxtyn that Pastor Ashton, the head of the AME Church, where Marcus had been spending so much of his time, was on board with the idea also.

Marcus arranged a conference call with his parents and Jaxtyn.

It was a difficult call. Both Walt and Cassy cried. "Everything's changing so fast," Cassy said, wiping at her eyes. "I know, my love," replied Walt. "But we can't keep trying to hold this life here together. It's not fair to our children to keep them…immersed in this. It's toxic."

It helped that Marcus had spent so much time with Pastor Ashton. He was able to describe the AME church—how friendly and welcoming everyone was, how the congregation was so diverse, ranging from fairly liberal to traditionally conservative. He stressed that regardless of their differences, the entire congregation was united in their Christian faith and their passion for following Jesus.

"Pastor Ashton says they have a special committee that helps orient Blacks who have relocated from other parts of the country, and there are plenty from South Carolina." Jaxtyn saw Marcus's parents exchange a look, and he suspected he knew what they were thinking: it wouldn't be people like them. It wasn't the wealthy elites who left to go north.

Marcus read the pause in the conversation correctly. "These riots are just accelerating things for everyone. I mean, where do we want to be when the dust settles? *If* the dust settles. It's not just the desperate who are leaving. No one wants to live under the influence of people like Pastor Logan." Then he delivered the coup de grâce. "Ella deserves a better life."

Walt and Cassy nodded and hugged each other, and Jaxtyn made a mental note—if any of this ever worked out—to talk to Marcus about a career as a lawyer.

They prayed together afterward, and Jaxtyn realized he'd held hands with the Johnsons more than he'd ever held hands with another person his entire life. He was getting used to it. And even the praying part was growing on him. They weren't as talkative as Daniel was during prayer, so Jaxtyn would try to sink into a meditative state, but it never worked. It was too difficult to center himself and empty his mind.

But the idea of praying *to* someone was growing on him as well. It didn't require an empty mind. Instead, it required a singular focus on something—*someone*, Jaxtyn corrected himself—outside of the person praying. It was easier to maintain focus that way, and it was comforting, reassuring—*and delusional*, Skylar whispered in his head—and yeah, probably delusional, too, Jaxtyn acknowledged.

But was it delusional if you found value in it, if you recognized the human impulse that drove people to it? Was it delusional if it worked? That is, if it worked in a way that achieved clarity, reduced stress, and provided perspective? Jaxtyn decided the *truth* didn't matter. While he was with the Johnsons, and hopefully, in the future with Daniel, he'd just go with it.

And so, he prayed to Jesus. And it was interesting that the Hollywood version no longer intruded on his thoughts. Instead, it was simply a loving presence, vaguely imbued with human characteristics, offering nothing but support, safety, assurance, and acceptance. It was nice.

It probably wasn't what most Christians experienced—well,

it almost certainly wasn't—but it was progress toward a shared understanding of a common experience, a starting point from which to build a future. He was so absorbed in this new experience, this loving embrace by…something, that he was surprised when Walt and Cassy gently pulled him back to the present. Cassy's eyes were shining. "He filled your heart with love, didn't he?"

At that moment, Jaxtyn felt closer to the Johnsons than he'd ever felt toward anyone, with the singular exception of Daniel the night they'd shared his bed.

He blinked away the moisture in his own eyes. "Yeah, I guess he did." And it wasn't a lie, because Jaxtyn didn't know the truth.

*

LUCK WAS ON their side. Two days later, Pastor Logan organized a prayer vigil at Sangre de Cristo for the following Sunday after services. The entire community was expected to turn out to pray for a final resolution to the political crisis plaguing the country. The Christian Nationalist Evangelicals, emboldened by the show of force in Washington, were ready for a hard break—a peaceful break, if possible, but a clean one, a national divorce, as it were.

Everyone would be there. But not Daniel, Cassy confirmed after speaking with his mother. Logan still wanted him kept out of sight.

On Saturday night, Marcus confirmed to Jaxtyn he was ready and in place. Walt went through the risks with Jaxtyn again, stressing the security cameras Daniel's family had in place around their home. They had Jaxtyn try on the "uniform" Walt had thrown together and practiced how he should hold the delivery parcel.

"You know you don't have to do this?" Walt asked. It was a rhetorical question. They'd been over it repeatedly. "There are lots of ways we can accomplish this part without you going there in person."

"I know," Jaxtyn replied.

"And you'll be cutting it really close," Walt continued. "He'll have, what, an hour to make the biggest decision he's ever had to make? What if he doesn't want to go along with the whole thing?"

"He will," Jaxtyn insisted. He *had* to. "I have faith." He offered Walt a wry grin at his choice of words. "Besides, I want to see him. I want him to see *me*. I need him to know I'm still here. And that I haven't given up on him." He swallowed thickly. "I hope he hasn't given up on me."

Walt clapped Jaxtyn on the back. "Well, that's the beauty of an abiding faith in God. You never have to give up. There's always a chance to make things right."

That was a comforting thought. He hoped Daniel felt the same way.

Chapter Twenty-Nine

HIS FATHER HAD seen the home security camera footage of Daniel slipping off without permission to visit Ruth. Since he was already "grounded" per Logan's advice and his parent's acquiescence, their only option was to admonish him and tell him what a disappointment it was he'd disobeyed a direct command.

They prayed on the topic of disappointment, and Daniel kept thinking, *if they only knew!*

His mother was dressed for church. It was Sunday morning, and both his parents were heading to the prayer vigil. She exchanged a look with his father as she buttoned her coat.

"Don't you *dare* leave this house, young man," his father said. "Spend the time praying that God forgives you for whatever sins you've committed Pastor Logan hasn't told us about." It was becoming painfully obvious that Logan hadn't sent Daniel home just to recover from the kidnapping, but that he'd written Daniel off entirely. He'd been erased from the history books as far as the church was concerned. Soon, Daniel would reveal everything, but he hadn't figured out the best strategy for doing so.

After he was alone, he went into his room to meditate, and if he needed proof that the last months had changed him fundamentally, he need look no further.

Since he hadn't been able to recapture the essence of prayer, hadn't been able to entice Jesus back into his heart, he'd taken up practicing the techniques Jaxtyn had taught him about mediation. It wasn't as cold and off-putting as it was the first few times he tried. Yes, it was still impersonal, but it was also calming to feel part of something so much larger than himself. And sometimes a surprising amount of time would pass without him consciously being aware of it. He understood now what the philosophers called transcendence. Maybe that's also what had been happening when he prayed to Jesus.

So many words for what might, essentially, be the same human experience.

In any event, meditation made him feel closer to Jaxtyn, and he wondered if he'd ever have the chance to set things right between them.

He'd just settled into that trancelike state of peacefulness when the doorbell rang.

He considered ignoring it, assuming it was one more busybody stopping by to badger his mother about what *really* happened on Daniel's mission. But then he realized all those people would be at the vigil, and curiosity got the better of him. He went to the front door and peered through the side panel's window.

Jaxtyn? But how…?

He was holding a package wrapped in brown paper and had a large pouch strung across his shoulder. He glanced meaningfully up at the security camera on the porch roof above the door. Daniel's eyes widened when he noticed the bicycle propped on its kickstand on the sidewalk and realized Jaxtyn was dressed like a bike messenger.

Daniel tried to make sense of it, but his mind was completely taken up with thoughts of *He's here*! *He's fine*! *He came to see me*!

Jaxtyn rolled his eyes and nodded his chin toward the door-knob.

Right! Daniel opened the door and drank in the sight of Jaxtyn, even as Jaxtyn immediately started speaking, "I have a package for Mr. James Harrigan. Are you Mr. Harrigan?" A nearly imperceptible shake of his head informed Daniel that, no, Jaxtyn wasn't asking him to lie. He should admit he wasn't Mr. Harrigan. He didn't know what was going on, but he was relieved Jaxtyn wasn't trying to leave a package for him. His father would surely check this footage, then demand to know what was in the thick envelope.

"No," Daniel replied. "There's no one here by that name."

"Oh," Jaxtyn said. He pretended to fumble for his pad, nearly dropping the package. "Let me double-check the address. Sorry. First day on the job. Would you hold this a second?" He held the package toward Daniel and grinned. Daniel had missed that smile. He took the package from Jaxtyn and felt a small object underneath it. He took the package in two hands, top and bottom, and felt Jaxtyn slide the smaller object into his grip.

He knew right away. A phone!

He waited while Jaxtyn checked his pad and realized he had

the wrong address. "Sorry. Wrong address. My mistake." He put his pad back in its holster and reached for the package. Daniel handed it back to him while simultaneously palming the phone and then slipping it into his pocket. Jaxtyn tugged the brim of his cap—a deep moss green that set off his blond hair, Daniel couldn't help but notice—turned without another word, got on the bicycle, and pedaled off.

Daniel rushed to his bedroom and turned on his burner phone. His heart pounded as he opened it. There were tons of missed messages from Black Beauty, and a second contact for Jaxtyn had been added. It was above the original with the image of the sitting Buddha. The new one read *Jax, temporary*, and it included a frowning face emoji.

He only had to wait a few minutes before *Jax, temporary* lit up with an incoming call.

"I'm so sorry," they both said at the same time. "No, no," they both responded, which prompted them to laugh, and then to ask, "Are you all right?"

"You first," Daniel said.

"I've missed you," Jaxtyn said. "I was afraid that ride in the van would be the last time we saw each other. And, well, I don't feel like it ended well between us."

"No," agreed Daniel. "I think we both need to work on our 'being a good kidnap partner' skills."

Jaxtyn laughed, and they both breathed for a moment, simply enjoying being with each other, even virtually. "Listen," Jaxtyn said. "I was going to try to be cool about this, but, *my God,* I've missed you. Please, please tell me you want to give us another chance."

"There's nothing I'd want more," Daniel replied. Jaxtyn released a long breath, and Daniel warmed with pleasure. "But I need to figure out a way out of this mess first. And how is it you're still here?"

"There's so much I need to fill you in on," Jaxtyn replied. "And you need to call Marcus as soon as we're finished. He's been frantic with worry. But we only have about an hour because the whole plan is already in motion."

"Plan?" Daniel asked, hope mixing with fear.

"Yes," confirmed Jaxtyn. "I'm getting you out of here."

He listened to Jaxtyn for fifteen minutes as he carefully explained everything. At first, he was incredulous. There was so much that could go wrong, and it was so complicated. But as he thought about it and challenged Jaxtyn on some of the details, he realized it *could* work. Maybe. "And Marcus is on board?"

"Yes. He'll tell you so himself as soon as you call him. And his parents are too."

"Let me think for a second." Jaxtyn didn't interrupt the silence. "Okay," Daniel said finally. "But there's something else we need to do that will make it even more complicated."

"Tell me. We'll make it work."

So he did, and then they spent another fifteen minutes tweaking Jaxtyn's plan. Well, it was more than a tweak, but by the end of their call, Daniel had moved from despairing to confident.

"Good," Jaxtyn said after they'd reviewed everything one last time. "Get ready. Call Marcus, and I'll see you in half an hour."

*

DANIEL TOOK DEEP, freeing breaths as he rode his bike next to Jaxtyn. His backpack carried everything he'd need, and Jaxtyn had only the clothes on his back. He rode with liquid grace, which surprised Daniel. "I didn't picture you as a guy who knew how to ride a bike."

"I used to ride one when I was little," Jaxtyn said. "And I haven't been on a bike in years. But like they say, once you learn how to do it, you never forget."

"Like meditating," Daniel said.

"Or praying," Jaxtyn added.

They smiled at each other, and Daniel had to quickly correct an unexpected wobble of the front tire.

"We're here," he said. They propped their bikes on the walkway leading to the porch. It didn't matter now if anyone saw them. He marched to the door, Jaxtyn right behind, and knocked loudly. He'd hoped Mrs. Deveraux would be at the prayer vigil, but no such luck.

She opened the door a crack and peered suspiciously at Daniel, and then squinted her eyes at Jaxtyn. "You should leave." She shut the door without waiting for a response. They heard voices raised inside, and it almost sounded like a scuffle before Ruth pulled the door open. "For God's sake, Mother, get a grip."

She stepped onto the porch and pulled the door closed behind her. The window curtains were pushed open, and Ruth's mother hovered in front of the glass, scowling. "This is insane," murmured Ruth. "It just gets worse and worse." She gave Jaxtyn a thorough assessment, and then smiled. "You brought me a present," she said to Daniel.

Jaxtyn blushed. "Ruth, this is Jaxtyn, the fellow I told you about. Skylar's roommate."

"Oh, that's a shame. But good for you, Dan."

"So," Daniel said, staring through the glass at Ruth's mother. "We're heading into the Blue. Want to come?"

Ruth blinked, and her mother's mouth widened into a shocked O.

"Yeah. I mean, of course I want to get out of here, but..." She lifted her pant leg to reveal the ankle bracelet.

"Daniel has a plan for that," Jaxtyn said. "We think it might work."

"Even if it doesn't," Daniel added, "what have you got to lose? Once we're up North, they're not going to be able to come after you."

The door flew open. "Ruth! Get in the house." She shook a trembling finger at Daniel. "The devil is working in you, Daniel Ridley. You boys leave right now. I'm calling the police."

"Get your bike, Ruth," Daniel said. "We have a plan."

Her mother reached out a hand to grab Ruth's arm, but Daniel stepped between them. "Ruth is an adult, Mrs. Deveraux. She can make her own decisions." It took less than three seconds for Ruth to decide. She ran down the steps and disappeared around the side of the house while her mother reached for her phone. "We'll watch out for her, Mrs. Deveraux," Daniel said.

She dropped the phone and sank to her knees. "No," she moaned. She managed to pick it up, and she began fumbling at the screen, but her hands were shaking wildly. Daniel wasn't sure if she'd manage to place a call—he imagined she would, eventually—but it didn't matter. Ruth was already pedaling around the front of the house.

*

IT WAS FIVE miles to Sangre de Cristo, and part of the way was through gently rolling hills. Daniel didn't know why Jaxtyn seemed to be taking it in stride while he and Ruth huffed and puffed up each incline. "Come on," he tossed over his shoulder. "We're already late."

Assuming Marcus was on time, Chief Stiles was the last piece of the puzzle that had to fall into place. But Daniel hadn't counted on Mrs. Deveraux calling the police. What if he went to Ruth's house instead of Sangre de Cristo?

When they crested the final slope and raced down the long drive into the manicured grounds of Sangre de Cristo, Daniel realized he had nothing to worry about. Chief Stiles was already there, as were two squad cars. And *of course* they were already there. Because, how could they not have been called? A bus with African Methodist Episcopal Church of Boston written in black, red, and green letters on the side was parked in the front courtyard of Sangre de Cristo.

Several dozen AME congregants had gathered outside the bus. They were all dressed for church, the men in suits and ties, the women in dresses and hats. Many of them had formed themselves into three rows next to the wide iron gates leading to the campus buildings. The gates were wide open, and some participants from the prayer vigil had already come out to see what was going on.

The AME congregants were singing "The Battle Hymn of the Republic." It was a rousing rendition, and their voices swelled when they reached the verse "As He died to make men holy, let us die to make men free." The cops standing by the squad cars nervously fingered the handles of their—still holstered for now, thank God—guns.

Next to the chorus of singers, Daniel noticed a film crew with multiple pieces of electronic equipment. They released a cloud of miniature camera drones above the scene. A news anchor Daniel recognized from his time in Boston stood talking to three camera operators, gesturing now and then to the scene before them. A sound technician held a headset to her ear while she adjusted something on her pad.

Daniel's heart swelled when he spotted Marcus standing in the front row, dressed in a stylish black suit with a green tie and polished shoes. *Truly, I couldn't ask for a better friend.* The chorus came to the end of the hymn, and at a signal from Marcus, who had obviously been waiting for Daniel and Jaxtyn to arrive, they fell silent.

Stiles whipped his head around when he saw the newcomers get off their bikes and walk toward him. "You," he spat out when he recognized Jaxtyn. "And Ruth Deveraux! Good Lord, does your mother know you're here? That's a parole violation, young lady." A cluster of camera drones zipped over to Stiles.

More and more members of the prayer vigil were walking between the gates and into the courtyard. Daniel walked up to Stiles and stopped a few feet in front of him. "Daniel Ridley?" Stiles seemed surprised, and why wouldn't he? Logan had probably assured him Daniel was out of the picture.

"Yes," Daniel said. "Chief Stiles, I need to report a kidnapping." More cameras overhead, and a hush fell over the assembled crowd. Stiles had the look of a man who suddenly had to walk through a landmine of lies. His gaze shifted toward Jaxtyn, and he reddened, then quickly turned back to Daniel.

"Right," he said. "Pastor Logan already told us about the unfortunate—"

"No. Logan lied. He ordered my kidnapping, me and Jaxtyn." Daniel nodded to Jaxtyn, as much for the sake of the cameras as anything else. And as if simply uttering the man's name conjured him from the depths of hell, Logan himself stepped through the gates and into the courtyard.

"What is the meaning of this?" he thundered.

Daniel leaned closer to Stiles. "Of course, you couldn't have *known* Logan lied about that, could you?" He looked pointedly at Jaxtyn. "I mean, no one would suggest you schemed with Logan, right? Or looked the other way while he committed crimes?"

Jaxtyn offered a discreet cough.

Stiles wasn't a stupid man, and Daniel saw him weighing his options. The deal was implicit but clear as day: Jaxtyn wouldn't share that Stiles had revealed he knew what Logan had done, but Stiles would have to throw Logan under the bus.

It made Daniel a little queasy to make the offer, but he and Jaxtyn had been over it, and he didn't see an alternative. If Stiles didn't have a way out of the mess, he'd go down fighting, and he'd have Logan on his side. There could be violence or worse in the courtyard. "It's a compromise, sure," Jaxtyn had said to Daniel when they'd first discussed the plan on the phone. "But it moves us toward justice." Daniel had a feeling there'd be a lot of compromising in his future.

Stiles's subtle nod told Daniel the gambit had paid off.

"Chief Stiles," Logan called out. "Arrest these people. All of them. They're trespassing, and this is private property." A bubble of camera drones peeled off to hover over Logan.

"Now just a minute, Pastor Logan," Stiles said. "You're not the law in this town." A murmur ran through the crowd. Apparently, that was news to them.

"Logan ordered my kidnapping," Daniel said loud enough for everyone to hear. "And the kidnapping of my friend Jaxtyn Keller. He had us thrown into a van where we were bound and gagged and driven for two days all the way from Boston. He admitted it to me last week when he threatened to accuse me of loving another man." Daniel swallowed as the cameras zoomed in. He hadn't thought about telling the truth of his kidnapping as a coming-out moment, but now that he'd said it, he realized that was exactly what it was.

An even louder murmur ran through the crowd.

It was only then that Daniel noticed his parents near the gates in the back. His father gripped his mother's arm, and they turned and walked away. *Well, some things are more important than others. I can make my own family.*

"It's true," said Jaxtyn. "I can testify to that."

"Me too," said a new voice from the direction of the bus. Sylvie! She stepped in front of the chorus. "I was in the apartment when the men he sent broke in. They stormed into my bedroom! They threatened to shoot me, and they knocked me out with drugs." The crowd's murmuring grew even louder. "I would never have known Jesus if it hadn't been for Daniel," she added, and Daniel thought it was an overly dramatic and entirely unnecessary thing to add. "Later, I learned they tied my friends up, dragged them out, and tossed them into a van. How could they *do* that?" The swell of indignation in the courtyard prompted Daniel to think maybe Sylvie knew how to read a crowd better than he did.

"He threatened me too," added Marcus. "After he had Dan kidnapped, he made me swear not to tell anyone about what happened to us in Boston. He said he wanted to make sure no one thought Daniel was successful in his ministry. Even though he was," he said, nodding to Sylvie.

"Marcus!" a young voice called from the back of the growing crowd in the courtyard. Ella ran to her brother and wrapped him in a hug, and a cloud of cameras followed her. "Did you ride down from Boston in that bus? Who are all these people?"

"Hey, El," Marcus said. "Yes, I did ride down in the bus from Boston. And these are my friends. We all go to the same church together."

Ella stared curiously at the group arrayed behind Marcus. "Is everyone at the church Black?" she asked. Chief Stiles looked increasingly uncomfortable.

"Mostly," replied Marcus. "And guess what? Every Saturday afternoon they have a party for kids."

Ella's eyes widened. "At the *church*?" Clearly, the idea of church and fun didn't go together in her experience.

"Yep. And—"

"Silence," demanded Pastor Logan in a voice trained to carry. "Stiles, arrest these people immediately. That's an order."

Chief Stiles frowned and stole a glance at the multitude of cameras pointed in his direction.

Time to bump it up a notch. "You know," said Daniel. "It should probably be Logan who's arrested. I mean, he's the one acting like a vigilante, having people kidnapped, roughing people up, telling them to lie, and taking the law into his own hands."

"Yeah, arrest Logan." Daniel wasn't sure who said it. He thought it might have come from a member of the AME chorus, but soon the demand was repeated by others. Within seconds, "Arrest Logan" could be heard above the increasingly agitated rumblings throughout the courtyard.

"Blasphemy!" shouted Logan. "I am doing the Lord's work. God is acting through me. These sinners must be smited." Unbelievably, that prompted a few snickers, and not just from the AME crowd.

"I think he means smitten," someone said, and that elicited actual laughter. "Or maybe smote," someone else offered. This was going better than Daniel could have hoped.

Logan had made his way to the front of the crowd, and he forcefully strode up to Chief Stiles. The crowd quieted. "Arrest them now, or I will fire you."

A muscle worked in the chief's jaw. "I don't work for you, Logan. And you're coming with me right now to the station for an interview about the kidnappings of Daniel Ridley and Jaxtyn Keller." He looked at Daniel and raised an eyebrow. *Satisfied?* he seemed to be asking.

"Almost," Daniel mouthed.

"You can't do this!" Logan complained. "I know everything about you, Stiles. I can destroy you!"

"You can try," Stiles replied, and then he turned to the two officers behind him. "Put him in the car."

Logan began shouting, but he was drowned out by a rousing rendition of "Onward Christian Soldiers" sung by the AME church choir.

"This is some really militant singing," Jaxtyn whispered to Daniel.

"Can't you just be happy for once?" Daniel replied.

Jaxtyn laughed and squeezed Daniel's shoulder. Stiles grimaced at the display of affection. "Are we done?" he demanded.

"Not quite," said Daniel. Stiles narrowed his eyes and waited. "It seems with Logan involved in all these crimes—"

"We all know you had no warning about Logan's plans, of course," Jaxtyn added. *That could change* said the withering glare he sent Stiles's way.

"Well," Daniel continued. "Logan might not have the time or inclination to push for the prosecution of Ruth."

Stiles held up a hand. "Now wait one minute. Ruth committed a serious crime, and around here, that's—"

"*Allegedly* committed a crime," Daniel corrected. "And now, obviously, her alleged co-conspirator isn't going to come anywhere near South Carolina, and I think even vigilantes only get one bite at the kidnapping apple—"

"That wasn't us—" Stiles began, but Daniel interrupted him.

"My only point," Daniel said as he waved his hand to take in the cameras and the crowd that stood gawking as Logan was stuffed into the back of a cruiser, "is that it's all connected, isn't it? Ruth's *alleged* crime, the kidnapping, the new…balance of power in Galatian Hills." Stiles stood silently, waiting to see what else would be asked of him. Daniel knew he had to be careful. He could only push the man so far, and it would still just be their word against his if it came to establishing Stiles was in on the kidnapping plot.

"Well?" Stiles prompted.

"Well, does she really need an ankle monitoring bracelet?" Then, for the sake of the cameras and to give Stiles a face-saving out, "That was all Logan's idea, wasn't it? To humiliate a young woman so publicly?"

Stiles paused only a moment, but his face reflected the calculations racing in his mind, and then he nodded. "It was Logan's idea. You're right." He took a deep breath and turned to the officer behind him. "Woodrow, get the key."

"Yes sir," she said and headed to the patrol car. A minute later, she was back, and Logan nodded to Ruth's monitoring bracelet. Woodrow knelt and released the unit from Ruth's ankle.

"I expect to see you at your preliminary hearing, young lady," Stiles said sternly.

"Of course you do," Ruth replied with a sweet smile.

Chapter Thirty

DANIEL HAD BEEN far too quiet since they left Sangre de Cristo. They'd been afforded some privacy in the very back of the bus, but Jaxtyn hadn't been able to get Daniel to share more than just a few words. They only made it as far as North Carolina before stopping for the night. Someone in the choir had a cousin who ran what she insisted was the best barbeque in the state, and they were all outside under an open-air wooden pavilion, waiting for their food to be brought out from the kitchen.

Sylvie had taken Ruth under her wing, and the two young women were speaking animatedly on a nearby bench. Marcus was spending his time with the AME folks, and Jaxtyn thought it was his way of giving Daniel space to work through what had transpired that day. And it *was* a lot. Jaxtyn only wished Daniel would talk to him about what he was thinking.

"Take a walk with me?" he asked. Daniel agreed, and they

began making their way down a graveled road that ran behind the barbeque joint. Within minutes they were out of earshot of the pavilion, and the smoky aroma of roasting meats had been replaced by the heady scent of spring wildflowers.

"It's so peaceful here," Jaxtyn said. "I mean, right here, of course" — he waved a hand to take in the nature surrounding them — "but also, down here generally. If everyone wasn't armed, it would almost be relaxing." He nudged Daniel's elbow with his own. "I can see why people would like Galatian Hills, if you fit in, that is. If you shared all the same…expectations."

Daniel made a noncommittal sound, and they walked in silence until they reached a small stream.

"You could stay, you know," Jaxtyn said. "I mean, I sprang all this on you very suddenly. You didn't have time to think about…everything." They stood in a small clearing along the bank and watched a couple of chipmunks on the opposite side explore a tumble of river rocks. "It wouldn't be embarrassing or anything for you to change your mind, or to take more time."

"Is that what you want? Do you want me to stay here?" Daniel sounded uncertain, maybe even fearful.

"No!" Jaxtyn exclaimed. "I don't think you belong here — not anymore."

"But what *do* you want?" Daniel asked.

"I want us to have more time together in Boston. I want to get to know you. And that night we shared…" Jaxtyn hoped Daniel felt the same way, but they'd had no time to talk about that night afterward. "But it's not just about that. I mean, yes, I'm attracted to you, and I'd like very much to see where that goes. But if you're not attracted to me, or don't want to spend more time together…that way…that's fine. I still want to get to know you better and help you settle into a new life in Boston."

Daniel picked up a small stone and tossed it into the stream, causing the chipmunks to dart into the cover of the rocks.

"It's all happening so fast," Daniel acknowledged, and Jaxtyn's stomach dropped. It sounded like Daniel was looking to slow things down. He took a deep breath and readied himself to put on a brave face, and then Daniel surprised him. "But yeah, you're still my demon." He reached out and took Jaxtyn's hand in his.

"Oh, thank God," Jaxtyn said. But when Daniel didn't seem to share his relief or his enthusiasm for the months ahead, he asked, "So, what is it? What's causing you doubt?"

"I just feel so…" He shrugged. "Unmoored."

Jaxtyn squeezed his hand, encouraging him to continue.

"The thing is," Daniel began, "everything that was the foundation of how I lived my life—my church, my school, my parents—it's all been taken away. I don't know how to…be."

Jaxtyn had seen the way Daniel's parents had turned from him, and he could only imagine how much that must have hurt. "Maybe your parents will come around, eventually?"

"No. You didn't see how they were with me after Logan sent me home. I was practically in prison. They'd sooner believe Logan than ask me about what happened." Daniel let go of Jaxtyn's hand and picked up another pebble to toss into the water. "My mother thought the liberal Christians at that Atlanta church brought the firebombing on themselves because of their 'sinful ways.'"

Jaxtyn grimaced. No, they probably wouldn't be coming around.

"You have me," Jaxtyn offered.

"Well," Daniel said. "For now…"

And sure, that hurt some. But Jaxtyn shouldn't expect Daniel to have the same faith in their future as he did. The connection between them Jaxtyn had always known was more than the sum of its parts burned brighter than ever. Jaxtyn knew they were important together—could do great things together—but that was impossible to put into words. One just had to have faith.

Oh! Faith.

"You have your faith," Jaxtyn pointed out.

"Yes," Daniel confirmed. "I do. It's the only thing I have left. But that's just it. It's *my* faith, not yours. I just don't see how this—" He waved his hand between them. "—can work if we don't share even—"

"No, Daniel, stop." Jaxtyn wanted to say that maybe he could grow into Daniel's faith. Maybe with Daniel's guidance and teaching, Jaxtyn could…what? Become a Christian? No. It was ridiculous and false. Although he'd learned a lot from Daniel and was able now to see how prayer to a personalized idea of the divine could be valuable, he knew that wasn't the same as believing the details about Jesus and Grace and sin and redemption. "I think we just need to focus on—"

Both their phones went off.

Jaxtyn held his breath as he checked his screen. What new travesty now?

"Oh my God," said Daniel, studying his phone.

It was coverage of the Sangre de Cristo event. There was Logan getting stuffed into a police car, there was Ella hugging her brother, there was Sylvie, crediting Daniel for introducing her to

Jesus, and, yes, there was Daniel confessing his—" Wait! Had Daniel said *love*? The scene repeated. Yes. Yes, he had.

Daniel dropped his arms and let his phone dangle at his side. "That…that came out differently than I'd intended."

Jaxtyn wrapped an arm around Daniel's shoulders. "Well, I *like* how it came out. Listen, Daniel. I know we're just getting started, but I believe we're meant to be together. Call it what you will, but I have faith the universe brought us to each other for a reason."

The coverage of what happened at Sangre de Cristo was all over the news feeds. It was presented as a rare moment of unity: blue and red, Christian and non-Christian, all coming together to bring justice into the world—at least for a moment, at least in a small way.

But it had to start somewhere.

*

THE FOLLOWING MORNING, they continued their journey north, sticking to the back roads as the interstates were still a mess, and they wanted to go around Washington rather than through it. As the day wore on, first one, then two, then three news vans caught up with them, each releasing its own swarm of cameras. They'd become a sensation.

Shortly after they crossed into Virginia, they were waved to the side of the road by a group of men dressed in the telltale red and white of Christian Nationalist Evangelicals. The men were armed, and Jaxtyn felt a surge of anxiety. He wouldn't permit himself to be kidnapped again, and he wouldn't allow any harm to come to Daniel.

But the group simply wanted to congratulate the "Harmony Bus," as the media had dubbed them. "We're not all like that," the group's spokesman had told them. "Yes, we want to be able to govern our communities by our religious principles, but we don't support violence. We wanted to thank the AME church for showing the North that different types of Christians are still able to work together.

They handed out bottles of water and homemade baked goods. Jaxtyn's recent experience with Christian Nationalists was still too raw to allow him to trust the food, but everyone else enjoyed it, and soon the convoy of the Harmony Bus and the news vans continued on its way. Small groups of people began appearing along the roadside, some waving signs, some applauding as they went by, and, yes, there were a few protestors too, but they were far outnumbered by the well-wishers.

By the time they stopped for lunch, the media was filled with wall-to-wall coverage of their trip. People had been inspired by the show of cross-cultural cooperation. The biblical story of Daniel and the lion's den began circulating on both Christian and non-Christian social media, and soon, a spontaneous "Lion's Den" movement arose, where people from all sides of the political and religious spectrum would intentionally engage with others on the opposite side, setting up local groups for open and honest discussions about all the hard issues confronting society.

"You did all this," Jaxtyn said after reading one of the many news articles out loud to Daniel. They were in the back of the bus, transfixed by the sights they were seeing out the window, the increasing numbers of people lining the roads, waving and clapping as they passed.

"All I did was tell the truth," Daniel replied.

"Maybe," said Jaxtyn. "But speaking truth to power isn't always an easy thing."

"Hey," someone called out from the front of the bus. "Listen to this. The US Congress is locking itself into the Senate chambers, vowing not to come out until they've hammered out a deal!" Shouts of "Praise Jesus!" and "Halleluiah!" filled the bus, and Jaxtyn was uncomfortably aware he was the only non-Christian in the group. Although, privately, he still had his doubts about Sylvie.

The man continued reading. "It says the House chambers were ruined in the fire, so they've all piled into the Senate side of the Capitol. Imagine that." The bus fell quiet at the reminder of just how close the country had come to the brink. Perhaps they'd saved themselves in time, but maybe not. They'd have to wait and see. "Hey, Daniel. Check it out. They're calling it the Lion's Den Summit."

Daniel blushed, and Jaxtyn leaned in close. "You're probably the most famous CeeNee missionary to declare his love for another man on national media *ever*."

*

A STATE POLICE escort was waiting for the bus when they crossed into Massachusetts, and the number of media vans accompanying them had swelled to eight. Along the roadside, the crowds grew larger and "Welcome Home" signs were everywhere. And it *was* good to be home. But it was Jaxtyn's home, not Daniel's. Just like Christianity was Daniel's faith, not Jaxtyn's.

Daniel had grown more and more quiet as the bus approached Boston.

Both men must have been dwelling on the same challenges they faced because when Daniel said, "We're never going to agree about it, are we?" Jaxtyn knew he meant more than just religion. He'd been looking at Ruth, sitting four rows ahead with Sylvie, when he said it. He was talking about abortion.

And truly, even more than the nature of Jesus, or whether heaven and hell existed, or if mankind was born into sin and needed salvation — all esoteric, theoretical concerns, as far as Jaxtyn was concerned — abortion, and whether it was a fundamental healthcare right or the murder of a human being, seemed like a rock-solid, real-world stumbling block. Intractable, maybe even unresolvable.

"No, probably not." Jaxtyn sighed. He wanted to say more, something to show it didn't matter, but it *did* matter, didn't it? It was an important question, and one around which they both had passionate convictions, but their positions on the matter were profoundly unaligned. He struggled to find a way to fill the silence but came up blank.

"Dan, did you get it?" asked Marcus as he came up the aisle from the front of the bus. He was followed closely by both Sylvie and Ruth. "Oh my God, I can't believe it!" Sylvie said. "Check your messages."

Jaxtyn pulled out his phone at the same time Daniel looked at his. Daniel shook his head. "What?" he asked. "I don't see anything."

"That's because you're still using a burner," Marcus said. "They don't know how to get ahold of you yet."

Jaxtyn was reading the message with a mixture of disbelief and excitement. He tilted his phone toward Daniel. "Global Max wants to option our story!" he said.

Ruth was bouncing on her toes. "Movie, book interviews — the whole package," she said.

Some members of the AME church overheard the conversation, and the news started rippling forward on the bus. Whispers of, "Praise Jesus" and "Halleluiah" could be heard as the good news spread.

Jaxtyn finished reading the message, then did a double take. He looked up at Sylvie. "Is that in *new* dollars?"

"Yes!" She clapped her hands together.

They'd be rich. Or at least wealthier than he'd ever hoped to be.

Daniel had read the message and turned to look out the window at the waving crowds. He looked distant and speculative, and Jaxtyn wished, yet again, that he could see into Daniel's head.

Sylvie reached down and put her hand on Daniel's shoulder. "The Lord works in mysterious ways."

*

THEY STAYED UP late into the night telling the entire story to Skylar. Jaxtyn was only a little bit surprised to see how the crisis of the past week had brought Skylar and Marcus closer together. Watching them, he thought they had the look of longtime best friends. And maybe they were. Maybe the Tibetans were right, and there was a bardo where souls spent time between earthly lives. Maybe Marcus and Skylar spent time in the bardo together, joined in some inexplicable way, and reunited during each life they lived.

It was a lovely thought, and just as likely as Daniel's Jesus.

Sylvie and Ruth were yawning, and Daniel still looked uncertain about everything. He'd largely remained silent throughout the recounting, only speaking up to clarify a point or correct Jaxtyn *again* about the events in front of Sangre de Cristo. "I did *not* declare my love for Jaxtyn. You've all seen the footage. I said Logan planned on accusing me of loving another man."

Jaxtyn grinned. "Same difference." The others had all nodded their agreement.

"We're going to sleep," Sylvie said. She and Ruth were going to bunk together until they figured out what they were going to do. It wasn't as awkward as it could have been if they hadn't all known a big chunk of money was heading their way. The two women left the kitchen just as Skylar and Marcus came in from the hallway.

"I'm glad you made it back, Jax," Skylar said at the end of the night. "And I'm really glad I wasn't home when they came to kidnap me."

"Wish I could say the same," Jaxtyn quipped.

"Listen, Marcus and I are plotting the future. We're on a roll and want to keep going. Is it okay with you guys if I head back with him and spend the night at the CeeNee's hotel and Daniel stays here?"

Jaxtyn looked at Daniel. He didn't look thrilled at the idea, but he didn't object either. He seemed more resigned than anything else. They both knew they had to finally have the talk they'd been putting off.

"Sure," they said together.

Sylvie and Ruth were already in Sylvie's bedroom with the door shut, so once they were alone, Jaxtyn led Daniel down the hallway to his bedroom. He was pleased to see Skylar had cleaned up his mess. His bed was made, his clothes were put away, and his dirty laundry was in the hamper. His pleasure disappeared when he saw the pile of condoms and lube Skylar had left on his bed. There was a note on top of the pile reading, "Better Safe than Sorry." It was signed by both Skylar and Marcus.

Daniel blushed deeply, and Jaxtyn said, "I don't know which one of them is the more corrupting influence." The seated Buddha in the painting above Jaxtyn's bed smiled down at them. Perhaps he was recalling what happened the last time Jaxtyn and Daniel were in this room. If so, it wasn't only the Buddha having those thoughts; Daniel also looked nervous about being back at the scene of the crime. Jaxtyn scooped up the pile of condoms and lube and transferred them to the top of Skylar's dresser.

He sat on the edge of his bed and patted the mattress next to him. "Sit," he said.

Daniel moved across the room to Skylar's bed and sat.

Jaxtyn frowned. "We're back to that, are we?"

Daniel smiled. "Listen. I'm not the same man I was the last time I was here. I'm not pretending to be anything other than what I am. I have you to thank for that. I know that I'm gay now, and I no longer think it's just a hurdle God keeps putting in my way to test me."

"Good," Jaxtyn said. "That's good. But then, why are you way over there?"

"Because if I was sitting next to you, I know how easy it would be to start kissing you, and then moving on to what we did before, and then maybe moving on to other things too."

It was getting better and better. Jaxtyn grinned. "Okay, if

you insist."

Daniel shook his head but couldn't hide his smile. "But I don't think we should."

Ouch. "Why?"

"Because it can't work between us—not in the long term. And if we just keep fooling around, we're going to hurt each other. And I don't want that." Jaxtyn didn't answer. How could Daniel be so certain it wouldn't work? "I can't just be…casual…about this," Daniel continued. "It took too much pain to acknowledge the truth about myself. I can't treat it like it doesn't matter, as if it's just about physical pleasure."

Jaxtyn nodded. That made sense. Daniel was an intense guy.

Daniel grinned. "The funny thing is, I think I would have been like this with girls too if only I'd ever been attracted enough to one to find out."

Jaxtyn nodded. "Of course you would have. You have principles, and you don't want sex if it isn't part of a meaningful relationship with future potential. That's a beautiful thing about you, Daniel. I never thought what we had—what we were developing—was just about physical attraction."

The tinny sound of Sylvia's monitor could be heard through the bedroom wall, too indistinct to make out what they were watching.

"I mean, we can't see the future," Jaxtyn said, "but I think you and I have potential. Don't you?"

Daniel looked like he was taking time to compose his thoughts, but the silence was broken by Ruth's laugh. Daniel looked at the wall, as if he could trace the laughter right through it, and then turned back to Jaxtyn. "No," he said. "I don't."

Ruth. Well, not Ruth exactly, but what she had done—what it meant.

"Daniel, we can't agree on everything. People have different opinions, different beliefs. We need to make space for each other."

Daniel flopped back on Skylar's bed and sighed. "I *knew* you'd say that."

"See?" said Jaxtyn. "That just shows you how close we've become already."

"It's not a joke, Jaxtyn."

"I wasn't joking."

Daniel sat up. "I know people will have different opinions. I know that's healthy—even desirable—in a relationship. But they should agree about the big things. How can we have different opinions about the sanctity of life and still think we could be a couple? What could be more important than that?"

Jaxtyn stood and walked to Skylar's bed. He sat next to Daniel. "I respect your ideas about the sanctity of life. I just think they're *your* ideas, and that you shouldn't judge Ruth for the choices she's made."

"Oh, but that's just it! I don't judge her. I *want* to. I thought I could. But when I met with her, I realized I couldn't. I had no right."

"Daniel, I don't understand. Why is that a bad thing?"

"I wish I could explain it clearly. I've thought about it so much because…well, because of us. I *know*, deep down in my soul, that life is sacred. I *feel* it."

Jaxtyn picked up Daniel's hand and closed his own around it. "That's *good*, Daniel. That's passion."

Daniel sniffed. "But I can't *justify* it. I can't *explain* it. When I talked to Ruth, I could only know that what she did was wrong, but I couldn't fault her for making the choice she made. How can I be so certain of a fundamental truth when I'm not even able to confront someone who violates it?"

"It's your faith, Daniel. It's what you believe."

"Yes, but it's her faith too."

"But…maybe faith is personal," Jaxtyn said. "Maybe how your faith informs your life is different than how the same faith works in others."

"Maybe," Daniel acknowledged. He hadn't pulled his hand away from Jaxtyn's. "But how could we be together if I knew you didn't share my belief in the sanctity of life?" He shook his head. "If faith is that…intangible, isn't it important we both share the same framework about it? About the big things at least?"

Daniel's reticence was beginning to make more sense. "But I *do* believe in the sanctity of life," Jaxtyn insisted.

"It's not the same. You don't believe what I believe."

He was right. It wasn't the same. Jaxtyn knew that, but there were so many different ways to understand life and all its inter-connectedness. He was reminded of something Vishnu had told him when they first met.

"Do you remember Vishnu?"

Daniel shook his head.

"He was the meditation leader of the Open Lotus meetings last month."

"Oh, right. I remember him now," Daniel said.

"He's a Jain. Well, he was raised as one, anyway. He grew up in India."

"A Jain?"

"Yes," replied Daniel. "Jainism is one of the oldest religions in the world. It originated in India over 5,000 years ago. They practice nonviolence in everything and hold all life to be sacred."

"Okay?" said Daniel, clearly not certain what this had to do with him and Jaxtyn.

"Well, Vishnu told me when he was a boy living in India, there were Jain monks who carried a huge peacock feather everywhere they went, and they would sweep the ground in front of them when they walked so they could avoid killing any insects."

"Wow. That's…intense." Daniel twisted to face Jaxtyn directly. "But, what are you getting at? Bugs aren't the same things as human babies, and even if they were, I don't see how—"

"They are the same thing for Jains," Jaxtyn interrupted. "They believe all souls go through lifetimes of reincarnations, millions of times over, and depending on how you evolve in one life, you might come back as a more advanced being, or you might come back as a lower life form, even as a bug."

Daniel smiled. "So, the bug you step on might be your grandfather or something?"

"Maybe," Jaxtyn acknowledged. "But it's not about the relationships; it's about the continuous spectrum of life, from lowest to highest. *All* life is equally sacred to a Jain. Beings are born and die all the time, but the soul is a constant. You should never cause harm to any life because the individual unique soul is a constant. It never dies; it just transforms."

Jaxtyn searched Daniel's face for a sign he understood what Jaxtyn was saying. He was glad to see Daniel was thinking about it, nodding his head occasionally. "That's sort of like what Ruth told me when we talked last week." He let go of Jaxtyn's hand.

"She said people are born and die all the time, and sometimes we're complicit in those events and sometimes we're not."

"Yes, exactly," Jaxtyn said. He took Daniel's hand again. "It's like the Jains sweeping the sidewalk. When you think about it, everything we do has some impact on other living beings."

Daniel looked surprised. "She said that too."

"She's a smart woman." Jaxtyn said.

"But, what am I supposed to do? I can't equate killing bugs with killing unborn babies. I don't see it as the same thing."

"No, of course you don't. The point I was trying to make is even though the Jains *do* see it that way—see the eternal soul as present in all beings—they don't insist others share that view. Nobody else is expected to sweep the sidewalk in front of them when they walk."

"So, I'm supposed to not expect other people to refrain from killing babies?"

Now it was Jaxtyn's turn to drop Daniel's hand. He leaned back. "Come on, Daniel. Now you're just being provocative." Jaxtyn looked up at the Buddha and took a breath, then continued. "You know there's a big gray area here. You said yourself you felt like you couldn't judge Ruth. And, well, when it comes to souls and when they appear in the body, are you really so sure you have all the answers?"

Daniel reddened. "No, I'm not," he whispered. "That level of unjustified certainty has always been my problem. I'm working on it."

"Good." Jaxtyn looked toward the wall between his bedroom and Sylvie's. "You know, they'd come in here and bash our heads together if they heard us talking about how men need to decide about what abortion means and what women should or shouldn't be allowed to do."

Daniel smiled. "Yeah, I think that was part of Ruth's message too." He tucked his knees up underneath him and Jaxtyn did the same. They sat knees to knees, facing each other. "But what am I supposed to do? I can't ignore what I believe. How do I honor the fact life is sacred—I mean, without sweeping the sidewalk—if I can't try to convince people abortion is wrong?"

"You *should* try to convince people of your point of view if it means that much to you. After all, you changed Sylvie's life by doing that." Jaxtyn reached out a finger and traced a small circle on Daniel's knee. "You just shouldn't try to force people to live according to your view of things." Jaxtyn stilled his finger but left his hand resting on Daniel's knee. "What if…" Jaxtyn paused, thinking through what he wanted to say. It was a new idea, but it felt right. Compelling, even. "What if we worked together on a project that aligned with both our beliefs about the sanctity of life?"

"What do you mean?"

"Well, you think we can't be together because we don't share the same values about how sacred life is. But I think we *do* share those values." His finger started circling Daniel's knee again. "For instance, if you think the life of an unborn child is worthy of protection, then surely the life of a living child is equally deserving, right?"

Daniel nodded. "Of course," he said.

"So, rather than focus on where we *disagree*, why don't we work together on things where we *do* agree? We could volunteer at an agency supporting refugee children, or immigrants, for instance."

Daniel was nodding again. "I can see that," he said. "And the more people engage on the things they do agree on, the more likely they might be to keep an open mind on the other things."

"Yes," said Jaxtyn. "Like, how, ever since I got to know you, I have a better understanding of what Jesus means to Christians, and how praying to Jesus can actually be useful."

"Exactly," agreed Daniel. "And how, because of you, I can see how meditation is a useful tool for obtaining mental focus."

"Right," said Jaxtyn. "It seems like, as long as we respect each other and know we're each being open and honest about what we believe, and we're willing to keep an open mind and have a true dialogue about our differences, then…well, then we should be able to do anything."

Daniel cocked his head. "So, I can believe passionately about a soul being in an unborn baby from the very beginning, and you can believe just as passionately that the soul is everywhere, and in existence all the time—"

"Actually, that was the Jains who believe that," Jaxtyn interrupted.

"Really, Jaxtyn? Just when I'm starting to work my way around to agreeing with you, you start correcting me?" He knocked his right knee against Jaxtyn's left.

Jaxtyn slapped his forehead. "I'm clearly not operating in my own self-interest here. Please, go on."

"No, I think I'm finished. It makes sense, I guess. It just feels…unsatisfying, to have to watch people make morally flawed decisions. But I get it, everyone has to be true to themselves."

Jaxtyn reached forward and grabbed both of Daniel's hands.

"And what's the alternative, anyway? Either I force you to conform to my way of thinking, or you force your views on me. I guess we could choose only to be with people who share exactly our same opinions, but that feels wrong too. It's…" Jaxtyn trailed off, trying to articulate just how much worse that forced conformity was.

"It's Galatian Hills," said Daniel. "And that works for Logan and Stiles, or it *did* anyway, but that's no way to live either. It didn't work for Ruth, that's for sure."

"Or for you," Jaxtyn added.

"True," said Daniel. "How did you get to be so smart? How come every time I have an existential crisis, you're able to show me the bigger picture and why everything isn't as bad as it seems?"

"It's what demons do, isn't it?" Jaxtyn asked.

Daniel leaned forward and rested his forehead against Jaxtyn's, running his hands up Jaxtyn's arms. "I think," he whispered, "You didn't read the demon job description."

"Oh, but I did! And as your demon, I feel compelled to point out you could be kissing me right now."

"Now you've got it," said Daniel.

The Buddha above them offered his mysterious smile.

Chapter Thirty-One

"SO, YOU GUYS are like a thing now?" Marcus asked.

"Yeah," Daniel responded. He'd spent the last three nights with Jaxtyn, and he was still trying to get used to the idea that there was no guilt associated with it. It was going to take a while. "Are you okay with that?"

"Of course I am, Dan. I just want you to be happy. You are going to be happy up here, aren't you?"

Daniel considered the question. There was too much uncertainty in the world for him to really be happy. Although Jaxtyn made him happy, mostly. "Maybe. I need to find a purpose, or at least a job."

Marcus snorted. "We don't need jobs, Dan." He held up the "Brother Thomas" name tag and raised a questioning eyebrow.

"Ugh. Leave it," Daniel said. "Put in on the CeeNee pile." The growing CeeNee pile on Marcus's bed included their missionary uniforms, their church-issued phones, a handful of pamphlets advocating for state-sponsored religion, and now their apostle name tags.

It was moving day, and they were leaving the King's Royal Court Hotel—and their former lives—behind. They'd taken a short-term rental in the same neighborhood where Jaxtyn, Skylar, Sylvie, and now Ruth, lived.

Daniel was looking at the brick wall outside of their window for the last time. It was early morning, but already there was street traffic and distant sirens. Always sirens. How much of Boston's ubiquitous background soundtrack had his church's fingerprints on it? His former church, he reminded himself. It was an uncomfortable thought and added to Daniel's sense of dislocation.

"I know we don't *need* jobs," he said. "But it's important to keep busy."

"Being rich will keep us busy enough," Marcus said, as he stuffed the rest of his clothes into his duffel.

"We don't have the money yet," Daniel replied.

"Oh, come on. The advance we received from Global Max is more money than you would have earned in a year with any job you could find here, and the agent Skylar's parents got us means we'll all be set for life. You've already got speaking gigs lined up. You're famous, Dan."

It was true. But it was another uncomfortable departure from his formerly structured and predictable life. He moved to his bed and reviewed the contact information he'd entered into his new phone earlier that morning. Jaxtyn, of course, and Marcus. But Sylvie now, too, and Ruth and even Skylar. He'd added Marcus's parents because they'd been so helpful to Jaxtyn, and he wanted to help them too as they planned their move to Boston. He'd even added his own parents because he remained hopeful that maybe someday they'd return one of his messages.

His phone beeped every few minutes with notifications, and he realized he'd have to put more effort into learning how to use the sensitivity settings. It was still startling how often his name was mentioned in the media. "Any word yet from Congress?" Marcus asked in response to the latest alert on Daniel's phone. The Lion's Den Summit had been in session for days, with no official word on progress, but many encouraging rumors.

At least the terror attacks had stopped, and there were no further riots in the Capitol. The entire country was holding its collective breath, waiting.

Marcus finished packing and came to sit next to Daniel on his bed. "How did we not see it, Dan? How evil he was, I mean?"

"I've been thinking about that," Daniel replied. "We grew up in it, I guess. And we had no other perspective. I wonder about our parents though." He looked at his phone again. He'd sent three messages to his mother and father. They hadn't responded. "I get why my parents would have gone along. They wanted the same things as Logan. But your parents? They seem so much more reasonable."

"They are. But we're Black."

Daniel flinched inwardly. Some things were harder to get over than others and pretending not to notice color had been ingrained in him from the beginning. But he was committed to learning and immediately recognized, and rejected, his instinct to dismiss Marcus's statement.

"How does that matter?" he asked. Marcus frowned. Daniel

held up his hand to forestall the objection. "No, I mean that honestly. I'm trying to understand."

"Being Black in Galatian Hills was weird," Marcus said. "It was like we had a secret, and Ella and I had to learn about our history privately. You know those science fiction books with alternate realities?" Daniel nodded. "It was like that," Marcus continued. "There are so many things you weren't taught, Dan. Or were taught in an entirely different way. Like, how Blacks lived their lives under Jim Crow laws."

Daniel blushed because he knew Marcus was right. "I don't know what those are," he said.

"Of course you don't," Marcus replied. "And that's the point; you weren't meant to know that part of history. It was erased for you. It's not your fault, but it sets you at a disadvantage when it comes to understanding how the world works — how and why people fight for justice."

Daniel had never thought about his education as being inadequate before. Quality education was one of the things religious communities like Galatian Hills prided themselves on. The town had one of the top-ranking public school systems in South Carolina. Could his understanding of history be so censored and distorted?

"When we learned Skylar's friends called themselves the New Riders and that they were modeled after the Freedom Riders of the 1960s, did you even know what that meant?"

"No. I guess I have a lot of remedial work to do."

"Yep. But that's okay. I can help you now. It was hard before when I had to be sensitive to the fact that you lived in a color-blind world. Which brings me back to my point about my parents. They lived in that world too, but it was difficult for them. They had to be White."

Daniel was trying to follow, but he tripped up on that one. "How could they be White?"

"This is so hard to explain to you."

"Marcus, we've known each other most of our lives, and I never knew all of this was happening to you. Please help me understand. I know I have a lot of work to do, but I promise I'll try. I'm beginning to feel like our friendship might have been built on false premises, and that's not good. I want to be an honest friend for you."

"Thanks, Dan. I'll try. Here's the thing. My family is wealthy. You always knew that, right?"

"Yes." The Johnsons were one of the richest families in Galatian Hills and lived in one of its grandest homes. Marcus and Ella often had private tutors and were frequently involved in extracurricular activities while Daniel and his friends were out riding their bicycles in the afternoon.

"Well, for people like Logan—really, for all the powerful people in Galatian Hills—they may truly believe they live in a community where race doesn't matter, where no one *sees* color. But for that to work, there has to be nothing to see."

Daniel squinted. That made sense, sort of.

"So, my family needed to make sure everyone in Galatian Hills saw just a darker version of a wealthy White family. And it wasn't that difficult. We were Christian Evangelicals, just like everyone else, and we had the same community values around family and faith and safety. It's just that, on Martin Luther King Jr. Day, we couldn't talk about his more radical side, and we had to have a private backyard barbeque to celebrate Juneteenth, and—"

"What's Juneteenth?" Daniel asked.

Marcus took a deep breath. "See!" he said, not bothering to conceal his exasperation.

No, Daniel didn't see, but he put his question aside. He suspected there would be many more where that one came from.

"My point is," Marcus continued, "my family had to work hard to fit itself into a mold. And there were plenty of other well-to-do, informed families in Galatian Hills who saw what was happening around them. It shouldn't be on the one upper-class Black family to have to risk everything by calling it out."

Marcus paused there, and Daniel was grateful. He had so much to learn if he was to become a useful member of his new society. And he had every intention of doing just that.

"Thank you, Marcus, for being patient with me and giving me a chance."

Marcus punched him in the shoulder. "Oh, come on, Dan. You're like the pasty-white brother I never had. I've got your back."

They were all packed, and Marcus surveyed the room. "Nice place," he said. "Five-star luxury at a bargain price."

Daniel laughed. "Dinosaurs."

"Hey, Dan?"

"Yeah?"

"Can we pray together here, one last time?"

Daniel smiled. "I'd like that."

They got on their knees next to the CeeNee pile on Marcus's bed, clasped their hands together, and invited Jesus to fill their hearts with His love.

Chapter Thirty-Two

PROFESSOR RINGLE SHIFTED restlessly in the front of the class-room, checking his notes and scrolling through his pad as he prepared for the start of the session. The title "Missouri Compromise" filled the left side of the display wall behind him, and "Virginia Compromise" occupied the right.

Congress's Lion's Den Summit had ended in the creation of the Virginia Compromise—widely lauded as a victory for all sides. The riots ended, and the terror attacks subsided—most people had relaxed into a guarded sense of relief. The years of increasing trauma and fear had left their mark, and it was startling to have that constant anxiety suddenly removed, like the relief one experiences after an abscessed tooth is pulled.

Congress had offered a path forward, and although the Virginia Compromise disappointed many on both sides, the media said that was a good thing. No one can have everything they want;

that's not how political progress happens.

The people of Boston had been at a breaking point. Something had to give, and if that meant allowing the red states to break off from the union, then so be it, as long as the constant attacks stopped. But finally, there was a solution. The entire city breathed easier, walked lighter, and even smiled at one another.

Not Professor Ringle though, thought Jaxtyn as he watched the man fidget with his notes and wipe sweat from his brow.

He looked up from his notes, cleared his throat, and faced the class. "Good morning," he said. "It's a momentous day. The first day of the Virginia Compromise." There was a smattering of applause, and many eyes shifted to Jaxtyn. They'd all seen the footage from Sangre de Cristo and followed the Harmony Bus's ride home. Jaxtyn was famous, but most of his fellow students were still trying to decide what they thought of the campus's Buddhist meditation leader ending up with a CeeNee boyfriend. A boyfriend who quite possibly had saved the country from disaster.

Jaxtyn was still struggling with how to think about all that too.

"Now, the more astute members of the class will have noticed I've put the Missouri Compromise on the wall alongside the Virginia Compromise. Who can tell me what the Missouri Compromise was?"

Jaxtyn knew it had had something to do with slavery before the American Civil War, but he didn't remember the details and looked down at his notes, along with most of the rest of the class, to avoid being called upon. They were all saved by a young woman in a hijab who raised her hand and said, "It was an agreement reached by Congress allowing Missouri to become a state that permitted slavery while bringing a new Northern state in at the same time—Maine, I think—that outlawed slavery. The idea was to keep the balance of slave-holding states and non-slave-holding states the same."

Professor Ringle nodded. "Thank you, Ms. Awad. You've restored my faith in the youth of Boston."

He turned to address the class. "And yes, that's exactly right. The Missouri Compromise also drew a literal line on the map and established a rule that future states below the line could allow slavery but those above the line couldn't. It seems absurd to us now, but in the 1820s, slavery was becoming a divisive topic in the still quite young United States. Congress wanted to keep everything in balance, so as not to throw fuel on the fire."

He displayed a map on the wall showing the demarcation line running straight through the new territories. "Now, as you know, within three decades, the nation was plunged into a bloody civil war that claimed over half a million battlefield deaths and countless civilian lives. Who can offer an explanation as to why the Missouri Compromise didn't work?"

More heads turned to their desks. It didn't help that Professor Ringle was clearly anxious about something and seemed ready to snap. A young man in the front of the classroom raised his hand. Jaxtyn recognized him as one of the recent Bangladeshi immigrants displaced by the rising sea levels in their home country. Jaxtyn had an uncomfortable moment when he was struck by how newcomers to the United States often seemed more informed about the country's history than the native-born were. He'd try to remember to talk to Daniel about that.

"Is it because the compromise didn't answer the essential question about slavery itself? It didn't address the morality of the practice at all."

Professor Ringle cocked his head. "You'd think so, Mr. Khatun, wouldn't you? At least that would have been a more honest death for such a flawed arrangement. But no. Turns out, just thirty years after it was adopted, Congress killed it. See, the rich and powerful wanted to build a railroad across the continent, and the business interests wanted it to run through Chicago, but the Southern states didn't want the new railroad running only through territories that would have to become non-slave states, because they were above the line. So Congress said, fine, let's junk the Missouri Compromise and instead we'll just let the people in these territories decide for themselves. They can incorporate "with or without slavery as their constitutions may prescribe."

"It was called 'popular sovereignty.'" He paused and surveyed the class. "Does that remind you of anything you've heard about in the news recently?" He gave an exaggerated nod to the words Virginia Compromise on the wall over his left shoulder. "So, please, someone tell me why the Virginia Compromise will work when the Missouri Compromise and the idea of popular sovereignty failed?"

The class was silent. They wanted to be excited about the future, and Professor Ringle was being a wet blanket.

"I'm serious," he said. "We all want the new compromise to work, don't we? So go on, give it your best shot. Convince me."

More silence.

Professor Ringle waited. Finally, an older student in the back spoke up. "It's already working," he said. "There have been no attacks in over a week." There were a few murmurs of agreement, but generally, the room remained silent. Jaxtyn was tempted to speak up; he had his own doubts about the Virginia Compromise, but he was already so publicly associated with its genesis he didn't feel like he should criticize it.

Ms. Awad came to his rescue. "But don't you see?" She directed her question to the man who'd said it was working. "It's only working right *here*, right *now*. But once individual jurisdictions start establishing their own state-sponsored religions—which is what the Virginia Compromise permits—then it won't be working *there*, will it? Not for everyone. Not for all the people living there who don't want to suffer under religious rule."

"Well, it's hardly 'religious rule,'" the man shot back. "And the point is they don't need to *stay* there. That's the beauty of the compromise. Any jurisdiction that chooses to establish a government religion needs to contribute to a fund that supports the resettlement of people who no longer want to live there. Housing, transportation, job support—it'll all be part of the fund."

"Oh, please!" someone else said "Like this fund—which is *never* going to have enough money in it, by the way—will help some poor teenager in Alabama start a new life somewhere else."

"Well, it might," someone said. "It's not like they'd have to move north. The compromise specifically allows local jurisdictions to opt out. I heard this morning Ashville's city council already announced they'd opt out if North Carolina goes ahead with establishing Christianity as the state's official religion."

That's when the comments started flowing.

"Too many people are too powerless, or under the control of others, to take advantage of that though."

"Come on, we can't fix everything for everyone."

"It's a start."

"It buys us time to keep persuading."

"I don't care what else it does if it stops the terror attacks." That one silenced the room. It was the guilty thought they'd all shared, even though most of them thought it was wrong. Why not sacrifice the powerless stranger down South if it meant you could stop sheltering in place in your classroom? There were lots of good answers to that question, but they all required bravery and fortitude.

A young man near the door stood suddenly and gathered his things. "Fuck you," he said to the room. "You don't know what it's like to be a thirteen-year-old gay boy growing up in a family and a community that tells you you're going to hell. I won't abandon my brothers to the religious police in some red state. If that means civil disobedience, then sign me up." He stormed out of the room, and the room fell silent again.

After a moment, the man who had earlier said it was already working spoke up again. Jaxtyn was surprised he had the balls to offer a counterpoint after what had just happened. "But if it stops another civil war?" he asked. "If it avoids another million deaths? Shouldn't we all be willing to make some sacrifices?"

This was becoming too painful. The students looked urgently to Professor Ringle to put an end to it. But rather than reading the mood of the room, he did the very worst thing he could. "Mr. Keller," he called. Jaxtyn cringed. "Might I ask you a question about your personal observations during your recent visit to Galatian Hills?" He said *visit,* but everyone heard *kidnapping.*

"I'm not really allowed to talk about it," Jaxtyn responded.

"Yes. Your media deal." Professor Ringle replied. He said *media deal* the way he might have said *syphilis*. "I'm aware. But to the best of your ability…?"

"What would you like to know?" Jaxtyn asked guardedly.

"I'd like to ask about the woman who was at the center of this…scheme…by that nationalist church. What was she like?"

Ruth. Jaxtyn hadn't gotten to know her well. And now that he thought about it, he probably never would. They just didn't have much in common. Ruth struck him as one of those people who make up the background noise in life, going about their business not too interested in things outside their day-to-day. She was pleasant, but he doubted she would ever go anywhere in life, although of course, he hoped she'd be happy.

She and Sylvie had hit it off anyway—but that could be mostly about the Jesus thing. He wondered if she voted, or if she preferred not to get involved.

"I'm sorry, Professor Ringle. I didn't get a chance to know her."

"I see. All right. Fair enough. But let me ask you this, if the Virginia Compromise had been in effect for a couple of years now, would her situation have been any different?"

Jaxtyn had thought about this a lot since his kidnapping. Galatian Hills already lived under a Christian legal structure; it just wasn't officially law. But the technicality didn't matter. Once the police had Christian crosses on their badges and cars, the lines had already been erased.

"No, sir. I don't think anything would have been different."

"So then, Mr. Keller, as you see it, since obtaining an abortion is illegal now under South Carolina law, it most likely would continue to be against the law if the state established Christianity as its state religion?"

Jaxtyn nodded.

"And I imagine this young woman would still have been charged with a crime, and perhaps prosecuted?"

Of course. It would only be worse in the future under the Virginia Compromise, not better.

"But I suppose—" Professor Ringle continued as if he was thinking about what options Ruth might have under the new Virginia Compromise. "—she could have left, used the relocation funds available under the compromise, started a new life somewhere else before she ran into her…difficulties?"

Jaxtyn shook his head. "I don't think it would have worked that way," he replied. In fact, it was an offensive idea. Ruth didn't *plan* to get pregnant any more than she carefully planned the rest of her life. Things just happen. Especially to people like Ruth, who seem to be pulled along in life's currents more haphazardly than others.

"Unlikely, yes" Professor Ringle agreed. "One last question, please."

Jaxtyn increasingly felt like he was testifying at a trial.

"Did Galatian Hills strike you as the kind of community where it would have been easy for a young woman to learn what her options might be? Either before or after becoming pregnant?"

Chief Styles's voice echoed in Jaxtyn's head. "*You're not in Kansas anymore, son,*" he'd replied when Jaxtyn had asked about a court-appointed lawyer.

"No sir, not at all."

Professor Ringle nodded and turned away from Jaxtyn.

Whatever point he wanted to make, he'd made. "So, under the Virginia Compromise, millions of women in these states with newly established religions will continue to live under threat of prosecution, only it will be worse now. State laws will be tighter, enforcement will become more draconian. Men will be more emboldened." He paused and scanned the room. Jaxtyn sensed other students preparing to follow the lead of the one who'd already left.

"But as you say, sir," Professor Ringle addressed the voice in the back who'd insisted the compromise was working. "If it prevents a new civil war…"

He moved back to his lectern and opened his pad. "Now, this is where today's lesson should end—a robust debate on the pros and cons of the Virginia Compromise, ending on a hopeful note for out-and-out war avoided."

The class let out a sigh of relief.

"Instead, I'm going to treat you to a little bit of performance art." He displayed his pad's screen on the wall, revealing a draft email titled, "My Resignation—effective immediately." A murmur ran through the room. "Today is my last day teaching here."

Were they supposed to clap? Protest?

"But as my last hurrah, I'm going to tell you the truth—a truth I imagine the university would caution me against sharing." He hit the Send button, and his message shot off into the ether.

"The Virginia Compromise is a filthy piece of misogynist *shit* crafted with the sole purpose of aggrandizing the egos of weak, powerless men." The room had never been so quiet. No one dared look around, but phones were surreptitiously raised throughout the room.

"None of this has ever been about religious rights. They *have* religious rights. They always have. This is entirely about controlling women's bodies, and thereby controlling women themselves, limiting their choices, defining their places. And why? Because they can! Because it makes them feel powerful in a world where they're terrified they have no real power.

"And it's not about letting people decide for themselves — like criminalizing women's choices is somehow the result of a democratic process. You want to vote on it? You want to go with the majority? Fine. But let the half of the population that has to deal with the consequences be the only ones who vote. See what happens then. Sure, there are a number of women who sincerely believe their faith requires them to oppose all abortions for all women, but a vote of only women would resoundingly support women's autonomy and choice — by wide margins.

"So, it's all about the men. And their fear. And their insecurity. And the fact that other men are more powerful than they are, so they need to be more powerful than someone else. That's why we're in this ridiculous position. Just like poor Southern Whites needed to feel superior to newly emancipated slaves! It's the same dynamic, over and over again. And we keep making the same mistakes!

"I'm old enough to remember when Dredd Scott was the worst Supreme Court case in history — the one that said enslaved people weren't citizens, so they had no federal protections — and then Dobbs came along, and for the first time ever, the court started taking away constitutional rights that had been enshrined in the law for decades, and suddenly women were vulnerable again, and subject to the religious fantasies of the men in control of state legislatures. And then—my God—Slater! Overturning Marbury vs. Madison!

"There was a time when we knew all this! When it wasn't considered a victory to sacrifice half the country to fascists. When we understood what it meant to live in a liberal, pluralist democracy, and when we guarded our freedoms against power-hungry politicians. When we knew how to live our lives and let others live theirs in peace, respecting differences, and—"

The door opened and campus police entered. They stepped to either side of Professor Ringle and—gently at first—grasped him by the arms. "Come with us, please." But he resisted and they started pulling him toward the door.

"You're going to have to learn this all over!" he yelled as they led him away. "You're going to have to rebuild the country because you let it fall apart!" And then he was gone, and the door swung shut behind him.

*

THE MEDITATION TIMER chimed, indicating an end to the session. Jaxtyn and Daniel sat cross-legged on mats on his bedroom floor, and at the sound of the chime, they opened their eyes, smiled at each other, and then helped each other up. Jaxtyn poured tea from the pot he'd brewed earlier, and they sat on the edge of his bed with their cups.

"That was a good session," he said, and Daniel nodded his agreement. Daniel hadn't seemed at all distracted by the absence of Jesus as a focal point for his mind, but Jaxtyn would have to remember to suggest Daniel lead them in a more traditional prayer session next time. Keeping that balance would be important as they continued to learn from one another.

Recently, Skylar had been spending more nights at Daniel's apartment playing VR games with Marcus, while Daniel spent the night with Jaxtyn, learning new things about each other, exploring, trying to decide if their crazy intuition they were meant to be together was more than just the first blush of attraction and desire.

From the beginning, Jaxtyn had been sure there was something mysterious between them—part of a hidden universal plan—and that conviction had only grown stronger since they returned from South Carolina. "Trust the universe when it tries to tell you something, Daniel," he said. "It doesn't matter if you don't understand right away. Have faith."

"Isn't that supposed to be my line?" Daniel asked.

Jaxtyn put his cup on the table, turned, and draped an arm across Daniel's shoulder. "You haven't cornered the market on faith, my friend. There's room for all of us." Daniel groaned. He'd told Jaxtyn many times he thought his little fortune cookie quips on faith and the universe were silly, empty pablum masquerading as wisdom. Jaxyn smiled. He liked getting a rise out of Daniel. "The you who is you is not the you who you knew." He ruffled Daniel's hair.

"Now you're just being obnoxious," Daniel responded. But he tapped Jaxtyn's bicep with his fist before he stood and walked to the desk and picked up his phone. "I've been thinking about that video of your professor's…what would you call it? Meltdown?"

Jaxtyn pushed himself back on the mattress to sit cross-legged and rest his back against the wall. The candles lighting the room had burned low, and it was difficult for Jaxtyn to distinguish between the white of Daniel's T-shirt and the nearly translucent, shimmering white of his skin. "Hmm. I'd call it a principled last stand in the defense of truth."

Daniel shrugged his shoulders. "Maybe," he said. He came back to the bed and sat. "But it's not the whole truth — or even the *only* truth. If there's one thing I've learned since I came up here, it's that there are more ways of seeing the world than I'd ever known could exist."

Jaxtyn reached forward and tugged the waistband of Daniel's sweatpants. "I'd say there are a few things you've learned up here." He didn't try to hide the innuendo.

"Ha," Daniel replied, but he made no move to follow up on the implied invitation. "I don't think we were all like that. Men where I come from, I mean."

We. Jaxtyn knew how hard it was for Daniel not to see himself as part of the community. Even though he'd managed to escape, he was certainly still a product of it. Eventually, he'd have to learn to see that world as a significant part of his past, not as an anchor in his present. But those were lessons for another day.

"To be fair," Jaxtyn replied, "he didn't say all men were like that. I think he suggested it was enough if just the ones who controlled the laws were that way."

"But, wouldn't I have noticed? If the men around me hated women?"

Jaxtyn had spent some time thinking about that question after listening to Professor Ringle's swan song. He had stressed the whole misogyny angle, and Jaxtyn had doubts about that. But was Jaxtyn capable of seeing through the layers of his own socialization to assess the "truth"?

He didn't know, so he'd asked Ruth. He wanted to talk to her anyway, to apologize for how he came across in the video when he'd said he hadn't really known her. "But you *don't* know me," she replied. "You were only telling the truth."

"But I should have made an effort to get to know you," Jaxtyn insisted.

"I don't see why," Ruth had responded. "I doubt we have much in common."

It was actually the exact sentiment Jaxtyn had been thinking as he listened to Professor Ringle. "But, what did you think about what he said? Is he right?"

"See?" Ruth had said. "This is what I mean. I don't care what he said. I don't think any of it really matters. I'm just happy to have gotten out of that house."

Jaxtyn hadn't been able to think of a way to continue the conversation from there, and he'd gotten no further with Ruth's input than he had on his own. He shook his head and returned his attention to Daniel. "I know he used the word misogyny, but I think what he talked about was power and control—that these men who run the state houses and get sent to Congress only feel powerful when they can control the lives of other people, and controlling women is the easiest way to do that, and it lets them feel higher in the pecking order."

Daniel frowned. "I disagree that's what it's about," he said. "And I know I have a lot to learn about how other people see things, but I think the objection to abortion is about ending the life of the unborn child. It just seems wrong, even if it isn't clear exactly when a soul exists, or when the fetus becomes something more than a collection of cells. But I think a fully developed fetus deserves the benefit of the doubt."

"I know you feel that way," said Jaxtyn. He rubbed his hand on Daniel's knee. "And I'm not going to try to convince you you're wrong." He let his hand settle on Daniel's thigh. "I love how compassionate you are. I could see that in you right away, even through your frosty know-it-all missionary persona."

Daniel sighed. "Um…thanks?" He put his hand on top of Jaxtyn's. "It's just that Professor Ringle is so sure of himself. How can he not feel at least a little bit conflicted about ending the life of a fetus that would have gone on to become a baby? How can that *not* make him uncomfortable? It seems to me you'd have to be pretty cold not to feel *something*…"

"Listen to you criticizing other people for being so sure of themselves," Jaxtyn said, but he turned his hand over and entwined his fingers with Daniel's to show he meant the comment in a loving way. "I'm proud of you, Daniel."

"Well, I'm learning, and I have you to thank for opening my eyes to so many things. I'm no longer the cocksure missionary who arrived here a few months ago."

"Speaking of cocksure…" Jaxtyn reached out and tugged at Daniel's sweatpants again, and this time Daniel allowed himself to be drawn in.

"It's such a new sensation for me," Daniel continued. "The more I learn, the less I know! It's a good thing though. It's very freeing."

"How's that?" Jaxtyn asked, pulling Daniel to his side and running a hand through his hair.

"Well, all this uncertainty leaves room to grow. That's got to be good, right? I mean, how are you going to be open to other people's ideas if you're already sure you have all the answers?"

Jaxtyn nodded, and for just a moment, he felt the universe coalesce around them, embrace them in an affirmation of the destiny Jaxtyn always knew lay in their future. This was it. It was happening. He didn't know yet what or how, but the universe had been leading them to this moment. Something important was being born.

Daniel rested his hand over Jaxtyn's heart. "I think I've found an answer to what I've been searching for," he told Jaxtyn, who was not in the least bit surprised to hear it. "I want to make that my life's work. I want to spread uncertainty, and doubt, and openness and questioning—to everyone, everywhere. I want to build a better world."

"You will, my love. You will."

The Buddha smiled above them, and deep inside Jaxtyn's heart, the Hollywood Jesus winked.

Epilogue

"WELCOME BACK TO the Lion's Den, your source for open, honest, *respectful* debate on the day's most challenging issues," Daniel said. "Today is a very special day for us. It's our one hundredth episode! I'm your host, Daniel Ridley, and the handsome demon to my left is your co-host, and my husband, Jaxtyn Keller." Jaxtyn offered a namaste for the cameras.

"Today, we're going to be talking reparations, so buckle up." Daniel turned to Jaxtyn.

"As you know," Jaxtyn began, "the City of Boston has sued the State of South Carolina for damages it suffered over years of increasingly violent terror attacks meant to demoralize its citizens and force the so-called blue states to acquiesce to a renegotiation of our national union to allow for state-sponsored religion.

"You can argue about whether that strategy was successful—I would say it was, given we now live under the highly problematic Virginia Compromise—but whether that compromise was a result of the terror campaign or not, the harm to Boston and other Northern cities was real, and the suffering enormous."

Jaxtyn turned to Daniel, who picked up the introduction to the discussion they were about to have. "Through the criminal investigations and trials surrounding the Christian Nationalist missionary churches—which are all now defunct—we have learned of the extensive collusion that took place between those churches and the states that housed them. The most notorious case, of course, is that of Sangre de Cristo. Although its leader is now in prison, there is no denying his trial revealed a well-documented evidence trail showing the State of South Carolina funded much of the church's operations through misdirected taxpayer dollars and had an active say in the more political activities it undertook."

The cameras panned to the Lion's Den's two guests while Daniel continued speaking. "Leaving aside for the moment the legal question of restitution, assuming the court finds South Carolina liable, there is a larger question of moral culpability. To what extent should state governments be held responsible for the actions of private companies they supported during those dark years that almost led us into another civil war? In other words, should South Carolina need to atone for its sins, and if so, how?

"Joining us now to debate this question are two people who regular viewers, or those who've watched the many dramatizations of my life during that time, will recognize immediately. Please welcome Former University of Massachusetts Professor of Constitutional Law Howard Ringle. Professor Ringle will be arguing the position that restitution is essential to renew the nation's faith in the rule of law but is also morally required to demonstrate that actions have consequences. Joining him today, and arguing the opposite side of the issue, is South Carolina's newest federal Congresswoman, Ruth Deveraux."

Daniel looked over to Jaxtyn and winked. Boy, had he pegged her wrong!

"Congresswoman Deveraux, let's start with you. Welcome to the Lion's Den."

"Thank you, Dan."

Jaxtyn winked back at Daniel. Childhood names never went away.

"Congresswoman, why don't you believe South Carolina should be held accountable for the harm it caused in Boston? The cleanup costs for the dirty bombs alone have already exceeded a billion dollars. And the legal theory of accomplice liability would clearly—"

"Oh, Dan," the congresswoman interrupted. "You were always so head-in-the-clouds! The people of my district didn't elect me to get mired in fancy legal theories. They hired me to look forward, not dwell on the past."

Maybe Jaxtyn had been mostly right about her after all.

"Besides, where would it end? Boston is angry at South Carolina. South Carolina is angry at these fraudulent churches that distorted Jesus's message. Everybody is angry at Texas. The colonies were angry at England—"

"Well," Daniel tried to interrupt.

Congresswoman Deveraux plowed right over him. "And besides, it's just too expensive. South Carolina doesn't have that kind of money. The amount of tax dollars we pay into the Virginia Compromise's relocation fund has been hundreds of millions higher than we anticipated!"

Professor Ringle rolled his eyes. "Who would have guessed," he mumbled.

"Forgive and forget, I say," she continued. "Let's look at the future as one country and stop trying to open old wounds. The past is the past; what's done is done…"

And so it went.

Predictable, not particularly helpful, but open, honest, and respectful.

Still, one hundred episodes! It wasn't their best one—far from it. But collectively, those episodes represented years of intelligent debate, an ever-expanding circle of viewers challenging their own assumptions and reassessing what they'd previously been certain about.

And with each episode, and with each year, Daniel's own awareness of a mysteriously complex and unknowable universe deepened. Jaxtyn said Daniel was experiencing anatta—a Buddhist concept he claimed meant there was no such thing as an individual self, but instead, everything was infinite and impermanent.

Daniel always smiled pleasantly when Jaxtyn said that. And who knows, maybe for Jaxtyn it was true.

But Daniel thought he had a better explanation: he was at peace with God and placed his faith in Jesus to guide him where he needed to go.

About the Author

John Patrick is an author and a Lambda Literary Award finalist who lives in the Berkshire Hills of Massachusetts, where he is supported in his writing by his husband and their terriers, who are convinced they could do battle with the bears that come through the woods on occasion (the terriers, that is, not the husband).

John is an introvert and can often be found doing introverted things like reading or writing, cooking, and thinking deep, contemplative thoughts (his husband might call this napping). He loves to spend time in nature—"forest bathing" is the Japanese term for it—feeling connected with the universe. But he also loathes heat and humidity, bugs of any sort, and unsteady footing in the form of rocks, mud, tree roots, snow, or ice. So his love of nature is tempered; he's complicated that way.

John and his husband enjoy traveling and have visited over a dozen countries, meeting new people, exploring new cultures, and—most importantly—discovering new foods.

Email
john@johnpatrickauthor.com

Facebook
www.facebook.com/JohnPatrickAuthor

Twitter
jpatrickauthor

Website
www.johnpatrickauthor.com

Instagram
johnpatrickauthor

Other NineStar books by this author

Paradise Series

Franklin in Paradise
Undercover in Paradise

Tides of Change Series

Dublin Bay
Turtle Bay
Havana Bay

CONNECT WITH NINESTAR PRESS

WEBSITE: NineStarPress.com

FACEBOOK: NineStarPress

X: @ninestarpress

INSTAGRAM: NineStarPress

BLUESKY: NineStarPress

THREADS: @ninestarpress

www.ingramcontent.com/pod-product-compliance
Lightning Source LLC
Chambersburg PA
CBHW060310100726
47907CB00002B/358